FALLS OF IRON

Christopher Mitchell is the author of the epic fantasy series The Magelands. He studied in Edinburgh before living for several years in the Middle East and Greece, where he taught English. He returned to study classics and Greek tragedy and lives in Fife, Scotland with his wife and their four children.

Brigdomin Books Ltd
First Edition, January 2021
ISBN 978-1-912879-50-2

For Vicky

ACKNOWLEDGEMENTS

I would like to thank the following for all their support during the writing of the Magelands Eternal Siege - my wife, Lisa Mitchell, who read every chapter as soon as it was drafted and kept me going in the right direction; my parents for their unstinting support; Vicky Williams for reading the books in their early stages; James Aitken for his encouragement; and Grant and Gordon of the Film Club for their support.

Thanks also to my Advance Reader team, for all your help during the last few weeks before publication.

DRAMATIS PERSONAE

From the City

Corthie Holdfast, Champion
Blackrose, Dragon
Aila, Shape-shifter
Naxor, Demigod
Maddie Jackdaw, Dragon Rider
Belinda, God

Falls of Iron

Irno, Count of the Falls of Iron
Vana, Sister of Irno and Aila; cousin of Naxor

Alea Tanton

Sable Holdfast, Spy
Gantu, Blue Thumb Gang Boss
Millen, Gantu's younger cousin
Adlin, Blue Thumb Training Manager
Sanguino, Captured Bloodflies Dragon
Latude, God; Governor of Lostwell
Baldwin, God; Patron of the Deadskins
Felice, God; Patron of the Blue Thumbs
Kemal, God; Patron of the Bloodflies
Isa, Servant in the Governor's Residence

Implacatus

Renko, Ancient; Commander of Taskforce
Joaz, God assigned to Taskforce
Maisk, God assigned to Taskforce

Banner of the Golden Fist

>**Van Logos,** Captain
>
>**Ahito,** Major
>
>**Sohul,** Lieutenant
>
>**Baku,** Lieutenant

Others

>**Karalyn Holdfast,** Dream Mage
>
>**Silva,** Former Courtier of Belinda
>
>**Gadena,** Trainer of Mercenaries

CHAPTER 1

FAITHLESS

Alea Tanton, Tordue, Western Khatanax – 12th Dunninch 5252

The noon sun beat down from the cloudless sky, its rays illuminating the blood-soaked sand. Sable Holdfast suppressed a grimace, while around her, the crowds on the stone benches of the arena watched, their attention on the violence below them.

A dozen slaves had been pushed out onto the sands, of whom four remained on their feet, each grasping one of the weapons that had been left in a pile in the centre of the arena. Around them lay the bloody remains of the others, hacked to pieces in the initial chaos and carnage of the confrontation. The crowds had cheered and bayed at the grisly spectacle, but their attention was already starting to drift as the survivors circled each other on the sands.

The well-built man to Sable's right grunted. 'Get a move on, you useless assholes.'

One of the slaves raised the large cleaver he was carrying, and lunged at a fellow survivor. The crowd's interest flickered, then boos and jeers arose from the half-filled benches as the intended victim turned and ran.

'Remind me, Gantu,' said Sable; 'what is the purpose of this? Beyond our entertainment, of course.'

'It's the qualifiers, ain't it, babe,' said the man to her right, the muscles in his thick neck bulging. He stretched out his bare arm and placed it over Sable's shoulder.

She ignored the urge to shrug his arm off, keeping her eyes on the action in the arena below them. Only two of the slaves were still standing. One was gasping for breath as he huddled by the high wall surrounding the circular area of sand, while the other was approaching, a long spear clutched in both hands. The crowd quietened as they watched from the tiered stone benches, then let out a roar as the slave drove the spear through the torso of his last rival. The victorious slave turned to the crowds, raising his hands to accept their acclaim.

Gantu removed his arm from Sable's shoulder so he could applaud the victor.

'What happens to him now?' she said.

'He gets a chance to join the greatest team in the city,' he said.

Sable frowned. 'This is how the team gets new recruits?'

'It's one of the ways,' Gantu said.

She picked up a growing sense of irritation from him at her questions, and nodded instead of asking another. He liked showing her off to his friends and cronies, who sat around them in a large group on the stone benches, but seemed to prefer it when she said nothing. It annoyed her, but was a small price to pay. Her gaze drifted over the crowds lining the arena as guards emerged from gates and strode across the sands. More slaves ran out, and began clearing up the remains of those who had fallen, while the victor was led back through one of the entrances that dotted the circular wall.

'Ah, there's the little runt,' Gantu muttered, his eyes squinting at a row of seats to their right. He nodded to a few of his friends, and then he and several of them rose to their feet. 'Stay here,' he grunted to Sable, then they walked away.

She watched as Gantu led the others over to where another group was sitting, then she noticed the eyes of a younger man on her. She turned, and the man glanced away, blushing.

Sable smiled. 'What would Gantu think,' she said, 'if he knew his little cousin was staring at me?'

The man's eyes widened. 'But... I wasn't...'

'Relax, Millen,' she said; 'I'm joking. Come over here and sit next to me.'

'Um, I don't think I should.'

'Do it, or I'll tell Gantu that you were staring at me.'

She felt a twinge of guilt as fear shone from Millen's eyes. He shuffled along the bench towards her.

'So,' she said, waving her hand at the arena; 'what's next?'

'It's the, uh, executions,' he mumbled, 'and then the team has their practice session after that.'

'And those seats opposite us,' she said, 'is that where the gods usually sit?'

'Yeah.'

'Will they be coming today, do you think?'

Millen shrugged. 'Maybe. They always show up for the big matches, but on practice days like today, then normally only Lady Felice bothers to attend.'

'Felice?'

'Yeah, she's the patron of the Blue Thumbs; they're her team.'

Sable sniggered.

'What's so funny?'

She thought better of telling him that she found the names of the three teams of Alea Tanton ridiculous, as the locals took the whole competition so seriously.

'Nothing,' she said, raising a hand to shield her eyes from the harsh sunlight as she glanced around the arena. 'When does the free food arrive?'

Millen lifted his eyes to her. 'I can buy you some if you're hungry.'

She smirked. 'Are you trying to avoid me?'

'No,' he said, his voice a little strained. 'It's just, you know... my cousin Gantu can get a bit... possessive.'

Sable turned her eyes to glance over at where Gantu was sitting, his cronies surrounding him as he spoke to a small group of terrified-looking men. There was no doubt that the man was a brute, but he had already proved his usefulness to her, providing her with not only food and somewhere to stay in the city, but also with a level of protection that her association with him entailed. Not that she needed protecting; she was perfectly capable of looking after herself, but no one bothered her, their fear of Gantu enough to keep all straying hands and glances away from her.

The crowd's attention turned back to the sands of the arena as a gate opened. Armoured warriors emerged, leading a long line of ragged and shackled prisoners out of the shadows of the underground tunnels that ran under the arena.

'The condemned?' she said.

Millen nodded. 'Yes. Today's batch of executions.'

Sable's eyes narrowed as she watched the prisoners be escorted out into the middle of the arena. The attention of the entire crowd was on them, and a hushed excitement percolated over the stone benches. The condemned were a mixture of the young and the old, men and women, all dressed in rags and covered in red weals and stripes from the whips held by the armoured guards. Sable hardened her heart. She had a job to do, and the suffering of the people inhabiting the festering city of Alea Tanton was none of her concern.

The prisoners were led to a long line of upright posts that ran down the middle of the arena, and the guards secured their chains – one captive to each stout pole. Two of the prisoners had a green tinge to their skin, and Sable realised that they must be Fordians – a people who made up a third of the population of the city, and who were the greatest rivals of the Blue Thumbs.

'I thought the Fordians had their own arena,' she said.

'They do,' said Millen, 'but any caught breaking the law in our part of the city are executed here in the Central Pits. And, obviously, they're not allowed to compete in the qualifiers. There's no way any of *them* would be allowed to join the Blue Thumbs; just like they would never let any of our folk into their team, the Deadskins.'

The armoured guards pulled back as soon as the last prisoner had been secured to a post, and they filed out of the arena through a gate that closed behind them. The crowd stilled, their gazes on the sand.

Sable frowned. 'What happens to them now?'

A large iron gate in the arena wall began to open before Millen could respond, and an ear-splitting shriek rose into the air. A beast emerged from the opening as soon as the gate was lifted, and Sable suppressed a cry as she stared down at it. It had a large, almost rounded back of thick, dark green skin, and each of its long forelimbs ended in a set a vicious-looking claws. Its back legs were scrabbling against the sand beneath it in its haste to reach the prisoners, but a thick chain around its ankle was keeping it back. It slashed out with its claws as its large jaws clacked open and closed, its teeth glinting in the strong sunlight.

The prisoners cried out from the posts where they had been secured, but there was no escape, no matter how much they writhed and struggled as the beast slowly approached.

'A greenhide,' said Millen; 'that's what happens to them.'

The crowd whooped and cheered as a long section of the beast's chain was loosened, and the monster charged forwards, its shriek echoing off the round wall of the arena. It reached the line of posts in seconds, and Sable glanced away as its claws tore through the first prisoner.

'Enjoying the show?' said Gantu as he sat back down next to her. He gave a glare to Millen, who lowered his head and edged away.

'Hmm,' said Sable. 'I'm not sure if "enjoying" is the right word.'

Gantu laughed as he watched the greenhide tear through the prisoners, then placed his arm over Sable's shoulder and pulled her closer. She noticed his eyes as he stared at the slaughter unfolding on the sand below them, and she didn't need to enter his mind to know the pleasure he was getting from watching the prisoners die.

It was none of her business, she told herself. Lostwell wasn't her world, and Alea Tanton wasn't her city. She had seen plenty of death in her twenty-eight years of life; much of it caused by her, but she had never taken pleasure in it, never actually *enjoyed* it. She had done some terrible things, but they had been for a greater cause, and it wasn't her fault that the cause she had been fighting for had turned out to be a sham.

She struggled against her feelings of revulsion as the crowd bayed for the slaughter of the prisoners. Gantu was rocking with laughter, his hand gripping Sable's shoulder tightly, his eyes fixed on the spectacle.

'Hector's hungry today,' he said.

Sable frowned. 'Hector? You mean that beast has a name?'

'We give all our greenhides names,' he said. 'The Blue Thumbs have six of them just now.'

'Seven,' muttered Millen.

Gantu turned and cast a glare of contempt at his younger cousin. 'Smart ass. Why don't you go and fetch some drinks for me and Sable, eh? Do something useful for a change.'

Millen got to his feet, looking pleased at the opportunity to get away from his cousin's presence for a while.

'Little toerag,' Gantu muttered to Sable. 'I hope he wasn't bothering you when I was talking to those guys.'

She shrugged. 'No more than usual.'

'Good. I'll break him in two if he so much as looks at you the wrong way.'

The crowd began to settle as the final prisoner was torn to bloody pieces by the greenhide. The beast crouched by the remains of one of the bodies, eating its fill, its teeth and claws dripping red onto the sand.

'Does this happen every day?' Sable asked. 'Not just here, but at the arenas of the other two teams as well?'

'Yes.'

'That's a lot of executions.'

Gantu snorted. 'Alea Tanton is a rough place.'

'Still, that's over a thousand executions a month.'

He gave her a glance that she interpreted as him wanting her to be quiet. She frowned, wondering how much longer she needed to humour him. He had connections – people Sable wanted to meet, but at the same time she was starting to tire of him. She turned to the sands of the arena. The chain attached to the greenhide was being wound back as slaves turned a large winch, and the beast was being dragged across the ground, its claws grasping onto chunks of flesh as it shrieked in protest. More slaves entered from another gate and, under the close supervision of armoured guards, began gathering the scattered body parts into great baskets.

Millen appeared, carrying a tray up the steep steps that ran by the stone benches. He eased his way past the groups of spectators, and lowered the tray next to Gantu.

'About time,' the older cousin said. 'I was dying from thirst.'

Sable watched as Millen picked up a jug of wine and filled two ceramic mugs with the red liquid. Behind him, down on the sands of the arena, the greenhide had been hauled back through a gate, which closed with a loud clang of metal. At the opposite end of the round arena, another gate opened, and the crowd let out a great roar as two columns of warriors ran onto the sand.

'Get out of the way,' Gantu cried, pushing Millen to the side and getting to his feet.

The younger cousin ducked down, and squeezed onto the stone bench as Gantu raised his fists and cheered.

'Is that them?' whispered Sable to Millen. 'The fabled Blue Thumbs?'

Millen nodded.

The two columns of warriors continued onto the middle of the sand then halted, lifting their weapons to salute the crowd. Each was wearing a different assortment of armour; some in leather, others in steel, with a variety of shields, helmets and weapons. All, however, had a dark blue sash over their shoulders. A tall, broad man walked into the midst of the two dozen warriors, a blue plume atop a bronze helmet that covered his face.

'Kelito!' roared Gantu, his fists punching the air.

The warrior in the centre circled slowly, taking in the applause and cries of the crowd.

Sable raised an eyebrow at Millen.

'He's the team captain,' he whispered.

The warriors turned as one, and saluted the high benches where, Sable noticed, a woman had appeared. She was tall, and dressed in flowing blue robes, while around her stood thick rows of soldiers. She rose from her seat, and lifted her hands into the air.

The crowd started to chant: 'Felice; Felice,' and the woman smiled benevolently at them. She then turned her gaze down to the team on the sands, and clapped her hands together. At once, the warriors paired off, and began sparring as the woman returned to her seat.

Sable stared at her. She turned to ask Millen a question, but Gantu sat down between them and picked up his wine.

'The boys are looking good,' he said as he drank; 'and just as well. With only nine days before we have to play the Fordian assholes, we can't be taking any chances.'

Sable's attention drifted away as Gantu continued talking about the team, and their prospects of defeating the hated Fordians. She gazed over the arena at the god sitting on the high benches across from her. It had taken Sable five days in the city to catch her first glimpse of one of the immortal rulers of Alea Tanton. She felt for her vision powers and sent her sight towards Lady Felice as Gantu chattered about team tactics.

The god was sitting alone, her guards keeping a space clear around her, and Sable pushed her vision into the woman's head, entering through her open eyes.

The first emotion she encountered was a frustrated and angry boredom. Lady Felice may have been smiling, but her inner thoughts betrayed the contempt in which she held the assembled crowd of Blue Thumb supporters.

Never mind that, thought Sable, pushing the god's feelings to the side; where's her Quadrant? The Holdfast mage had been keeping an eye on the high benches, and had seen no sign of the god arriving. She delved into the god's recent memories, keeping her presence hidden, and found what she needed – a recollection from a few minutes before, of Felice tucking the copper-coloured device deep within her robes.

Sable smiled. Gotcha. Then she frowned. Someone was saying her name.

She pulled her vision back to her body to see Gantu glaring at her.

'Are you ignoring me?' he cried, his face red with fury. 'I've been speaking to you, and you give me nothing but a blank stare?'

Sable glanced around. Several of Gantu's cronies were watching as their boss berated her, while Millen was wearing an expression of unsettled fear.

'I was listening, honey,' she said, 'but sports aren't my favourite passion; you know that.'

She darted into his mind before he could say anything else.

You're not angry with me. Everything's fine. You're happy that I'm here.

Gantu opened his mouth, then hesitated, his eyes blinking. His frown dropped, and he smiled.

'Tell me more about Kelito,' she said; 'he seems like a pretty decent captain.'

Gantu grinned. 'Oh, he is, babe; he's the best captain we've had in years.'

His cronies relaxed and turned back to the arena as Gantu chattered on about how wonderful Kelito was. Sable nodded and tried to look interested, then took a sip of wine. Millen caught her eyes for a second, then he flushed and looked away.

They watched the team practise on the sands below them for an hour, as Sable kept half an eye on Lady Felice. The god applauded and cheered at the appropriate points, doing almost as good a job of hiding her true feelings as Sable was, then a loud gong sounded, and the team stopped their drills. They lined up in front of their captain, and Kelito inspected them as the crowd watched. When he reached the end of the line, they turned to face Lady Felice, and bowed as one. Applause echoed round the arena as the team strode towards one of the gates that led into their training quarters, and the crowd began to get to their feet.

'That's the signal that it's time for the food dole,' said Gantu.

Lady Felice raised a hand, stilling the crowd. A courtier approached the god, bowed, then turned to face the rest of the arena.

'Before you depart,' he called out to the crowd, his clear voice carrying to the furthest benches. He waited a moment as the spectators settled again. 'Following our victory here eleven days ago against the Bloodflies...' he paused to allow the crowd to cheer; 'the most noble Lady Felice, patron of the Blue Thumbs, has a special treat for you today.' He gestured with his right hand, and a large gate began to open, the largest of any that ran round the walled perimeter of the sand.

The crowd turned, staring in anticipation.

'Behold,' cried the courtier; 'Sanguino, the dragon captured from the Bloodflies.'

'Ha!' yelled Gantu, jumping to his feet along with most of the crowd. They stared down at the gate as the iron frame was raised. Warriors emerged, followed by slaves who were gripping onto two lines of chains. The crowd roared with savage elation as the large head of a beast appeared in the entrance, a muzzle shackled to its face. The slaves pulled on the chains, and dragged the beast out onto the sands.

Sable narrowed her eyes. She had been told about these creatures, though she had scarcely believed it. At that moment, she realised how wrong she had been. The dragon was enormous, its bulk barely squeezing through the open gate, its scales shimmering in a deep red. Its limbs were linked with thick shackles, and its ripped and ragged wings had been secured to its back with long chains. Captain Kelito had returned to the arena, and he strode to where the head of the dragon was being held in place by the gangs of slaves. He raised a long spear, its point shining in the bright sunlight, and jabbed it up into the dragon's face.

The beast cried out in pain as the crowd cheered and roared. Thousands were on their feet, their fists in the air as they jeered at the captured dragon.

'Kill him!' screamed Gantu, his face red.

Captain Kelito raised the spear again, jabbed the dragon's neck, and a fresh line of blood dripped onto the sand. The dragon struggled and flailed, but the mass of slaves was keeping its body steady.

The slaves began to haul the dragon back through the open gate, and the cheers turned to boos, the arena reverberating with the angry cries of the crowd. Sable shuddered as the dragon disappeared back into the large tunnel. It wasn't so much pity she felt for the tormented beast, but more revulsion at the bloodlust of the crowd. A chant of 'kill, kill,' rang out from the stone benches, and the courtier raised his hands for silence. The crowd slowly settled, though many, including Gantu, remained on their feet.

'The dragon Sanguino,' the courtier called out, 'will die, of that there is no doubt. Captured in fair combat by the mighty Blue Thumbs, this beast, the prized champion of the Bloodflies, shall meet his end, here on the legendary sands on the Central Pits – but not today.'

The crowd muttered aloud, and more booing rose up.

'In a little over two months from now,' the courtier went on, 'we shall be hosting, here in the Central Pits, both the Bloodflies and the Dead-skins. What better way to start the games that day than with the death of Sanguino? Imagine the shame the Bloodflies and their supporters will feel, having to watch as their champion is put to the sword!'

Excitement rippled through the arena, and Lady Felice stood and waved to the crowd, smiling as they roared their approval. Then, without warning, she vanished, and the spectators began making their way towards the steps that led out of the arena.

Sable frowned as she got to her feet. No one in the crowd had looked surprised to see the god disappear, therefore, she reasoned, they must be used to such events. Still, the main purpose for her attendance at the Central Pits that day had been fulfilled – she had located a Quadrant. She smiled at Gantu as he escorted her down the steps, and he beamed back. It was clear from his expression that he was revelling in the jealous and admiring glances that Sable was attracting from the other spectators. Occasionally she found her beauty a hindrance, but not often.

Gantu led Sable and his cronies down into the interior of the arena.

The dole was underway within a central courtyard, and slaves were handing out large baskets of food and drink to anyone with a Blue Thumb tattoo. The free supplies were the main reason most of the spectators came to the arena each day; with unemployment so high, it was one of the few reliable ways to stave off hunger in Alea Tanton. Millen had told her that similar doles occurred daily at the arenas of the Bloodflies and Deadskins within their districts of the vast city that sprawled along the coast between Old Alea and Old Tanton.

While most of the crowd formed queues to receive their baskets, Gantu barged to the front, making a show of his strength and influence among the supporters of the Blue Thumbs. Some lowered their eyes as he passed, while others called out greetings to him. He nodded to a few, and those he chose to ignore quickly looked away. At the head of the line, the slaves bowed before him, and handed over two baskets to each of Gantu's cronies, while the guards glanced the other way.

They were approached by another large group as they were making their way out into the bright sunshine. A broad man was at their head, his hands tattooed blue all over, and he nodded to Gantu.

'Braxa,' Gantu said, returning the nod as the two groups of gang cronies eyed each other.

'I propose a truce, Gantu,' the broad man said, his arms folded across his chest.

Gantu said nothing.

'In a few days, the Blue Thumbs will visit the Deadskins' arena,' Braxa went on. 'We should be planning what to do, instead of fighting each other.'

'Well, well,' said Gantu. 'Is that an admission of defeat?'

Braxa scowled. 'No. I'll be more than happy to resume our battles after the game, but why should we help those Fordian assholes? We need to be at full strength when we go to the Northern Pits. The Deadskins will piss all over us if we're fighting among ourselves.'

Gantu twisted his fingers through his long moustache for a moment, and Sable darted into his mind. She could sense the intense loathing Gantu felt for his rival gang-leader, and his stubbornness. His pride meant he would rather go down fighting than show any sign of weakness, even when he knew that what Braxa was suggesting was reasonable. If Sable did nothing, there was a good chance violence would break out, and she couldn't risk Gantu getting injured or killed; not when he was her way to getting her hands on the Quadrant.

Tell him you agree to the truce. It will make you look magnanimous and powerful.

Gantu blinked, his eyes tightening. 'Fine. You can have your damned truce.'

Braxa raised an eyebrow, looking a little surprised. He nodded. 'See you at the Northern Pits.'

Gantu waited until Braxa and his group had walked away, then turned to his own cronies. 'Come on, let's get drunk.'

Sable stood alone on the roof of the high apartment block, smoking in the warm night air. Tobacco was a habit seemingly only enjoyed by Fordians in the city, and Gantu had forbidden her from lighting up anywhere inside the building that he and his gang inhabited. She didn't mind; it gave her an excuse to escape his attentions, and, more importantly, to use her vision powers in peace.

After five days, she still only had a sketchy idea of the layout of the city. In the north spread the slums of the Fordians, which came to an end by the walled harbour town of Old Tanton. The central districts were taken up by the Torduans – the peoples who followed the Blue Thumbs, and then, further south, lay the slums of the Shinstrans, clustered for miles around the pits that were home to the Bloodflies. Beyond that was the high promontory where Old Alea sat, towering above the rest of the city. Old Alea was where the gods of Lostwell, including Lady Felice, dwelt in luxury, and although it was twenty miles from Gantu's apartment block, it was where Sable knew she needed to go. She had a mission; a task – find a Quadrant at any cost, and deliver it to her niece Karalyn Holdfast.

Sable gazed down at the narrow warren of streets and flicked ash over the low wall that surrounded the rooftop. Her niece hated her. Despised her. Sable didn't blame Karalyn for that; after the pain she had caused the rest of her family, she deserved to be hated. She should have been executed for what she had done, instead of being dragged off to Lostwell in an attempt to find Karalyn's brother, a boy Sable had never met. Karalyn could have taken anyone she wished to Lostwell, but instead had chosen Sable and Belinda, to save them from the wrath of the Empress.

They had been offered a second chance, and Sable was determined not to wreck it. Her family might loathe her, and expect her to fail, but she would show them; she would prove to them that she could be trusted, and she would prove it to herself at the same time.

A low rumble distracted her, then she felt the building shake. She gripped the top of the low wall, her eyes wide as screams arose from the streets and housing blocks around her. Tiles toppled from rooftops, and an excruciating sound of stone grinding against stone filled her ears. In seconds it was over, and Sable glanced around.

She heard a sound behind her and jumped.

'It was an earthquake,' said a voice.

She turned. 'Damn it, Millen, don't sneak up on me like that.'

The young man smiled. 'Sorry.'

'You don't look it.' She lit another cigarette, her hands trembling. 'An earthquake?'

'Yes – a mild one. The city gets half a dozen of those a year, it's nothing to worry about.'

Sable glared at him. 'Who's worried?'

Millen strode up next to her and peered down at the streets. 'I thought you'd be used to earthquakes; I thought they were common where you come from.'

Sable frowned. Her cover story was that she was from the Kingdom of Kinell, a small realm on the eastern coast of Khatanax, and before leaving Karalyn, she had briefly studied the customs and culture of its people. She couldn't remember reading anything about earthquakes though, so merely nodded and said nothing.

'Well?' he said.

'Well, what?'

'Are there earthquakes in Kinell?'

Sable sighed, then entered his mind.

You will stop asking me questions about Kinell. You don't care. You are content with me changing the subject.

'So,' she said, 'did you want me for something, or did you just fancy getting some night air?'

'Gantu sent me.'

'Oh.'

'He was looking for you. He says he's ready to retire for the evening and, well... he wants you.'

Sable nodded. 'Right.'

Millen caught her eye, a melancholy look on his face. 'How do you do it?'

'Do what?'

'How do you put up with him? You seem smart, and you're way too beautiful for that stupid thug. I don't understand it, you should be...'

'Shut up,' she said, shaking her head. 'You're drunk; you shouldn't be saying things like that to me.'

'I can't help it; I...'

'Listen to me, Millen,' she said; 'don't trust me, I mean it.'

His eyebrows furrowed, but he said nothing. Sable crushed the cigarette butt under the heel of a sandal and strode past him, heading for the stairs.

'There you are!' Gantu cried as she entered his dimly-lit chambers. He gestured to the small group clustered on the low couches, and they rose, bowed, and departed.

Sable smiled and sat next to him on the long couch. He placed one arm round her shoulder, and she smelled the alcohol on his breath as he kissed her neck.

'You are gorgeous,' he mumbled, his hand straying up her leg, 'and mine.'

She took his hand in hers and stood, then led him to the enormous bed chamber that lay next to his reception room. She lit a small lamp as Gantu began pulling his clothes off, his eyes never leaving her.

She put her hands on her hips. 'Get onto the bed.'

He grinned, and reclined onto the thick mattress.

'Good,' she said as she entered his mind.

Sleep.

His eyes snapped shut, and his head crashed down against the pillow.

Dream about us lying together, and when you awaken in the morning you will believe it really happened.

A smile crept over his sleeping face, and he started to snore.

Sable slipped out of her dress and let it fall to the floor. She stretched, got into the other side of the bed, and settled down for a good night's rest.

CHAPTER 2

DUN KHATAR

Dun Khatar, Southern Khatanax – 12th Dunninch 5252

A warm wind gusted across Aila's face, and she lifted a hand to her eyes to shield them from the harsh sunlight, and from the sand that was swirling around them. She turned, and saw everyone who had left the City standing close by.

'Are we there?' she said to Corthie. 'Are we on Lostwell?'

Naxor pulled his cloak up to cover most of his head. 'Yes.'

'I don't recognise where we are,' said Corthie.

'That is unsurprising,' said Naxor, 'seeing as your experience of Lostwell was confined to Gadena's training camp.' He glanced at the others. 'We should get out of this wind.'

The dragon lifted her head above them, as Maddie sheltered among her large, scaled limbs. 'Like Corthie,' said Blackrose, 'I do not recognise this place.'

Naxor muttered under his breath. 'Again, unsurprising.'

Aila felt the wind pick up. Around them stretched a series of ruins – low sandstone walls, and the remains of gigantic buildings that had half-collapsed. A thick layer of sand and ash was covering the ground, and the wind was throwing it into their faces as they blinked under the sun.

'Follow me,' said Naxor as he began to stride off, his boots crunching over the thick carpet of pale sand.

The others watched him for a moment, then Belinda shrugged, drew her sword and followed him. Aila and Corthie went after her, then Maddie and the dragon a few paces to their rear. Naxor walked down what had once been a wide boulevard, with ruined structures on either side, and a line of empty marble plinths running down its centre. Nothing was growing among the ruins; no grass or shrubs, and there was no sound except for the howling wind. Ahead of them loomed a large building, the tallest structure that Aila could see. Several of its towers had fallen, and fragments of weathered masonry lay scattered across the ruined streets. Naxor made directly for an arched entrance-way, which was still standing, despite wide cracks that ran down its ashlar blocks. He climbed a set of uneven steps and strode under the archway, disappearing into the interior shadows of the building.

Blackrose lowered her head to the entrance, then turned to Maddie. 'I think I might remain outside.'

Her rider frowned. 'Why? I know you're a little on the large side, but you'll fit through there.'

The dragon tilted her head. 'I am more concerned about the building collapsing on top of us. It does not appear to be very stable.'

Naxor re-appeared at the entrance. 'It's been standing for hundreds of years; it's perfectly safe.'

Aila glanced at Corthie. 'Anything's better than being out here in this wind.'

He frowned, and cast a suspicious glance at Naxor. 'I get the feeling your cousin is trying to trick us.'

Naxor shook his head. 'Suit yourselves. You dragged me here because I was the only person who knew anything about Lostwell. Well, here we are. If you don't like it, we could always go back to Pella.'

'No, thanks,' said Belinda. She climbed the steps and entered the building, her sword gripped in her right hand.

The others hesitated for a moment, then followed her. Aila walked up the steps, and strode into the dark building, welcoming the immediate relief from the wind. She shook her hair, and a shimmer of sand fell from her locks as she gazed around. They moved further into the building as Blackrose squeezed through the archway, temporarily cutting off the only source of light in the interior. Once the dragon was through, she moved to the side to allow the strong daylight to shine through the entrance.

'This is the old Palace of the Ascendants,' said Naxor. He pulled the cloak from his face and lifted a water-bottle to his lips. 'It may look a little shabby now, but believe me, it was quite a glory in its day.'

Maddie glanced at him from where she was unstrapping a bag from the dragon's side. 'And how would you know that?'

'Because, young lady, this was one of the first places I visited when I started travelling to Lostwell. For over sixty years, it was to this palace, in this city, where I would bring salve to trade for champions.'

Maddie pulled the bag to the dusty ground and knelt by it. 'And then what happened?'

'Lostwell was invaded.'

'Who cares?' said Aila. 'Why are we not at my brother's castle? I thought we were going to the Falls of Iron.'

Naxor laughed. 'What, with Maddie in charge of the Quadrant? If it had been up to me, I could have taken us directly to Lord Irno's castle in the Falls of Iron.'

Maddie frowned. 'Did I do something wrong?'

'You have no idea what you're dealing with, do you?' Naxor said, shaking his head. 'What you did, little Maddie, was this – you used the Quadrant to return us to its place of origin; the place where our world, the world of Pella, Auldan and the Bulwark, was created.' He sat on a fallen block of stone and stretched his legs out. 'We are in Dun Khatar, the old capital city of Khatanax. It was here that one of the Ascendants – Nathaniel I believe his name to be – created our world.'

Aila glanced at Belinda, who was frowning. 'Did you hear that?' she said. 'Your old boyfriend used to live here.'

Belinda shrugged.

Naxor laughed. 'Why was I unaware of this? Belinda and Nathaniel?'

'Did you ever meet him?' said Corthie.

'No. I used to deal with a god by the name of Agatha before the invasion that destroyed Dun Khatar. When the fighting was over, I had to be a lot sneakier, as agents were searching for the source of the salve.'

Maddie lifted some parcels of food from the bag and unwrapped them on the ground. 'We should eat, and then we can go to this Falls of Iron.'

'And how do you intend to get there?' said Naxor.

Maddie frowned at him. 'With the Quadrant.'

'I see. And you know how to get it to take us to the Falls of Iron, do you?'

'Well, no, but you can show me.'

Naxor snorted. 'Forget it. If, however, you were to lend me the device, then I shall take us all there.'

'Out of the question,' said Blackrose. 'You have already proved to us that you cannot be trusted with the Quadrant.'

Maddie took the copper-coloured device out from under her cloak, and glanced closely at it.

'Good luck learning how to use it without my help,' said Naxor. 'Remember, get it wrong, and you could appear in the middle of a mountain, or above an ocean.'

'Screw you,' said Maddie. 'Blackrose knows how to use it – she can teach me.'

Naxor smirked at the dragon. 'Go on then.'

'Unfortunately,' Blackrose said, 'the treacherous little demigod is correct.'

'What?' said Maddie. 'But you told me you knew how it worked.'

'I do, but without knowing the precise location of the Falls of Iron, I cannot show you how to take us there.'

Naxor laughed again.

'Shut up,' said Aila.

Belinda glanced over, the sword still in her hand. 'I could torture him until he tells us.'

'Let me help,' said Corthie; 'please.'

'Enough!' cried Aila. 'What is wrong with us? We've only been gone from the City for ten minutes, and already we're shouting and threatening each other.'

'I have a simple solution,' said Blackrose. 'I know enough to instruct Maddie on how to transport us directly to my world – Dragon Eyre. I propose we leave now. Anyone who wishes can depart with us. Or not.'

'What?' said Aila. 'You would abandon us on Lostwell?'

'I would.'

Maddie shook her head. 'We can't,' she said to the dragon. 'We need to find Corthie's sister, and then we can go.'

Aila glared at Naxor. 'You knew we would end up among these ruins, didn't you? Why didn't you tell us before we left?'

'What, and miss all the fun? Call it my way of getting a little revenge, cousin. Now, let's all calm down, and I'll do what I was asked to do.' He picked up a stick and began drawing on the thick layer of dust and sand on the ground. He sketched a shape. 'This is Khatanax.'

'I thought we were on Lostwell,' said Corthie.

'We are,' Naxor said, 'but there are several continents on Lostwell, and the one we are on is called Khatanax. The wars of the gods turned most of the other continents to ash; either that or they were infested with greenhides and rendered uninhabitable. Khatanax was spared the worst of the damage, at least until the final invasion, which occurred almost two hundred and fifty years ago. That was when the city where we are sitting was reduced to rubble.' He scratched a mark within the outline of the continent. 'Dun Khatar, close to the southern tip of Khatanax. North of us is the Shinstran Desert, and then the Fordian Wastes. Before the invasion, they were the fertile regions of Shinstra and Fordia, but nothing lives there now – the land was poisoned by the gods who attacked. Up here in the west is Tordue, where the city of Alea Tanton lies. Before the invasion it was nothing more than a couple of small fishing towns, but millions live there now – refugees from Fordia and Shinstra mostly, along with thousands of peasants forced off their land. It's where the ruling gods of Lostwell are based, but I would strongly advise against visiting Alea Tanton; it is a pestilent cesspit.'

'For once I agree with you,' said the dragon, her head lowered as she glanced at Naxor's map in the sand. 'Alea Tanton was where I was imprisoned for ten years, and forced to fight in the pits. From what I remember, it is nothing but a never-ending sprawl of slums, where the reek of death and rot is all pervasive.'

'Buckler also came from there,' said Naxor, 'and I remember the state you were both in when I purchased you.'

The dragon glared at the demigod, her teeth bared. 'Never refer to having "purchased" me again, insect. I have never been yours to own.'

Naxor shrugged. 'I'll bear that in mind. Anyway, to the east of Tordue is Kinell, which is nominally a separate kingdom, but in reality it's controlled by the gods who dwell in Alea Tanton. It escaped the ravages of the invasion by submitting immediately, as Shinstra and Fordia should have done.'

'And what about the Falls of Iron?' said Corthie.

'It's here,' said Naxor, planting his stick just south of Tordue. 'It's part of a region called the Four Counties. Like Kinell, they survived the invasion by surrendering to the new regime.' He glanced at Aila. 'It's where Irno has his castle.'

She smiled. 'I can't wait to see him; he was always my favourite out of my brothers and sisters. For three hundred years I thought he was dead, and now he's living in a castle with Vana.'

Naxor nodded. 'Unless the Holdfasts have killed them by now.'

'Karalyn wouldn't have done that,' said Belinda. 'Sable maybe, but not Karalyn.'

Aila frowned. 'Sable?'

'Sable Holdfast,' said Belinda. 'Corthie's aunt.'

'Really?' said Corthie. 'Then why have I never heard of her?'

'Ask your sister.'

'I'm asking you.'

Belinda shook her head. 'And I'm telling you to ask your sister. I don't want to get involved in Holdfast family business.'

Corthie frowned and folded his arms.

'Where is Sable?' said Aila.

'The last I saw her,' said Belinda, 'she was in the Falls of Iron with Karalyn but they weren't, ah... getting along very well.'

'Why not?' said Corthie, his eyes dark.

The god looked away. 'I don't want to tell you. It's not my place.'

Aila saw anger rise up in Corthie's features as he clenched his fists.

'Back to the map,' said Maddie. 'How far are we from the Falls of Iron?'

Naxor pursed his lips. 'Maybe two hundred miles?'

Every eye turned to the dragon.

'Yes?' she said.

'Could you fly us there?' said Aila.

Blackrose lifted her head, her red eyes gleaming in the dim light of the abandoned building.

Naxor laughed. 'It's either that, lizard, or you give me the Quadrant, and we could all be there in moments.'

'Forget it,' said Maddie. 'We all know what happened the last time you had a Quadrant.'

'I could hold my sword to his throat,' said Belinda.

'That wouldn't be necessary,' he said. 'You can trust me.'

'Do you think we're out of our minds, Naxor?' said Maddie. 'You must, otherwise you'd never suggest such nonsense. This is like a big game to you, isn't it? You don't care about me and Blackrose, or about getting Corthie back to his family. I've seen you eye up the bag of salve strapped to the harness; all you want to do is steal it and vanish, so you can go off and live like a debauched king somewhere. You don't give a rat's ass about any of us; well, except maybe Belinda, but that's only because you want to get inside her pants.'

Belinda's face flushed. Naxor glanced from her to Maddie and back again.

'And,' Maddie went on, 'Blackrose isn't a ferry service; she's not here just to carry you lot about all day.'

'Fine,' said Corthie; 'then we'll walk.'

Naxor shook his head, though his eyes were still darting towards Belinda. 'You wouldn't get far.'

'Why not?'

'Were you not listening, young champion? The Shinstran desert is a poisoned wasteland. Nothing lives out there, and there's no water – none.'

Maddie glanced up at Blackrose. 'Maybe we should have a quiet word; just the two of us.'

'As you wish, rider,' the dragon said. She turned her body within the large chamber, then she and Maddie went back to the arched entrance.

Aila frowned at her cousin. 'Was she right?'

'About what, dear Aila?'

'Are you chasing after Belinda?'

Naxor narrowed his eyes. 'And what business is it of yours?'

'None, but if it's true then I might need to have a word with Belinda regarding your previous record with women.'

Belinda frowned. 'I don't need any warnings from you.'

'Hey,' said Maddie before Aila could respond; 'you'd better come and look at this.'

They got up and walked over to the archway, where Maddie was pointing towards the horizon. Aila glanced outside. The first thing she noticed was that the sunlight had faded, and she looked up. To the south of the ruined city was a tall range of mountains, with several peaks in a row, separated by long, high ridges. Smoke was belching up from two of the highest peaks, while a rumble rolled down the hillside. A flutter of light grey material was swirling through the air; a little like snowfall.

'Volcanoes,' said Blackrose.

Aila raised an eyebrow. 'What?'

'We don't have any on our world, cousin dear,' said Naxor, 'but there are several in Khatanax, caused, I believe, by the gods' invasion. Some of the ruling gods in Alea Tanton have power over rock and stone; it was they who levelled this city, not any army. But in doing so, they seem to have caused deep fractures in the ground, from which fire and smoke sometimes spew.'

'Fire?' she gasped.

Naxor nodded. 'And molten rock.'

Aila held out her hand and a wisp of light grey material landed on her palm. 'This is ash?'

'Yes,' said Blackrose; 'the ruins are thick with it.'

A deep rumble echoed from the mountainside, and a great blast of thick dark smoke rose from the tallest peak, spreading out to join the other plumes that were starting to cover the sky.

'There are many volcanoes on Dragon Eyre,' said Blackrose; 'it is the mechanism by which new islands are formed. If there is a risk that an eruption may be imminent, then I do not wish to fly. I have seen what can happen to dragons caught in a shower of burning rocks.'

'But are we safe here?' said Aila. 'I mean, if it... erupts?'

The dragon tilted her head. 'Probably.'

'The mountains are twenty miles away,' said Naxor; 'we're safer on the ground than in the air. Safest of all would be if you just gave me the Quadrant.'

The others turned, and began moving back into the shelter of the large, empty chamber.

Naxor shook his head at them. 'Does no one trust me?'

They sat and ate in the dusty chamber while the light outside faded. The occasional rumble would ripple through the ruins, but Aila saw no sign of burning rocks whenever she glanced through the archway. They had brought enough supplies for several days, but Blackrose's appetite was vast compared to that of the others, and Aila knew they were relying on her to get them across the desert to the Falls of Iron.

No one talked much as they had their meal. Belinda and Naxor would swap the odd glance or two when they thought no one else was looking, while Corthie sat in silence, his eyes heavy and brooding. After a few curt responses, Aila left him alone and sat glumly as she made her way through her rations of dried meat and fruit.

'I have come to a decision,' said Blackrose, breaking into the silence.

Maddie turned to her. 'You have?'

'Yes, rider. Once the smoke from the mountains has settled, I shall take the advice you gave me by the archway and transport everyone to the Falls of Iron.'

Aila sighed in relief. 'Thank you.'

Blackrose inclined her head towards her. 'You are most welcome. To abandon you all here would be dishonourable, and I have no doubt that Maddie would never let me forget it. It has been over twenty years since I was last in Dragon Eyre – a little longer shall not make much difference. I have been told that Karalyn Holdfast does not require a Quadrant to travel between worlds, therefore I am sure she will have no objection to Maddie holding onto the one she currently has in her possession. Does that sound fair?'

'It does,' replied Aila. She glanced at the others, but they said nothing. 'Can you fit us all on your back at once?'

Maddie shook her head. 'There's not enough room on the harness for everybody.'

'Quite,' said Blackrose. 'I shall have to make two trips. For the first, I shall carry Maddie, of course, and also Corthie, so he may be reunited with his sister and aunt. Naxor will be my other passenger.'

'Me?' he said.

'Yes, you, little insect. There is a fair chance that neither of the Holdfasts will be present in the Falls of Iron, and if that is the case, then you will be required. However, I have a condition. If you ask to "borrow" the Quadrant again, I shall drop you into the middle of the fearsome desert you keep talking about, and you can make your own way to Lord Irno's castle. Understood?'

'Um, yes.'

The dragon glanced at Belinda, then turned to Aila. 'For those left behind, we shall leave sufficient supplies for a day and a night. Each two-hundred mile stretch will take me four or five hours to complete, and I shall need to rest once we arrive at our destination.'

Aila nodded, though the prospect of spending a day and a night in the company of Belinda did not fill her with any joy.

'I'd rather Aila came with us on the first trip,' said Corthie.

'I thought you might,' said Blackrose, 'but Naxor must accompany us. You will not be apart for long, and Belinda's skills with a sword should keep your beloved safe.'

Aila cringed a little. She hadn't felt much like Corthie's beloved since they had arrived. He was wrapped up in nerves about meeting his sister, she told herself, but already she missed the days they had spent together in Cuidrach Palace in Pella.

The dragon turned from them and made her way to the archway to gaze out at the smoke filling the sky.

'Looks like we'll be here all night,' said Maddie. 'Anyone know any songs?'

Corthie pulled himself to his feet and strode off into the darkness, heading away from the light coming from the archway.

'I guess that's a "no" from him,' said Maddie.

Aila stared at the ground for a moment, then got to her feet.

'Maybe you should give him some time, cousin,' said Naxor.

'He's mortal,' she said; 'he doesn't have much.'

She set off after Corthie, walking until the shadows engulfed her at the far end of the vast chamber. She glanced around, but there was no sign of him, then she noticed a large opening to her right, through which a faint grey light was seeping. She turned for it, and went under a broad archway. Ahead of her was a wide set of stairs, with an ancient-looking window at the top, the glass long gone, leaving a tall rent in the side of the building. Corthie was seated on the wide ledge, his gaze on the view outside. Aila climbed the stairs in silence.

'Hey,' she said as she reached him.

He glanced at her, then turned back to look through the window. Aila followed his glance and gazed across the sprawling landscape of ruins. They seemed to go on for miles. Desolate streets lay half-filled with sand and ash, while collapsed and weathered structures lined them, making a recognisable grid. Several buildings still rose above one storey, but the majority had crumbled, their interiors exposed to the howling winds.

'This must have been some place,' she said.

'Aye,' he muttered.

'You'll get to see your sister soon. That must feel good.'

'If she's there.'

Aila fought back her irritation at his attitude. 'This is the first time I've seen you like this,' she said. 'Setbacks don't usually bother you.'

He turned to her. 'Belinda's keeping something from me. I don't know what it is, but it must be important.'

'About your aunt, you mean? Sable? It's strange you've never heard of her.'

'I guess, but there's more to it than that. There's something I can't quite put my finger on, but it's filling me with apprehension about meeting Karalyn. Something's wrong.'

'Maybe it's this place,' she said. 'It wasn't what I was expecting, I admit. Remember that I've lived in the same town for nearly eight centuries. I'm slightly terrified if I'm being honest.'

'Do you regret coming along?'

'No, but I feel like someone who has stepped outside their front door for the first time, and found that the world is not as welcoming as they'd hoped. The City felt like a prison at times, but at least it was familiar.'

He took her hand. 'Whatever happens, we'll face it together.'

'Alright, but that means no more storming off on your own. If something's bothering you, tell me.'

'You've lived the equivalent of a dozen full lives,' he said; 'sometimes, you must think that I'm a child.'

'Yes, but don't take offence – I think that way about every mortal I meet, not just the ones who are only nineteen. The second century was the hardest, when every mortal I knew in my youth had died, and the years started to merge into a blur; decades would pass, and I would wonder what in Malik's name I had done during that time. Only two things have ever made me feel young again – Yendra's rebellion, and you. With you the world seems fresh and new, and a little bit scary.'

For the first time since arriving, Corthie's frown began to fade, and she felt a tingle down her spine as he gazed at her.

'We should go back to the others,' she said.

He reached out with his hand, and his fingers touched her face, drawing her in close to him. 'Not yet.'

CHAPTER 3
REFINED

Dun Khatar, Southern Khatanax – 13th Dunninch 5252

As soon as Maddie's eyes opened, she reached beneath her to make sure the Quadrant was still there. Curled up as she was among Blackrose's limbs, she doubted that Naxor would have been able to steal it from her, but she still felt reassured when she felt the metal device against her fingertips. She stretched and scrambled to her feet, stepping round a giant, scaly forelimb.

Bright sunlight was shining through the archway at the end of the vast hall, and she could see a perfect blue sky framed against the summits of the mountain range. She strode to the entrance and leaned against the stone blocks. A strong wind was blowing from the west, and there was no smoke left in the sky.

'Good morning,' said a voice next to her.

'Morning, Belinda,' she said. 'Did you sleep well? Sorry if Blackrose's snoring kept you all awake; at times I couldn't tell if the rumbling was coming from her or the volcano.'

'I didn't sleep,' the god said; 'I was up all night with Naxor.'

Maddie flushed. 'Oh. Um... that's eh... Right.'

'We were talking, that's all. Talking.'

'Of course you were. It's none of my business what you get up to.'

'Naxor wanted more, but I...' Her voice tailed away into silence as she gazed out at the view of the mountains. 'Can I ask you something?'

'Sure.'

'How do you know if someone actually likes you, or if they just want to, well, as you put it, "get into my pants"?'

Maddie blinked. 'Um, I don't know if you're asking the right person, Belinda. I'm clueless when it comes to relationships. My entire experience with guys amounts to a few drunken fumbles in the dark. Maybe you should ask Aila.'

Belinda shook her head. 'I don't think she likes me, and it would be strange to confide in someone so old.'

'But you're eons older than her; thirty thousand years against her eight hundred.'

'Yes, but I only remember the last few years. That's my problem; I'm thinking like a mortal, not as a god. It's humiliating. Naxor and Aila look down on me like a child, whereas you... well, you are a child, really.'

Maddie frowned.

'When we find Karalyn,' Belinda went on, oblivious to Maddie's embarrassment, 'I intend to ask her to restore the rest of my vision powers, at a minimum. That way, I'll be able to read Naxor's thoughts and find out the truth for myself. Until then, I think I'll be keeping my pants on.'

'I'm not sure I'd want to see what was going on inside his head. If you like him, then there's nothing wrong with just having some fun.'

'Fun? Are you serious? He makes my insides twist whenever he looks at me; whatever I'm feeling, it's not "fun".'

'Malik's ass, you're not in love with him, are you?'

Belinda lowered her eyes. 'I don't know. How is it supposed to feel?'

'Again, you're asking the wrong person. Sorry I'm not much use, but I've never been in love, not unless you count me and Blackrose, but that's not quite the same as you and Naxor. The only thing I would say is that, well, he doesn't exactly strike me as very trustworthy. I slept with my hand on the Quadrant all night.'

'He's trying to change; people just need to give him a chance to show it.'

Maddie raised an eyebrow.

Belinda sighed. 'We should wake everyone up. The volcano might start rumbling again, and Blackrose should get into the air while the skies are still clear.' She glanced at Maddie. 'Thanks for listening.'

'Any time,' Maddie said, though she wondered what possible help she could have been. She turned as Belinda strode back into the huge chamber, and saw Aila and Corthie appear from wherever they had spent the night. They looked happy enough, but Maddie remembered her sister's words, about how their relationship was doomed.

Love, she thought; who needs it?

Two hours later, the dragon rose into the bright morning sunshine, with Maddie, Corthie and Naxor strapped to the harness that spread across her shoulders. Maddie sat in the middle, with the ex-champion to her left, and the demigod to her right. Below them, Aila and Belinda were watching from the shadows of the palace ruins, their hands up to shield their eyes from the sun.

Corthie waved down to them, then settled into the harness, his eyes troubled.

'It's so bright here,' Maddie said as she glanced around. 'Wow. The city is huge. The ruins go on forever. Tell me what I'm seeing, Naxor.'

'If I must,' the demigod said. 'Your Quadrant took us directly to the centre of Dun Khatar, because, I guess, that was where Nathaniel was when he created our world; the world of Auldan, Medio and the Bulwark. That's why all of the buildings look so big; they were the palaces and towers from where the rebel gods ruled the whole of Lostwell. I'm not sure how many people lived here before the final invasion, but it must have been millions.'

Maddie glanced down, her eyes making out the old street layout. Below them, where the Palace of the Ascendants stood, was a series of concentric rings, from where several wide boulevards extended, like the spokes of a wheel, she thought, though the spokes were all ranged on a single side of the central circle.

Naxor pointed down at a dark ribbon that wound through the streets. 'The river Flaxon,' he said; 'now silted up and barren. Whatever the invading gods did to destroy this place, they somehow made the rivers all dry up. They changed the entire climate of the continent, making it hotter and drier. Once, the whole land was green and fertile, and now only Tordue and Kinell are still inhabitable, along with a small strip by the Southern Cape.'

'Why did they invade?' she said.

'Who knows? The wars of the gods go back millennia. I'm not sure what first started it all.'

A snorting sound came from the dragon. 'Tell her the truth, insect.'

Naxor looked puzzled. 'I am telling the truth. I have no idea why the gods of old started killing each other.'

'That's not what I meant,' said Blackrose, 'and you know it. The wars of the gods ended ages ago; both sides had utterly exhausted themselves, and Lostwell lay in peace for thousands of years before the final invasion. Tell her why the wars restarted, insect. Tell her the cause of the final invasion.'

Naxor glanced away as both Corthie and Maddie turned to him.

'Well?' said Maddie.

'Salve,' Naxor muttered.

'What?' said Maddie. 'You mean they wanted salve so much they went to war for it?'

'Yes.'

'But that's not the whole story,' said Blackrose.

Naxor scowled. 'Then why don't you tell it?'

'Very well. The wars had consumed world after world in an unending cycle of carnage and annihilation, until, finally, they petered out. Why? Because the gods themselves, the Ascendants, and the Ancients, had aged over millennia and had become too decrepit to continue. Their offspring, and the offspring of their offspring, found their powers diluted with every generation. Given another thousand years, and the rule of the gods would have been over, forever. Instead, salve made its appearance. Withered old husks who had barely moved from their thrones in centuries were suddenly reinvigorated, and their pride and lust for power awoke anew, and refreshed. They conquered Lostwell to ensure that they would be the ones who controlled the supply of salve, not the rebels, and then they spread, giddy with youth and power, and took the last remaining refuges that had eluded them up to that point.'

'You mean Dragon Eyre?' said Maddie.

'Indeed, rider. My world was one of those devastated by the second spring of the gods. Were it not for salve, then I would still be queen.'

Maddie turned to Naxor, her eyes narrow.

'Look,' he said, 'I had no idea that any of that would happen. All I knew was that I needed champions to save the City from the green-hides. How was I supposed to know that the gods would go wild for salve? Besides, I was under orders from the God-King himself; I was only doing what I was told.'

'How much salve did you bring here?' said Corthie.

'I'm not sure exactly. Many tons over the years, I suppose.'

'Tons?'

Naxor shrugged. 'I was good at my job.'

'And what will happen,' Corthie went on, 'now that the City has shut off the supply?'

Maddie groaned. 'Whatever it is, it won't be good.'

'It is addictive to gods,' Blackrose said, 'and mortals. There could be trouble when it starts to run low.'

'That doesn't have to be the case,' said Naxor.

'What do you mean?' said Maddie. 'You heard what Queen Emily said – there are to be no more shipments of salve from the City to Lostwell.'

Naxor smiled. 'Technically, the high valley in the mountains where we found that rich seam of salve is not actually in the City.'

'So that's why you're after the Quadrant?' said Corthie. 'You want to return there and start mining it out?' He shook his head. 'You shouldn't have told us.'

'Who else would I tell?' said Naxor. 'We are among the very few who are aware that there is another source of salve. Think about it for a moment before dismissing it. Blackrose – you need funds to raise an army to retake your world from the gods; you cannot do it on your own. Where will you find such resources? It would only take us a few days to amass an enormous amount of salve; we could refine it in Irno's castle in the Falls of Iron, and the delightful Queen Emily would never need to know.'

Corthie glared at him. 'I knew you were trying to trick us.'

Naxor laughed. 'Trick you? I'm not trying to trick you – if I were, would I be telling you this? All I am doing is making a simple suggestion. A business proposal. Even if I were in possession of a Quadrant, which, quite clearly, I am not, it would still be in my interests to bring you in on this. I can't do it alone, and I certainly have no desire to tell others about the location of our secret little salve mine. You already know.'

'Then we could do it without you,' said Maddie.

'You could try,' Naxor said, 'but I am the only one among us who knows how to refine the raw mineral, and I am the one with connections to the merchants of Alea Tanton. It's taken me decades to build up a discreet network of contacts through whom I can safely distribute the salve. I'd say that I would bring a fair amount to any partnership.'

Maddie glanced away from the demigod, his words triggering a cascade of ideas and emotions within her. What he had said about Blackrose needing resources to fund her takeover of Dragon Eyre had struck deep, and for the first time she tried to imagine what that would mean. Had she been foolish to believe it would be as simple as returning to Blackrose's world, and perhaps burning a few gods? Were they going to need an army?

Her eyes narrowed as a sharp glare of blinding light came from beneath them.

'What is that?' she gasped.

'The beginning of the Shinstran Desert,' said Naxor. 'It would be advisable to shield your eyes, as much of the sand was turned to glass, such was the heat of the inferno that consumed the lands below us.'

'Can you fly with this light?' she cried to the dragon.

'Fear not, rider,' said Blackrose. 'Though it pains me, I can cope with the glare. I will make for the range of mountains to the north-west, where we will be more protected from the light.'

Naxor glanced at Corthie. 'Now do you understand why it would have been impossible to walk across this desert?'

Corthie grunted, but said nothing, a hand up at his eyes. They endured the dazzling glare for over an hour, then approached the brown, barren slopes of the mountains that stretched out to their left. Maddie's head was throbbing by that point, the sea of glass below them reflecting the bright rays of the sun as it rose towards its noon peak. Above them, the sky was a deep blue, with no clouds anywhere, and she missed the soft pinks and peaches of the skies above the City, feeling a pang of homesickness inside her for the first time.

Blackrose soared over the rising hillsides of the mountain range, and Maddie squinted in relief at the dull, dead browns of the lifeless rocks. The temperature dropped as they climbed higher, then Blackrose dipped, following a narrow valley that snaked among the ragged ridges and broken peaks. Far to their left, a pillar of grey smoke was rising from a blackened summit.

She pointed. 'Another volcano?'

'Yes,' said Naxor. 'I think that one spews its lava down into the ocean. If it's the one I'm thinking of, then I once saw it erupt while I was sailing to the Falls of Iron.'

Corthie opened his mouth to speak, then narrowed his eyes and frowned. 'Is that a cloud ahead of us?'

Maddie turned from the sight of the distant volcano to gaze to their front. Below them, the desolate slopes of the valley wound, but she couldn't see anything that looked like a cloud.

'Blackrose,' said Corthie, 'do you see it?'

'I do,' said the dragon; 'directly in front of us; like a small raincloud.'

Naxor frowned. 'I don't see anything.'

'I guess Corthie and Blackrose's eyes are better than ours,' said Maddie. 'He has battle-vision, remember.'

'So do I,' he said.

Maddie raised an eyebrow at the demigod.

'Fine,' he said; 'it might not be as strong as Corthie's, but I'm not terrible in a fight. I just prefer to avoid them if possible.' He squinted into the distance. 'Oh. Yes. I see it now. Blackrose, I think it might be better if you fly around it.'

'Why?' said Maddie, as she finally saw what they were talking about. A dark-grey smudge, just below the horizon. It seemed to be moving, rippling in the wind.

'Because,' said Naxor, 'it's not a cloud.'

Blackrose began to bank to the right, but the hazy smudge seemed to grow larger with every second, and a dull, droning sound echoed across the valley. The dragon picked up speed, but the smudge turned, moving into her path. Maddie heard a low gasp from Naxor.

'What is it?' she said.

He stared at her. 'Bloodflies.'

The droning increased in pitch, and Maddie's mouth opened. The smudge was made up of thousands of flying insects, each as big as her fist.

'Cover your skin!' Naxor cried, pulling a cloak from a harness bag.

Blackrose started to ascend, but the swarm rose up to follow, and within seconds the dragon was enveloped. Maddie yelled in fright as she grabbed a heavy cloak and threw it over herself. The noise became unbearable; a high buzzing drone that surrounded them. Blackrose cried out in pain as the enormous flies attacked her flanks and wings, thousands of the flying beasts alighting on her scales to feast upon her blood. Maddie felt rough impacts all over her body as she hunkered down on the harness saddle, the cloak pulled tightly around her. Tears came to her eyes as she felt a sharp, searing pain in her left ankle, and she cried out as she buried her head into the cloak.

Blackrose roared, and a blaze of fiery heat swept over Maddie. She opened her eyes a slit and peered through a tiny gap in the cloak. All around, the sky seemed to be on fire. Blackrose was moving her head from side to side, sending out huge sprays of flame, in which thousands of the Bloodflies were burning. The heat, stench and noise made Maddie's senses spin, and she clung on to the harness as dizziness flowed through her. Her ankle throbbed in agony as the acrid smoke and flames surged around them, then the heat died away, and a cold wind cooled her skin. With a start, she realised that the sound of the flies had gone, and she glanced around.

Blackrose had risen high into the sky, higher than Maddie had ever experienced before, leaving the swarm behind them. Maddie pulled the cloak from her head, then stared in a mixture of pity and revulsion at the dozens of red blisters covering the dragon's scales. Her eyes went to her ankle, and she saw the bite – an angry sore the size and colour of a ripe plum.

'Amalia's sweet breath,' Naxor muttered, his gaze on the swarm a hundred feet below them.

Maddie turned to Corthie. Like her, he had been bitten, and there were two red weals on his left forearm. He grimaced as he stared at them, then he glanced at the dragon's injured wings and back.

'Blackrose!' Maddie called out. 'Are you alright?'

The dragon did not respond. Instead, she soared ever higher into the sky, until the mountains grew fainter beneath them. Maddie started to feel dizzy, her breath shallow, and the temperature plummeted.

'That's high enough,' yelled Corthie; 'we're going to freeze.'

Blackrose said nothing, but Maddie guessed that she must have heard, as she levelled out. She surged a burst of speed, and the three passengers clung on as the dragon raced across the sky. She took a route between the volcano to their left, and the desert of glass on their right, the miles sweeping by below them.

After what seemed an eternity, Maddie felt the dragon start to descend. Shivering and short of breath, she lifted her face to watch as Blackrose soared downwards, heading towards a long, dark ridge of rock. Rather than circle round as she usually did, Blackrose plummeted down, only slowing as the ground rushed up towards them. She landed on a steep bank of barren hillside, shuddered, then her limbs collapsed beneath her and her head sank to the ground.

Maddie tried to unbuckle herself from the harness, but her hands were too cold to grasp the straps properly.

'Blackrose!' she cried.

Next to her, Corthie pulled his straps free and jumped down to the ground. He ran up to the dragon's head, his eyes roaming over the dozens of livid bites from the Bloodflies.

He turned back to Maddie. 'Her eyes are closed. What do we do?'

'The salve,' she yelled as she continued to struggle with her own straps. 'It's in a bag, attached to the harness.'

Corthie hurried back, and began searching among the stacked luggage and packs.

'Damn it,' Maddie cried as she ripped a fingernail to the quick on the steel buckle.

'Allow me,' said Naxor, reaching over.

He released the buckle, and Maddie almost fell off the broad shoulders of the dragon, her legs still numb from the cold. She slid down to the ground, using her arms to lower herself.

'In there!' she cried to Corthie, pointing at the harness.

Corthie lifted the large leather bag, and undid the strap connecting it to the harness, while Maddie stared in anguish at the still form of the dragon.

'How do we use it?' said Corthie as he opened the bag.

'I'm not sure; we could spread it over her wounds, or maybe burn it so can breathe in the vapours.'

Corthie picked out a piece of raw salve from the bag. His eyes widened, and he dropped it.

'My hand's tingling,' he said, gazing at the chalky residue on his fingertips. 'Is that normal?'

'Yes,' she said, 'and don't waste any. Smear your fingers along your bites.'

He did so, then grimaced in pain as the skin on his arm bubbled, giving off a noxious odour of burning flesh and poison. The bubbling settled and Corthie wiped the remains from his arm, revealing the skin whole and healed underneath.

'Woah,' he said. 'That nipped a bit, but it worked.'

'Of course it worked,' said Naxor, walking towards them. 'The pain was due to its raw state; refined salve doesn't sting at all.'

Maddie glared at him. 'Very interesting, but possibly a little irrelevant right now. We need to get a fire going.'

Naxor glanced around. 'With what? There's nothing to burn up here on this barren mountaintop.'

'Then we'll have to spread it over her by hand.'

'You're joking, yes? That will take hours, and you'll absorb more through your hands than the dragon will; her scales are a lot thicker than your skin.'

'Then what do you suggest, smartass?'

'Do you trust me?'

'No.'

Naxor shrugged. 'A pity.'

Corthie appeared behind the demigod, towering over him. 'What do you want, Naxor? If you know a way to save Blackrose, do it; and then we'll trust you.'

Naxor glanced over his shoulder at the ex-champion, a slight smirk on his lips.

'Give me the salve,' he said, 'then fetch as much alcohol from the harness packs as you can carry; in fact, bring it all.'

Corthie turned to Maddie. She frowned, then nodded, and Corthie passed the sack of salve to Naxor. The demigod smiled, then carried it over to where the dragon's head was lying on the ground. He sat and peered into the large bag. 'Oh, and bring me a cooking pan and a ladle.'

Maddie and Corthie raided the luggage for every jug of Taran brandy that they had been gifted back in Pella, and dumped it all by Naxor, along with a broad steel pot, and a thin, long-handled ladle.

'Thank you,' said Naxor. He lifted the bag and placed it into the pan, then turned the edges of the sack over the wide metal rim. 'This is rather a crude method, grant you,' he said as he opened the first jug of brandy. 'Normally, one would use pure, distilled alcohol and a whole manner of sieves and strainers, but this will have to do.' He took a large swig of brandy, and then poured the rest over the heap of salve resting in the pot. It sizzled and popped, emitting a cloud of fumes. 'Don't breathe that,' he said. 'It's rather toxic.'

Maddie took a step back.

Naxor chuckled as he emptied two more jugs onto the salve. He poured the final two jugs into the pot, then stirred the bubbling, roiling contents with the ladle. When the fumes had died down, he pulled up the edges of the fabric, and lifted the sack clear of the pot, letting a milky-white liquid seep through the cloth in a torrent of heavy drips.

'Behold,' he said, as the liquid filled the pot to a level of two inches, 'almost-refined salve. Not bad if I do say so myself; it reminds me of the countless experiments we carried out in the mine behind the Royal Palace in Ooste. Now, for the next part I'm going to need Corthie's assistance.'

Maddie frowned. 'Why not me?'

'Because you, my dear, lack the brute strength necessary to prise open the jaws of an unconscious dragon.'

'Oh. Alright.'

Naxor stood and pulled the sack away from the pot. He set it down on the ground, then lifted the pot with both hands. He nodded to Corthie, who strode towards Blackrose.

'Sorry about this,' he said to the dragon, then he leaned over and grasped hold of her mouth, his left arm raising her jaw open a few inches as his boots dug into the ground. Naxor edged over, handling the broad pan with care.

'Don't drop it,' shouted Maddie.

'I might if you keep yelling at me.' He lifted the pot close to Black-rose's face, then began to pour the salve into her open mouth. Some of it splashed against the thick tongue, while some ran off the sides of her fearsome teeth. When about a quarter of the contents had been poured in, Naxor stepped back and lowered the pan to the ground, and Corthie let go of the dragon's jaw.

Naxor raised his hand. 'Now, let me wake her, so she can swallow it.'

Corthie backed off to where Maddie stood as Naxor's eyes hazed over. The dragon's body convulsed and shuddered, and she let out a cry of agony, her eyes snapping open. She raised her head, then lowered it again, the claws on her forelimbs gouging through the earth under her. Maddie's eyes scanned the black scales, and she gasped as she saw the salve begin to work. All over the dragon's body, the vicious-looking weals and blisters were healing, and she emitted a low groan of relief.

Her eyes blinked, and she gazed down at Maddie and the others. 'You saved me.'

'It was Naxor,' said Maddie. 'He knew how to refine the salve so you could drink it.'

'Everyone helped,' said Naxor, 'but yes, it was my idea.'

'Thank you,' said the dragon. 'You know, when I return to collect Aila and Belinda, I think I'll fly over the ocean.'

They set off again after Blackrose had rested, Naxor using the time to pour what was left of the refined salve into three of the empty brandy jugs. Blackrose stayed at a high altitude, and they soared up the middle of the long mountain range. Two hours of flying saw them leave the mountains behind, the land below transforming into a grassy plain, criss-crossed with fields and small settlements.

'The Four Counties,' said Naxor. On our left are Cape Armour and the Glebe, while to our right lies Kaulsnaughton. The Falls of Iron are directly ahead.'

They passed a river below them, and Naxor instructed the dragon to follow it upstream, towards another range of mountains. As they approached the heights, Maddie saw that they ended in a colossal cliff face that ran across the plain, beyond which the mountains rose like a wall.

'On the far side of those mountains is Tordue, and the city of Alea Tanton,' said Naxor.

Maddie nodded. 'And the Falls of Iron?'

Naxor pointed at where the river met the cliff face. Gathered at the base of the sheer cliffs was a large cluster of white cubes, protected by a tall wall running in a semi-circle across the plain. More white cubes were clinging onto the side of the cliff in tiers of ever-rising terraces cut into the face of the rock. The river leaped down the cliff in a series of high waterfalls, on either side of which were more structures gouged into the stone, all painted white like the others. Near the summit of the cliff stood the largest building of all, a towering fortified keep, with walls and turrets, all dazzling white in the afternoon sunshine.

To the left of the fortress was a long, narrow plaza, which led up to a large set of gates.

'I'm going to use my vision powers,' said Naxor, 'to let those inside know that we're friends. There are wild dragons on Khatanax, and we don't want to start a panic.'

His eyes hazed over.

Blackrose circled over the high cliffs for several minutes as Maddie and Corthie stared down, then Naxor jolted, his eyes clearing.

'Take us down,' he said to Blackrose. 'The guards have been told not to loose upon us.'

The dragon began to circle lower. On the battlements of the fortress, Maddie could see soldiers running and shouting, while others were pointing up at the descending dragon. The gates of the fortress started to open, and a stream of guards poured out.

'Are you sure they're friendly?' said Corthie.

'This is merely an honour guard,' said Naxor. 'I spoke with my cousin Lord Irno, the Count of the Falls of Iron; he is coming down to greet us.' He bit his lip. 'That's the good news.'

Maddie frowned. 'And what's the bad?'

'The Holdfasts,' he said; 'they're not here.'

CHAPTER 4

IMPLACATUS

Serene, Implacatus – 13th Dunninch 5252

Thump-thump-thump.

Van's head throbbed to the rhythm. Reflexively, his hand moved out from the comfortable bed where he lay, to feel across the small table that sat close by. His fingers found the ashtray, and scoured around until they located the stick of dullweed that he had been smoking the night before.

He picked it up, and shoved it between his lips.

Thump-thump-thump.

'Aren't you going to answer that?' said a voice. 'Whoever it is, they've been knocking for five minutes.'

'Get me a light,' Van muttered, his eyes still closed, 'and I'll think about it.'

A slender arm stretched out over Van's chest and he heard a match being struck close to his face. He inhaled, and felt his aches and pains dull away to nothing. He opened his eyes and stared at the low ceiling of the cramped bedchamber.

Thump-thump-thump.

'Well?' said the woman lying next to him.

'I'm still thinking about it.'

'Asshole,' she muttered, and slid her long legs out of the bed. Van watched her as she pulled a fur-lined gown from a chair and draped it over her shoulders, tying the belt at her waist.

'Coming,' she called out to the sturdy door.

Van took another draw of the weedstick then stubbed it out in the ashtray. He placed an elbow behind his head and glanced at the door as the woman unbolted it, then opened it wide. Outside in the hallway were several soldiers.

'Can I help you?' she said.

'We're looking for Captain Van Logos, ma'am. Is he in?'

The woman turned her head towards the bed and stepped aside. 'There he is.'

Four soldiers entered the room.

'Captain Logos?' said one.

Van frowned, the old pain in his chest flaring up. 'I want to get dressed before you arrest me.'

'Arrest you, sir? We're not here to arrest you.'

'Then let me guess; my Banner has summoned me?'

'Our orders come directly from the most noble Lord Renko, sir.'

Van's face fell. 'I think I'd rather be arrested. What does Renko want with me?'

'All officers of the Banner of the Golden Fist have been ordered to gather at the court of his Lordship, sir.'

Van said nothing for a moment, as a familiar knot of anxiety grew in the pit of his stomach. A summons could only mean one thing.

'Wait outside,' he said.

The soldiers saluted, then filed back out of the room. The woman shut the door and turned to him.

'I don't get it,' she said. 'You spend every evening complaining about having nothing to do, and now that something's come along, you look more miserable than ever.'

'I don't remember asking for your opinion,' he said as he pulled back the thin sheet. He swung his feet onto the cold floor, then picked up a half-empty bottle of vodka from the bedside table and took a swig.

'Are you trying to kill yourself?' she said, folding her arms across her chest.

'Why do you care?'

She narrowed her eyes.

Van scratched his head and stood, swaying slightly. His hangover had yet to fully kick in, and he suspected he was still a little drunk from the night before. He coughed, feeling the pain flare across his chest, then leaned over, picking up his clothes from where they lay scattered across the floor. Dizziness whirled through him as he straightened, and he sat back down on the bed.

'Where are my boots?'

'I don't know; probably where you left them.'

She walked over to the narrow window, and eased back the thick wooden shutters, letting in the pale morning light. Van scrunched up his eyes, the glare making his head throb. He pulled his clothes on, ignoring the fact that he had worn them the previous day. Half of him hoped that Renko would take one look at his dishevelled appearance and dismiss him from the service; but the other half was terrified at the prospect of his life losing the only meaning it had ever had.

He found his boots under the bed, laced them on, and stood up.

'How do I look?'

The woman shook her head. 'Like crap.'

He nodded. 'What are you going to do with your day?'

'I'm going straight home to have a shower,' she said. 'You really need to get yours fixed; you live like a pig.'

'And will I see you tonight?'

She frowned. 'I guess.'

'Try not to sound so enthusiastic.'

'You don't pay me enough for enthusiasm.'

He reached into his pocket. 'That reminds me.' He pulled out a handful of coins and dropped them onto the unmade bed. 'For you. Don't steal anything while I'm gone.'

'As if. You have nothing worth stealing, Van.'

He avoided the stained and cracked mirror as he walked to the door, his limbs heavy and tired. His officer's uniform jacket was hanging from a peg by the door, and he pulled it over his shoulders. A silver cigarette case was in the inside pocket, but it was empty. He patted his other pockets, and found a crushed packet buried among a collection of loose coins. He extracted it, then teased out a cigarette that had remained unbroken. He struck a match and lit it, then coughed as soon as he had inhaled.

The woman shook her head at him. 'Have a good day. Try not to die.'

'Be careful,' he said; 'you almost sounded like you cared.'

He opened the door and walked out into the long passageway. The four soldiers were standing close by, and they saluted again as they saw him.

They set off without a word, striding along the cold passageway, passing countless doors that led to tiny apartments identical to his own. There was no natural light in the corridor, and it was lit by a succession of wall lamps that gave off a pale blue glow. At the end of the passageway was a large, high-ceilinged hall, with one wall made entirely of glass. The bright daylight stung Van's eyes as they passed, and he averted his gaze from the panoramic view of sky and clouds. The city of Serene had been built into the side of a vast mountain, thousands of feet above the forests and plains of the land far below. Carved over millennia by the ruling gods, the city was home to a vast number of mortals, all working for the glory and benefit of their divine masters.

Opposite the enormous window was a gargantuan statue of an Ascendant, its marble form artfully poised to make it appear as if it were holding up the ceiling with a raised hand, while the other held a globe symbolising Implacatus. An elegant staircase wound up from the base of the statue, seeming to float as it passed the muscled torso of the sculpted god. Van followed the soldiers up the steps, passing civilians moving up and down the levels of the housing district. At the top of the stairs, they turned right, and emerged into the open air.

A cool breeze was brushing the face of the mountain, rustling the leaves of the trees planted out on the wide terrace. Van stubbed his cigarette out and searched the pack for another one, but the rest were split and broken, and he frowned.

At least the fresh air was clearing his head, he thought. He had spent the previous few days within the chambers and halls of the mountain, barely glimpsing the sun, never mind feeling its rays against his skin. He yawned and scratched the stubble on his face. At the far end of the wooded terrace were a few stone benches, and then a sheer drop down the mountain side. A few of Van's fellow officers were standing around, or sitting with their legs stretched out in the sunshine.

He spotted one of his lieutenants and ambled over, his four-soldier escort saluting and turning back towards they way they had come.

'You got a smoke?' he said.

The lieutenant glanced up, then stood and saluted. 'Yes, sir,' he said, putting a hand into the inside pocket of his immaculate uniform.

Van glanced around. Every other officer was as well turned out as the lieutenant.

He nodded as the lieutenant passed him a cigarette. 'Did I miss something, Sohul?'

'Sir?'

Van lit the cigarette and gestured to Sohul's uniform. 'I was woken up half an hour ago by soldiers at my door. Something tells me that you weren't.'

'Letters were posted out two days ago, sir,' Sohul said. 'Did you not get yours?'

Van narrowed his eyes, then recalled having seen a pile of mail when he had returned from the dullweed den the previous evening. He had ignored it, his mind focussed on separating his companion from her clothes. 'I must have missed it. What did it say? I mean, besides telling us to come here.'

'Not much, sir. There were no clues about what the operation could entail.'

Van grunted. As long as it wasn't Dragon Eyre again, he told himself. Anything else he could handle. A major arrived, and started walking through the groups of officers, nodding at the captains and lieutenants. His eyes went cold as he saw Van.

'Captain Logos,' he said, his tone unmistakable. 'You stink of alcohol and... is that dullweed I can smell on your uniform?' He glared at Lieutenant Sohul, who saluted and edged away swiftly.

'Sorry, sir,' Van said. 'I was given no time to get ready. The four soldiers at my door were quite insistent I follow them immediately.'

The veins on the major's forehead bulged. 'Your past service record is the only reason you are still an officer in the Banner of the Golden Fist, Captain, but you cannot live on old glories forever.'

Van straightened his spine and stood to attention. 'Have I ever let you down on an operation, sir?'

'No, Captain, but your behaviour whilst on leave discredits your uniform.' He sighed. 'What happened to you, Van? You had such promise.'

'I don't adjust very well to civilian life, sir.'

'Well, for the sake of the Banner's reputation, and your career, perhaps you should turn around and go home. There are already a couple of absences among the officer corps from sickness; one more won't make much difference. If Lord Renko sees you in this state, he's liable to...'

Van glanced over the major's shoulder. 'It might be too late for that, sir.'

The major turned. A dozen yards away, a slender arc of stone was rippling its way through the air towards the edge of the sheer cliff. Standing on it was a tall, broad man in purple robes, looking every inch the god he was, while behind him was a small group of similarly-dressed immortals. The end of the stone bridge settled onto the terrace, and the gods strode down, their sandaled feet gliding over the grass.

'The most Noble and Ancient Lord Renko,' said a courtier, bowing low as the purple-robed figure approached the officers, who were forming into neat lines.

'Stay at the back,' muttered the major as he walked forwards to greet the gods.

Van did as he was asked, and positioned himself at the rear of the group as the major bowed before Lord Renko.

'Major Ahito,' said Renko as his eyes scanned the group; 'is this the entire officer corps of the Banner of the Golden Fist?'

'Almost, your Grace,' the major said. 'Two lieutenants are currently unwell.' He gestured to the officers. 'Gathered here are eleven captains, twenty-nine lieutenants, and four majors, including myself.'

Renko nodded, then faced the assembled group. 'Thank you for answering our summons. Her Highness Arete, the Seventh Ascendant, has commissioned me to lead an operation. I shall command. We require an entire regiment of the Banner's finest soldiers, fully equipped and ready to depart Implacatus within a month. Veterans only. The operation is deemed to be of critical importance, and so the highest rates of pay shall be offered to those selected.' His gaze went over the officers, then he gestured to two of the other immortals next to him. 'Lord Maisk and Lady Joaz shall also be part of the operation.'

Van suppressed a curse. He had worked with Maisk before, and it had not been a pleasant experience.

'For now,' Renko went on, 'all officers apart from the majors shall return to the Banner headquarters and begin the preparations for the regiment's departure. The majors shall accompany me to an audience with the Seventh Ascendant. Her Highness wishes to say a few words.'

The ancient god nodded, and the majors stepped forward. Renko turned, and stepped back onto the slender bridge. The majors and the other immortals joined him, and the bridge lifted, the surface of the rock structure rippling as it pulled away from the edge of the cliff face. The assembled lieutenants and captains saluted, and waited until it was out of sight, lost in the clouds, before relaxing.

Van scratched his stubble as the other officers started to chat, their voices rising amid the peaceful wooded terrace. He located Lieutenant Sohul among the crowd and beckoned him over.

'Yes, Captain?' said the lieutenant.

'Give me a cigarette and five minutes of your time.'

A frown crossed Sohul's face for a moment. 'Yes, sir.'

They walked into the woods as the officers began to disperse. Sohul took a cigarette from a packet, lit it and passed it to Van.

'I need this job,' said the captain.

Sohul said nothing.

'You heard Renko; one regiment – that means five captains, maybe six at the most. I have to be one of them. I assume you want to be part of this operation as well?'

'Yes, sir. Though, don't you think it was a little odd that they didn't tell us where it would be?'

'Who cares?' Van said. As long as it's not Dragon Eyre, he thought. 'You help me; I help you.'

'And how can I help you, sir?'

'I need a thousand in gold.'

'I, uh, don't have a thousand, sir.'

'Don't give me your crap; I know you have the money. Here's the deal – you help get me selected, and I'll give you back double when we're paid, and I swear I'll pick you as my senior lieutenant.'

Sohul's eyes lowered. 'I don't know, sir.'

'Come on; how many times did I save your life on Dragon Eyre?'

'Three times, sir.'

'So? Don't you think you owe me?'

'But, sir, what if I lend you the gold and you aren't selected?'

'Let me worry about that, Lieutenant.'

Sohul sighed in resignation. 'And you'll pay me back double, yes?'

'Of course,' Van said, a small smile creeping over his lips; 'you have my word.'

Six hours later, Captain Van Logos strode along a wide corridor within the mountain. Above him, deep shafts were letting in streams of daylight from the outside, while behind him, two porters were pulling his equipment along on a small cart. It had cost Van three hundred in gold to redeem his uniforms, armour, weapons and other Banner kit from a pawnbroker. He had gone from there to the office of a doctor he knew, and then onto a prestigious bathhouse, where another fifty gold had seen his clothes laundered and pressed, his hair washed and cut, and the stubble shorn from his features.

The Banner of the Golden Fist had its large headquarters on the southern-facing slope of the mountain. It was piled up on several levels, with bastions and tall towers jutting out from the rocky hillside. Van smiled as he approached the grand entrance gatehouse; a solid structure of gleaming red granite. The Banner had been his employer for almost half of his life. He had enlisted as a fifteen-year-old, following in the footsteps of his mother and father, who had both served in the military. There were other Banners, but Van had never once considered joining any of them – the Golden Fist was the best, and everyone knew it.

Soldiers saluted as he passed through the wide, arched opening. He slipped a couple of gold pieces to the porters, and passed them a slip of paper with directions on how to find his rooms, then turned for the giant administrative building in the centre of the complex. His chest twinged as he entered, though whether the sudden pain was from nerves or his old condition he couldn't guess. The hallways and passageways were busy, with slaves, clerks and soldiers bustling around, the commission from the gods having sparked the place into life. He climbed the steps of a tall tower, and knocked on the door of the grand offices of Major Ahito.

A clerk opened the door. 'Captain Logos?'

'I'm here to see the major. Is he in?'

'I'm afraid he's rather busy at present, Captain. Perhaps if you were to come back tomorrow?'

Van held out a small pouch of gold. 'It is rather urgent.'

The clerk pocketed the gold and nodded. 'Come this way, Captain.'

Van was led into a large reception room, and the clerk pointed to a seat.

'Please wait here, Captain.'

Van frowned, then walked over to the chair and sat. He glanced up as the clerk entered another room by a side door. The walls of the reception chamber were lined with huge paintings, each depicting landscapes from previous operations of the Banner. A dozen different campaigns from a dozen different worlds, all of them victorious. The most recent painting displayed a scene from Dragon Eyre, and Van avoided looking at it, not needing to be reminded of its horrors.

'Captain Logos?' said the clerk.

Van looked over to the door.

'The major will see you now.'

He got to his feet, smoothed the front of his dress uniform, and strode across the marble floor towards the room. Inside, Major Ahito was sitting behind his desk, an enormous window at his back letting in the light from the setting sun.

'Thank you for seeing me, Major,' said Van, standing to attention in front of the desk.

'At ease, Captain,' said the major. 'How can I help you?'

Van reached into his uniform jacket and withdrew a leather pouch containing five hundred in gold. He placed it onto the desk.

'I would like to be considered for the coming operation, sir.'

The major glanced at the pouch for a moment. 'Take a seat.'

Van nodded and sat himself down in front of the desk.

'You will be aware, Captain,' the major said, 'that you are not the only officer to visit me this afternoon bearing gifts?'

'I assumed that would be the case, sir.'

'The only difference is, they were all here hours ago.'

Van's heart started to sink, but he kept his chin up. 'You know my record, sir.'

'Indeed. If it weren't for that, you wouldn't have got through the door. Now tell me, why should I pick you over anyone else?'

'Because I'm the best captain in the Banner, sir.'

The major nodded, his lips pursed. 'And how is your health these days?'

'I'm in great condition, sir, mentally and physically.'

'Then the rumours I hear have no substance to them?'

'Rumours, sir?'

'Yes. Reports that say you are close to burning out; that a combination of too much salve, dullweed and alcohol has rendered you unfit to serve. That your heart is liable to give out.' He shook his head. 'I've seen it before, Captain, all too often. Young, promising soldiers who think they're invincible in their late teens, only to be confronted with the bitter truth ten years later. You're twenty-eight years old, Van. How much longer do you think you will be able to take the amount of salve necessary for you to perform in the field?'

'Many years, sir. My heart is sound.' He reached back into his uniform and handed the major a letter, one that had cost him almost a hundred in gold to procure. 'This is from my doctor, sir. As you will see, he has proclaimed me fit and healthy.'

The major took the letter, and read it in silence.

'Does that satisfy you, sir?'

The major folded the letter and handed it back to Van. 'Such declarations can easily be bought for a small bribe, Captain.'

Van tried to look shocked. 'I would never dream of asking a doctor to falsify my health records, sir.'

The major glanced at the pouch of gold sitting on the desk. 'Of course you wouldn't.' He drummed his fingers for a moment, then glanced at the clerk standing by the door. 'How many captains have been selected so far?'

'Five, sir,' said the clerk.

'Very well. Please add Captain Logos to the list. He shall be our final selection.'

Van grinned. 'Thank you, sir.'

The major frowned. 'Don't make me live to regret this, Captain. Dismissed.'

'I told you it'd be fine, Sohul,' Van said, slapping the man on the back. 'And I kept my word – your name was at the top of my picks for lieutenant.'

Sohul nodded, a wry smile on his face. 'Thank you, sir. Any clues as to where we're going?'

'Not yet, but that's where I'm headed next, to a briefing.'

The lieutenant glanced around the busy bar, one of several within the Banner complex. 'Then do you think you should be drinking, sir?'

'I'll pretend you didn't say that.' The captain dug into his pocket and threw a small bag of gold at Sohul. 'Take this, and use it to buy a beer for every sergeant who's going on the operation – and make sure you tell them it's from me.'

Sohul frowned at the bag. 'Isn't this my gold, sir?'

'It's what's left of it.' Van downed the last of the vodka in his glass and stood. 'See you tomorrow, Sohul; bright and early.'

'Yes, sir. Bright and early.'

Van nodded to the lieutenant, then strode to the main doors of the bar. A dull ache throbbed through his chest for a moment, but he ignored it. He descended a flight of steps and entered a lamplit hallway, where a door was being guarded by two soldiers. They opened it for him and he walked into a large chamber, with wood-lined walls and a fire blazing in a hearth. Seated at a table were five other captains from the Banner, along with a few staff officers.

Van took a seat.

'Logos?' said one of the other captains. 'How did you get on the list? I thought you had a weak heart.'

'Yeah? Well, you thought wrong.'

The captain shook his head. 'You were good in your prime, I'll grant you, but your operational days should be over.'

'Buddy, I'm twenty-eight; I've not even reached my prime. And anyway, how would you know? You were still in shorts when I was on my first operation for the Banner.' He glanced around the table. 'I've done five tours of Dragon Eyre. Five. If anyone has a problem with me being here, let me know, and I'll show you a few of the tricks I picked up on that lizard-infested cesspit.'

A side door to the chamber opened, and the officers jumped to their feet as Major Ahito strode in, followed by another major and one of the immortals who had been up on the wooded terrace.

'Please sit, gentlemen,' said Ahito. 'This is Lady Joaz. She has come down from the Divine Mountain to speak to you.'

The god's eyes scanned the room, her features expressionless.

The officers sat, while Ahito, Joaz and the other major took their places at the head of the table. Slaves entered the chamber, bearing wine, and filled the glasses of everyone present.

'Officers,' said Joaz, her voice piercing the silence; 'greetings. Her Highness Arete, the Seventh Ascendant, and the most Noble and Ancient Lord Renko, have sent me here this evening to brief you on the operation. What I say to you must not be repeated outside of this chamber. Anyone who disregards this shall face the severest penalties. You may not know me, but I have vision powers, and can see into each of your minds, so you know that this is not an idle threat.'

The officers glanced at each other, saying nothing.

'The operation,' Joaz went on, 'is on Lostwell. Have any of you been there?'

Of all the officers present, only Van raised his hand.

Joaz turned to Ahito. 'I thought we requested veterans? Why is this man the only one to have been to Lostwell?'

Ahito's face reddened. 'Every officer here is a veteran, my lady. The Banner of the Golden Fist has not conducted an operation on Lostwell for ten years.'

Joaz nodded. 'I see. Sometimes I forget that the lifespan of mortals is brief, especially that of salve-mercenaries.' She glanced at Van. 'What is your name?'

'Captain Logos, ma'am.'

'Well, I'm glad at least one of you will have some prior knowledge of our destination.' She took a long breath. 'Our mission is simple, but of extreme importance. For three centuries, the Ascendants, Ancients, and every other god and demigod on Implacatus have depended upon a single substance above all others – salve.' She paused for a moment. 'We have been keeping two secrets regarding this substance, and I am about to reveal them to you now. The first is that Lostwell remains the sole source of salve. It does not originate there, but the supply is channelled through that world. The governors of Lostwell were tasked with locating the ultimate source of it, but they have failed. The objective of this operation is to step in, and do what they have been unable to do – locate the source, and bring it under our control. The need for such measures has, up to now, been unnecessary, as the supply of salve coming from Lostwell has been sufficient to meet all of our needs. This is where the second secret comes in. Supplies have recently become intermittent, and there is a real prospect of a shortage. This *cannot* be allowed to happen.'

Complete silence fell over the chamber as the officers listened. Van frowned. Run out of salve? His mind raced at the implications.

'Therefore,' Joaz went on, 'the most divine Ascendants have decreed that Lord Renko will have the full powers of a plenipotentiary, with the authority to govern Lostwell in any way he sees fit. His word will have the force of ultimate law, as if one of the Ascendants was there in person. We must locate the source of the salve, and having found it, control it – whatever it takes; whatever the cost.' She glanced around the table. 'Any questions?'

Van raised his hand again.

'Yes, Captain Logos?'

He smiled. 'When do we leave, ma'am?'

CHAPTER 5

THE THIRD ASCENDANT

Dun Khatar, Southern Khatanax – 13th Dunninch 5252

Aila glanced at Belinda as they ate their cold lunch in silence. The god had barely spoken two words to her since Blackrose had carried Corthie, Naxor and Maddie away that morning, and Aila was starting to wish she had made more of a fuss about being left behind.

She had tried to make conversation but each time, Belinda had just nodded, or grunted a monosyllabic response. The god hated her, it was obvious; but why? Aila had assumed that Belinda's dislike of her had stemmed from the fact that Corthie would have remained in the City to be with her, rather than travel to Lostwell to be reunited with his family; but Aila's decision to leave did not seem to have changed Belinda's opinion of her. Aila was no stranger to being disliked; many within her own family had loathed her, but she was disappointed that Belinda seemed to think so little of her. Other people's views of her didn't usually bother her, but Belinda was close to Corthie and the other Holdfasts, and she worried about getting off to a bad start with Karalyn.

She thought about asking Belinda straight out for her reasons, but that would only prove to the god that she cared. It was better to continue acting nonchalantly around her, to give the impression that nothing got under her skin.

'I wonder what they eat in the Falls of Iron,' she said.

Belinda shrugged, her eyes on the dusty ground.

'I mean, I know it's food, obviously,' Aila went on, 'but what type? Are there cows on Lostwell? I assume they drink alcohol; do you think they have wine and brandy here? I've never seen you drink; do you?'

'No.'

'Oh. Probably sensible. I used to drink a lot when I was younger, and when I was under house arrest, but I guess I needed something to do to pass the time.'

Belinda frowned. 'Could you be quiet for a minute? I'm trying to think.'

Aila's face fell, and for one horrible moment she thought her eyes were about to well up. She pushed herself to her feet and stomped off just in case; she didn't think she would be able to bear the humiliation of crying in front of Belinda, especially for being told to shut up. She strode over to the arched entrance of the palace and looked out at the ruins of the ancient city. She glanced up into the clear, blue sky, irrationally hoping to see the sight of a dragon coming to collect them, even though she knew Blackrose would not be returning for many hours yet.

No tears came, and after a few minutes her hurt gave way to anger. Belinda was rude, arrogant, and she treated Aila like she was the least important member of their party. She might be a thirty-millennia-old god, but she behaved like a child. And she was scary. Scarier in her own way than even the God-Queen had been as, unlike Amalia, it was impossible to tell what Belinda would do next.

She felt a low rumbling vibration come up through the soles of her boots and she looked down just as it stopped.

Weird, she thought.

Before she had time to imagine what could have caused it, the ground shifted beneath her, jolting and shaking. A cry escaped her lips as she clung onto to the side of the arch, while behind her in the palace hall, she heard a great crash as stone blocks toppled down from the ceiling. She stared out at the city as the ruins swayed and shook. A jagged crack tore through the courtyard in front of the palace, swallowing up thick flagstones in its wake.

Aila's heart raced. Was the world ending? She felt an urge to run, but her boots were slipping on the rippling ground.

'Stay where you are,' said Belinda, as she strode up to where Aila was clinging to the side of the arch. 'It'll be over in a moment.'

Aila stared at the god. 'What's happening?'

The vibrations ceased as suddenly as they had begun, and Aila sank to the stone ground, her hands trembling. She coughed as a cloud of dust and ash swirled around them.

'It was just an earthquake,' said Belinda.

'A what?'

'An earthquake.'

Aila pointed towards the mountains. 'Is it related to the volcanoes?'

'Presumably.'

'Amalia's ass; I thought the world was ending or something.' She glanced back into the dark palace. 'Did the ceiling collapse?'

Belinda sighed. 'No, just a couple of loose blocks.'

'I'm not going back in there again. What if there's another earthquake? The whole palace might come down.'

'I doubt it. This place probably gets earthquakes all the time.'

'How can you be so blasé about it? I thought we were going to die.'

Belinda shrugged. 'Earthquakes are beyond our control, and there's no point in worrying about things you have no control over.'

'It's that simple, is it?'

'Yes.'

Aila got to her feet, her eyes tight. She dusted the grime and ash from the front of her clothes and took a step outside. Nothing much seemed to have changed, but as the city was already in ruins, it was hard to tell. Maybe Belinda was right; maybe Dun Khatar experienced frequent earthquakes. Still, it had been among the most terrifying minutes of Aila's long life.

'I'm going for a walk,' she said. 'My nerves are frazzled.'

Belinda nodded. 'I'll come with you.'

'You don't have to.'

'I know that.'

Aila turned away, shielding the scowl on her face from Belinda. They descended the steps from the palace entrance, taking care to avoid the new crack that had opened up along the surface of the plaza. A road led off to their left, and they took it, passing between rows of single-storey ruins, each fronted by pillars, most of which were lying in pieces amid the thick layers of sand and ash. There was no wind, and the sun burned down from the clear sky, and after a few minutes Aila wished she had brought some water.

She turned. The palace was so huge that it would be easy to find their way back. Belinda was gazing at the ruins they passed, her eyes scanning the streets and buildings.

'Recognise anything?' said Aila.

'Of course not.'

'But, if Nathaniel was here when he made my world, and you were with him, then you might have once lived here.'

'You sound like Queen Amalia. She too seemed to believe that my memories were submerged somewhere deep within my mind, ready for some trigger to restore them. They're not. Karalyn obliterated my mind, and everything in it.'

'And you're not angry with her for that?'

'I was strangling her – she lashed out.'

'But...'

'I've said everything I want to say on the matter.'

Aila closed her mouth, and fell silent. They walked on, passing a square lined with huge ruins, with a fountain in the middle piled deep in sand. They came to the stone banks of a river, but Naxor had been right, and it was dried up and barren. It cut through the city in a straight line, and the only bridge within view had collapsed long before. They gazed at the far bank for a moment, where the ruins of the city spread out into the distance, then turned right and walked along the old embankment. Ahead of them sat a huge, rounded boulder, so big that it was almost blocking the wide path, but as they got closer, Aila realised that it was the head of a colossal statue. The upper surface of it was weathered and smooth, but the features of a face were visible on the sheltered side.

'An old woman,' she said, peering at the carved marble. She glanced at Belinda. 'Could it be Agatha? You know, the god that Naxor said he dealt with when he first started coming to Lostwell.'

Belinda shook her head. 'It's not Agatha.'

'How do you know?'

She frowned as she stared at the statue, as if unsure whether or not to tell Aila. 'Agatha,' she said after a while, 'was the leader of the gods who invaded Corthie's world. I was also one of them. After my memories were destroyed, I fought against her.'

'Did you kill her?'

'No. Karalyn did.'

'How?'

Belinda said nothing. She turned her gaze from the marble head and pointed. 'More of the statue lies ahead of us.'

'It must have been as big as the two Michael statues in the City.'

They walked on further, passing gigantic stone limbs, and an enormous piece of torso.

'Why doesn't the City have a proper name?' said Belinda.

'It has lots of names – Auldan, Medio...'

'Yes, but why doesn't the entire city have a name? You can't keep calling it "the City".'

'The City was its name. It was all we knew.'

'I'm going to call it Pella from now on. It's where the king and queen live, so that will suffice.'

Aila opened her mouth to object, but Belinda started hurrying down the path, heading for a large blocky structure of stone. Aila followed, watching as Belinda crouched down by the base of the structure. It was the ancient pedestal, where the colossal statue of the old woman had once stood.

Belinda glanced up at her. 'Flowers.'

Aila looked down. Set out by the base of the pedestal were several bundles of cut flowers, their withered stalks tied together with ribbon. The stubs of more than a dozen candles were also set out, and blackened scorch marks were streaking the stone of the pedestal, showing where they had been lit.

'The most recent bunch is less than a month old, I'd guess,' Belinda said, her hand stretching out to touch a small pile of desiccated petals.

'I thought nothing grew here.'

'It doesn't. Someone must have brought them from far away.'

'Someone who comes here regularly, by the looks of it. This seems like a shrine, or a memorial.'

'To the old woman,' said Belinda, her voice low.

'Yeah. She must still have her supporters, whoever she was.'

Aila glanced around as Belinda continued to gaze at the dead flowers. The pedestal sat next to a wide boulevard that led to another collapsed bridge over the dried-up river. On the other side of the road was an identical pedestal. A giant sandaled foot remained atop it, with part of a leg up to the lower shin surviving. Aila crossed the road to take a closer look, noticing more parts of the statue lying scattered beyond. On the side of the pedestal facing the river, she caught a glimpse of large, carved letters cut into the face of the stone. She walked back as far as the edge of the river and glanced up, reading.

The Fourth Ascendant – the Blessed King Nathaniel

Nathaniel? Aila frowned. It made sense, she supposed; after all, he had once been powerful, and he had lived in Dun Khatar. She glanced back at Belinda, who seemed to have had the same idea. She was pushing away sand from a thick pile that lay against the side of the pedestal facing the river, uncovering the letters that lay hidden beneath.

Aila went back across the wide road, and glanced up. Belinda was crouching on the pile of sand, staring at the inscription.

'What does it say?' said Aila. 'I can't read it; you're in the way.'

Belinda said nothing, then she lifted a hand to her face. Aila narrowed her eyes. Was she crying? Did Belinda cry? Aila began to climb up the pile, her boots sinking into the soft sand. She reached the level where Belinda was crouching, and glanced at the carved words.

The Third Ascendant – the Blessed Queen Belinda

Aila's eyes widened. 'Oh.'

'I thought you didn't drink?' said Aila.

Belinda pulled the stopper from the jug of Taran brandy and glugged it down. She wiped her lips. 'I'm making an exception.'

She sat on a block of stone, close to where they had eaten their lunch. Her eyes were still red, but her tears had ceased somewhere on the road back to the old palace. Belinda's palace, Aila realised.

'Pass me some,' she said.

Belinda shook her head. 'There's another jug in the luggage. This one's mine.'

Aila reached over from where she sat and pulled a large leather case towards her. She rooted around in it for a moment, then pulled out the jug of fine brandy. She hesitated for a second. It was supposed to be a gift for Irno and Vana, but she remembered that there were several jugs among the baggage Blackrose had taken to the Falls of Iron, so she removed the stopper with a yank.

She took a swig. Lovely.

'I was a queen,' Belinda said, her voice barely more than a whisper.

'I thought you knew all that,' said Aila. 'Didn't Amalia tell you about your past?'

'Yes, but it didn't seem real; none of it seemed real. I knew it was me, but at the same time it wasn't really me. The old Belinda was like a story in a book; a character that people told me about. But that statue. That was me.'

'The Third Ascendant,' said Aila; 'what does that mean?'

Belinda glared at her. 'How should I know? Amalia didn't mention anything about that to me.' She took another large swig of brandy. 'Blessed Queen,' she muttered, then started to laugh.

Aila frowned. Was Belinda getting drunk already?

'I was the queen,' the god went on, 'of a city that has been destroyed by earthquakes and volcanoes – an appropriate metaphor for my life, don't you think? My mind is in ruins; my memories annihilated, my identity wrecked, my history forgotten.'

'Not by everyone,' Aila said. 'Somebody left those flowers.'

'So? They could walk through that entrance right now and I wouldn't recognise them. Sometimes I think it would have been better if Karalyn had killed me. The Empress wanted to execute me; maybe she should have.'

'Don't say that.'

'Why not? No one likes me. You hate me.'

Aila said nothing. Was Belinda's calm and ruthless demeanour only a façade? Was she in pain?

'I see you're not denying it.'

'I don't hate you, Belinda.'

'Yes, you do. You look at me as if I'm a child, except you fear me too. Why? Didn't I save your life in Ooste? Haven't I proved countless times that I'm on your side? What else do I have to do? Maddie's frightened of me too, and Blackrose will never trust me again, not since I threw her rider into a horde of greenhides; but I only did that so the dragon would intervene and save your stupid city. Even Corthie looks at me differently now.' Rage passed over her face, then she started to cry again.

Aila watched her in silence.

'You've turned him against me, haven't you?' Belinda said through her tears. 'You were jealous that we used to be close, and you've poisoned his mind. Karalyn will see through you – she'll read your thoughts and see what you've done. He's just a boy, and you're an eight-century-old demigod. You'll be lucky if she doesn't kill you on the spot.'

'That's not fair,' Aila cried. 'I love him. I didn't mean for it to happen, and I tried to stay away from him, but... I can't help how I feel.'

Belinda stared at her, her eyes narrow, then her features softened and she looked away.

Aila swallowed. 'Do you really think I'm in danger from Karalyn?'

'Probably not. She doesn't like killing people. But, she... never mind.'

'And Corthie loves you; he's acting weird because he thinks you're keeping something from him.'

Belinda nodded.

'Well? Are you?'

The god said nothing.

'Naxor likes you.'

Belinda's eyes met Aila's. 'Does he? Has he told you that?'

'Yes, a couple of times.'

'So, he's not just trying to get me into bed?'

Aila swithered for a moment. She wanted to reassure Belinda, but at the same time she felt it might be a little rash to make any promises on Naxor's behalf.

'He, uh, might be trying to get you into bed. In fact, he probably is. He does like you, Belinda, but I'm not sure you should completely trust him. I know he's my cousin, and I love him, I do, but, well, he's Naxor.'

'He told me last night that he wants us to run off together. That once we've delivered Corthie to his sister, then we'd be free to do whatever we liked. We could have adventures, he said. Wealth, power, castles, servants, but I don't want any of that.'

'What do you want?'

'I don't know.'

'Malik's ass, Belinda; you're a mess.'

Belinda's eyes darkened for a moment, and Aila felt fear trickle down her spine.

'Sorry. I...'

'It's fine,' said Belinda. 'At least you're being honest with me. For once. I am a mess.'

Aila sipped her brandy as Belinda stared at the dusty ground. 'Can I ask you something?'

'You can ask. I might not answer.'

'How can Corthie have an aunt he's never heard of?'

Belinda took another long swig. 'She's the illegitimate daughter of

Corthie's grandfather and the old queen of the Holdings. They were having an affair, apparently.'

'Sable's a princess?'

Belinda snorted. 'No. She's a bitch.'

'Oh. You don't like her much, then?'

'She doesn't care about anyone but herself. She uses people, then discards them. Karalyn made a mistake bringing her here, and Corthie... well, let's just say that he's not going to be very pleased when he discovers what Aunty Sable's like.'

'Do you think she'll be in the Falls of Iron?'

'Who knows? When I left to go to Pella, we didn't make any definite plans on where or when to meet if I managed to bring Corthie back.'

'So they might not be waiting for us in Irno's castle?'

'They were going to start searching for a Quadrant,' Belinda said.

'Why? I thought Karalyn could travel without one.'

Belinda frowned. 'Damn it.'

'What?'

'I shouldn't be drinking. I've already said too much.'

'This is the most we've ever talked,' said Aila. 'I don't hate you, you should know that, but I am scared of you.'

Belinda raised her glance, her eyes red and sad. 'Why?'

'Because you're dangerous, and unpredictable. You gutted the God-Queen like a fish, and you threw Maddie off a dragon.'

'I told you, I only did that to get Blackrose to intervene. I know how much she loves her rider. I risked my own life to do that – I honestly thought the dragon was going to rip my head off, but I did it anyway. Corthie and Yendra would have died if I hadn't. Of all the things that fill me with dread, having to return to Lostwell to tell Karalyn that Corthie was dead is the worst. I need to prove to her that I've changed; that I can be trusted again. I did a terrible thing, and bringing Corthie back here is the only way I can redeem myself.'

'And once they're reunited? What then?'

'They go back to the Star Continent; back to their own world.'

'I meant for you; what happens to you?'

Belinda swigged from the jug.

'I remember,' said Aila, 'that you told Amalia that only Karalyn could bring your powers back. Are you going to ask Karalyn to restore them?'

'Yes.'

'And will she?'

'Probably not. Like you, she thinks I'm dangerous. I don't think she wants to see me fully restored. It's stupid; I could have ended the war against Agatha in a few days; instead, we slogged it out for years.'

'But you still won?'

'Yes, but only because Karalyn was so wracked with grief and rage that she found the strength to destroy Agatha and her armies. That's why...'

'That's why what?'

'Nothing.'

Aila nodded. 'Corthie's right, isn't he? You *are* keeping something from him.'

Belinda shrugged.

'Is it serious?'

The god laughed, though there was no joy in it. She lifted the jug to her lips and drained it, swaying on the stone block where she was sitting. She stared at the empty jug for a moment, then threw it over her shoulder, and it smashed against the ground.

'You finished it?' said Aila, an eyebrow raised.

'Yes. Can I have yours now?'

Aila frowned.

Belinda swayed again, then put a hand to her mouth. 'I think I'm going to be sick.' She fell forward, her knees cracking off the stone floor, then vomited, a stream of foul-smelling liquid gushing from her mouth.

Aila jumped up to avoid being splashed, then sighed and walked round to where Belinda was kneeling. She crouched down next to her and placed a hand on her back.

'Use your self-healing powers,' she said.

Belinda turned her face towards her, vomit dribbling down her chin. 'What?'

'You're a god, Belinda; you can sober yourself up in seconds if you want.'

'I can do that?'

'Of course. I'd never drink if I had to experience a hangover.'

Belinda groaned, her arms wrapped round her torso. 'I'm too drunk to know how.'

'Just relax; picture your condition as an illness, and...'

'Leave me alone,' Belinda cried, shrugging off Aila's hand. 'I don't want to be sober.'

Aila stood and took a step back. 'Alright.'

Belinda staggered back onto the stone block and sat there, her head lowered and her arms hanging loose by her side. In front of her, the pool of vomit was spreading out across the dusty ground. Aila turned to go.

'Wait,' said Belinda.

'What?'

'If I tell you, you must promise not to say a word of it to Corthie.'

Aila hesitated. If it was serious, then it would be better to know. 'Alright.'

Belinda glanced at her. 'Something *is* wrong. Very wrong.'

'Go on.'

'A few months before we left to start our search for Corthie, Karalyn had twins.'

'Did something bad happen to them?'

'No. Well, I don't think so. As far as I know, they're fine.'

'Then?'

'Damn it, I don't even know how to begin. Corthie's nineteen, right?'

'Yeah.'

'And he was fourteen when he was abducted.'

'That's right; that's what he told me.'

Belinda shook her head. 'He should be fifteen.'

Aila frowned, then crouched back down next to the god. 'What?'

'He was missing for one year, not five. He was abducted a little over a year ago. Karalyn, Sable and I have only been looking for him for a few months.'

'That doesn't make any sense, Belinda.'

She laughed. 'You think I don't know that? None of it makes sense. He was missing for a year, and then we travelled to Lostwell. We found the Falls of Iron, and I went to Pella, but instead of Corthie being fifteen, he was nineteen.'

'But what happened to the missing four years? Does time work differently on different worlds?'

'I considered that, but I don't think so. I asked Naxor, without telling him why, and he told me that time works the same on Lostwell as it does in Pella. And he's travelled between the two many times, so he would know.' She started to cry again, and put her head in her hands. 'There's only one explanation I can think of, but if it's true, then... then Karalyn is going to... her heart is going to break in two.'

Aila leaned in closer. 'What explanation?'

'You know that Karalyn didn't use a Quadrant to get to Lostwell, right? She used her own powers, but what if something went wrong? It was the first time she had done it, so maybe she didn't understand what she was doing. Maybe, somehow, the journey took us four years. It seemed to pass in an instant, but what if it didn't? What if we were trapped in some kind of limbo for four years?'

'But then...'

'Then she won't have been gone from her twins for a few months; she'll have been apart from them for four years. They'll be almost five by now, and she will have missed nearly all of it.'

Aila breathed out, her mind spinning.

'Karalyn is six years older than Corthie,' Belinda went on, 'except, she's not any more. She's still twenty-one, and he's nineteen. As soon as she sees him...'

'Why didn't you tell him?'

'Because I'm still not sure, and I didn't want to panic him. I'm only telling you now, because if Karalyn is in the Falls of Iron, then they will have already met, and they'll both know. If that's the case, then perhaps you should be prepared.'

'Prepared for what?'

'Anything. Karalyn's rage, and her grief. The last time she was pushed to the edge she wiped out gods and armies, annihilated them without mercy. This time?'

'What should we do?'

'Finish the brandy,' said Belinda, 'and then, when we get to the Falls of Iron, stay out of Karalyn's way, if you can.'

The next morning, Aila and Belinda sat on the steps in front of the palace with their luggage piled up around them, waiting for Blackrose. The god had not mentioned anything to do with what they had been talking about, and Aila hadn't asked. She was still a little scared of Belinda, but felt that she had gained some understanding of what drove the god.

Belinda pointed at the sky. 'Here she comes.'

The dragon circled overhead, transforming from a tiny speck in the clear heavens, until her great size became visible. Maddie was sitting up on the harness, and she waved down at them. Aila and Belinda stood as the dragon lowered herself onto the wide plaza.

The god looked around at the ruins.

'Saying goodbye to your city, Queen Belinda?' said Aila.

'Something like that.' She glanced at Aila. 'Remember, not a word.'

Aila nodded.

Maddie climbed down from the side of the dragon as Blackrose folded her wings and stretched.

'Hey,' said Maddie. 'You have fun while we were away?'

Aila smiled. 'We refrained from murdering each other.'

'Yeah? Well, there will be plenty of time to do that in the Falls of Iron.'

'Why?' said Belinda.

Maddie shrugged. 'Because Karalyn's not there.'

CHAPTER 6
ACTING ON IMPULSE

Alea Tanton, Tordue, Western Khatanax – 1ˢᵗ Tradinch 5252

The arena shook as the voices of seventy thousand people roared. Gantu was on his feet, the veins on his neck bulging, and his arms in the air as he unleashed a torrent of abuse at the red-clad supporters on the benches opposite. A quarter of the arena was taken up with the followers of the Blue Thumbs, their numbers limited for their visit to the Southern Pits – home of the Bloodflies. Armoured soldiers stood along the high fences separating the rival groups of supporters, their crossbows ready.

Sable had already seen several supporters from both groups being beaten half to death by the soldiers, their bloodied bodies being dragged away to be thrown out of the arena. The carnage up in the stands was nothing, however, compared to the slaughter that had been going on amid the sands beneath the tiers of stone benches. The day's entertainment had commenced with a dozen executions. The supporters of the Bloodflies had cheered and laughed as the blue-clad Torduans were slowly impaled upon long stakes, while the Blue Thumbs had raged at the sight of their brethren suffering. The arena announcer had proclaimed the dozen Torduans to be criminals, but Gantu had assured Sable that this was lies – the victims were innocent

Blue Thumb supporters who had been arrested for no reason other than to be executed.

Following that, the games had begun in earnest. Sable had been informed at length by Gantu about the myriad rules governing the fights taking place on the sands, but she hadn't paid him much attention. To her, there didn't seem to be any rules. For the first round, four warriors in red took on a similar number in blue; they had hacked and stabbed at each other until the sand was spattered in blood. Points were awarded by a panel of judges sitting high in the stands, and behind them sat two gods. Sable recognised Felice, whom she had seen several times in the Central Pits while attending the Blue Thumbs' practice sessions, but the other one was new to her.

'Bloodflies scum!' Gantu screamed, his finger out-stretched and pointing at the hordes of red-clad supporters. 'I'll rip off your heads and take a dump down your necks, ya goat-shagging Shinstran bastards!'

Sable sat back on her bench and suppressed a sigh. How much more of this was she going to have to endure? She had been in Alea Tanton for nearly a month, and there hadn't been a single word from Karalyn in that time. Her niece had been clear that she wasn't to make her move until expressly ordered to, but Sable was growing tired of waiting.

She glanced up over the walls of the arena. The Southern Pits were located only a few miles away from the high promontory of Old Alea, where the ruling gods of Khatanax dwelt, and she could see the line of high cliffs in the distance. That was where she needed to be, not stuck with some ignorant oaf and his idiot friends. On her left, Millen was also sitting, a bored expression on his face.

'Enjoying the games?' she said, keeping her voice low so it wouldn't carry up to Gantu amid the cacophony in the arena.

He gave her a wry smile.

'Who's winning?'

Millen glanced over to a high, wooden panel above where the judges were sitting. 'Three points each,' he said, 'but there are another five rounds of fighting to go.'

'Five rounds? My head will explode from this racket. What a noise.'

'If you think this is bad, just wait until we execute the Bloodflies' dragon next month. The Shinstrans will go crazy. There will be riots outside the arena after the games finish today, but they'll be nothing compared to what'll happen next month.'

Sable nodded. 'There will be riots today?'

'For sure, yes. There always are, following each game.'

The crowd roared again as Round Two began. Three greenhides were released into the arena, each with a daub of thick red paint across their shell-like backs, while, at the other end of the sands, ten Blue Thumb warriors ran through an open gate, armed with nets and long pikes.

'Get stuck into them!' Gantu yelled, his fist in the air. He groaned aloud as one of the greenhides swung its razor-sharp claws, slicing a Blue Thumb warrior in two in a spray of blood. Gantu turned to Sable and Millen. 'Did you see that? Clueless, absolutely clueless. He should never have been let onto the team. Useless asshole.'

Sable nodded. 'Terrible,' she said.

Go back to watching the game. Never mind about us.

Gantu turned back to gaze at the sands.

She glanced at Millen. 'I'm going for a cigarette. Do you want to come?'

'Um, I'm not sure I should.'

'Come on. What if I get harassed by some thug? Gantu will be happier knowing that you're there to keep an eye on me.' She stood, and nudged Gantu's elbow. 'I'm going for a smoke – your little cousin's coming along to make sure no one hassles me.'

'What?' muttered Gantu, his eyes still on the game. 'Yeah, whatever.'

She headed for the stairs, leaning past several Blue Thumbs supporters as they stood, cheering and shouting at the top of their voices. She descended the steps, without bothering to check if Millen was following. She smiled to herself. Of course he was. At the bottom of the stairs was an arched tunnel, one of many that led away from the tiers of stone benches. She squeezed past vendors selling hot meat on sticks, all of it smeared with that awful fish and pepper sauce so beloved by the inhabitants of Alea Tanton. At the far end of the tunnel were more stairs, and a small alcove that was open to the outside. She went and sat on the ledge, and gazed out at the city as she lit a cigarette.

'I thought you told Gantu that you were going to give up smoking?' said Millen as he appeared beside her.

'No, I told him I'd consider it.'

'He hates it.'

'I know.'

Millen smiled and sat next to her. 'Something tells me that you don't care.'

She glanced at the young man. He was slim, above average handsome, and a little taller than most. He might do, she thought, though he would need some working on before he would be of any use to her. She turned her eyes back to the city.

'That other god,' she said; 'who is he?'

'Lord Kemal,' said Millen. 'He's the patron of the Bloodflies, which is why, you know, he's wearing red.'

'And there are four gods currently in Alea Tanton, including Latude, the Governor of Khatanax?'

'Yes.'

She nodded. 'Have you ever been to Old Alea?'

He laughed. 'Of course not. No one gets in there without permission. There are soldiers guarding every entry point up onto the top of the cliffs. Thinking of carrying out a robbery, are you?'

'As a matter of fact, yes, I am.'

Millen's laughter cut short and he made a strange choking sound. 'You're joking, right? I mean, I was joking, just in case that wasn't clear. No one robs the gods up in Old Alea. It would be suicide.'

She smiled.

He shook his head. 'So, you were joking. Ha, ha.'

'You fancy helping me?'

He looked away. Sable watched him. She hoped he would say yes, otherwise she would have to kill him, and Gantu would most likely be quite upset if that happened. She would have to blame it on some supporters of the Bloodflies, or maybe a rival Blue Thumbs gang.

'Well?' she said.

'Well what?'

'What's your answer?'

'Answer to what?'

'Oh, I see,' she said; 'you're pretending I didn't ask if you would help me rob some gods in Old Alea. So let me ask again – will you help me rob some gods in Old Alea?'

'Gantu's put you up to this, hasn't he?' said Millen. 'He's trying to test me, is that it?'

Sable thought for a moment about what she was going to do next. She knew how Millen felt about her, and a twinge of guilt echoed through her thoughts for a moment. She suppressed it, then lifted her hand to Millen's face, touching his cheek. He stared at her wide-eyed, then she kissed him.

'Do you want to live in that fool's shadow all your life?' she whispered. 'Or do you want to leave the arena with me?'

You want to come with me more than you've ever wanted to do anything else in your life. And, you're brave enough to do it.

'When?' he said, his face pale.

'Now.'

He stared out through the opening by the ledge, and she slipped her hand into her robes, feeling for the hilt of her dagger. Her powers of persuasion sometimes struggled to work if the subject's heart was set against whatever she was telling them to do, or if they were particularly strong-willed. With Gantu it had been easy; he had been like a puppet in her hands, but Millen?

'If I do this,' he said, 'will I ever see my home again?'

'Probably not, but would that be such a bad thing? Gantu treats you like a slave, when you could be so much more.'

'Who are you?'

She smiled. 'Sable Holdfast.'

'Are you really from Kinell?'

'Give me your answer first. Are you with me? Yes or no.'

'Why me?'

'Yes or no, Millen, and this is the last time I'm going to ask.'

He gazed into her eyes. 'Yes.'

She stood, releasing the grip on the dagger. 'Then let's get out of here. Follow me.'

She hurried down the next flight of stairs, and they came into a large courtyard, lined with pillars that were holding up the main structure of the arena. The area was packed, with vendors selling food, drink and narcotics, and groups of Blue Thumbs supporters were standing around. Sable reached out with her line-vision, sending her sight outside to look for a way through the crowds, then pressed on, heading for the nearest exit.

What she had done was impulsive, she knew, maybe even reckless, but she was fed up waiting for a signal that might never come. Karalyn hated her, and maybe she had decided to abandon Sable in Alea Tanton. If that was the case, then gaining a Quadrant would put her in a powerful position, if she could figure out how to work it.

First things first, she thought as they emerged into the blazing sunlight. Time to put some distance between them and the arena. She quickened her pace, and darted through the crowds, turning into a wide street, then taking a right leading away from it. She paused for a moment in the shadows of an alleyway, then sent her vision back out, lifting it up to the top of a spire close by, from where she could get an aerial view of the street layout. She quickly memorised a route, using a touch of battle-vision to amplify her senses, then she felt her arm being nudged.

She glanced at Millen.

'What were you doing?' he said. 'Your eyes went all weird.'

'I have vision powers.'

She entered his mind, and saw that he didn't believe her. She could also see that he was starting to regret leaving the arena, but his desire for her was keeping him going. No, not just desire. He actually liked her. Damn.

'I know you don't believe me,' she said. 'That's fine. I have an intricate plan, one that I'm perfectly capable of carrying out myself. An accomplice would be very handy, but I'm not going to beg. Begone if you don't want any more part of this.'

'You have a plan to rob the gods?'

'I do,' she lied.

'Rob them of what?'

'Walk with me and we'll talk,' she said, turning to go. She glanced back at him. 'That's if you're coming?'

He closed his eyes for a moment, and lowered his head. 'Alright,' he said; 'but only to stop you from being killed. These streets are rough.'

'Then you'd better remove that blue sash before we go any further, otherwise it'll be you getting killed.'

He pulled the sash from over his shoulder, and let it fall to the ground.

'How's your Shinstran accent?' she said as they began to walk.

'Terrible.'

'Then don't talk; just listen.'

He nodded as they entered a busier street, filled with Bloodflies supporters heading towards the arena, several of whom were armed. Sable and Millen stayed to the left of the passing stream of people, Sable pausing occasionally to get her bearings.

'I'm after one item in particular,' she said, keeping her voice low. 'You'll have no idea what it is, so I'm not going to bother you with the details. To get it, we'll have to get up onto the cliff-top plateau and enter Old Alea. To do that, we, and by "we", I mean you, will need to look the part. We're going to play husband and wife; you happy with that?'

He nodded again, his face flushing slightly.

'Now,' she went on, 'it's six miles to the base of the cliffs of Old Alea, but only two to the edge of the walled merchants' district.'

'There's a walled merchants' district?'

'Yes, for the rich mortals of the city. Where did you think they lived? It's not a particularly big area, so I'm guessing they aren't too many inhabitants; maybe three or four thousand. That's where we're going first.'

He nodded, though he was glancing warily at the Shinstran locals out on the street.

Be brave. You're doing great.

The main road that stretched down the spine of the city was named the Artery, and Sable led Millen onto it. They hailed a pony-carriage, and paid a few silver coins to be transported the two miles to the beginning of the merchants' district. It sat on the right hand side of the Artery, opposite a massive complex of shanty dwellings and slums, deep within Shinstran territory. Around the district was a high wall, tall enough to deter any climber. Sable had scouted the guarded entrances and they headed towards the ocean coast, where she knew a smaller trader's gate was located. Armoured guards stood sentry along the base of the wall, while others patrolled up and down, or checked the traffic heading in and out of the gate. Sable began to catch the scent of the ocean as they approached, though it smelled nothing like the Inner Sea she knew back home.

It stank. Sable crinkled her nose, trying to ignore the rancid, salty and oily odours emanating from the vast body of water.

'Now I know why the fish sauce tastes so bad,' she muttered.

Millen glanced at her. 'What's the next part of the plan?'

'Don't you worry about that; it's all under control.'

She scanned the gate, drawing on her battle-vision. A queue of loaded wagons was waiting to enter the merchants' district, and guards were questioning the drivers and checking their identification papers. Any attempt to get in that way would likely result in a fight, and that left too much to chance. If she were alone, then she would have attempted to talk her way in, but Millen's presence rendered that option unviable. The guards would know something was wrong as soon as he opened his mouth. She considered ditching him, but knew how useful he could be, if she could manage to get him inside the wall. She sent her vision up to the top of the battlements that ran across the high barrier, glanced down from the vantage point, and smiled.

'This way,' she said. 'Let's go somewhere a bit quieter.'

They strode past the gate and continued walking for a further half-mile, until they came to the shore of the ocean. A high embankment had been raised, and they had to climb it before the dark waters became visible. Sable suppressed the foul stench, and they walked down the far slope and onto a path that ran by the shingle beach. The waves of the ocean were surging onto the beach fifty yards from the path, and the ground in between was littered with debris – garbage, dead animals that might have been seals, and raw sewage. Gulls shrieked and squawked overhead, while others stood upon the bloated corpses of the animals, pecking at the grey flesh with their beaks.

'What a charming sight,' said Sable. 'Truly delightful.'

Millen snorted. 'This is as close as I've ever been to the ocean.'

'Somehow that doesn't surprise me.'

Six guards were standing at a stone gatehouse where the path met the wall, blocking access to the foreshore of the merchants' district. Beyond them stood a series of abandoned quays and old harbour buildings, their windows boarded-up.

'Stay behind me,' Sable whispered as they approached.

'Officers,' she said in her best aristocratic voice. 'I require your assistance, if you please.'

The guards frowned as she got closer, their hands resting on the stocks of their crossbows.

'I went for a walk,' Sable went on, 'and I appear to have got lost. My servant seems to be rather useless; perhaps you could do me a favour and give him a good beating.'

The guards glanced at each other.

'Look at me,' she said. 'That's better.'

Sleep.

The six guards toppled to the ground in a clatter of armour and weapons. Sable bent over without breaking her stride and plucked a sheathed sword from one of the guard's belts. She tucked it into her robes as Millen stared, his mouth hanging open.

'What did you do?' he gasped.

'I hate repeating myself,' she said. 'I have vision powers. Top-notch as well; the full range, plus a few extras thrown in courtesy of my dream mage ancestry.'

'Am I supposed to understand what that means? You're a mortal. Aren't you?'

'Quit talking and get a move on,' she said, stepping over the last guard and easing through the half-open gate. She glanced around, and started walking towards a long quayside.

Millen scampered up next to her, his eyes wide. The quayside was deserted, and Sable hurried past a derelict warehouse. On the other side was a street leading to rows of large houses, each with a small, tended garden at the front. Flowers were blooming in each, helping to block out the stench coming from the ocean. A guard was posted at the entrance to the street, and Sable ducked into the dark eaves of the warehouse, Millen tucking in behind her.

She waited until the guard was facing in their direction.

You are desperate for a pee. Go relieve yourself somewhere nice and quiet.

The guard's face flushed. He glanced around, then rushed off in the other direction, towards a stand of elm trees.

Sable strode out of the shadows, poised confidently. She belonged there, she told herself. They reached the paved walkway that lined the road, and walked down the quiet street.

'I never knew anywhere this beautiful existed,' said Millen as he glanced at the large houses on either side of the road. Trees fronted most of the mansions, their branches thick with luscious green leaves. Hanging baskets filled with flowers hung from lamp posts, mirroring the blooms in the little gardens.

Sable shook her head. 'Your expectations are pretty low.'

'I've lived in the slums all my life.'

'Then how come you can read?'

He flushed. 'How did you know that?'

She stared at him. 'I'm not repeating myself again.'

'You mean... you looked into my mind?'

'Of course I did. One can never be too careful. But notice that I knew you could read, but not why? That shows that I haven't gone rummaging around in your memories.' She was lying; of course she had raided his memories. Best not to mention that, she thought. 'So, tell me, why can you read?'

'I taught myself,' he said. 'I found a picture book that had been thrown into the trash, and took it. After that, I starting stealing books from a school in Old Tanton, the one for the children of the mercenary officers garrisoned there. I never told Gantu though; he wouldn't have liked it.' He glanced at her. 'I still can't believe it; how is it possible to have vision powers unless you're a god? But if you're a god, then why don't you just walk up to the gates of Old Alea and tell them? They'd let you in. Are you from Implacatus?'

Sable frowned. 'Where? Wait, I'll read it out of your head later; we've got work to do.'

She spotted a bench by a small patch of grass and trees in the centre of a junction, and strode over to it. She sat, took a deep breath of the flower-scented air, then lit a cigarette.

Millen sat next to her. 'You call this "work"?'

'Patience,' she said. 'We need to find somewhere suitable for us to transform into a rich, married couple.'

She lifted her vision again, and began to search the nearby houses, darting into each to check who was inside. Within the seventh mansion she found what she was looking for, and she pulled her vision back to her body. A low ache was throbbing behind her temples from so much use of her powers, but she wasn't going to show that in front of Millen. She smiled at him, and they got to their feet.

'Did you find somewhere?' he said, his eyes still a little sceptical.

'Indeed I did. A nice cosy mansion, where the lord and lady are currently not at home. It's perfect.'

Twenty minutes later, they were in a dark storeroom of the mansion, and Millen was staring at Sable as she finished tying the two servants to sturdy wooden chairs. Gantu's little cousin had been of very little use, but Sable guessed he was still in shock from the whole experience. She fastened the gags round the servants' faces, then checked that the cords securing their wrists and legs were nice and tight. The old man had a bruise running down the side of his face; but it was his own fault. If he hadn't tried to resist, than Sable wouldn't have had to hit him. Opposite him was a younger woman, who hadn't stopped crying since Sable and Millen had broken in.

She stood back and folded her arms, admiring her handiwork. 'That'll keep them quiet for a while.'

They left the storeroom, and Sable closed the door, wedging another wooden chair under the handle. Millen said nothing, his face pale, and his hands trembling.

She frowned at him. 'What's the matter with you?'

'I thought you said this place was empty?'

'No, I said that the lord and lady of the house were out. Come on, let's raid the pantry. And then I might have a long, hot bath. I wonder if there's a wine cellar...'

Millen backed away from her. 'You're insane.'

'Oh, Millen. Did I kill them? No, they're still alive. A few hours tied up in a cold, dark storeroom won't do them any harm in the long run.'

'You hit that old man.'

'So? He was trying to escape. Imagine if he'd managed it, then I would've had no choice but to kill him. This way, when the owners of the house return, the servants will be above suspicion.' She shook her head at him. 'And I thought you were brave. Maybe I chose the wrong guy.'

She strode off into the adjacent chamber, which was lined with crates, sacks and boxes of food and supplies. She knelt down and pulled out a bottle of something from a low rack. She eased out the stopper and took a sniff.

'Eww. I don't know what this is, but none of it will be passing my lips.' She paused, noticing Millen's brooding presence over her shoulder. 'Look,' she went on, keeping her eyes on the rack of bottles by the floor, 'we'll be out of here in the morning, once we've rested and got ourselves all dressed up in some fancy clothes. There's a carriage out in the backyard next to the little stables, did you notice? We'll hitch it up to the ponies and head off to Old Alea as soon as it's dawn.'

Millen said nothing.

Sable selected a different bottle, then stood and turned to him. His hands were shaking, and he looked like he wanted to bolt. She opened the bottle and held it out.

'Take a drink,' she said; 'calm your nerves.'

He stared at her, his eyes wild with panic. 'What am I doing here?' he cried. 'Why did I come? This can't be happening. Gantu's going to kill me. Already he'll be freaking out, and he'll have sent his goons to look for us. My life is over, I...'

She slapped him across the face. 'Get a hold of yourself. It's too late for regrets; besides, Gantu will never find us.' She swigged from the bottle. 'Hmm. Not bad.'

She strode off, climbing some stairs to the main living quarters of the small mansion. She found a large sitting room, and closed the thick curtains. She glanced around the well-furnished chamber, lit a few oil lamps, then sat on a long comfortable couch. She kicked her boots off, leaned back, and took another swig from the bottle. She heard the floorboards creak by the doorway, but didn't turn.

'Who are you?' said Millen.

She sighed. 'I told you. I'm Sable Holdfast.'

'Yes,' he said, walking over and sitting on an armchair opposite her, 'but who are you? Are you a god?'

'No. I'm mortal, just like you.'

'You're nothing like me.'

She narrowed her eyes a little. 'Did you not yearn to be free of Gantu? Did you not long for your life to change? You should be thanking me.'

He lowered his eyes. 'I don't know if my heart can handle this. I don't know why I agreed to come with you.'

She smiled. 'Yes, you do.'

'Why, then?'

'Because you like me. Because you've liked me from the moment we met.'

Millen said nothing. His hands had stopped trembling, but his face looked forlorn, and anxiety shone from his eyes. She felt a sudden pang of guilt for what she had done to him, but quashed it. He had hated his life in the shadow of Gantu, and she had done nothing but show him a glimpse of something better. She passed him the bottle, and he took a drink, then steadied his breathing.

'Feeling any better?'

'A little,' he said. 'Sorry for freaking out in the pantry. I guess... I guess that today didn't turn out as I'd expected.'

She laughed. 'It was fun.'

He raised an eyebrow. 'You have a strange idea of fun.'

'Yeah, maybe.'

She glanced at him. She had been right before – he was handsome, and his grey eyes were gazing at her as if she was all he had ever wanted.

She patted the space next to her on the couch. 'Come and sit over here.'

He took another swig from the bottle and moved round the low table to join her on the couch.

She took his hand. 'Are you nervous?'

'We're breaking into Old Alea in the morning, so, yes. I mean, how are we...'

'Not about that,' she said, lifting a hand to his face. 'About this.' She kissed him.

His arms went round her as their lips touched, then he kissed her neck and she shivered as her desire awakened.

It was just fun, she told herself; nothing serious, then she pulled him down onto the couch, her nails digging into his back.

CHAPTER 7

THE BETTER PART OF VALOUR

Falls of Iron, Western Khatanax – 1st Tradinch 5252

'The answer remains no,' said Count Irno, his eyes dark over his thick black beard.

Maddie folded her arms, her gaze fixed on the tall throne where the count sat. 'This is totally unfair. Isn't Blackrose a guest here, just like I am?'

'Blackrose is a wild beast,' Irno said. 'She has already proved that, by flying low over the town and terrifying my people. She's lucky I didn't turn the castle's ballistae on her.'

'No, you're lucky,' Maddie said. 'If you'd done that, then she would have burned the place to the ground, and you'd deserve it, too. All I'm asking is that you treat her with a little respect, and allow her to land in the forecourt, and to sleep in the deep caves behind the castle. She's not like all those wild dragons everyone keeps telling me about.'

Irno raised an eyebrow. 'So you say. However, you appear to have very little experience of wild dragons, whereas I, unfortunately, have had many dealings with them. Flying, fire-breathing serpents are not to be trusted; I learned this the hard way. Besides, if the authorities in Alea Tanton were to discover that the Falls of Iron has a dragon setting up home within its walls, then the consequences for all of us could be profound. And that, my dear lady, is my final word on it.'

'Asshole,' Maddie muttered.

Irno spluttered. 'How dare you address me like that? I should have you locked up and thrown in the cells.'

'Try it,' said Maddie, 'then you might get a glimpse of how wild Blackrose can be.'

The count stared at her. 'Get out of my sight.' He nodded to his guards. 'Escort Miss Jackdaw from my presence, immediately.'

Maddie clenched her fists as the guards approached. 'Don't even think about touching me.' She turned to leave the audience hall, then glanced back to Irno. 'And remember, little Count, between me, Blackrose, Corthie and Belinda, we could kick your ass, and the ass of everyone else in this stupid town.'

She stormed from the chamber before the guards could reach her. She passed through the tall doorway, and out into the bright sunshine, the glow from the whitewashed stonework dazzling her eyes.

'That go well?'

She turned, and saw Aila sitting on a bench by a low wall overlooking the town. 'Take a guess.'

'I don't need to,' Aila said, 'not if the expression on your face is anything to go by.'

Maddie walked over and sat by her on the bench. 'Sorry, Aila, but your brother's a buffoon. He thinks he's all high and mighty because he rules over some little town in the middle of nowhere. "Count", ha, what even is a "Count" anyway? Stupid title.'

'Did you threaten him again?'

'I might have done. So what? Aren't we supposed to be his guests?'

'Yes, but come on, Maddie. Irno's letting us stay here, even after everything that Karalyn did when she arrived. You saw his face when he caught sight of Belinda – I thought he was going to have a heart attack and drop dead on the spot. Karalyn, Belinda and Sable really scared him, and Vana, when they passed through looking for Corthie a few months ago. The Holdfasts imprisoned them, interrogated them, and then nearly drained them dry when they sent Belinda to Pella.'

Maddie frowned at her. 'You mean the "City"? I'm not calling it Pella. The Bulwark, maybe, but not Pella.'

'Don't change the subject; put yourself in Irno's shoes for a moment, that's all I ask.'

'Fine, but then why is he taking it out on Blackrose? She didn't do any of those things you mentioned, and her patience is fast running out. If I told her half of the names that Irno's called her, she'd probably go berserk.'

'Please ask her to be patient for a bit longer.'

'Why don't you ask her yourself?' said Maddie. 'I'm heading up to the top of the cliffs just now. Come along, unless you've got anything better to do.'

Aila frowned. 'I haven't, as a matter of fact.'

'What's wrong? You had a falling out with the big guy?'

'No.'

'Then where is he?'

'Drinking.'

'Again?'

'Yes, again.'

Maddie nodded. 'Wow, Corthie can really put the booze away.'

'I know.'

'You should tell him not to drink so much.'

'I did. He called me a hypocrite. He said that if I could spend two centuries in an opium daze, then he could spend a few days drinking while he waits for his sister and aunt to turn up.'

Maddie chuckled. 'He's got you there.'

'Don't you start. That was different; I was under house arrest, not trying to get my bearings in a new world. Karalyn could arrive any day, or she might never return. We need to make a plan.'

'Let's start with talking to Blackrose,' said Maddie, standing.

The demigod got to her feet, a miserable expression on her face. Maddie glanced at her, then turned towards the rear of the castle's long, narrow courtyard. There was something going on; Maddie could feel it. Something to do with Aila, Corthie and Belinda. A secret of some kind. It probably had nothing to do with her, but she was curious all the same. Maybe she could help? She led Aila to the base of a tall tower that rose high against the side of the cliff, and they began to climb the stone steps upwards. There were slit windows running up the side facing south, and the bright sunshine lit their way.

'Malik's sweaty crotch, I'm knackered,' Maddie said as they reached the halfway point. 'This climb always takes it out of me.'

Aila glanced up at her. 'I can see why you want Irno to let the dragon sleep by the base of the castle.'

'I know. I have to do this every day; sometimes twice in the same day.'

They stopped at a window slit and gazed out at the view. The plains were spread out before them, in shades of brown, and green where the irrigation channels fed water to the fields from the river that wound its way down to the coast. Tiny white cubes were dotted about the landscape – the farmhouses and barns of the county. On the horizon reared the dark line of the mountains that stretched all the way south-east towards the ruins of Dun Khatar, and above that the sky was a deep blue, with the bright, hot sun blazing down.

'It's been sunny every day since we got here,' said Aila.

'Yeah, it's been great. I love the feel of the sun on my skin, and I hate being on Blackrose's back when it's cold and rainy. There's only one moon though, which is a bit weird. I miss the little moon.'

Aila glanced at her. 'I wonder how things are in the City.'

'Oh, so you're calling it the City now? What happened to "Pella"?'

'It's the world that we both come from; we can call it that when we're alone. Do you think you'll ever go back?'

'Part of me hopes so,' said Maddie, turning back to the stairs and continuing to climb; 'part of me doesn't care.'

It took a further twenty minutes of climbing to reach the long, wide ledge where Maddie met the dragon each day. The ledge was a hundred feet from the top of the cliffs, but far enough from the town to be acceptable to Count Irno. Maddie panted as she stepped up onto it, sweat running down her back.

'I would have thought the climb would have toughened you up by now, rider,' Blackrose said, her wings folded in, and her head resting on her large forelimbs. Her jet black scales were shimmering in the heat, and she looked like she had been sleeping.

'Morning, Blackrose,' said Maddie, leaning her palms on her knees. 'I brought some extra company today.'

'Who? Ah, I see. Corthie's paramour.'

'I have a name,' said Aila as she climbed onto the ledge.

Blackrose ignored her.

Maddie let out a sigh. 'Do we have to go over this again? You can't be holding ridiculous grudges, Blackrose. It makes you seem petty.'

The dragon raised her head a foot. 'Who said I was holding a grudge? Surely, one is allowed to dislike someone without necessarily holding a grudge?'

'I don't care if you dislike me,' said Aila. 'I've had nearly eight centuries of people disliking me. I've found they generally fall into two categories – those who don't know me at all, and those who know me too well.'

'Well, I like you both,' said Maddie. 'Obviously, I'm Blackrose's rider, and I'm not Aila's... rider. Um, forget I said that; anyway I think actually you two have a fair bit in common. You're both cynical, grumpy misanthropes; I mean I can't exactly imagine either of you dancing or singing at a party. And, Aila usually dresses in black, so there's that too.'

'Hearing you speak,' said Blackrose, 'makes me realise I've missed other company. Maybe, it would be acceptable to me to hear the voice of a fellow grumpy misanthrope.'

'Then I guess I'll stay,' said Aila. 'The rest of our party are far too cheerful for me to handle.'

Blackrose tilted her head. 'And what do they have to be cheerful about? Have the fabled Holdfasts returned at last?'

'No. One is drunk out of his mind, and the other two are in love. Well, one of them's in love, the other? I'm not so sure.'

Blackrose nodded. 'One consolation of being exiled to the cliff top is that I'm spared having to witness the spectacle of Naxor and Belinda fornicating like goats in spring.'

'Eww,' said Aila.

'Exactly,' said Maddie. She frowned. 'I worry about Belinda. I think she might get hurt.'

'Then you should worry about Naxor,' said Aila, 'because if he hurts Belinda, then I fear for his life.'

'You know what I mean,' said Maddie. 'Belinda is like... Malik's ass, this makes me sound patronising, but she's like a child; a teenager. Yes, I know I'm still a teenager, but Belinda doesn't seem to have the first clue about, well... anything. Oh, she's smart, and she kicks ass, and don't forget it was her that sealed the breach in the Outer Walls.'

'What?' said Aila. 'Why did no one tell me that? I asked about it, and was told it was all of you: you two, Belinda and Rosie.'

'No,' said Maddie, 'it was pretty much Belinda. She didn't want to take credit for it at the time. She didn't care about any of that stuff.'

'She leapt from my back,' said Blackrose, 'after I had expressly ordered her not too. She has valour.'

Maddie glanced at Aila. The demigod was frowning, as if she was bearing a burden. Maddie chewed her lip, then turned to Blackrose. 'She certainly does, though she and Corthie haven't been getting on.'

'Why not?' said Blackrose.

'No idea,' said Maddie, catching the dragon's glance. 'There's no point asking *me*.'

Blackrose tilted her head for a moment, saying nothing. She turned to Aila. 'Demigod, what is your opinion on lying? Is it necessary, or is it the ultimate proof of the weakness of humanity?'

Aila raised an eyebrow, and Maddie smothered a low chuckle.

'Four years? Twins? Malik's damp patch, could it be true?' Maddie shook her head as if trying to dispel a hangover.

Aila glared at them. 'That wasn't fair, you assholes! Maddie, is that why you asked me up here, so you could get Blackrose to play her mind games on me? You sneaky, treacherous little witch.'

'Hey!' said Maddie. 'I didn't bring you up here for that purpose exactly, but well, you know, I suspected something was going on, and if it affected me or Blackrose then I kind of needed to find out.' She cringed. 'Um, wow. I guess I am a treacherous little witch.'

Aila slumped to the stone ledge, sitting down hard, her head in her hands.

Blackrose leaned forward with her head, and gently nudged Aila's shoulder. 'I have released you from your compulsion, but one question I didn't ask – why haven't you told Corthie of this?'

'I've tried,' Aila said.

'Not very hard, it seems.'

'I wanted to have a serious discussion with him, but he's been drunk for days.'

'Then tell him not to drink so much.'

Aila narrowed her eyes at the dragon.

'You should tell him before Karalyn gets here,' said Maddie.

'If she gets here,' said Blackrose. 'I am starting to suspect she may never return. Perhaps she has already learned the truth, and has returned to her world.'

Maddie frowned. 'She wouldn't do that, would she? She wouldn't abandon Corthie and Belinda.'

'I cannot answer that. Regardless, perhaps it is time you and I moved on, rider. We are accomplishing nothing by remaining here. Every day that passes is another day that Dragon Eyre suffers under the oppression of the gods.'

Maddie glanced at Aila. 'I hate to admit it, but she might be right.'

'You mean you're going to leave us?' said Aila.

'That was always our objective,' said the dragon. 'I feel sympathy for Karalyn's predicament, if indeed Belinda's theory is true, but it remains no business of ours.' She lifted her head and gazed out over the panoramic view of the landscape below them. 'Lostwell is a broken land, groaning in torment. Yes, I have decided. We shall leave.'

'When?' said Maddie.

Blackrose turned to her. 'Tomorrow. That will give you time to say your farewells to the others in our company.'

'They'll want to see you too,' said Aila. 'I'll speak to my brother, to see if he'll make an exception to the rules about you not being able to land by the castle. If he knows you're going, then he might relent.'

Blackrose's eyes glimmered. 'I'm sure Count Irno will be delighted to see me depart.'

Aila nodded, then got to her feet. 'Alright. I'd best go down and tell everyone.'

Maddie turned to the dragon. 'I'll come back up here later tonight and let you know the plan.'

'Very well; I shall be watching for you. In the mean time, I will go flying, and hunt some of the furry beasts that inhabit these mountains.'

Maddie grimaced, then she and Aila turned for the stairs.

'Are you going to tell Corthie?' she said, as the two women started to descend.

'Yes.'

'When?'

Aila sighed. 'When we get to the castle, I guess.'

'Good. He needs to know.'

'Malik's ass,' Aila muttered; 'I'm getting nagged by a nineteen year old.'

Maddie shrugged. 'You're going out with a nineteen year old.'

'You disapprove, don't you?'

'It's not my place to disapprove,' said Maddie, 'though I do think it's a bit weird. I know you won't want to hear this, but it can't possibly end well.'

'Does any mortal relationship?'

'It's hardly the same, Aila. When Corthie's in his sixties and seventies, you'll still look twenty-one. And what if you have children? I assume you've at least considered it. Are you prepared for what that will mean? Mortal children.'

'So what's your advice? Or are you just being a bitch?'

Maddie frowned at her. 'Don't call me that. I don't like it.'

'Do you blame me? I trusted you, Maddie, and you tricked me. You dragged me all the way up these endless steps so that Blackrose could squeeze the truth out of me. It was horrible – she could have made me say anything.'

'I know what it feels like; she's done it to me.'

'That makes it worse. You knew, and you still did it.'

'Then you shouldn't have been keeping secrets.'

'But it has nothing to do with you; it's none of your damn business. You know, I'm glad you're leaving tomorrow; the sooner you're gone, the better.'

She stormed off down the stairs, leaving Maddie trailing behind.

Damn it, she thought; *I might have gone too far.*

There was no sign of Aila when Maddie finally reached the bottom of the steps and emerged from the base of the tower. She took a moment to rest in the shade of the cliff side, catching her breath from the climb down. She wandered over to a small water fountain built into an alcove in the sheer face of the cliffs, leaned over and took a cool drink. The weather in Khatanax was so hot, hotter than she had ever known it back in the City, excepting that one time when Blackrose had flown her and Rosie out into the desert. She straightened, peeling her sweat-soaked tunic from her back.

'Miss Jackdaw.'

She turned. 'Naxor.' She glanced around.

He frowned. 'Who are you looking for?'

'Your shadow. Where is she?'

'Belinda happens to be taking a nap.'

'Tire her out, did you?'

'Don't be vulgar, Miss Jackdaw.'

Maddie narrowed her eyes. 'Were you wanting something?'

'I was merely taking a stroll.'

'And you happened to bump into me as soon as I come down the stairs? Come on, Naxor; do you think I'm stupid?'

'Perhaps I shouldn't answer that. However, I did see Aila a few moments ago, and she looked a little less than pleased. What have you and Blackrose been doing to her?'

'We've decided to leave Lostwell tomorrow; maybe she was sad about that.'

Naxor blinked. 'You're leaving?'

'Yeah, that's right. So, you can say goodbye to your hopes of stealing the Quadrant.'

'But what about our secret little salve mine? Surely you can't be intending to go to Dragon Eyre as you are, with no gold and no army. You do realise that Blackrose's world is a rather dangerous place to be?'

'We'll manage.'

Naxor said nothing for a moment, then he nodded. 'Walk with me, please.'

'Where?'

'It won't take a moment.'

He led her through the castle courtyard until they came to a high curtain wall, then they climbed the steps to the battlements. A warm wind was blowing from the south, and Maddie squinted in the harsh light.

'The Falls of Iron,' said Naxor. 'The most impregnable fortress in the whole of Khatanax. The town below is shielded by a high wall, but even if invaders managed to breach it, then the sheer cliffs would stop them getting any higher. There's abundant fresh water, not only coming from the river, but there are deep pools within the dozens of caves and caverns behind the cliff face, along with huge stores of gold and supplies. At the base of the hills are tunnels leading to rich seams of iron, a resource that has made the county very rich. It's no coincidence that I chose this location for my cousin Irno to reside. It's the perfect base.'

'What do you mean you "chose" this location? Actually, I don't want to know.'

'What I am saying, dear Miss Jackdaw, is that perhaps you and your reptilian friend shouldn't be so hasty. Stay here a while, and allow me to fill a few caverns with raw salve. I'll split the proceeds fairly, and then you can go to Dragon Eyre with the harness bags filled with gold. Overflowing with gold. Think about it.'

'Why would I want to stay somewhere that won't even let Blackrose land? She's been exiled to the cliff top.'

'I know, but it's only been a few days – let me work on Irno. He's a decent chap, and once I've explained to him about the salve mine, then I'm sure I could win him round. A dragon might draw attention, but she would also be very useful in scaring off anyone who got too inquisitive.'

'You haven't told Irno about the salve mine?'

'Of course not.'

'Don't you trust him?'

Naxor sighed. 'It's not a matter of trust, Miss Jackdaw. If he knew, then any god would be able to read it out of his head – just as I read the real reason for Aila's distress out of yours while we were standing by the fountain a few minutes ago.'

Maddie glared at him. 'You what? You snake.'

Naxor shrugged. 'She's my cousin and I was worried.'

'Then you know about...'

'About the so-called missing four years? Yes. I read that out of Aila's mind several days ago. Ironic; the only person from our party who doesn't know is Corthie.'

'Do you believe it?'

'Who can say? Perhaps we'll only discover that when Karalyn shows up. But if it is true, then that's another reason why we should act now. We should be transporting as much salve here as possible before she arrives, because when she does, I imagine she'll want to return to her world immediately, taking Corthie and Aila with her.'

'And Belinda?'

Naxor shrugged. 'She hasn't decided what to do.'

'I hope you're not stringing her along, Naxor.'

He laughed.

'I'm serious. To you it might be just another conquest, but I don't think Belinda sees it that way. Her emotions are fragile.'

'And why do you care? Just a moment ago you told me you were leaving us here so you can go off to Dragon Eyre to get killed. What goes on between Belinda and me is none of your business, little mortal girl.'

Maddie turned and started to walk away. 'Asshole.'

'Wait,' he called to her; 'you'll think about what I said, yes? About the mine. It would make us all very rich.'

She ignored him and kept walking. She entered the massive keep of the castle, and waited a moment for her eyes to adjust to the dim light. She needed to speak to Count Irno, to ask him if Blackrose could descend to the castle forecourt in the morning in order to say goodbye to everyone, but dreaded it. Instead, she headed towards the ale room. It was early for getting drunk, but it was her last day in the Falls of Iron.

She heard Corthie's voice before she opened the door to the ale room. He was laughing, and shouting something, his words slurred. She smiled as she entered. The room was low-ceiling, and thick with smoke from the little white sticks that the locals inhaled. She coughed.

Corthie turned from where he was sitting by a table. 'Maddie! Get your arse over here. Aila told me you're leaving tomorrow.' He clicked his fingers towards a serving girl. 'Hey, doll. Get us some more beers.'

The girl nodded, a weary expression on her face. Maddie squeezed past the busy tables and sat down by Corthie.

'Aila's spoken to you, has she?'

'Aye, you just missed her. She's away to talk to Irno about the dragon coming down here tomorrow before you leave.'

'Is she? Excellent, then I don't have to.'

Corthie slapped her on the back, and she nearly fell off the chair.

'I going to miss you,' he said. 'You and the flying lizard.'

The girl returned from the bar with two large tankards of ale, and set them down on the table.

'Cheers, doll,' grinned Corthie.

'So this is where you've been for the last few days, eh?' said Maddie.

He eyed her. 'If you're here to nag me about drinking too much, then the door's that way.'

She shrugged. 'It doesn't bother me. I guess Aila's been giving you a hard time about it?'

'Aye. You could say that. But, I mean, what's a few days getting smashed compared to two hundred years of smoking opium? She just doesn't understand how bored I get.'

'When you're not killing greenhides, you mean?'

'Exactly.'

'Did you and Aila fight?'

'No, it was perfectly shivilised... I mean civilised. She told me about her wee trip up to see old scaly-face.'

'She told you about that? She told you what we discussed up there?'

'Aye.'

'And what do you think?'

He shrugged. 'It's not really sunk in yet. It might when I sober up, but who knows when that'll be, eh?'

'You're taking it pretty well,' she said. 'Poor Karalyn. Imagine losing four years of your life, and not getting to see your kids grow up. She's going to go absolutely mental.'

Corthie squinted at her. 'Karalyn? What?'

'What?'

'What are you talking about – four years? What kids?'

'Uh, isn't that what Aila told you?'

'She told me all about your plans to leave tomorrow.' He narrowed his eyes. 'What did you think we were talking about?'

'Nothing.'

'Is Aila keeping something from me?'

'Um...'

Corthie pushed himself to his feet, sending the two full tankards flying, their contents spilling over the wooden floor.

'Stick it on my tab,' he yelled over to the serving girl, then he staggered from the ale room.

Maddie shrank into her chair. *Bollocks.*

CHAPTER 8
LOCAL KNOWLEDGE

Serene, Implacatus – 1st Tradinch 5252

Van stared into the bathroom mirror, a cigarette hanging from his lips. The buttons on his uniform shone in the reflected glow of a small lamp, and he smeared a little soot from the base of the lamp over them with his thumb, to dull them down. In his left hand he held a small vial, containing a tincture of salve. It was enough for half a dozen doses, maybe more if used sparingly, but his stomach was already twisting at the thought of taking some. Emergencies only, he told himself; he was a good soldier, he didn't need salve to fight. He slid the vial into a pocket, and heard the glass clink against his silver cigarette case.

Ash fell into the deep stone sink, as smoke spiralled and weaved by Van's face.

He was ready.

'Captain Logos, sir?' came a voice from outside the bathroom.

He dropped the cigarette into the sink and opened the door.

'Sir,' said the corporal; 'Major Ahito wants you.'

Van nodded and strode out of the bathroom and into the shadows of the large marshalling yard, where a thousand salve-soldiers of the Banner of the Golden Fist were assembled, lined up in their companies. Grouped to the rear of the soldiers were dozens of loaded carts and wagons, with hundreds of slave porters and guards. Each column of soldiers was headed by a standard bearer and a small cluster of officers, while Lord Renko, his two deputy gods, and the senior officers of the Banner had gathered in front of the massed troops.

Major Ahito hailed him as he approached. 'Captain Logos; over here if you please.'

Van saluted the major, then bowed before Renko and the other two gods.

Renko nodded at him. 'You are the officer with previous experience of Lostwell?'

'Yes, my lord.'

'Have you been to Alea Tanton?'

'I have, my lord. I was garrisoned within the walls of Old Alea.'

'Perfect.' He nodded to Lady Joaz. 'Captain Logos will escort you.'

She bowed. 'My lord.'

'Captain,' Renko went on, 'select two dozen soldiers and accompany Lady Joaz to the departure point.'

Van saluted. 'Yes, my lord.'

He strode towards the massed lines of soldiers until he reached his company, where a soldier was holding aloft a standard bearing a large eagle, a winged snake captured in its talons. He gazed down the column for a moment.

'First and second squads, along with Lieutenant Sohul and an artificer, follow me. Lieutenant Baku, you are now in command of the rest of Eagle Company.'

Van led the soldiers back across the huge yard, the soldiers marching behind him, as Sohul caught him up.

'Have we been chosen to go first, Captain?'

'That we have, Lieutenant. We're going to Alea Tanton.'

'Where?'

'Lostwell.'

The lieutenant frowned. 'All this is for Lostwell? What could possibly be important enough on Lostwell to warrant such a force? I heard it was a backwater.'

'When I'm allowed to brief you, I will.'

They reached a low tower at the edge of the marshalling yard, where a wall ran along the edge of a precipice. Lady Joaz and a handful of demigods and servants were waiting a few yards away from the tower.

Van and Sohul bowed before her, and the two squads lined up behind them.

Joaz nodded. 'Captain.'

'Ma'am. This is Lieutenant Sohul, an up-and-coming young officer.'

Sohul bowed again.

She gave him a polite nod. 'Gentlemen, we shall be heading the expeditionary force this evening. Our destination is the city of Alea Tanton. We shall be arriving somewhere within the walled fortress town of Old Alea, where our first objective will be to locate and secure an area of land large enough to set up a portal link. Any questions?'

'No, ma'am,' said Van. He turned to the squads. 'Form a perimeter around Lady Joaz and her party.'

The soldiers rushed to obey, each squad peeling off until they had circled the god and her assistants. They held their light shields to the outside, and unslung their long, powerful crossbows. Each had a sword strapped to their waists below their steel breastplates, and a spear clenched in the same hand as their shields.

'We're not expecting a hostile response,' he said to the soldiers, 'but allow no one to approach Lady Joaz.' Van nodded to her. 'Ready when you are, ma'am.'

She extended a hand, and one of the demigods passed her a copper-coloured device. Joaz took it, and traced a finger along the engravings in a pattern. Van watched her closely. He had seen Quadrants being used many times, but their workings remained a mystery to him.

'What's Old Alea like?' Sohul whispered.

'Residential,' said Van; 'rich. It's where the gods of Lostwell live.'

Joaz raised her head, and turned towards where Lord Renko was standing by the other god, Lord Maisk. She lifted a hand in the air, and

Van saw Renko gesture in reply. A second later, the air around them grew hazy, then shimmered. Their surroundings disappeared for a fraction of a second, and then they were in Alea Tanton, their boots on the paved surface of a narrow, tree-lined road.

Van glanced up and down the street. On either side stretched walled gardens leading to enormous, palatial mansions. Ten yards to their left was a sturdy iron gate.

'First squad,' he yelled, pointing; 'get that gate open. Artificer, accompany them.'

He heard a cry from the other direction and spun on his feet. A small group of people were standing on the road twenty yards away, gesturing at the newcomers.

Van nodded to a sergeant. 'Keep those civilians back, but no unnecessary casualties.'

'Yes, sir,' cried the sergeant, and the soldiers of his squad closed ranks facing the group. Van strode over to the gate where the first squad was busy, and peered through the steel bars. It led onto a large, landscaped garden, with small groves of bay and olive trees, and an ornamental lake. In the distance rose a huge mansion, streaked with dark ivy.

The artificer had the bolts barring the gate cut within moments, and the soldiers pulled them open.

Van gestured to Lady Joaz. 'This way, if you please, ma'am.'

She walked across the road, her retinue following, along with the second squad, who kept their lines intact as they withdrew.

Van bowed before the god. 'These gardens should suffice for the portal-link, ma'am.'

'I must say, Captain,' she said, a slight smile on her lips; 'you are awfully efficient.'

One of her assistant demigods smirked. 'More lucky than efficient, I'd say. What were the odds of arriving so close to a large open space?'

'The odds were high, my lady,' said Van, bowing again. 'Old Alea is filled with large public squares and enormous gardens.' He pointed at a pair of high towers over to their right. 'Governor Latude's residence is in that direction, about half a mile from here I'd say.'

The demigod frowned and strode away as Lady Joaz laughed softly. 'Lead on, Captain,' she said.

Van ordered the two squads through the gates, posting a sergeant and a handful of soldiers to secure them as they moved on into the heart of the gardens.

They reached a flat open area of short grass, and Van halted.

'Lieutenant Sohul, I want you and the first squad up on the driveway by that fountain, in case the lord or lady of the mansion decides to unleash dogs or militia against us. Send a pair of soldiers with a message, informing the owners that we have come from Implacatus and are not to be hindered in any way.'

Sohul saluted. 'Yes, sir.'

Joaz brandished the Quadrant as the lieutenant led the squad away. She traced a finger over its surface again, and a dark, black void opened up a yard from her, a swirling mass of nothingness, twelve feet wide, and the same high. A moment passed, and then the swirling faded away, revealing the marshalling yard from the Banner's headquarters. Lord Renko was standing there, while Lord Maisk was clutching another Quadrant, its power holding the portal open from the other side.

Lord Renko stepped through, his boots striding onto the grass of the garden. He glanced around, nodded, then gestured to Major Ahito in the marshalling yard. A whistle blew, and the companies of mercenary soldiers began marching through the portal, led by the major.

'This way, sir,' said Van. 'The glade behind me is large enough for the regiment.'

Ahito nodded, then gestured to the first columns. He turned back to Van as the soldiers began spreading out across the grass.

'Good job, Captain.'

'Thank you, sir.'

Lord Renko strode over to join them and nodded at Ahito. 'Put the plan into motion as soon as the entire regiment has made it through, Major.'

Ahito bowed. 'Yes, my lord.'

Van stepped back as the majors and gods entered a discussion. He glanced over to the driveway, and could see Lieutenant Sohul there with his squad. Lights had been lit within the rooms of the enormous mansion, and the sound of dogs barking rose up into the evening air. He took a deep breath, and a flood of memories came back to him as he recognised the sour tang of the polluted ocean that bordered the city on one side. He waited until his own company had marched through the portal, and joined them as they assembled in lines upon the grass.

Lieutenant Baku saluted. 'Sir; do we have orders?'

'Not yet,' said Van. 'Welcome to Lostwell.'

Baku glanced around. 'Not bad.'

'This is the highly fortified residence of the gods and demigods who live here,' Van said; 'the rest of the city is a complete dump. With any luck we'll be garrisoned up here. We want to keep out of the slums if at all possible.'

The lieutenant nodded. 'Is that where the smell is coming from, sir; the slums?'

Van nodded. 'The slums and the ocean. It's hard to tell which stinks worse.'

A sergeant hurried over to him. 'Sir, we have a problem.'

Van narrowed his eyes.

'The mansion, sir. Our messengers have met with some resistance from the locals.'

Van glanced back at the portal for a moment. Hundreds of soldiers were still moving through from the marshalling yard, and the senior officers were in deep discussions with Renko and the other gods.

'Show me,' he said to the sergeant.

They strode up to the driveway, and Van heard raised voices as they approached.

'You will pay for this outrage!' cried a low voice dripping with anger.

A man was standing in a dressing gown, his fists clenched. He was glowering at Lieutenant Sohul and the other soldiers, who were blocking his path.

'Can I help you, sir?' Van said.

The man turned to him, his eyes lit with fury. 'Are you this idiot's commanding officer?'

'I am Captain Logos.'

'Then tell this fool to get out of my way. You soldiers have no right to be trampling all over my garden.' He raised his right hand. 'Do you realise I could kill you all in a single second?'

'That would be inadvisable, sir,' said Van, easing his way to stand between the god and Sohul. He folded arms across his chest. 'You should return to your home.'

'Do you know who I am, you mortal fool?'

'No, sir, nor do I care.'

'I am Lord Baldwin, one of the most powerful gods on Lostwell, and you are trespassing on my land.'

Van nodded. 'Lord Baldwin, go home before you embarrass yourself any further.'

The god swung his hand back, as if to strike Van.

'Sergeant,' Van said, 'send a message to the most Noble and Ancient Lord Renko; let him know that one of the divine residents of Old Alea is having a tantrum.'

The sergeant saluted, and made to leave.

The god hesitated, mid-swing. 'Lord Renko?' His features paled.

Van raised a finger to halt the sergeant. 'That's right,' he said to the god; 'Lord Renko is here, on a commission from the Seventh Ascendant, Lady Arete. Are you hindering us, sir?'

'You're from Implacatus?'

'Indeed.' He gestured. 'The mansion, sir?'

Hatred shone from Baldwin's eyes, but it was tempered with a raw fear. He remained where he was for a moment, then slowly turned and strode up the driveway, his head bowed in shame.

Van glanced at his lieutenant. He and the squad were staring at him. It was probably the first time in their lives that any of them had seen a mortal stand up to a god. There was a touch of awe in their eyes, but also anxiety.

'Back to Eagle Company,' he said. 'Let's go.'

'Was that wise, sir?' whispered Sohul as they headed down the driveway away from the mansion.

'It's not often I get the opportunity to antagonise an arrogant son of a bitch like Baldwin.'

'But he'll tell Lord Renko how you treated him, sir.'

'So? I have a feeling that our divine commander isn't too pleased with the current government of Lostwell at the moment.'

They reached the long grassy glade, which was packed with soldiers. The last of the supply wagons were rumbling through the portal, and Van headed towards the cluster of senior officers, leaving Sohul and the squad with the rest of his company.

'Ah, there you are, Captain,' said Ahito.

'Apologies, sir. I was delayed by having to deal with a certain Lord Baldwin. He objected to our presence in his garden.'

Renko glanced over. 'Who?'

Van bowed. 'Lord Baldwin, Commander. I advised him to get back indoors.'

Renko said nothing for a moment, then nodded. Behind him, the final wagon trundled onto the grass of Lord Baldwin's garden, and Lady Joaz lowered her arm. The portal shimmered then vanished with a slight pop. A moment later, Lord Maisk appeared at her side, the other Quadrant in his hand. Renko beckoned them, and they strode forward.

'Lord Maisk,' he said, 'take two companies of soldiers and secure the entrances to Old Alea; hold the gates to the rest of the city, and ensure that no one tries to leave the plateau via the harbour. As of this moment, Old Alea is sealed off. No one is to enter or leave without my permission.'

Maisk bowed.

'Lady Joaz,' Renko went on, 'you shall accompany me and the other three companies of the regiment directly to the Governor's residence. I trust you did your research and you know where it lies?'

'Yes, my lord,' she smiled. She gestured over to the pair of tall towers that Van had pointed out earlier. 'It's half a mile that way.'

'Very good,' he said. He nodded to the assembled officers of the Banner. 'See to your companies.'

The officers saluted.

Eagle Company was among those selected to escort Lord Renko to the Governor's mansion, and Van gathered his soldiers. Renko led the way in person, striding through the gates with Lady Joaz by his side, and the three companies followed; six hundred soldiers in all, followed by the porters, the wagons, and a small rearguard.

By the time they were underway, a small crowd had gathered further down the street, staring at the arrivals as they marched north across the high promontory. On either side, more mansions were situated, lying amid their spreading garden estates, along with neat rows of small cottages for the mortal workforce that tended to the needs of the rulers of Alea Tanton. Van strode near the front, just ten yards behind Renko, leading Eagle Company in a double column as they marched towards the Governor's residence. Van remembered it well. The street layout probably hadn't altered in centuries, and it was exactly as he recalled.

Ahead lay a large circular junction lined with tall beech and cypress trees, with fountains spraying cool water into the warm evening air. A patrol of local militia was guarding the road that led to the Governor's residence. They took one look at the approaching soldiers and bolted, fleeing back along the road as fast as they could. The soldiers of the Banner ignored them, and pressed on, passing the fountain as their boots clacked over the smooth flagstones beneath them.

The streets were well lit with regular oil lamps hanging from tall iron posts, and Van saw the massive mansion belonging to the Governor loom up before them. It had a tall tower at the end of each wing, and the central block rose to half their height. Around it was a low wall, with a steel fence atop it, and a great gate lay along its length.

The column halted, and Van saw Renko talking to Joaz and their demigod aides. Lady Joaz nodded, then spoke to Major Ahito, who was standing close by. The major bowed low, then walked towards the head of the columns.

'Captain Logos,' he said. 'Lady Joaz has requested that your company accompany her to the rear of the residence.' He glanced at the other captains. 'The rest of will be going straight through the front door. You are not to initiate hostilities, but deal ruthlessly with any armed resistance. Lord Renko wants the entire mansion and its grounds occupied as smoothly as possible. If any of the leadership of Alea Tanton attempts to flee, detain them, with force if necessary.'

The captains saluted. Van walked to his company, where his two lieutenants and eight sergeants were waiting for him. He passed on the major's orders, and he saw their eyes widen at the prospect of trying to detain a god by force.

As they were getting ready to depart, Van felt a niggle behind his temples.

Captain Logos.

It was Lady Joaz's voice in his head.

He smiled. *Yes, ma'am?*

I trust you know the route to the rear of the residence?

I do, ma'am.

Picture it in your mind for me.

He took a breath, closed his eyes and concentrated on the street layout surrounding the Governor's mansion. He then focussed on a set of gates set into the wall by a small courtyard. Part of him hated when gods went into his head – he had so many bad memories, and many of his thoughts were far from pure or noble, and he always worried that they would see more than he wanted them to see.

Got it, she said in his mind; *thank you, Captain, and I would appreciate your discretion in this matter. After all, I would hate for Lord Renko to discover that I had neglected to conduct the required research.*

Understood, ma'am.

She left his head, and Van opened his eyes. He nodded to Sohul, Baku and the sergeants. 'Follow me.'

The company marched forwards, leaving the other two on the main road with Renko and Major Ahito. Lady Joaz joined Van at the head of the company, and they took a street to their right, passing rows of accommodation for the mortals of Old Alea. Eyes glimpsed out at them from behind thick curtains and painted wooden shutters, but no one opened their doors.

Joaz glanced at Van as they walked. 'Tell me, Captain; what did you do to annoy Lord Maisk? He positively loathes you.'

'Did he tell you that, ma'am?'

'Yes. He bristled when your name was mentioned at a briefing.'

'Four years ago I served with him on Dragon Eyre, ma'am. He reported me for insubordination.'

'Really? And how did that go?'

'The tribunal acquitted me, ma'am. There were several inconsistencies in the lord's account.'

'I would be very interested in hearing all about it, Captain.' She smiled. *Perhaps when the residence is under our control, we could find some time alone to discuss it further.*

He caught her glance, and gave a slight nod. 'I am at your service, ma'am.'

I know you are, Van Logos.

He cleared his mind of the thoughts whirling about it. He had been seduced by gods before, and by demigods looking for a casual affair with an experienced Banner officer. It meant nothing to them, and so it meant nothing to him. He wondered how long Lady Joaz had been alive for. She wasn't an Ancient, so she would be under ten millennia old, but as all of the gods took salve, they all looked around the same age. Joaz would pass for mid-twenties in the world of the mortals, but so would Lord Renko, and he *was* an Ancient. Van shook his head. At twenty-eight, he already looked older than the gods. He wondered what age he would be when they lost all interest in him.

It took a further ten minutes to reach the rear of the residence, and the company halted in front of the gates that led to the back steps of the palatial mansion.

Lady Joaz's eyes glazed over for a moment as she contacted Lord Renko, then she glanced at Van.

'Order the company in, Captain. Lord Renko has given the order to proceed.'

Van signalled to his lieutenants and sergeants. There was no need for words – they had drilled together for so long that each knew their role. The first and second squads charged across the courtyard, and were up and over the gates in seconds. They secured the local militia in the blockhouse, and cut the chains securing the gates. The other squads flooded in, their crossbows cradled in their arms. Van left a squad with Joaz, and led the way up the paved path to the back of the mansion. Screams were rising into the night air as the soldiers burst down the rear doors, and entered the huge building. Chaos reigned inside. Servants, clerks and militia were running through the vast hallways in panic. Many were rushing towards the rear door, then skidded to a halt as they saw Van's approaching company.

'On your knees!' he cried at the crowd, drawing his sword. 'In the name of Implacatus and the Seventh Ascendant, I command you; get on your knees.'

Within minutes, Van's company was occupying the rear of the mansion. Guards had been posted to the main stairs and passageway junctions while others were standing by the rear gates, blocking anyone from entering or leaving.

A god by the name of Kemal had been apprehended lurking in a room on the upper floor. He had surrendered without a fight, and Van decided to escort him in person to the central suite of rooms, where Renko had established control of the building. Lady Joaz accompanied them, along with a squad of soldiers. The residence had been virtually undamaged in the occupation, the officers making it clear that looting and vandalism would not be tolerated. The soldiers hardly needed to be told, their training was extensive, and their pay good enough for most to be able to resist the temptation.

Van found Lord Renko in the heart of the complex, just as the god was about to enter the Governor's personal quarters. The Ancient acknowledged Joaz, the captain and their prisoner, then ordered a squad from another company through the main doors. They had been barricaded from the inside, and the soldiers smashed them down, then clambered over the debris. Inside, a man was standing, holding a sword in his hand, and wearing nothing but a bathrobe. Behind him, four young women were huddled together, staring at the soldiers as they charged in. The interior was as luxurious as anything Van had seen on Implacatus. Chandeliers glittered from the ceiling, their glow illuminating the gold and silver on display, along with long, silk-covered couches, tables over-flowing with food and drink, and, in the corner of the chamber, a huge sunken bath, large enough to easily accommodate a dozen bathers.

Renko waited until the small group had been surrounded, then strode in, followed by Joaz, Van and the other officers present.

'Governor Latude,' Renko said, his expression showing what he thought of the trembling god in the bathrobe; 'your reign in Lostwell is at an end. This residence, Old Alea, and the entirety of Khatanax is now under my authority.'

Latude stared, his mouth hanging open.

Renko frowned. 'Put the sword down.'

'Whoever you are,' Latude said, 'you have no right to enter this world. I was appointed by Implacatus.'

'And it is from Implacatus that I have come,' said Renko.

Van saw his eyes glaze over, and knew he was using his vision powers to communicate directly with the governor.

Latude's face fell. He dropped the sword and collapsed to his knees. 'Forgive me! I thought Old Alea was under attack – I had no knowledge that you would be coming here.' He whimpered, and lowered his head to the floor. 'Forgive me, my lord.'

Renko shook his head. 'Pathetic.' He glanced at a soldier. 'Get those girls out of here. Place them in my harem.'

'Yes, sir,' the soldier said, shouldering his crossbow.

Renko glanced around the room as the soldier took the four young women away. His gaze roved over the opulent décor and fine furniture, then his eyes widened. Van frowned, then followed the Ancient's gaze, over to a long glass cabinet sitting horizontally in an alcove at the back of the room.

Rage passed over Renko's face, and he strode towards the cabinet. Van and a few others moved closer to look. Lying inside was the badly-preserved corpse of a man, the skin leathery and grey, the face shrunken. Brown teeth still clung to the jaws, and wisps and tufts of hair partially covered the skull.

Renko stared at the corpse for a long time, saying nothing, then he slowly turned to Latude.

'Governor,' he said, his voice filled with disgusted loathing; 'explain this desecration.'

'It is the remains of a great traitor, my lord,' Latude said from his knees.

Renko clenched his fists. 'I know who it is!'

He drew his sword, and clubbed the cabinet with the hilt. The glass shattered, then Renko sheathed his sword and reached inside. With great care, he lifted the withered corpse out of the cabinet and laid the body down onto one of the couches. He began wrapping it in a silk covering, while Joaz and the officers stared in silence.

When Renko had covered the body, he turned back to Latude. 'Someone will pay for this sacrilege.'

'It wasn't me!' cried Latude. 'It was Lord Kemal! He brought the corpse back here; it was him.'

'Kemal?' said Renko. 'Where is he?'

'We have him, my lord,' said Lady Joaz. She nodded at Van, who bowed. He turned back to the door, and gestured to the soldiers from his company to bring their prisoner in.

Lord Kemal was brought forward. His face betrayed no emotion, and Van wasn't sure if the god had heard what had happened from outside the chamber.

Renko waited until Kemal was standing a yard from him, then he raised his hand. 'Tell me, Lord Kemal, how is it that the body of the Fourth Ascendant Lord Nathaniel came to be on display here?'

Kemal bowed, seemingly unaware of the tension in the room.

'Certainly, my lord,' he said. 'Several years ago, I led an expedition south into the mountains beyond Dun Khatar, following a report that the rebel and traitor Lady Agatha was hiding there, along with others in her group. We found a deep ravine where the rebels were based and, after a brief siege, we broke through. Unfortunately, though we destroyed their base, Agatha and the others escaped. They had a Quadrant, my lord. I believe this was all in the report we submitted to Implacatus.'

Renko took a breath. 'And the body?'

'We found a tomb within a cavern in the side of the ravine, and took possession of the remains of the traitor Nathaniel, my lord. We brought it back here as proof that the rebellion was finally at an end.' He glanced over and noticed the glass lying on the carpet next to the empty cabinet, and his eyes narrowed.

Renko swept his fingers through the air, and Kemal's head exploded, showering the room with blood, gore and fragments of bone. The body stayed upright for a moment, then wobbled and toppled to the floor, blood flowing from the severed neck.

Latude let out a wail.

'Silence,' said Renko. 'You were the Governor; it should have been you. Fortunately for you, I still require your obeisance for now, otherwise your brains would also be decorating the furniture.' He glanced at the others in the Chamber. 'Leave us. I wish to thoroughly question the Governor on the present situation in Khatanax. And then I shall make arrangements to transport the body of the Fourth Ascendant back to Implacatus for a burial worthy of his name and renown. He may have fought against us, but he was one of the twelve Ascendant Gods and a master world-builder.' A tear rolled down his cheek. 'Our lives are the lesser for his loss.'

The officers and others present bowed, then filed out of the chamber, leaving Renko alone with a cowering Latude.

Outside, Lieutenant Sohul was waiting for Van.

'Sir,' he said, 'do you have a moment to go over the dispositions of the company forces, and the allotment of supplies for our stay here?'

Van frowned.

Now, that sounds dull, said Joaz's voice in his head; *instead, Captain, how about you grab a bottle of something nasty and meet me upstairs – I have been assigned some beautiful quarters, and I think you might enjoy the view.*

'Sorry, Lieutenant,' said Van, 'but I'm afraid I'm going to be unavailable for a while. Don't worry; I'm sure you'll manage fine.'

CHAPTER 9
HOT AND COLD

Falls of Iron, Western Khatanax – 2nd Tradinch 5252

Aila lay alone in bed as the first rays of dawn entered through the shutters of the small chamber. It had been a hot and airless night in the castle and she had slept little, her mind going through the same conversations over and over, half-awake, half-asleep, until she had felt as if she might be going mad. She was exhausted, but had come to no conclusions.

She was also angry.

In many ways, Corthie was perfect for her. He understood her better than people who had known her for decades or longer, and although they were different types of people – he was out-going while she was reserved, and he was an optimist, while she often dwelt on everything that could go wrong – they complemented each other. Or so she had thought. It pained her to acknowledge it, but their happiest times together had been while he had been busy killing greenhides in the City; without fighting to distract him, his attention drifted into apathy and boredom, his mind seemingly incapable of relaxing or of being content with an ordinary life. He needed the thrill of battle-vision like it was a drug; remove it, and the only thing he wanted to do was drink himself into oblivion each night.

She couldn't understand – if he loved her like he said he did, then why wasn't she enough for him? His time was short, so why would he rather spend it getting drunk than being with her? She could get drunk with him, of course, and had done a few times when they had first arrived in the Falls of Iron, but given the choice between the ale room and a sober night with her, she knew which he would choose.

She wondered what Princess Yendra would have to say about it. She missed her aunt more with each passing day; longed for her advice and company. Maybe they should have remained in the City, but with the greenhides defeated, would Corthie be acting the same way if they had stayed?

He had shouted at her for not telling him about the missing four years. It had been the first time she had seen him drunk and angry at the same time, and although she had never been worried that he would raise his hands to her, he had raised his voice, and had left her with a sickening feeling in her stomach; a twisted knot of emotions that she had spent half the night trying to untangle.

Did she love him? Yes.

Was she infuriated by him? Also yes.

Was she prepared to admit that she might have made a mistake? No. She refused to contemplate it. She had left behind everything she knew – her home, Yendra, Cuidrach Palace; all to be with Corthie, and if it had been a mistake then… No. He was young, and had been through more in the last few years than most people experienced in a lifetime. All that violence and killing had done something to his brain, and she needed to be patient as he worked through it. She suppressed a scream of frustration. Patient? His mortal lifespan felt like water seeping through her fingers, draining away before her eyes.

She pulled back the sweat-soaked sheet and got to her feet. The stone floor was cool and for a moment she considered lying down upon it to get some relief from the heat. She noticed her skin was dotted in little red marks – bites from the blood-sucking insects that plagued the town and castle after dusk, and so she powered her self-healing until they vanished, watching the blotches disappear. The effort tired her out, and she sat back onto the bed. The new day had arrived, but all she wanted to do was lie down and sleep. She couldn't. It was Blackrose and Maddie's last day, and despite their disagreements, she still wanted to say goodbye to them before they departed. She lowered her head, trying to summon the will to get washed and dressed.

Hello, said a voice in her head.

Aila jumped, her heart racing.

Don't panic, said the voice. *I don't have long to speak. This is the furthest I've ever been able to send my vision powers... Um, Aila, is it? Oh, you're a demigod. Interesting.*

Who are you?

Me? I'm Sable Holdfast. I was looking for Karalyn, but in her absence you'll have to do.

Sable? I thought you were with Karalyn; where are you?

Alea Tanton. I've been waiting for ages for Karalyn to contact me, but so far, nothing. I have a message for her.

Aila nodded, though she had no idea why. She waited for the voice to continue, but there was nothing but silence.

Are you still there?

Yes, said Sable; *I was just reading some of your memories, and, um... Hang on a minute.*

There was a glow of light in front of Aila, and a woman appeared in the room.

Aila stifled a scream. 'How did you do that? Do you have a Quadrant?'

'Not yet,' the woman said, an infectious gleam in her eyes. 'I'm doing a vision trick; making you see me as if I were really there, or here; wherever. A bit like what you can do with your powers, when you make people see you as a different person.' She smiled, a hand on her hip. 'I wonder if I could try that? Anyway, so that was a lot to process – Corthie's back, and he's your drunken boyfriend, and he's aged four years, or rather, Karalyn and I haven't aged four years. Hmm, so I should be thirty-two, but I'm still only twenty-eight? I knew there had to a silver lining somewhere.'

Aila peered at the vision. 'And you're Corthie's aunt? You look more like you should be...'

'His sister? Thanks. Sorry; one benefit of being in your mind is knowing what you're going to say next.'

Aila smiled. She knew she should be annoyed, but instead she felt relaxed, even happy.

'I wonder if Karalyn's discovered the truth yet,' Sable went on. 'If she has, that would explain her absence. She's probably gone back to see her brats. What a terrible mother, not seeing her children for four years. And it's a pity Belinda's back – couldn't you have left her in that City-world-place you come from?'

Aila laughed, unable to help herself.

'So, as I was saying, I've been waiting in Alea Tanton for my beloved niece to contact me, and I've been getting a little restless, so I've decided to act, with or without Karalyn's permission. That's my message to her. If she complains, which she will, then tell her she shouldn't have left me for a month twiddling my thumbs.'

'Act?' said Aila. 'What are you going to do?'

'Steal a Quadrant, if possible. I'm going to break into Old Alea today, where the gods of Lostwell live, and if I'm successful, then you might be seeing me in the flesh before too long.' She smiled again, and Aila thought to herself what a beautiful smile she had. 'Once I figure out how to use it, of course. Only, I've run into a potential problem. I was scouting out the ways into Old Alea, about an hour ago, and something's changed overnight. There are soldiers everywhere, and they've come all the way from Implacatus.'

'Where?' said Aila.

'God-land. God-world, whatever you want to call it – where the God-bosses live. And they're on a mission. Have you heard of a substance called salve? Oh, you have? Wait a minute. Ah.'

'Salve? What about it?'

'Oh dear, Aila; it appears that your world might be in a spot of danger. A little army has arrived with the sole purpose of finding the source of salve. I was in the mind of one of the most stupid gods I've have the misfortune to read; an oaf by the name of Lord Maisk. He's part of the task force sent from Implacatus. They have complete authority to do whatever they please in order to find out where the salve is coming from, and then they intend to take over the source.'

'Damn it,' cried Aila; 'and now you know about my world too. What if they read it from your head?'

Sable laughed. 'I'm a Holdfast. No one will be reading my head. This might be bad news for your world, but it could be good for me. If they're distracted by this salve business, then I might be better able to sneak about and do my thing. Tell you what; I'll lay down some misinformation for them, and send them off in the wrong direction for you.'

A deep sense of gratitude washed over Aila. 'Thanks.'

Sable smiled. 'No problem. Right, I'd better go; I'm working at the limits of my powers. Pass on my message to Karalyn, if she ever turns up. Oh, and tell Belinda she can kiss my arse. Bye.'

The vision dissipated, leaving Aila staring at the empty space in the room where Sable had been. It was strange, but Aila almost missed her already. She smiled and stood, starting to look forward to passing on Sable's message to Belinda.

The god's eyes narrowed as Aila related the conversation to her, while Naxor sat on the next chair along, barely able to contain his mirth.

'She sounds quite interesting, this Sable,' he said.

Belinda gave him a cold stare. 'She's a bitch. Stay away from her.' She shook her head as she turned back to Aila. 'She was playing with your mind.'

Aila blinked. 'No, she wasn't.'

Belinda sighed. 'Let me guess. She was rude, selfish, and raided your thoughts and memories without asking, and yet you felt nothing towards her but joy, even gratitude?'

'What? No, I... wait, was that what happened?'

'I'm immune,' said Belinda, 'but I've seen her do it to other people plenty of times. She could steal from you and leave you bleeding in a ditch, and you'd thank her for it, and beg her to do it again.'

Naxor laughed as Aila's face fell.

'No,' she said, unable to believe it. She squinted at Naxor. 'And why are you laughing? Did you not hear the part about our world being in danger?'

He shrugged. 'They've been searching for the source of salve for hundreds of years.'

'But Sable said they'd brought an army with them this time. I don't know; it sounds pretty serious to me.'

'What does?' said a voice from the other side of the courtyard.

They turned, and saw Corthie approaching through the bright sunshine. He was squinting in the light, and walked over into the shade where the others were sitting.

'Aila's worried,' said Naxor. 'Apparently some gods have arrived, looking for the source of the salve.'

Corthie sat. His eyes were bloodshot, and his face was unshaven and had a grey tinge about it. 'Arrived where?'

'Alea Tanton,' said Naxor.

'You look terrible,' said Belinda. 'And you stink. When's the last time you took a bath or a shower?'

'Shut up, Belinda,' he said. 'I'm on my way to get washed just now.'

Aila frowned. So far, he hadn't even glanced in her direction.

'And what are your plans for today?' Belinda went on. 'Or is that question too obvious to answer?'

'Stop nagging me; you're not my mother.'

'No. Your mother would give you a good slap if she saw you like this.'

'Pyre's arse, can a man not have a few drinks now and again?'

Belinda snorted. 'And what about Aila?'

His bleary eyes narrowed. 'What about her?'

'You're treating her like crap.'

Aila cringed, wishing she could disappear.

Corthie got back to his feet. 'Well, maybe if you and Aila had been honest with me, I wouldn't feel the need to get wasted.'

'Don't give me that!' Belinda cried. 'You don't need an excuse to get wasted. You're behaving like a child.'

He smirked at her. 'Aye, well you would know about that.'

He turned and strode away, disappearing into a side door of the castle keep.

Aila groaned and put her head in her hands.

'That went well,' said Naxor. 'I suppose it makes a change from everyone being annoyed with me.'

Belinda glanced at him. 'Do you think I went too far?'

'You do have a rather blunt manner at times, but as I've said before, it's one of your traits I find endearing. I never have to worry that you're not being completely frank with me. I love that you're so honest.'

The god smiled, and Aila felt like vomiting. She got up from the bench, leaving Belinda and Naxor gazing into each other's eyes, and walked to the wall surrounding the courtyard. It was hot in the sunshine, and a shimmer was rising from the lands below her. She wondered if she should go after Corthie and have it out with him, but dreaded the prospect. She sighed. For the first time in ages, she wished she had some opium to smoke, so she could forget about everything for a while.

She thought about Sable. The young Holdfast woman was alone in a foreign city, in a strange world, yet she seemed in charge of her own destiny. Maybe she should try to be more like Sable, she thought. Despite Belinda's comments about her, Aila still found it hard to believe that her emotions had been manipulated. Maybe Belinda was jealous.

A shadow flickered overhead and Aila gazed upwards into the deep blue sky. She shielded her eyes from the sun, and saw the silhouette of a dragon circling above them.

She turned back to Naxor and Belinda. 'They're here.'

They walked across the courtyard, and left the castle through the main gatehouse. The large forecourt was empty, its flagstones baking in the heat. The dragon began lowering in the sky, sweeping past the cliff-side until Aila could feel the breeze coming from her wings. She alighted onto the forecourt, her claws landing on the flagstones.

She brought her head down. 'Greetings.'

'Hi, Blackrose,' said Aila.

'Are you all set to go?' said Belinda.

'We are,' said the dragon. She turned her head as Maddie scrambled down from the harness. 'My rider has packed everything we need.'

'You're going to a war zone,' said Naxor. 'You need soldiers, and a massive amount of gold. Just a few days, and I could get you the gold.'

Aila turned to him. 'Are you still going on about that salve mine, even after what Sable said?'

'Sable?' said Maddie.

'Yes,' said Aila; 'she's been in touch. She said that the gods have brought an army to Lostwell to find the source of the salve.'

Maddie raised an eyebrow. 'That doesn't sound good.'

'It's fine,' said Naxor. 'They'll never find our world. The City is perfectly safe.'

'Pella,' said Belinda.

'Yes, dear. Pella. That's what I meant to say.'

Aila glared at him. 'You don't know if it's safe. What if the gods find one of the merchants you were dealing with?'

'That wouldn't help them locate your world,' said Blackrose. 'Ideally, they would need a Quadrant that had travelled there, or else they could possibly read it out of Naxor's head.'

'But someone might lead them here,' said Aila, 'to the Falls of Iron.'

'You worry too much,' said Naxor. 'I've been very, very careful.'

Blackrose peered into the distance. 'Ah, here's Corthie. I wondered if perhaps he would be too inebriated to join us this morning.'

Maddie leaned in towards Aila. 'Sorry about, you know. I didn't mean it.'

'It's alright,' she said; 'you saved me from having to tell him.'

Corthie nodded to Blackrose as he approached. 'I'm sorry you're leaving.'

'It's what I wanted from the start,' said the dragon; 'to get back to my world. I thank you for your help; I thank you all for your help.'

'I didn't help you,' said Naxor; 'I actively tried to prevent this from happening and I still think it's a mistake. The conflict on Dragon Eyre didn't end with your surrender and capture.'

'Which is another pressing reason why I should return. My people are suffering.'

'I understand your reasons,' said Corthie, 'but maybe Naxor's right for once. Maybe you need to go when you're ready for a war.'

'I agree,' said Belinda.

Blackrose tilted her head. 'This reminds me of when you all tried to persuade me to save the City that imprisoned me. I did, and yet you are still not satisfied.' She turned her long neck in Aila's direction. 'I notice that you haven't given your opinion, little demigod. What say you?'

Aila shrugged. 'It's your decision.'

'It is. Are you still upset about what happened yesterday? Perhaps I shouldn't have compelled you to tell the truth; if it has hurt you, then I am sorry.'

Maddie looked up at the dragon. 'You've never once apologised to me. Not ever.'

'I've never done anything to you worthy of an apology, rider. In Aila's case however, I pried into something that turned out to be none of my business.'

'It's fine,' said Aila. 'I should have told Corthie as soon as Belinda told me.' She turned to the god. 'And you should have told us all long ago.'

Corthie glanced at Belinda. 'Why didn't you?'

'Because it might not be true,' she said; 'there might be another explanation for what's happened. None of us understands anything about how time works, especially when you go from one world to another.'

'I understand,' said a voice from the cliffside.

Everyone turned. A woman was standing in the shadows by the cliff, leaning against the rock as if exhausted. She was tall, almost as tall as Yendra, and her skin was as dark as Sable's.

Belinda let out a gasp.

'Karalyn?' said Corthie, his eyes wide.

'Brother.'

He ran over to her, racing past the dragon, and gathered the woman in his arms, his sobs punctuating the silence. She put her arms round his back, and they held each other in a tight embrace. Aila glanced at Belinda. The god's face was still, her eyes wary.

Corthie took his sister's hand, and they walked over to the others. He wiped his eyes. 'This is Karalyn.'

The dragon raised her head. 'Karalyn Holdfast. Well met.'

'Blackrose,' she said.

Her gaze scanned the others in the forecourt. Her face looked drawn and taut.

'Nice to meet you,' said Maddie. 'I'm Maddie Jackdaw.'

'I know.' She glanced at Aila. 'I know who you are, as well.'

Aila looked away as Karalyn's green eyes pierced her, and despite the heat, the demigod felt a cold shiver run down her spine.

'Where did you come from?' said Maddie. 'I didn't see you walk up the forecourt.'

Karalyn turned to her. 'I arrived a while ago.'

'I do not wish to doubt your word,' said Blackrose, 'but I would have sensed your presence if you had been here. Do you have a Quadrant, or are you able to move without one?'

'Karalyn could have been here the entire time,' said Belinda, 'and none of us would have known.' She glanced at her. 'How long were you standing there for?'

'An hour, maybe. What does it matter? In answer to your question, dragon, I can travel around Khatanax without a Quadrant. It's what I've been doing since I sent Sable to Alea Tanton. Something had been troubling me ever since I read the mind of Vana, Aila's sister. Her memory contained an image of Corthie that I knew couldn't be right; or at least that's what I thought. So, to be sure, I went to a mercenary training camp that Irno knew about – the one that prepares the champions for travelling to the world you've all recently come from.'

'Gadena's camp?' said Corthie.

'Aye,' she said. She shook her head as she looked at him. 'Four years.' She lowered her head. 'You spent four years in that camp. I refused to accept it at first, but now I realise that I must have made a mistake when I brought myself, Belinda and Sable to Lostwell. It was my mistake, but I am far from being the only one who has paid the price for it.'

'You have my sympathy,' said Blackrose. 'I understand what it is like to be separated against my will from those I love.'

'Then will you do me a small favour?' she said.

'Name it.'

'Stay a few more hours? I want to talk to my brother, but I also have a great many things I could tell you about; things I have learned since I arrived here.'

Blackrose tilted her head. 'Very well. A few hours, you say?'

'Until sunset?'

'Then I shall leave you to speak with your kin, and return an hour before the sun sets this evening. Maddie, do you wish to stay, or come flying with me today?'

'I'm curious to find out what's happened,' Maddie said, 'but... well, it's none of my business, I guess.'

'Precisely,' said the dragon, 'and we shall speak to her when we get back.'

Maddie nodded to the others, then clambered up the harness until she reached the dragon's shoulders. Blackrose extended her wings and lifted into the air, powering upwards and sending a wash of warm air across the forecourt.

'Shall we get a drink?' said Corthie.

Karalyn nodded, and they turned for the castle.

'Were you really standing there for an hour?' said Naxor as they walked.

She glanced at him.

'I assume you know who I am?' he said. 'You've been in my head, am I right?'

'She can go into everyone's head,' said Belinda, 'including mine and Corthie's.'

'What?' said Aila. 'But Corthie's immune from all powers.'

'Not all,' said Karalyn. 'I sealed him up against ordinary mage and god powers, just as I did with Sable and Belinda, but dream powers are not ordinary. And yes, Naxor, I arrived here before the dragon landed. I was tired, and I knew she was coming.'

'You were spying on us?' said Aila.

'I was finding out what I needed to know.'

Aila shuddered.

They entered the keep and walked into the ale room. Inside, Corthie hailed the bar staff, then sat by a table near an open window.

'Ale for everyone,' he said. 'And a bottle of raki for the table.'

The others took their seats. Naxor and Belinda sat to Karalyn's left, while Aila sat at the other end of the table, next to Corthie on Karalyn's right. Two serving girls brought drinks over for them, setting out tankards, and small glasses for the raki.

Aila glanced at Karalyn. Her eyes were downcast and she looked tired. Aila tried to imagine how the young mortal woman was feeling; how someone so powerful could have made such a terrible mistake, and she felt a pang of sympathy for her. She had left her children behind to do the right thing and search for her brother, and she had paid a heavy price.

'You have twins?' said Corthie. 'I remember you being pregnant when I was abducted.'

Karalyn glanced at him, then lit a cigarette, sending a thin trail of smoke spiralling up to the low ceiling. 'Aye. Cael and Kyra. They had just turned six months old when we left our world. And now, they will be almost five.'

'Did you make up with Lennox?' Corthie went on. 'Is he there, looking after them?'

She turned to Belinda. 'Didn't you tell him?'

'No. I didn't think it was my place.'

Karalyn nodded. 'Lennox and I did get back together, but he was killed in the final battle against Agatha.' Her eyes tightened, but no tears came. Aila wondered if she had cried so much that she had run out.

Corthie lowered his head. 'Lennox is dead?'

'I left the twins with Thorn and Keir,' Karalyn said, her voice a whisper. 'They probably imagined that they'd be looking after them for a few months, not four and a half years. The twins will see Thorn as their mother; she'll be all they remember, all they know.'

'Keir's with Thorn?'

'They got married.'

'Thorn married that numpty?'

Karalyn narrowed her eyes. 'He's our brother. He's a Holdfast. You can call him what you like when we're alone, but not in front of strangers.'

'Aila and Naxor aren't strangers.'

'They are to me.'

'I can't even imagine the pain you're in,' said Aila.

'Of course you can't,' said Karalyn; 'you're a demigod. You should go back to your own world and leave us alone.'

Aila bit her tongue. If she opened her mouth, she knew she would regret it.

'Don't speak to her like that,' said Corthie. 'I love her, and she's coming with us when we go home.'

'What happened to you, brother? I looked into your mind when you were out on the castle forecourt – so much blood, so much death. Would Aila stay with you if she truly understood how dark your thoughts have become? How you live for violence? That without it, your life feels empty and meaningless. You say you love her, but if that is so, then why have you done nothing here in Lostwell but drink yourself into unconsciousness each day?' She shook her head as the rest of the table sat in silence. 'It's my fault. If I hadn't made such a mess of getting here, then I could have got to you before Gadena turned you into a killer; but it's too late now. The brother I knew is gone forever.'

Belinda leaned forward. 'My oath to you has been fulfilled. I found Corthie, and brought him to you.'

Karalyn nodded. 'Aye. I release you from your vows. Go where you please; do as you please.' She glanced up at the god. 'But I would advise against trusting Naxor.'

'Is that it?' said Belinda. 'You release me? What about my powers? I used to rule Lostwell, did you know that? Nathaniel and I. They called me the Third Ascendant, and Queen. You can't just discard me; you can't just leave me without the powers that are my birthright; it's not fair.'

'Shut up, Belinda.'

The god rose to her feet, fury in her eyes. 'You never had any intention of giving me my powers back, did you? You used me to find your brother, and now you're pushing me aside.'

'You're alive, aren't you?' said Karalyn. 'The Empress would have taken your head from your shoulders if it weren't for me. You won't be coming back with us, is that clear?'

'Perfectly. But know this; I'd rather die than go back with you. I want nothing more to do with you, or any of the Holdfasts; but before you leave, I want my powers back.' She glanced at Naxor. 'Let's get out of here.'

Naxor rose, then nodded to Karalyn. 'It's been... enlightening.'

Aila watched as Belinda and Naxor left the ale room, then started to wish she had gone with them.

'Why did you do that?' said Corthie. 'Why are you acting like this? I know you're hurting, but you'll be back with your children soon. Belinda did everything you asked of her, and more. She's a damned hero, sister; she saved the City where we were living; she saved the lives of thousands of people by her actions.'

'If you think I care about the inhabitants of that world, or of any world other than our own, then you are mistaken, brother. I care about one thing, getting home to my children.'

'Why are you being such a bitch?'

'A bitch?' Karalyn said. A cold smile appeared on her lips. 'Brother, I have barely begun.'

CHAPTER 10

UNPROFESSIONAL

Alea Tanton, Tordue, Western Khatanax – 2nd Tradinch 5252

Sable exhaled, sending a plume of smoke up to the ceiling of the wood-panelled office, her high-heeled boots up on a stool in front of her. She would have rather been sitting out on the veranda, but was making do with gazing at the dawn light through a narrow slit in the curtains. Her head ached a little from her vision trip to the Falls of Iron, but the pain was worth it for the information she had picked up from the demigod.

Aila had seemed friendly, and had proved highly susceptible to Sable's powers. Sable knew that it was partly down to Aila's emotional exhaustion, but she still felt a twinge of pride that she had managed to make a demigod relax and laugh so easily. She had learned a lot from her mind, but Karalyn's absence was the most relevant. Where was she? Was it possible that she had fled back home, abandoning Sable and Belinda to return to her children?

Sable hoped she had. She feared Karalyn in a way that she feared no one else. If she had truly left Lostwell, then Sable would be free, but free to do what? She didn't know, but getting her hands on a Quadrant still seemed to be the wisest course of action.

Next to Karalyn's absence, the fact that they might have spent four years frozen as they had travelled from their world to Lostwell seemed almost inconsequential. After all, what did it matter to her life in Khatanax? And if she ever returned to her own world, then a few years might have lessened the Empress' anger towards her.

She almost laughed as she imagined her half-sister Daphne having to help look after her two dream mage grandchildren for four years. Served her right for being such a stuck-up cow. Even better, Sable had gained four years on her, and would still be at her fighting peak, while Daphne would be well into her forties. She pictured herself getting a Quadrant, going back to the Holdings and kicking her sister's arse. Half-sister, she reminded herself. Sable's mother had been a queen, and she had royal blood flowing through her veins, as well as the Holdfast variety. Daphne may be an aristocrat, but she was a peasant compared to her.

None of it made up for the gaping hole in her life caused by the collapse of her faith. She still felt stupid when she thought about the fact that she had worshipped a being that hadn't been a god; just a highly-powered mage with an unlimited lifespan. Was that what gods were? No. Powers didn't make them divine, not in the way she understood it. To the mortals of Lostwell, she was like a god, and that was ridiculous.

She heard the floorboards creak outside the room, and decided to try something out.

When you walk in, you think I am Gantu.

Millen opened the door and strode into the chamber. He glanced over, paused, and did a double-take.

'Hi, Sable,' he said. 'That was weird. For a second I thought Gantu was sitting there. My nerves must still be on edge from yesterday.'

Sable nodded. 'Yeah, maybe. Everything prepared?'

'Yes. I've loaded the wagon with the contents of the cellar, and the ponies have been fed and watered. And, as you can see, I've dressed up to look the part.'

She smiled. 'You look like a different person; very smart and handsome. Are you ready to brave Old Alea with me?'

Of course you are, she implanted into his mind; *you are confident and courageous, and you trust me completely.*

'I think so,' he said. 'Wow, I can hardly believe we're doing this. Robbing a merchant is one thing, but breaking into Old Alea? Did you find the permit?'

She nodded. 'It was in the desk drawer; first place I looked.'

He gazed at her. 'You look amazing. I mean, you were beautiful before, but seeing you in that dress...'

'I won't be wearing it for long.'

His face flushed.

'It'll do until we get through the gates of Old Alea,' she said, 'but it's utterly impractical for fighting.'

'Do you think there will be any fighting?'

'I hope so. I haven't killed anyone in ages.'

He nodded as if he assumed she was joking. She knew from reading his thoughts that he had no idea she had battle-vision. She should probably tell him, she thought, weighing up his need to know, with the satisfaction she would get from seeing his face if he saw her in action. She stubbed the cigarette out and stood, the black folds of her dress reaching the floor and covering her boots. She picked up a small shoulder bag, cursing the dress's lack of pockets, and checked to make sure she had put her cigarettes and the permit card inside.

'Shall we, husband?' she said.

'Certainly, my good wife,' he replied, extending his arm.

She took it and they strode from the room. The two servants were still tied up in the storeroom, but Sable wasn't too worried. She had lied to Millen about the owners of the house, telling him that they were due to return that evening, but what he didn't know wouldn't hurt him. They left the house via the back door, and walked down to the wagon. Millen assisted her up onto the padded driver's bench, then he began hitching the four ponies to their harnesses. The rear of the wagon had a high canvas covering, and inside were a dozen large crates, and three barrels. The mature cheese in one of the crates was giving off a tart aroma, and her stomach rumbled as she watched Millen attach each pony to the front of the wagon. When the last was in place, he ran to the end of the yard and opened the two large gates.

Sable cracked the whip over the heads of the four beasts, and the wagon jerked forwards, its wheels rumbling over the worn flagstones. It rolled through the entrance, then Sable pulled on the reins while Millen closed the gates behind them. He leaped up onto the driver's bench and Sable handed him the whip and reins.

'Straight ahead,' she said, 'then the third road on the left.'

He nodded, and they moved off, entering the street by the little square. A gardener was pruning the bushes by the bench where Sable and Millen had sat the day before, and he glanced up, his brows furrowing as he caught sight of the wagon.

Our presence is of no concern to you.

The gardener's eyes went back to his work, and he started to whistle a tune Sable had heard at the arena when the Bloodflies had been hosting the Blue Thumbs.

'Who do you think won the game yesterday?' she said to Millen.

He frowned. 'The Bloodflies. Shinstran assholes.'

'And how do you know that?'

'Did you not hear the noise from over the walls last night? That was the sound of celebrating.' He shook his head. 'Unbelievable. I'm glad we didn't stay to watch the end.'

'Do you really care?'

He shrugged. 'I don't like to watch the butchery that goes on in the arenas, and I hate the gangs and the violence; and Gantu for that matter, but I'm still a Blue Thumb, and will be until the day I die.'

'You do realise,' she said, 'that the ruling gods of Alea Tanton set up these teams so that you would keep fighting each other, instead of freeing yourself from their grip?'

'That might be objectively true, but I can't help it; I feel it in my bones. I was brought up to loathe the Fordians. That horrible green skin, like rot or mould; decay. There's no better feeling than seeing the Blue Thumbs thrash the Deadskins.'

She raised an eyebrow. 'Really? No better feeling?'

'Alright,' he said, a smile creeping across his lips, 'last night was better.' His eyes drifted away for a moment. 'Anyway, it's the same with the Shinstrans. I admit we don't hate the Bloodflies as much as the Deadskins, but not by much. If they beat us yesterday...'

'Then what?'

'Then Gantu's gang, and many other Blue Thumbs gangs, would have rioted all the way back to our part of the city. I guess that's another reason I'm glad I wasn't there. Yesterday might rank as the worst day Gantu's had in a long while. First he lost you, and then the Blue Thumbs were defeated.'

'He lost you too.'

'Yes, but I don't imagine he cares too much about that.'

Sable pointed. 'There's the third road on the left. After that, take the next right, and we'll be on our way to Old Alea.'

Millen nodded, and guided the wagon down the street. The paved walkways on either side were getting busier, with workers delivering goods to the mansions, and gardeners and oil lamp-fillers out preparing the merchant's district for another hot day. They took the next right, and joined a wide road where several wagons were heading towards a large gatehouse in the distance. Above it rose the high cliffs of the promontory where Old Alea sat. A wall with battlements stretched round the perimeter of the small plateau, and a wide ramp had been cut across its face, alongside, Sable noticed for the first time, the gargantuan faces that had been carved into the rock next to it.

Even though the cliff was a couple of miles away, the faces were large enough for her to pick out their individual features, and she sent a burst of line vision in their direction to take a closer look. She recognised the face of Felice, the patron of the Blue Thumbs, and also Kemal, who filled the same role for the Bloodflies. The largest face was of a god she didn't recognise.

'Is that Governor Latude in the middle?' she said, pointing at the cliff in the distance.

Millen squinted. 'I don't know. I've never been this far south, and have only heard stories about the great images of the gods carved into the side of Old Alea. That face is the biggest, so I'd guess it must be Latude.'

Shops on either side of the road were starting to open, and a few gentlemen and ladies of the district became visible; out for their morning strolls, or overseeing the work of their servants. The wagon moved onwards, and they reached the gatehouse, where armed guards waved them through. They left the merchant's district, and went along a road that had high walls on either side. To their right stretched an enormous fortress, home to the city's militia garrison, and ahead of them was the start of the ramp that led up the steep slope. A few wagons were already making their way up the ramp, towards the entrance to Old Alea. Another gatehouse was embedded into the walls that circled the promontory, and its gates appeared to be closed.

'Is that normal?' said Millen. 'Why would the gates be shut?'

'That reminds me, there's something I should probably let you know about. Last night, hundreds of soldiers arrived in Old Alea. They came from Implacatus.'

Millen's eyes narrowed. 'What? From Implacatus? But why would they...'

'Salve,' she said; 'they want to find the source of salve.'

'Maybe we should rethink this.'

'Why?' she said, smiling. 'Are you the source of salve?'

'What?'

'If not, then we have nothing to worry about.'

'Let me get this straight – the gods think salve comes from Lostwell?'

'It appears so,' she said, deciding that it would be best to keep all knowledge of Aila's world from him. Sable's mind might be impenetrable to all but Karalyn Holdfast, but Millen's was vulnerable to anyone with vision powers.

A few hundred yards ahead of them, the first wagons were starting to line up by the closed gates, and Sable could see the drivers jump down, and speak to a handful of soldiers who were present. After a few moments, the gates opened, and the wagons rolled under the wide archway and disappeared into Old Alea.

'See?' said Sable. 'Nothing to worry about. I imagine the soldiers up there have been ordered to prevent the local gods and demigods from fleeing. They will have been instructed to allow supplies to enter.' Something caught her eye as she glanced up at the gates. 'Do you see that?'

Millen squinted. 'What am I looking for?'

'There's a body hanging from a beam over the gatehouse. It's Kemal, I think. I recognise his red outfit from yesterday, but without his head, I'm not completely sure.'

Millen gasped. 'Lord Kemal? But... but...'

'Indeed. It seems that someone from Implacatus is giving everyone a little demonstration of their power.'

'They executed the patron of the Bloodflies?' Millen said. 'The Shin-strans are going to go berserk. I hope Lady Felice is alright.'

She frowned at him. 'There are perhaps more important things going on than the fate of a team patron.'

'Not to the inhabitants of this city. The Implacatus gods can't go around killing our patrons like that; and hanging him up for the people to see? Are they trying to provoke the biggest riot in history? Even the Torduans and Fordians will think it's a step too far.'

'Why would supporters of the other two teams be upset? Don't they both hate the Bloodflies?'

'Yes, but the patrons are sacrosanct. The idiots up there have no idea what they've unleashed.'

'Interesting. Either the invaders don't know, or they do, but don't care. I wonder which it is.'

The wagon inched up the slope until it reached a level area in front of the gatehouse. Sable turned, and glanced at the view of Alea Tanton stretching out behind them. It clung to the coast of the ocean, only a few miles wide, but over thirty miles from north to south. The fortress and the merchant's district were easily recognisable, but much of the rest of the city was a chaotic sprawl of slums and shanty dwellings, with a grey haze lying over the rooftops.

Four soldiers approached. Unlike the city militia, they were dressed in identical steel breastplates, and were heavily armed. Professionals, Sable realised at once.

'Good morning,' she said to them.

One stuck his hand out. 'Permit.'

Sable reached into her small bag and withdrew the folded card.

'Here you are, officer,' she said, handing it to him.

He scanned it, then passed it back. He glanced up at Millen, then peered into the rear of the wagon.

'All supplies have been requisitioned for the use of the Banner, ma'am,' he said. 'Please report to the Governor's residence.'

Sable nodded. 'I trust we shall be suitably recompensed?'

'Of course, ma'am. The Banner are not thieves.'

'The Banner?'

'The Banner of the Golden Fist, ma'am.' He gestured for them to proceed, then stood aside.

Millen cracked the whip, and the ponies moved off. They skirted round a large pool of blood directly beneath the body of Kemal hanging above the gates, and passed through the archway. More soldiers were assembled on the other side, preventing any traffic from leaving Old Alea. Several carriages and wagons were parked by the side of the road, their owners protesting to the soldiers blocking their departure.

Millen glanced from them to Sable. 'What's the Banner of the Golden Fist?'

'I don't know.'

'Why not? Didn't you read that soldier's mind?'

'No. Contrary to what you might think, I don't go around reading everybody all the time, and even when I do, it's usually just for specific pieces of information.'

A soldier on the road halted them before they had left the gatehouse compound. He eyed them for a moment, then clambered up to the driver's bench.

'I'm your escort to the Governor's residence,' he said, sitting himself down to Sable's left.

'And why do we need an escort?' she said.

He gave her a wry smile. 'To make sure you don't get lost on the way, miss.'

'How helpful,' she said, as Millen got the wagon underway again. 'Tell me, what is the Banner of the Golden Fist?'

'We're the best mercenary outfit on Implacatus, miss,' he said.

Sable nodded. 'Do you know why Lord Kemal is dead?'

'I heard it was because he disrespected Lord Renko.'

'And he is?'

'Our commander, miss. He's an Ancient, and not someone you want to get on the wrong side of.'

'I see.'

'Take a right here,' the soldier said to Millen.

Sable suppressed a frown. From reading Lord Maisk's mind earlier that morning, she estimated that there were up to a thousand Banner soldiers in Old Alea, a number so high that they would need to requisition dozens of wagons a day to feed them; it made no sense, therefore, that they would be interested in her and Millen's little wagon. So why were they being so careful about making sure she went to the Governor's residence?

She glanced at the soldier to her left and dived into his mind. After a quick rummage through his memories, it became clear that he knew very little about the precise strategy of his commanders. She focussed on the orders that he had been given, and saw that he and the rest of his company had been told to ensure all merchants that entered Old Alea were taken to the Governor's residence, but they hadn't been told why.

Her nerves jangled as she tried to think what it could mean. They weren't interested in the meagre supplies in the back of the wagon – they wanted merchants. Perhaps they wanted to negotiate contracts for supplies? No. They seemed too professional to go about their business in such a haphazard manner. Then it was information they were after, but what information could merchants in Alea Tanton have that the gods of Implacatus could possibly need?

Her stomach tightened as she realised the answer. She glanced around the street. It was quiet, but soldiers were patrolling the route between the gates and the tall towers that marked the location of the Governor's residence. The sun had risen over the height of the high wall surrounding Old Alea, and she squinted in the bright light.

She needed to act. She glanced at Millen, cursing herself for bringing him along. If he ended up captured and questioned, then the soldiers would be looking for her. He didn't know much about her, but he knew she had vision powers, and that alone would be enough to raise the suspicions of the new rulers of the city. If it came to it, she would have to kill him.

Stay silent, she whispered into his mind. *Don't nod, or gesture, and keep your eyes on the road. We're heading into a trap. They're using the residence to interrogate any merchants who arrive, to see what they know about the trade in salve. Get ready to follow me. You are brave, Millen. Trust me, and everything will be fine.*

She withdrew her vision from Millen's mind, and sent it up to the roof of the nearest house. She scanned the route, checking the position of every soldier on sentry duty along the way. There were only a couple of places that were not in the direct sightline of any one of them, and neither were ideal. She pulled her sight back, and thrummed her battle-vision. Whatever happened, she could not risk being taken into the residence and captured. Even with Karalyn's protections shielding her from the powers of the gods, she was still only a mortal, and as she knew, mortals died pretty easily.

Sable readied herself as the wagon approached the first blind spot. It was halfway along a curving street with cottages on either side, and a line of trees ran down the centre. She slipped her hand beneath the folds of her dress, feeling for the hilt of her knife.

She turned to the soldier. 'So, how long have you been in the Banner of the Golden Fist?'

He shrugged. 'It's been four years...'

Her hand lashed out, powered by battle-vision, and the knife blade ripped through the soldier's throat. She grabbed his arm to stop him falling off the wagon, and pushed him into the back.

'Stop the wagon,' she hissed to Millen.

She shoved the soldier's body down among the crates, then picked up a large bag and slung it over her shoulders. Millen had brought the ponies to a halt, and Sable jumped down to the flagstones.

'We've got about two minutes to get out of here,' she said to him. 'Come on.'

She ran in her high-heeled boots, cursing that day's choice of footwear. A few curtains were twitching in the windows of the cottages, but no one was on the street. She ducked down a narrow alleyway that ran between two rows of houses, hearing the steps of Millen behind her. They entered another street and slowed down, passing a few of the lower classes who were standing outside their cottages, chatting in soft voices. Her dress attracted a few questioning looks, while others glanced down the alleyway from where they had emerged.

They crossed the street and took another alley, breaking into a run as soon as they turned a corner. The alley switched left, then right, and they skidded to a halt before a high wall blocking the end. On either side were low out-buildings at the rear of the cottages, and Sable began climbing. She pulled herself up onto the roof of a garden shed, and kept low as she helped Millen up. In the distance echoed a cry, followed by shouts a few moments later.

'Over the wall,' she said, glancing up. 'Can you make it?'

He nodded.

She sprang up, and caught hold of the top of the wall, then swung her legs over. She caught a glimpse of a wide sweeping landscape of gardens, then jumped down into a thicket of dense bushes, her dress ripping on the long thorns.

Millen dropped next to her a moment later, and they struggled through the undergrowth. Ahead of them were stands of trees basking in the sunlight, and a fountain glittered by a pool to their right. In the distance, a large mansion stood – a structure the size of a palace, made up of an eclectic mixture of styles. One section looked like a fortress, with a tower and battlements, while another swept in a gentle arc of colonnades and red tiles like a villa in the Holdings.

Sable and Millen reached a clearer spot, and she pulled the bag from her shoulders. She slipped off the ripped dress and stuffed it into the bag, then took out another set of clothes. She caught Millen's eyes on her as she changed, but she didn't mind; after all, it was nothing he hadn't seen the previous night. When dressed, she unlaced her boots and replaced them with servant's shoes to match the rest of her outfit.

Millen took the bag, and they set off. They crept along the base of the wall for a mile, staying as close to the shadows as they could without getting tangled in the dense undergrowth. Sable halted by a large tree that stood close to the wall, and directed her vision to a high branch. On the other side of the wall was a row of large stone warehouses, and then streets lined with cottages, with the sea wall in the far distance.

She nodded to Millen, then jumped, gripping onto a branch and climbing the tree, her battle-vision guiding her. She leapt the gap to the wall, then lowered herself down into the street, dropping the last five feet.

She dived into the shadows of a warehouse. The lanes running between the buildings were empty and silent, though sounds were coming from the street at the far end. She heard Millen land a yard away, then she sensed him crouch beside her.

'What now?' he said.

'It's time to find somewhere safe to hide for a bit, and regroup.'

An hour later, Sable and Millen were sitting on the sea wall. After walking for three miles through the streets of Old Alea, they had reached a derelict area by the decaying sea walls, and had broken into a half-collapsed turret that over-looked the ocean several hundred feet below. Its lower storey had an intact roof, and Sable had scouted the entire area with her powers. If the Banner of the Golden Fist undertook a serious search of Old Alea, then they would be found, but she guessed that they probably had a day or two before that happened. The surface of the promontory covered over twenty square miles, and there were plenty of places to hide.

There was another reason that she had chosen the sea wall. She glanced at Millen. She should never have brought him; it was unprofessional, and sloppy. He was untrained, a hindrance, and if she didn't have to constantly look out for him, then she would be free to infiltrate one of the mansions that they had seen. There was no way he would be up to the job of going undercover; he was liable to freeze, or do something stupid that would get them both killed.

It was a shame, but he had to go.

She lit a cigarette, and moved a little closer to him. Their legs were dangling over the edge of the wall, and there was nothing below them to break any fall until the ragged rocks at the base of the cliffs, where the ocean's swell crashed in foaming plumes of white.

She moved her left hand to the small of his back.

'I can't wait to see the sunset from here,' he said. 'It'll be beautiful.'

'I'm sorry,' she said.

He glanced at her. 'For what?'

She braced her hand, ready to deliver a sharp shove; all she needed to do was push, and her life would become a lot simpler.

'For dragging you into this,' she said.

He laughed. 'I came here of my own free will, and besides, these have been the best two days of my life. I have never felt more alive.'

Sable cursed her weakness. How could she kill him when he was gazing at her like that? Her life would be simpler, but how would she be able to live with the guilt? She had done many terrible things in her life, but that didn't mean she had to keep on doing them. She was a bad person, she knew it, and deciding not to murder someone who trusted her wouldn't suddenly turn her into a good person, but, well, it was a start.

She removed her left hand from the small of his back and sighed.

Weak, and unprofessional.

CHAPTER 11

A BITTER TASTE

Falls of Iron, Western Khatanax – 2ⁿᵈ Tradinch 5252

The sun was lowering over the vast ocean, and Maddie felt grateful for the drop in temperature. It had been a blisteringly hot day of almost no wind, and the baked ground was too hot for bare feet. Blackrose had told her that Dragon Eyre also enjoyed a warm climate, but at least there was always a sea breeze, as well as a chance of a short, sharp shower of rain. On Khatanax it never seemed to rain, or maybe they had just arrived in a dry season, like summer back in the City.

The dragon had found them a comfortable spot to relax in all day, with a bit of shade from the sun, and a small mountain stream that trickled its way down the high rocky slopes to the ocean. Whenever Blackrose got too hot, she would take off, and surge down to the huge, rolling waves that crashed against the rough shoreline, soaking herself in the cooling spray. And then, when she returned to where Maddie was sitting, her shimmering scales would dry in minutes, leaving patches of salt covering her like a thin film of white crystalline dust.

Blackrose was impatient to be off, they both were, but their promise to Karalyn Holdfast had kept them tied to Lostwell. Maddie hated long goodbyes. Once she had said farewell to someone, that was it; she didn't want to keep bumping into them, it made the whole thing awkward. It didn't matter, she told herself; they would soon be in Dragon Eyre, with all the danger and excitement that entailed.

'Should we head back?' she said to the dragon, who was basking in the sunlight next to her.

'Soon. We are only ten miles from the Falls of Iron, rider; we can be back there in a few minutes.'

'I wonder what Karalyn wants to tell us.'

'To be truthful, I doubt it will be anything of much use. I agreed to her request because I sympathised with her plight, not because I felt her information was required.'

'It was a nice thing to do.'

'It was respectful. Please do not accuse me of being "nice".'

Maddie opened the pack by her side and took out the Quadrant. She held it in her left hand, and ran a finger over some of the etchings.

'Be careful, rider,' the dragon said. 'You do not want to inadvertently trigger the device.'

'I'm just trying to remember your instructions for getting us to Dragon Eyre. It's a bit more complicated than what I had to do to get us here.'

'You'll be fine.'

'What if I make a mistake?'

'You won't.'

'And we'll arrive... where exactly?'

'High up in the sky,' the dragon said. 'I felt that would be the safest course. We should be above the islands close to my old capital, where my palace was situated. It will be cold, but better than risking somewhere too close to the ground.'

'And there's no chance of us losing four years?'

'None.'

'Are you excited?'

The dragon glanced at her. 'Apprehensive. So much will have changed in twenty years. Some of my old friends and kin will be dead, others will be in chains. It will be a time of tears as well as joy. Our first task will to discover the fate of my mother's older brother.'

'What's his name?'

'That is not something I am willing to tell you, rider. If he lives, then he may decide to tell you himself. To the mortals of Dragon Eyre, he was known as Greysteel, just as I was known as Blackrose.'

'Wait, is he the one that named you Nathara? Your old mentor?'

'Indeed. He fled the capital shortly before it was surrounded and captured by the gods. He advised me to leave with him, but I refused. As Queen, I knew my place was to remain by my throne, to the bitter end. Except, it wasn't the end. The noble death that I had expected, perhaps even yearned for, did not occur. The gods knew well that captivity would be more shameful to me than death.'

'Yeah? Well, I have a feeling they're going to regret not executing you. We're going to kick ass in Dragon Eyre, though I...'

'Though you what?'

'Nothing.'

'Come, Maddie, don't be coy.'

'Well, it's just that I think I'm going to miss human company. I had to leave Rosie and Tom behind, and now we're leaving the others as well. It's all very well having a dragon as a friend, but someone nearer my own size would be nice too.'

'It's what happens in life; people move on. I for one wish Buckler were here, even though he frustrated me incessantly while we lived in Arrowhead.'

'Life is stupid. People annoy the crap out of you, and yet you still miss them when they're gone.'

'From that am I to gather that you are going to miss our little party?'

'Yeah. Funny, I'm probably going to miss Aila the most, even though she doesn't like me very much. She's the most normal out of them, despite being a demigod. I hope Corthie realises what he's got with her.'

'The champion needs a cause to fight; I fear he will never be content with a peaceful life. If I could choose to bring one more human with me to Dragon Eyre, it would be him. He would be a mighty lord, a captain of my armies.'

'I wouldn't mention that to Karalyn, not after everything she's gone through to find him.'

Blackrose turned her head to glance at the position of the sun. 'I estimate that sunset is an hour away. Let us go, and make our final farewells.'

Maddie packed the Quadrant back into her bag, then climbed up the straps of the harness. The sky to the west was lit up with vibrant reds and pinks, and it reminded Maddie of home. She buckled the waist strap, and Blackrose took off, ascending into the air. She swooped down to the left, and followed the coastline south for a few miles, until the small harbour town belonging to the Falls of Iron came into sight. Boats were tied up alongside the piers and wharves, and the white-washed buildings were reflecting the warm glow of the setting sun. Blackrose veered to the east, and soared inland along the edge of the cliffs. She disturbed a flock of grey herons, scattering them in all directions, then she ascended above the level of the cliffs, the sun at her back.

The town of the Falls of Iron looked peaceful, its white houses tinged with pink from the light, and its waterfalls glistening. Blackrose circled a few times, and lowered herself down to the castle forecourt, her claws out as she landed onto the smooth flagstones. Blackrose glanced around.

'I would say that we are alone,' she said, 'but with Karalyn's powers, who knows?'

Maddie unbuckled her strap, and clambered down to the ground. She peered into the lengthening shadows.

'Karalyn, are you there?'

'I'm here,' she said, appearing directly in front of them.

Maddie let out a small yelp. 'Please don't do that. It's weird beyond words.'

'Sorry,' said Karalyn. 'I was waiting out here on my own, and I didn't want to attract attention.'

Maddie nodded. 'I'll bet invisibility must have its uses, yeah? Sneaking about, and finding out what people really think of you.'

'I can read their minds for that,' Karalyn said. 'I mostly make myself unseen when I don't want to be bothered by people.' She glanced at Blackrose. 'Thanks for staying. I know how eager you are to leave, and it means a lot to me that you came back this evening.'

'It's perfectly fine,' said the dragon, 'I could see that you were keen to speak to your brother. It is good that you have been reunited with him. He often talked about you, and possessed an unshakable confidence that you would find him.'

She nodded. 'Do you mind if I sit while we talk?'

'Of course not.'

Karalyn walked towards the base of the cliff, where a row of white-painted stone benches were laid out. She sat down on one, and lit a cigarette, while Maddie joined her.

'The sky is beautiful,' said Karalyn, her gaze on the sunset.

'Can I ask you something?' said Maddie.

Karalyn nodded.

'On your world, how much time passed between Corthie being kidnapped, and you starting your search for him?'

'Almost a full year,' she said. 'We had a Quadrant, but didn't know how to use it, and we had to finish the war against Agatha and the other gods. As well as that, I was pregnant for half the time, and had two babies to look after.'

'I wasn't criticising,' said Maddie. 'It's amazing that you managed to get here at all. When you did arrive in Lostwell, why did you send Belinda to the City, rather than go yourself?'

'I wanted to send a fighter, and I trusted Belinda more than Sable. I was aware that your world was infested with greenhides, and I'm useless with a sword. It was also to do with how much power I needed. I had to pull strength from Irno and Vana, and neither are particularly powerful, so in the end, I only had enough to send Belinda.'

'She performed admirably,' said Blackrose. 'She did everything you asked of her, and more.'

'And I have released her from her vows. She is no longer bound to me; she is free.'

Blackrose nodded, though there was a touch of impatience in her dark eyes. Maddie turned back to Karalyn. 'You said you had some useful stuff to tell us?'

The woman smiled. 'I do. This is meant only as advice, so don't take offence, but I think you might be making a mistake returning to Dragon Eyre.'

Blackrose snorted. 'You sound like Naxor. That demigod has never ceased telling me that he thinks I should not go home. I have been away for twenty years, Karalyn. I am going back, and I will allow nothing to stop me.'

'I agree that you should go back; it's the timing that concerns me. I read Gadena's mind thoroughly when I visited his training camp. I was looking for evidence that Corthie had been there for four years, but I also found much about Dragon Eyre in his head. As well as training champions for the world Maddie is from, he has also been busy recruiting mercenaries from Lostwell to fight on Dragon Eyre. There are a lot of landless, poor people in Khatanax, and Gadena has sent thousands of them to fight on the side of the gods, against your people. They have also been using greenhides.'

'None of this surprises me,' said the dragon. 'The gods started using greenhides on my world while I was still there.'

'Aye, but did you know that almost half of the entire landmass of Dragon Eyre is now infested with the creatures? And the other half is packed with soldiers. Naxor might have a point – perhaps you need an army.'

Blackrose said nothing for a long moment, then she lowered her head. 'Half?'

Karalyn nodded. 'Sorry to be the one to have to tell you. Believe me, I wish you every success against the gods, but I wouldn't want you throwing your life away.'

'And what would you suggest?'

'There are colonies of wild dragons living far to the north-east of here, close to the borders of Kinell. Some of them have escaped from captivity, and they have bred over several generations. From what I understand, they hate the gods as much as we do. Perhaps they would be willing to help reclaim your world?'

'Wild dragons?' said Blackrose, anger colouring her voice. 'I think not. They would be ungovernable, chaotic, and none of them would understand the customs and traditions of Dragon Eyre. I thank you for your advice, Karalyn Holdfast, but escaped dragons from the pits of Alea Tanton would be of no use to me.'

Maddie frowned. 'But you told me that you wished Buckler was with us. Wasn't he from the pits?'

'Yes, rider, but that was one, young dragon, whom I had known for a decade. A colony of wild dragons would not listen to me, not unless I fought each one of them first, and came out victorious. It would take years to civilise them and bring them under my authority, and we don't have years.' She glanced at Karalyn. 'Was that everything you wished to tell me?'

'Almost. There is one more thing.'

'Yes?'

Karalyn stubbed out her cigarette and lit another. Maddie could see the strain in her eyes, and wondered when she had last slept a peaceful night.

'As you know,' Karalyn said, 'I made a mistake when I came here. On my world, I had just mastered the ability to move around without a Quadrant, and I stupidly thought that meant I also knew how to travel between worlds. I got the location right, but it wasn't as simple as that. I think each world exists within its own time, and any leap between them risks something going wrong with that aspect. Although it seemed to pass in an instant, we were trapped... somewhere, for four years. Maybe it was nowhere; I still don't really understand it.'

'But you must have fixed the problem,' said Blackrose.

Karalyn raised an eyebrow.

'After all,' the dragon went on, 'you sent Belinda to Maddie's world without any such difficulties.'

'I did,' Karalyn said, nodding, 'but that was before I'd realised that we'd lost four years getting here. If I had known, then I wouldn't have risked sending her. The problem is, I don't know what I did differently that time. Was it something to do with it being only one person travelling? Or maybe, it was because I wasn't going myself? Apart from my twins, I'm the only person alive that possesses dream powers. Corthie, Sable, and others in my family have traces of it, but only I am a full dream mage. That means there's no one I can talk to about what I did wrong.' She glanced up into the dragon's eyes. 'I need to ask another favour of you.'

Blackrose remained very still, saying nothing.

'What favour?' said Maddie.

'I'm sorry, Karalyn,' said the dragon, 'but my answer is no.'

Maddie frowned. 'But she hasn't even told us what she wants.'

'She doesn't need to. She wants the Quadrant.'

'I cannot risk travelling home without one,' said Karalyn. 'What if I make the same mistake? My twins would have aged another four years. What if I make a greater mistake, and I am held within nothingness for forty years, or four hundred?'

'I understand your need,' said Blackrose, 'but my answer remains no. I sympathise, believe me; you have suffered, and you are in pain, but I too need to return home.'

'But you don't need to return now,' said Karalyn; 'in fact it would be foolish to do so. Lend me your Quadrant, and take your time preparing for your return. My aunt, Sable, is currently in Alea Tanton, searching for a Quadrant. If she finds one, then you can take it.'

'And what about Sable?' said Maddie. 'How would she get home?'

'I don't think Sable wants to go home. I chose her to come along because she was under a sentence of death. She fought for Agatha and the other invading gods, and did things that were unforgivable. There are some in my family that can take life without remorse or a second thought, and Sable is one of them. If you give me the Quadrant, then I will be taking Corthie, and no one else.'

'Eh, what?' said Maddie. 'You'd abandon Aila and leave her here?'

'Her brother and sister live in the Falls of Iron, as well as her cousin Naxor. And Belinda too, if she chooses to stay here. Corthie will be upset, I realise that. He will probably hate me for it, but it's for the best. Mortals and demigods don't belong together. If you look into your heart, you'll see that I'm right.'

'None of this is of any consequence,' said Blackrose, 'for my answer remains the same. I will not be handing over the Quadrant, and I make no apologies for that. It was given to me by the rulers of Maddie's world as a just reward for saving their City. It was promised to me, by Corthie, by Aila, and by others. It is mine, Karalyn.'

The Holdfast woman nodded. 'I feared you would say that.'

'I would still like us to part on amicable terms, Karalyn. I understand why you had to ask, but I cannot acquiesce. Perhaps you should take your own advice – wait for this Sable to find you a Quadrant, and then you can return to your children.'

Karalyn shook her head. 'No.'

'No? What other choice do you have?'

'The only one there is – I take the Quadrant from you.'

The dragon laughed, a harsh sound that echoed off the cliffside in the dwindling light. 'And how would you do that? You are weak, mortal, you cannot physically overcome me; and your powers might be strong, but they are no match for me.'

Karalyn stood. 'I am weak? Try to kill me.'

'Don't be foolish. You are letting your grief override your sense. If I wished to kill you, you would be dead in a second.'

'Then try it. *Now.*'

Blackrose glared at Karalyn, and raised a forelimb, the claws extended. Maddie took a step back, her eyes wide as she stared at the woman standing in front of Blackrose.

'Go on,' said Karalyn. 'I command you, lizard, try to kill me.'

Blackrose froze, her dark eyes blinking. 'I... I cannot.'

'Of course you can't,' said Karalyn. 'I burned it into your brain the moment you landed. You cannot hurt me; you will never be able to hurt me.'

'How is this possible?' roared the dragon. 'What have you done to me?'

'Now,' said Karalyn, 'order your rider to hand the Quadrant over to me.'

'Forget it!' cried Maddie. 'You can't...' Her words dried up as she felt a presence in her mind, something that seemed to choke off all of her thoughts. She fell to her knees, cracking them against the flagstones.

Blackrose's mouth opened as if against her will, her eyes anguished. 'Give her the Quadrant, Maddie.'

Maddie tried to object, but she was no longer in control of her body. Her hand went to her shoulder bag, and she took out the copper-coloured device. Her fingers shook as she held it; a small part of her mind protesting vehemently, but she was powerless to stop herself stretching her hand out towards Karalyn.

'Thank you,' said the Holdfast woman, plucking it from Maddie's hands.

The presence left Maddie's mind, and she collapsed to the flagstones panting. Next to her, Blackrose's body seemed to loosen, and she lowered her head, her eyes closing.

'I didn't want to have to do that,' said Karalyn, 'but you gave me no choice. I tried to persuade you; you should have listened.'

Maddie felt tears flood her eyes as she struggled to her knees. 'I hate you.'

'I don't blame you.'

'I would tear you into a thousand pieces if I could,' said Blackrose, her voice strained and full of hurt and rage.

'I know you would. What's done is done, and the Quadrant is mine.'

Maddie grabbed Blackrose's limb and pulled herself to her feet as tears spilled down her face. The dragon turned to her, and the look she gave her reminded Maddie of the worst days of her imprisonment under Arrowhead – the helplessness, the frustration, the pain.

'I'm sorry,' Maddie wept. 'I had to give it to her; I couldn't help it.'

'It's not your fault, my rider, I know you. It was that Holdfast witch; she has destroyed us.'

'Don't exaggerate,' said Karalyn. 'There are other Quadrants on this world, and your haste is nothing compared to mine.'

Footsteps rang out from the entrance to the castle's gatehouse.

'What's happening?' said Belinda. 'I heard Blackrose cry out.'

'Karalyn betrayed us,' cried Maddie, pointing to the Quadrant held by the Holdfast woman. 'She made me give it to her.'

Belinda nodded. 'She compelled you.'

'You knew she could do this?' thundered Blackrose. 'Why didn't you tell us?'

'Because I never thought she would do it to any of us.' She shook her head at Karalyn. 'How could you?'

'You know the answer to that, Belinda. I must return home.'

Blackrose growled. 'Kill her, Belinda. I would, but she has bound me with her powers and I cannot harm her.'

Belinda's face fell. 'No, Blackrose.'

'Does she have you in her grip also?'

'No, she doesn't. I'm sorry, but I still love Karalyn, despite what she has done to you. She saved my life, twice over, and I would never hurt her, even when I think she's wrong.'

The dragon raised her head and roared, shaking loose rocks from the cliffside, and sending them hurtling down the slope. Maddie lifted her hands to her ears, and for a moment all she knew was the hurt of betrayal in her heart and the deafening roar of pain from Blackrose.

The dragon lowered her head again, and stared at Karalyn. 'I curse you, and all of the Holdfasts. May you never find happiness; may your children reject you and hate you as I do; may your life, and the lives of all your kin be filled with pain and fear; may those you love die in agony, alone and broken, and when your end comes, may it be filled with a despair that eats you from within.'

Karalyn's gaze remained steady. 'Begone, lizard.'

'Maddie,' cried Blackrose, 'climb onto my back. I cannot bear another second of being in this vile witch's company.'

Maddie glanced at Belinda.

'What about Aila, Corthie and Naxor?' said the god. 'They wanted to say goodbye.'

'Then they should have been here, Belinda,' said Blackrose. 'Maddie, now.'

Maddie ran to the dragon's flank, and started to climb. She felt sick, and heartbroken, and she could feel the dragon's rage rise like a wave about to crash against the rocks. Behind them, the sun had set, and the oil lamps in the town below were starting to be lit. Maddie strapped herself into the saddle, and the dragon beat her wings and rose into the dark sky. Beneath them, Karalyn was already walking back towards the castle, while Belinda stood alone, her face gazing upwards.

'I should burn this place,' said the dragon; 'this nest of traitors and friends who are not friends.'

'No, Blackrose,' said Maddie, 'please; let's just get out of here.'

The dragon turned to the north, swept out her wings, and they soared away through the night sky, the stars above them glittering down in their multitudes.

CHAPTER 12

MISDIRECTION

Alea Tanton, Tordue, Western Khatanax – 3rd Tradinch 5252

The soldiers cleared a path for Van to walk to the abandoned wagon. The body of the soldier had been removed, and transported to the Governor's residence, but the bloodstains remained, spattered over the driver's bench, and lying thick in the rear next to the crates and sacks.

'Has the back of the wagon been thoroughly searched?' he said.

'Yes, sir,' said a lieutenant. 'Wine, cured meat, two boxes of fruit, and a crate of cheese.'

Van nodded. At least he had discovered the source of the smell. 'No gold or weapons?'

'None, sir, and no sign of any contraband.'

'And the witnesses are sure the two fugitives weren't armed?'

'The woman had a bag over her shoulder, sir, but they didn't appear to have any weapons on them when they fled.'

'Alright,' he said; 'get the wagon moved to the Governor's residence, and make sure there are no more blind spots on the route from the gatehouse. This must not happen again, understood? Lord Renko is already chewing my balls over this.'

'Yes, sir.'

Van frowned at the scene, then strode away, a cluster of sergeants and soldiers following him. They came to the end of the curving avenue, and Van turned round, standing where the closest sentry to the murder had been. Just as he had reported, the middle of the road was shielded by the line of trees, and the wagon was invisible.

'Damn it,' he muttered. 'Get me a carriage.'

Back at the Governor's residence, Van went to a small chamber on the ground floor that had been turned into his office, and the command room of Eagle Company. Sohul was there, waiting for him.

'Good morning, Lieutenant.'

'Good morning, sir. Lord Renko has requested an update on your investigation into the killing of the soldier.'

'Thank you, Lieutenant. Unfortunately, I don't have much to tell him. One of our men was killed in broad daylight, and despite the two fugitives being seen by a dozen local witnesses, there's been no sign of them, beyond a scrap of black cloth in a thorn bush.'

'Do you suspect collusion, sir?'

'It's possible. They might have friends somewhere in Old Alea.' He sat at a table, which was covered in maps and documents, then looked up as the door opened. A servant walked in, carrying a tray with small cups and a ceramic coffee pot. 'We're going to have to order a full scale search of the town,' he said to Sohul as the servant poured his coffee.

'Sugar, sir?' the servant asked, a smile on her lips.

She had a nice smile; beautiful, in fact.

He nodded. 'Two.'

'Lord Renko might have some objections, sir,' said Sohul. 'A full search of Old Alea would take too many soldiers, and he said we'll need them to start transferring the population of the merchant's district up to the Governor's residence for questioning.'

Van bit his tongue. He needed to be careful around unknown servants, even if they did have beautiful smiles. Any one of them could be spying for Lord Renko, reporting his words to him. Van wasn't paranoid by nature, but he had experienced the paranoia of some of the gods, and it was always safer to assume that a spy could be listening. He frowned. The servant seemed harmless enough, and he began to feel sure that she wasn't a spy. He was a good judge of character.

'It might help, sir,' said Sohul, 'if I knew why the merchants are being questioned. It might be connected to the murder.'

'Alright. This is not to go to the lower ranks, as Lord Renko feels that it could impede his mission here. The fewer who know, the better – if word gets out, the merchants of Alea Tanton might panic and flee.'

'Understood, sir.'

'Lord Renko has reason to believe that some of the merchants living in the city have contacts with whoever is bringing the salve to Lostwell. My assumption is that the murder has nothing to do with our mission here, because there's no way the two merchants who killed the soldier and fled could have possibly known why they were being taken to the Governor's residence. More likely, they're guilty of something else, and thought they had been caught.'

He noticed the servant was still in the room, tidying away old coffee cups and placing them onto the tray, but he didn't need to worry.

The door opened again, and a sergeant walked in.

'Sir?'

'Yes, Sergeant?'

'You might, eh, want to take a look out of the window, sir.'

Van stood and walked to the tall window set into the northern side of the residence. Several plumes of smoke were rising over the city.

'The word from the gatehouse, sir,' said the sergeant, 'is that the entire city is rioting.'

'Is there a game happening in one of the arenas today?'

'No, sir. I believe the last game was a few days ago.'

'Games?' said Sohul.

'Blood sports,' said Van. 'The locals can get quite passionate about them.'

'Might the inhabitants be rioting because of our presence here, sir?'

'I doubt it, Lieutenant. The population couldn't give a rat's ass about the gods of Alea Tanton, except for... Oh.'

'Yes, sir?'

Van strode from the room without responding, and walked along the marble-panelled hallway to a set of dimly-lit stairs. He descended, Sohul and the sergeant following, and they came to the basement, and a row of dank holding cells. A soldier on guard duty jumped to his feet and saluted.

'At ease, soldier,' Van said. 'How many merchants do we have now?'

'Twenty-six, sir.'

Van nodded, and gazed through the bars at the well-dressed citizens within the first cell. A few of them got to their feet when they saw the two officers.

'I have a sports-related question,' Van said to them. 'Tell me, who are the current patrons of the three teams of Alea Tanton?'

'When are we getting released?' cried a man. 'We've done nothing wrong.'

'I asked a question,' Van said to him; 'are you refusing to cooperate?'

The merchant glared at him. 'Lord Baldwin is the patron of the Deadskins; Lady Felice the Blue Thumbs, and Lord Kemal the Bloodflies.'

Van groaned. He turned to Sohul. 'There's your answer. Come on; we'd better let Lord Renko know.'

'Are you telling me, Captain,' said Lord Renko, 'that the city of Alea Tanton is aflame because of these games?'

'They're protesting the execution of Lord Kemal, my lord. He was a patron of one of the teams, and the citizens look up to their patrons as, well, gods.'

Lord Renko stared out of the wide window of the tower. His view over the city was far better than that from Van's office, and the extent of the rioting was clear. There were at least a dozen large fires, and many smaller ones, and the grey smoke was billowing up over the slums.

'The entire city militia is out dealing with this,' Lord Renko said, 'when I need them to be sealing off the merchant's district.' He turned to

Van. 'Well, Captain? You've brought me the problem; I hope you've brought a solution too.'

'Appoint a new patron immediately, my lord, and have them use a Quadrant to travel to the three arenas, along with the patrons of the other two teams. Announce that Lord Kemal was found guilty of embezzling gold from the Bloodflies' veterans fund, and that you won't tolerate any corruption that hurts the ordinary people of the city. I'd also recommend announcing a generous upgrade of the arena facilities, and perhaps a doubling of tomorrow's food dole; conditional on the riots ceasing at once.'

Renko frowned at him. 'I don't like you, Captain.'

Van said nothing, keeping his face impassive.

'Lord Maisk has told me much about you,' Renko went on, 'and you have succeeded in distracting Lady Joaz from her duties. I find you to be one of those mortals who have an ingrained dislike of your betters; you hold the gods in contempt. There's no need to deny it; I can read it from your mind.'

'I wasn't going to deny it, my lord.'

Renko smiled. 'You think you're clever, mortal, but I have seen countless soldiers like you over my long life, and I'll see countless more long after you have died and faded into oblivion. Now, I hope you have some good news for me regarding the murder investigation.'

'I'm afraid not, my lord. We know that there were two of them, a man and a woman, both dressed as merchants. They weren't trying to smuggle anything into Old Alea, but for some reason they didn't want to be taken to the Governor's residence.'

'The route was guarded by soldiers, was it not? How did they get away?'

'There was a blind spot on the route, my lord, a place where a line of trees cut off the sight of the nearest sentry, for a distance of about five yards. From there, they ran through a few streets of peasant cottages, and then climbed over the wall into Lady Felice's estate. We have no knowledge of their movements after that.'

'A blind spot? And who was responsible for guarding the route?'

Van frowned. He had given the job to Sohul, who was standing two yards to his left, his eyes lowered.

'It was my responsibility, my lord.'

'That's right, Captain Logos,' said Renko, 'it was your responsibility. Your negligence allowed one of our soldiers to be murdered, and his killers to get away.'

'Yes, my lord. Should I order a full-scale search of Old Alea?'

Renko turned back to the window, his hands clasped behind his back. 'No. You have until this evening to apprehend the murderers. If you fail, then I will consider the case closed, as we do not have the resources to sweep the entire promontory. However, I will also hold you responsible for that failure, and there will be consequences. Dismissed.'

Van and Sohul bowed, then left the chamber. They descended the long spiral staircase through the tower until they reached the main wing of the residence.

'Consequences?' whispered Sohul as they made their way to Van's office. 'What consequences?'

'I'm not sure. If you're clever, you'll start to distance yourself from me. If Renko makes my head explode, you'll want to be far enough away so none of the blood spatters over you.'

Sohul's face paled.

'Don't worry,' said Van; 'I was being metaphorical. I hope.'

Sohul eyed him. 'Thank you for the advice, sir, but Lord Renko and Major Ahito already know that I was your top pick for the task force; I'm already too close to you. If you fall, then I do also. And thank you for taking responsibility for the mess-up over the sentry positions. I should have checked the route myself. Sorry, sir. It won't happen again.'

'It was an easy mistake to make; you trusted the sergeants to get it right; not that I'm blaming them either. How could the fugitives have possibly known where to strike? How did they know that there was a blind spot? Something doesn't add up, and we've got until tonight to figure it out.'

They reached the office and Van sat by the table. His eyes scanned the large map of Old Alea that was spread out upon its surface. The known route of the fugitives was marked out in red; a line that snaked along alleyways, then came to a halt within the gardens of Lady Felice's mansion. A piece of torn black fabric was lying by the edge of the map, the solitary piece of evidence they had collected.

Logos? echoed a voice in his mind.

Yes, Lady Joaz? he replied.

Come to my rooms.

Sorry, ma'am, but I have an urgent task to fulfil for Lord Renko.

There was a silent pause.

I thought you said you were at my service?

I am, my lady, but...

Joaz disappeared from his thoughts, leaving a vague feeling of trepidation in Van's mind. He ordered coffee, and ten minutes later the same servant from before entered the office, bearing a tray. She set the cups down onto the table and poured from the ceramic pot.

His staff sergeant knocked and entered. 'Sir?'

'Yes, Sergeant?'

'A crime report arrived for you while you were with Lord Renko.'

Van frowned. 'I'm already dealing with a crime; I'm not a damn police officer.'

'It came from the lower city, sir, not from Old Alea, and it was marked solely for your information. The militia down there thought it might be of interest to your investigation.'

Van raised an eyebrow. 'The militia go to the trouble of taking down crime reports in the lower city? I find that hard to believe.'

'They do when the crime takes place in the merchant's district, sir.'

The sergeant extended his hand and Van took the document. He scanned it quickly. A family had returned to their home that morning, and had found their two servants beaten up and tied to chairs in a storeroom. The servants claimed that a man and a woman had broken into the house while the family were away. The man, they said, had spoken like a Torduan, but the woman's accent had been harder to place. The owners of the house had reported that a wagon and four ponies had been stolen, and the report included an inventory. Van's eyes caught on the crate of extra mature cheese. The family had also reported the theft of some clothes and their permit to enter Old Alea, but apart from that, their home had been left intact.

Van laughed, then handed Sohul the report.

The lieutenant frowned. 'So, we're dealing with a local Torduan, and possibly a foreign woman? The description of the man says that his build was slight; he hardly seems like the man who cut the soldier's throat. The medics said that the blow had taken great strength.'

'But it ties in with what the soldiers at the gatehouse remember. They also said that the woman had a well-educated but strange accent. And the witnesses by the peasant cottages confirmed that the man didn't look well-built. Could we be dealing with a god?'

Sohul narrowed his eyes. 'I don't follow, Captain.'

'Forget the Torduan for a moment. So far, we've been assuming that it was the man who struck the blow. But what about the woman? She doesn't sound local, so she must have travelled here from elsewhere, possibly so she could break into Old Alea. Humour me for a moment. For the sake of argument, let's imagine that we have a rebel god on the loose in Lostwell; it was a haven for rebels for hundreds of years, remember? And this god wants to break into Old Alea. She steals a permit and a wagon, then up she goes. She used vision powers to see the blind spot, and she would have been strong enough to deliver the killing blow.' He paused as the servant placed his coffee before him. 'It can't be a coincidence that she went to Lady Felice's estate; perhaps she has something to do with it.'

'Sounds a little far-fetched, sir,' said Sohul.

Van raised an eyebrow. Sohul was right; it did sound a little far-fetched, especially the part about Lady Felice. He wasn't sure how that thought had entered his mind, but the more he considered it, the more it seemed as if it must be true. Lady Felice was involved somehow; she had to be.

A tinkling of cups distracted him, and he watched as the servant left the room.

Van sipped the coffee. It was excellent. He glanced at Sohul. 'I think we should pay Lady Felice a visit.'

Four hours later, Van and Sohul returned from Lady Felice's mansion. It had not gone well. The god had made them wait and then when she had finally agreed to speak to them, she had made her annoyance known. Halfway through the interview, it began to dawn on Van that he had made a mistake; Lady Felice had clearly nothing to do with the murder of the soldier, but it was too late, and the damage was done.

He dismissed Sohul for the rest of the evening and returned to his office alone, a sense of foreboding creeping up on him. He took a cigarette from his silver case, lit it, and gazed out of the window, and when the knock came at his door, he wasn't surprised.

'Captain?' said the sergeant. 'Major Ahito would like a word.'

Van nodded. He stubbed the cigarette out, and got to his feet. He followed the sergeant up a flight of stairs to the major's plush quarters and went in. The major was standing with a couple of his aides by a large, ornately-carved fireplace that looked like it hadn't been used in many years. He glanced in Van's direction, and dismissed the aides, who left the room without meeting the captain's eyes.

'You wanted to see me, sir?' Van said.

The major walked to a table and poured himself a glass of clear spirits. 'Do you have any idea what I've just been doing, Captain?'

'No, sir.'

The major sipped from the glass. 'Take a guess.'

Van frowned, but said nothing.

The major slammed the glass down onto the table. 'I've been clearing up your mess, you fool,' he cried. 'Lady Felice is in Lord Renko's rooms, in tears, and I had to spend twenty minutes being berated for your incompetence and impertinence. Lord Renko wishes to know why you were spending time harassing Lady Felice instead of catching those who had trespassed upon her property. In the name of all that is holy, what made you think that interrogating a god would be a good idea? You practically accused her of being responsible for the murder of our soldier.'

'Sorry, sir.'

'I'm afraid that "sorry" isn't good enough, not this time. Lord Renko is demanding action. He said there must be consequences for your idiocy. It took all the influence I possess to keep him from ordering your immediate dismissal from the Banner.' He shook his head. 'I've managed to save your rank as captain for now, but I'm removing you from your duties here in Old Alea; you're being re-assigned to work with the local militia down in the lower city.'

'Sir?'

'Don't give me that look, Logos; I'm trying to save your life as well as your career. You've managed to piss off Lord Renko, and most of the other gods up here; it's best if you keep a low profile from now on.'

Van gazed at the carpet. 'Yes, sir.'

'Collect your belongings and move down to the militia fortress tonight; and take Lieutenant Sohul with you; your actions have put him in danger too.'

'Yes, sir.'

'And,' the major said, his glance directed out of the window, 'you are to visit Lady Felice before you leave the residence, so that you can give her an unreserved apology.'

'Is she in Lord Renko's offices, sir?'

'No; Lord Maisk's.'

Van nodded, and he felt the knot in his guts tighten. He saluted and left the major's rooms, then walked to the tower by the western wing of the residence. He hadn't been inside Lord Maisk's quarters since the Banner of the Golden Fist had taken over the building, but knew where they were situated. He went over the day's events as he walked, trying to figure out what had possessed him to suspect Lady Felice. He had been so certain that she was involved; it had seemed obvious.

He knocked on a door, and one of Lord Maisk's aides opened it and showed him in. He was escorted to a large chamber, where Lord Maisk was reclining on a long, low couch, a glass of wine in his hand as he watched two young women dancing in front of him. Three other gods were present, lying on other couches, which together formed a square. Van suppressed a groan as he saw who they were. On Maisk's left was Lady Felice, and along from her were Lord Baldwin and, lastly, Lady Joaz.

Maisk gestured to the dancing girls, and they hurried from the centre of the square, picking up the clothes that they had been shedding for the pleasure of the gods.

'Lady Felice,' Van said, 'may I humbly offer you...'

'Silence,' cried Maisk. 'You will speak when I permit it, Logos.' He pointed to the clear area in the middle of the square of couches. 'Get on your knees.'

Van walked forwards, edging between Baldwin and Joaz. He reached the middle of the room and dropped to his knees, facing Lady Felice, who was gazing at him with a gleam of pure hatred in her eyes.

'Now, Logos,' spat Maisk, 'say what you have come to say.'

Van bowed his head. 'I apologise, Lady Felice. I made an error of judgement, and should never have accused you of wrong-doing.'

The room descended into silence for a moment.

'Is that it?' said Lady Felice. 'You humiliate me, and try to have me arrested for the murder of a mortal, and that's all I get?'

'Perhaps,' said Baldwin, 'we should flay the skin from his back?'

'I would enjoy watching that,' said Maisk, 'but I had to promise Lord Renko that I'd let him leave this room alive.'

'We can still hurt him, then,' said Felice.

'Mortal,' Baldwin barked at Van; 'it's my turn for an apology. Do you think I've forgotten the way you spoke to me when the Banner arrived through the portal into my gardens?' He raised a hand as Van slowly turned to face him. 'And remember, I can squeeze the life from you; make you experience pain on a level you would not believe possible.'

Van bowed his head again. 'And to you, Lord Baldwin, I also apologise. I should have treated you with the respect you deserve.'

Baldwin smiled, and clicked his fingers. Pain exploded across Van's body and he collapsed to the floor, writhing in agony. It felt as though his insides were burning, or as if he had drunk acid. He convulsed on the floor, the sound of the gods' laughter ringing in his ears. His eyesight went blurry, but he caught a glimpse of Lady Joaz. She wasn't laughing, but she had a smile on her lips.

You should have come to my rooms when I asked, she said in his mind.

He felt fingers grab hold of his hair, and his head was lifted from the carpet. Lord Baldwin smirked at him, then drove his fist into Van's face, breaking his nose. Lord Maisk pushed Baldwin to the side, then brought down his boot, stamping on Van's head and driving it back down to the floor. He stood for a moment, resting his boot on Van's face.

'One more blow like that and you'll kill him,' said Baldwin. 'The mortal's heart is weak from years of over-indulging in salve.'

'But you can bring him back, yes?'

'I can, but I hate wasting my powers on undeserving mortals.'

'You don't have to fully heal him,' said Felice. 'So long as he can crawl out of here.'

Van's body began to shut down, and his mind retreated from the crescendo of pain. At that moment he longed for death to end the agony.

'I want to take his life,' said Felice. 'Open his eyes so he can see me.'

Maisk took the boot from Van's face and crouched down, grabbing hold of his hair. He lifted Van's head up, then pinched open one of his eyes. Van could barely see anything; his eyes were streaming, and blood was trickling down his forehead. In front of him, Lady Felice was holding a knife in her hands, the blade glinting in the light of the lamps.

'Look at me,' she said. 'That's right. This is what you get when you think you're better than the gods. You are nothing, mortal; a slave, a worthless slave.' She brought the knife closer to his chest, then pushed it in, slowly, twisting the blade as she did so, her eyes burning with dark desire.

Van felt the knife, then his eyes closed and he felt nothing more.

Maybe a second passed, maybe minutes, Van had no way of knowing. He cried out, his mouth full of blood, then he vomited as pain reached every part of his body.

'You disgusting pig,' said Lady Felice.

'Maybe we should have moved him before I revived him,' said Baldwin.

'You didn't heal him completely, I hope?' said Maisk.

Baldwin laughed. 'No. He'll live, but he'll feel like death for days.'

Van felt a slap across his face and he opened his eyes. Baldwin, Felice and Maisk were all staring down at him as he lay on the floor in a pool of blood and vomit.

'Go on,' said Maisk, 'get out of my rooms. If you cross any of us again, then I doubt Lord Renko will allow you to live a second time.'

Van struggled to his knees, a hand on the edge of a couch, then he pulled himself up, swaying and gripping his aching chest. Ahead of him, Joaz was watching from her couch.

Leave, she said in his head; *quickly, before they change their minds about letting you live.*

Without a word, Van turned for the doors, and staggered over, ignoring the laughter from the couches. He passed a group of servants entering with mops and buckets of water, and made his way to the door, a fierce pain pounding behind his temples. Every step was agony, and he fell to the ground as soon as he had left Maisk's quarters. He felt arms lift him, and saw the sergeant who had escorted him to the tower, along with a couple of other soldiers from Eagle Company.

'Lean on me, sir,' he said. 'We'll get you to your room.'

The next twenty minutes were a blur of pain and exhaustion as the three soldiers helped Van down the stairs and into the bed chamber that lay next to his office. They laid him on the bed, and he had a coughing fit, bringing up more blood.

The sergeant thrust a mug of raki into his hands, and placed a lit stick of dullweed between his lips. Van opened his eyes. As well as the three soldiers who had helped him, another two sergeants were in the room, along with Lieutenant Sohul.

Van drew on the dullweed and took a swig of raki.

Sohul crouched by the bed. 'What did they do to you, sir?'

Van stared at him, unable to speak.

'They tortured him to death,' said the sergeant. 'I couldn't see it, but I heard it all.'

'Assholes,' muttered another sergeant.

'Get a wagon ready,' said Sohul. 'We'll transport the captain down to the lower city before they have a chance to change their minds and decide to kill him. Organise a squad to accompany us, along with two sergeants.' The lieutenant glanced around the room. 'Come on, move.'

The soldiers cleared the room, leaving Sohul alone with Van.

The lieutenant shook his head. 'The sergeant's right; they are assholes, sir.'

'No, Sohul,' Van said, his voice a gargled whisper; 'they're gods, and that's what gods do.'

CHAPTER 13

SOBERING UP

Falls of Iron, Western Khatanax – 3rd Tradinch 5252

'Wake up, Corthie,' said Aila.

No response, just the gentle rising and falling of his chest, and a sound of soft snoring.

She shoved him. 'Wake up. We need to talk.'

He groaned, and rolled over to face the window. Aila got up and opened the shutters wide, letting the harsh sunlight fall over Corthie's eyes.

He groaned again. 'What do you want? I'm trying to sleep.'

'We need to talk about what to do,' she said.

He turned onto his back and scratched his head. 'About what?'

She frowned. 'Do you not even remember? Were you that drunk?'

He glanced over at her as she sat down on the bed beside him. 'I was pretty drunk. We shouldn't have started so early. I can't even remember saying goodbye to Blackrose and Maddie.'

'That's because you didn't; they flew off in disgust after your sister stole their Quadrant.'

Corthie narrowed his eyes, then closed them. 'Bollocks; I remember now.'

'Karalyn forced a dragon to hand over the Quadrant; a dragon.'

'She's a dream mage,' he said; 'she can make anyone do whatever she likes. Still, I can't believe she would use her powers to do that. She must have also forbidden Blackrose from hurting her, otherwise she'd be a smoking pile of ashes by now.' He scratched his head again. 'I have a blinding hangover; that raki's lethal. I guessed we talked about all of this last night?'

'We did, but you're making a lot more sense this morning. Last night you were just ranting and raving, at least until you fell over.'

'Was Karalyn there?'

'No, there's been no sign of your sister since she took the Quadrant.'

'Then who was I ranting at?'

'Me, Naxor and Belinda. It was Belinda who told us what had happened – she saw it.'

Corthie leaned up on his elbow. 'Do I need to apologise to anyone?'

She shrugged. 'Are you going to get drunk tonight?'

'And if the answer to that is yes?'

'Then there's very little point in apologising. If you're really sorry then prove it by staying sober for a few days, or at least until we sort this mess out.'

He said nothing.

'I'm meeting Vana for breakfast now,' she said, 'so I'll leave you to get washed and dressed.' She leaned over and kissed him. 'See you later.'

'Aye, see you soon.'

Aila got up and strode from their chamber, entering a cool, stone passageway. The early morning was the best part of the day in Aila's opinion, before the sun heated everything up. Evenings were also a relief, but the muggy warmth often lingered on into the night. She strolled outside, and joined her sister at a little table over-looking one of the waterfalls.

'Good morning, Aila,' said Vana.

'Morning,' said Aila as she sat. 'Have you seen Karalyn Holdfast today yet?'

'Thankfully not,' Vana said. 'I try to avoid her if at all possible; she comes and goes as she pleases, and Irno and I are powerless to stop her.

However, I have found that if you stay out of her way, then she tends to leave you alone.'

'How bad was it,' Aila said, 'when she, you know, drained you?'

Vana put down her cup. 'It was awful; I could feel my life being pulled from me, and my self-healing could do nothing to prevent it. I honestly thought I was dying, and was a little surprised when I woke up in a dark room a few hours later.'

'She must have stopped it just in time.'

Vana pursed her lips. 'Lucky me. Coffee?'

'Yuck; no thanks,' said Aila. 'I confess I'm not overly fond of the food and drink here, especially the drink.' She pulled a face. 'Coffee and raki? And the wine's rancid. Malik's ass, I wish I had some Taran brandy.'

Vana lit a cigarette.

'And this?' Aila said, pointing at her. 'Are you trying to set yourself on fire?'

'Life here grows on you,' her sister said.

'You don't miss the City?'

'I miss some of the people, but not the place. I was terrified when Naxor first brought me here; Lostwell seems so huge compared to the City, but even then I was relieved to no longer be under the control of Prince Marcus. He was so obsessed with finding you, I had to hunt for you every day.'

'I know,' said Aila; 'I was very nearly caught every day.'

Vana smiled. 'Sorry.'

'It's fine; what else were you supposed to do? Listen, I'm a little worried about our City. After what Sable told me...'

Vana snorted. 'I wouldn't trust a word she says. She's the most manipulative person I've ever met; she would have told you that only if she thought she'd get something out of it for herself. The Holdfasts are a plague. I mean, apart from Corthie, obviously.'

Aila sipped from her glass of water, her gaze on the countryside below the cliffs. 'People keep saying things like that to me about Sable, but it's not the impression I got when I spoke to her.'

'Then you're another of her gullible victims,' Vana laughed. She nodded to the table, where bowls of food sat. 'Eat your breakfast, before it gets warm.'

Aila placed some meat and cheese onto her plate, and picked at them. She felt ashamed to admit it, but part of her wished that Naxor had abducted a different member of her family – Mona perhaps, or even Lydia. She hadn't got on well with Vana for hundreds of years, and their old quarrels, though never spoken about, seemed an insurmountable obstacle to the siblings ever becoming close.

'It feels good,' said Vana, 'just knowing that our resident flying lizard has gone at last. I can't begin to tell you how much anxiety the dragon's presence here has caused me, and Irno, of course. I could hardly sleep, wondering if it was going to burn us out of the castle.'

'Blackrose is a "she", not an "it".'

'Regardless, her departure is a weight off my mind.' She glanced at Aila. 'And next, I suppose, it'll be your turn to go. Now that Karalyn has her hands on Naxor's Quadrant, I'm sure she'll be keen to travel back to her own world.'

'I imagine.'

'And she'll be taking you and Corthie with her, no doubt, but what about Belinda? Please tell me that she'll be leaving as well.'

Aila shrugged. 'She's in love with Naxor; I don't know what she's going to do.'

Vana smirked and shook her head. 'If she stays for him, then she's a bigger fool than I thought. Don't frown like that, sister, you know fine well how our beloved cousin treats women. He's a cad, pure and simple. And Belinda? Dear, oh dear; she's behaving like a love-sick child. You did warn her, I assume?'

'I did. She didn't listen; she thinks he's misunderstood.'

Her sister laughed. 'She's not the first girl to think that, and she won't be the last.'

'She's a god, not a girl.'

'Do you think that one day she might start acting like one?'

'Maybe in a hundred years or so, once she's wrapped her head around the concept of immortality.'

'She's invisible to my powers, did you know that? Just like the Hold-fasts, which is why I didn't see them coming. I routinely scout the environs of the Falls of Iron, just in case any of the gods of Alea Tanton decide to pay a visit.'

'From what Sable told me, that might be soon.'

'And if Sable said that, then I'd expect the opposite to be true. Really, Aila, you used to be the least trusting of any of us, and now you're taking the word of someone you've never even met. Unfortunately for me, I have met her, and I've seen her in action. In her own way, she's as frightening as Karalyn; ruthless, and cruel – a killer. At least Karalyn doesn't kill people. Between them, Belinda and Sable accounted for almost twenty of our militia when they first arrived. By Amalia's breath, those two can fight.'

'Talking of Amalia, I hope you're scouting for her as well.'

Vana frowned. 'She wouldn't dare to come here, would she?'

'Not while Corthie and Belinda are living in the castle. And she'll avoid Karalyn too, if she finds out about her.'

'I doubt she'll know anything about the Falls of Iron. Naxor was always very careful to keep it secret, and if the same thing happened to the God-Queen as happened to you, then she will have arrived in the ruins of Dun Khatar, minus an arm. She'll need time to recover before she does anything else. No, I'm sure we've seen the last of her.'

'I hope you're right.'

'What does it matter to you, though? You'll be safely tucked up on Corthie's world, living with the Holdfasts; dwelling among all those mortals with god-powers. You know, when you get there, it might be a good idea to keep the fact that you're a demigod a secret. I don't think they like immortals very much. And then, of course, you'll need to have a plan for how you intend to get back, once, you know, Corthie has, um... passed.'

Aila said nothing. She put down the fork and glanced away.

'I'm just being realistic, Aila. I'm not deliberately trying to hurt your feelings, but... he is a mortal.'

'I'm aware of that, thank you.'

'There's no need to lose your temper. I can see that it's a painful topic, but am I supposed to avoid it? We've had our share of disagreements, but you're still my little sister, Aila.'

She suppressed a bitter laugh. 'Alright, so what would you recommend?'

Vana lit another cigarette. 'End it, now. The longer you leave it, the worse it will be. Failing that, then steel your heart. And, if you can, refrain from having any children with him.'

'But you had children with mortals, Vana.'

'Yes, I did. Over five hundred years ago, and their descendants are still living in Ooste and Pella. It nearly broke me, sister, having to watch them grow old and die, and I swore to myself I would never do it again. You think I'm callous, but it was the only way I could survive. Spare yourself that pain.'

Aila felt her eyes begin to well up, and she forced the tears away before they could start. She gazed at the waterfall, watching as a light breeze sent swirls of spray out into the sky where they glistened in the sunlight. The temperature was starting to rise, and the plains below them were shimmering in a heat haze.

'Good morning,' said Corthie.

She turned, and watched him approach. He had washed and was dressed in clean, smart clothes, his damp hair falling over his face.

Vana smiled at him. 'Good morning, champion.'

He laughed as he sat. 'I don't think you can keep calling me that. I'm not the champion of anything any more.' He glanced at Aila's full plate. 'You not hungry?'

'Not really,' she said.

Vana stood. 'I'll leave you two alone. Corthie, help yourself to breakfast; there's coffee in the pot.'

'Coffee?' he said. 'There's coffee here?'

She nodded. 'See you both later.'

Corthie took the coffee pot and filled a cup. 'How did I not know there was coffee on Lostwell?'

Aila frowned. 'Perhaps because you've been drunk every day?'

'You're forgetting that I lived on Lostwell for four years,' he said, adding sugar to his cup and stirring. 'Gadena must have kept it from the trainees. That and cigarettes.'

'They have those on your world?'

'Aye. Most of my family smoke, but I always thought it was a disgusting habit.'

'Did you ever hear of the Falls of Iron when you were at Gadena's?'

'No. We were kept within the confines of the camp, and told very little about the outside world.' He took a sip of coffee and sighed, stretching his feet out across the flagstones. 'Pyre's arse, that's good.'

She glanced at him. 'It's nice to see you cleaned up and sober for a change.'

'Well, maybe I might have, you know, overdone it a bit.'

'A bit?'

'A tiny bit.'

'What about Alea Tanton? Had you heard of that in Gadena's?'

'Aye, I'd heard of it. A few of the recruits had come from there.'

'Your friend Tanner, is that where he was from?'

'No, he was from a little village on the other side of Khatanax. Kinell, I think it was called. Why? Are you developing an interest in Lostwell?'

'I keep thinking about what Sable told me.'

He frowned. 'What did Sable tell you?'

'Corthie,' she said, shaking her head, 'we talked about this last night.'

'Remind me.'

'Sable said that the gods of Implacatus have sent an army to Alea Tanton to hunt for the source of the salve. I've tried talking about it with people here, but no one's taking it seriously. Naxor said that he's been so careful that it was impossible for the gods to track down the City, while Vana disbelieves anything that Sable says.'

'All I know about Sable is that Belinda hates her guts.'

'But what if she's telling the truth? What if an army really has arrived? Don't you think it's worth checking out?'

'Alright, let's imagine that Sable is right, and an army has come, along with some gods. I'd guess that at least one of those gods would have the power to read minds, so it might boil down to how much patience they have. Given enough time, they could read everyone, and eventually they might be able to piece it together.'

'That's what worries me,' she said. 'If they manage that, then they might be coming to the Falls of Iron.'

'Or they'd hear about Gadena supplying champions for Naxor.'

'And that would lead them here as well. And then, all they'd have to do is read Irno or Vana's minds, and they'd discover the truth.'

Corthie sipped his coffee and nodded.

Aila took a breath, unsure if what she was about to say was wise. 'Corthie, I have misgivings about travelling to your world knowing that the City could be in danger.'

He said nothing, his eyes on the view of the plains. She wondered if he would get angry, after all, he might think she was laying down unnecessary obstacles, or perhaps he would doubt if she really wanted to be with him.

'I understand,' he said, 'but what can we do about it?'

'I think that we could ask Karalyn; maybe she'd be willing to check out Sable's story. It might be just as Vana said, that Sable was lying to me. I mean, that's what I hope is true. It would put my mind at rest.'

He nodded. 'What if it turns out that Sable was telling the truth?'

'I don't know,' she said; 'I haven't worked that part out yet.'

'What's the worst that could happen? Yendra's strong.'

'She is, but even she couldn't withstand a concerted attack by several gods at once. Sable said that Implacatus wants to control the supply of salve – that would mean that they would occupy the City, and take over; and everything we fought for would have been for nothing.'

'Alright,' he said. 'Come on, let's find my sister and ask her.'

'Now?'

'Aye, now, unless you had planned on actually eating something for breakfast.'

They got to their feet, and walked back into the castle keep. Irno and Vana had kept a small suite of rooms available for Karalyn at the top of a tower, far away from the rest of the inhabited chambers, and they strode along the cool, stone passageways, passing the ale house and the kitchens on the way. Just as their eyes were getting used to the dim interior light, they crossed by an open window, and were dazzled by the sun again, the whitewashed stone gleaming bright. They reached a set of narrow stairs, and climbed up past a few levels to the top, where Aila heard a knocking sound, followed by voices.

'Try again,' said Naxor.

Thump-thump-thump.

'She's not in,' said Belinda.

Aila and Corthie emerged onto the landing, where Naxor and Belinda were standing outside a thick wooden door.

'Hey,' said Aila; 'you had the same idea as us, yeah?'

Belinda nodded. 'It's no good, though; we don't know where she is.'

Corthie walked up to the door. 'Karalyn? Are you there?'

'What if she's gone?' said Belinda. 'She could have used the Quadrant to leave.'

'No,' said Corthie; 'she wouldn't do that.'

'After yesterday,' the god went on, 'I'm not sure what's she's capable of doing. I've never seen her act like that – so cold.'

'Be careful,' said Naxor; 'she could be here right now, listening.'

Aila glanced around, a chill running up her spine.

'I don't care,' said Belinda. 'Karalyn!' she cried. 'If you're here, show yourself.'

Corthie stepped back from the door. 'Maybe we should wait downstairs. If she wants to see us, she can find us.'

'Wait,' said Aila. 'I hear something from inside the room.'

They all gazed at the door as it started to open. Karalyn peered out into the tower landing, her eyes bleary, with dark lines under them. She glanced at the four waiting outside her room.

'Good morning,' she said.

'Were you in there the whole time?' said Belinda.

'I was sleeping.'

'Can we talk?'

Karalyn said nothing for a moment, then nodded. 'You'd better come in.'

She opened the door and walked into her small chamber as the others filed in after her. Aside from the low, unmade bed, there was only a single chair in the room, and they stood around as Karalyn opened a set of shutters, letting the sunlight spill in.

'Sit on the bed,' she said.

They did so. Karalyn took the chair, and lit a cigarette. Naxor glanced around the room, and she gave him a wry smile.

'You won't find the Quadrant,' she said. 'I've hidden it from your eyes – you could be looking right at it, and you wouldn't know.'

'So,' said Belinda, 'you were sleeping?'

'Aye. I do actually sleep occasionally. I had a long night, learning how to use my new toy. I figured it out in the end, with a little help from the knowledge I pulled from the minds of Blackrose and Naxor.' She glanced at them as she smoked. 'You can stop looking at me like that. I know what I did was wrong, but what's done is done.'

'We didn't come here to accuse you of anything,' said Naxor, 'but to ask what your plans are.'

'That's not the only reason,' said Belinda.

'No,' said Aila; 'I have questions too.'

Karalyn gazed at them all in turn. 'Alright. Let's start with you, Naxor. I can see you're conflicted – part of you wants me to leave this world as soon as possible, mainly because I terrify you, but you also want to squeeze some information out of me first. The good news is that I'll be going soon. The bad, is that I don't know how many other Quadrants are currently on Lostwell, or where they might be located. I'm not omniscient. Alea Tanton is a good bet, which is why I sent Sable there. I also sense your worry, Naxor; you are concerned that I will reveal your selfishness and dishonesty to Belinda, but I have no intention of doing so. She is clearly in love with you and, harsh as it may sound, she needs to learn these lessons on her own.'

She turned to the god. 'Belinda, I know you hate me. I can feel your loathing and mistrust without having to read your mind. I'm sorry, not just for what I did to Blackrose and Maddie, but for everything. I've made a lot of mistakes, but my greatest ones were with you. If I'd given you all of your powers when the Empress ordered me to, then maybe Corthie would never have been abducted, and maybe Lennox would still be alive. I feared what you would become; I feared that I'd be responsible for the creation of a monster; instead, it was I who became the monster. I love you, Belinda; I have since the day you awakened in the attic of the Holdfast townhouse, when you were helpless and weak, without language or memories, and I'm proud of what you've become.'

Belinda glanced away as a tear slid down her cheek.

'Now, I know,' Karalyn went on, 'what you want from me, but first I must ask – what would you do with your powers if I restored them?'

'Defend myself,' said Belinda, 'and fight for those I love.'

'You used to rule worlds,' Karalyn said, 'do you not wish to do so again?'

'No.'

'The gods of Implacatus will be hunting you, as soon as they realise that you are alive. I know that you don't want to come back to the Star Continent with me, but I don't wish to leave you here defenceless against those who will try to kill you.' She raised her hand. 'There, it is done.'

Belinda blinked. 'What? But... I don't feel any different.'

Karalyn smiled. 'You won't, not for a little while. I've set your powers to return gradually, one at a time, so that you are not overwhelmed. The blocks I placed in your mind are extremely powerful, and any sudden dismantling would cause you a lot of pain, and might even send you mad. Be patient for a little longer. You will feel them return.'

The god began to weep. 'Thank you.'

Naxor raised an eyebrow. 'How do we know you're telling the truth? You could be fobbing her off, and then, when you've gone, it'll be too late to do anything about it.'

Karalyn turned her gaze to him. 'I guess you'll just have to trust me.'

'The way that Blackrose trusted you?'

'I know what you all think of me for what I did to the dragon. I wish there had been an alternative, but as you yourself said, sending Black-rose back to Dragon Eyre unprepared could have catastrophic consequences.' She turned to Aila. 'I know what you wish to ask.'

'About Sable?'

'Aye.'

'Well, is she telling the truth?'

'In this case, she is. Unbeknown to her, I read her thoughts yesterday evening. She is in Alea Tanton right now, infiltrating the newly arrived gods from Implacatus. Everything she told you is true – the gods mean to track down the source of this salve substance so that they can control it. Their leader, Lord Renko, is under instructions to use force if necessary to discover the source.'

'They don't have a chance,' said Naxor. 'They would have to interrogate every single merchant in Alea Tanton.'

Karalyn smiled. 'And that is precisely what they are planning to do. Orders have been given to bring the entire population of the city's merchant's district up to Old Alea for questioning. Renko cares nothing for the future of Lostwell; he has one aim – find the salve, and nothing else matters.'

'Amalia's breath,' said Aila, 'this is a nightmare. We have to do something to stop them.'

Karalyn nodded. 'You will have plenty of opportunities to try.'

'What?' Aila said, frowning. 'Why?'

'Because you are not coming back with me and Corthie.'

'Hold on,' said Corthie, his eyes wide; 'that's not your decision to take.'

'As I possess the Quadrant, brother, it is indeed my decision to take.' She looked from Corthie to Aila. 'Your relationship is doomed. Mortals and immortals do not mix. Aila knows this deep down; she fears what the future will hold. She dreads seeing you grow old, and the thought of watching any children you have wither and die makes her feel sick. If you love her, Corthie, then you would not wish to put her through this. If you love her, you will let her go.'

Corthie jumped to his feet. 'No. Screw you, Karalyn, you're acting like you think you're a god; well, you're not.' His face fell. 'Wait. Have you... seen what will happen? Have you had a vision of our future?'

'What?' said Aila.

'I could lie to you and say that I have,' said Karalyn, 'but no, I've had no vision involving you and Aila. The words I speak are coming from experience, not from any vision of the future.'

Aila's eyes narrowed. 'You can see the future?'

Karalyn nodded. 'Sometimes. Occasionally, I catch a glimpse of an event that is yet to happen when I look into someone's eyes.'

'But you haven't had a vision of us,' said Corthie, 'so you don't know what will happen.'

'This can't be right,' said Naxor, 'these powers are impossible.'

'I wish that were true,' said Karalyn.

Naxor glanced at Belinda, who shrugged and nodded. 'But...' he gasped. 'Have you... have you had any such visions about any of us since you arrived in Lostwell?'

'Just one,' said Karalyn; 'through Sable's eyes.'

'Does it affect us?'

'Aye.'

Naxor's eyes bulged. 'You have to tell us.'

Karalyn shook her head. 'No, I don't. I thought about telling you, but honestly, it would just make things worse.'

'Get back to me and Aila,' said Corthie. 'You won't separate us. Either she comes with us, or I'm staying here.'

'Don't be childish, brother.'

Rage and frustration clouded Corthie's features. 'Stop trying to control my life. I love Aila.'

'You're just a boy; what do you understand about love?'

'Do you have any idea what kind of life I've been living for the past few years, which, to you, passed in a heartbeat? Do you understand what the four years at Gadena's was like, or how I managed to fight thousands of greenhides in the City? I was a boy when I was abducted, but I'm a man now, just two years your junior, not six. I know how I feel, and if you try to separate me from Aila I will never forgive you, do you get it? Never.'

Karalyn glared at him, then she turned to Aila. 'And what do you say, demigod?'

Aila stared in silence for a moment, her eyes flitting between Corthie and his sister. She knew what she should say, what she was supposed to say. She should tell Corthie that Karalyn was right, that their love had no future, and that she would be unable to bear the sight of him withering and dying before her eyes. Vana had told her the same, and Maddie, Blackrose and Belinda too. They had all told her that her love for Corthie would end in nothing but tears and pain, and now Karalyn was saying the same thing. But then she remembered the words of Yendra, the sole person who had encouraged her to go with Corthie, to live her life with him, and to find some happiness, even if it wouldn't last. Nothing lasted forever.

'I want to be with Corthie,' she said.

Karalyn's face contorted with rage, and for a moment Aila thought she was going to lash out.

'You fools,' she cried. 'You stupid, selfish idiots. You want to be together, then fine, but you're not coming back with me.' She stood and pointed a finger into Corthie's chest as tears rolled down her face. 'This will destroy our mother, you know that. I'll return home, alone, after five years! All of this, everything I've sacrificed, was for nothing. What am I supposed to tell her?'

Corthie took Aila's hand. 'Tell her I've found happiness. Tell everyone in our family that I love them, but I'm not giving up Aila.'

Karalyn raised her left hand, and the Quadrant appeared in it.

'So be it,' she said through her tears. 'You'll regret this, brother, but so be it.'

Karalyn vanished.

Aila started to cry, and Belinda stood and hugged her, then Corthie joined them, wrapping his big arms around them both, his own eyes welling with tears.

'Malik's ass,' said Naxor. 'What now?'

CHAPTER 14

A DAY AT THE OFFICE

Alea Tanton, Tordue, Western Khatanax – 4th Tradinch 5252

Sable walked along the street as the sun was rising over the horizon to her left. Soldiers were lining both sides of the road, guarding a row of large, covered wagons.

'Excuse me,' she said to a sergeant as she squeezed past him.

He glanced at her for a second. 'Sorry, love.'

At the end of the road was the massive Governor's residence, the place where Sable had been working for the previous couple of days, and also the place where the wagons were being taken. Merchants and their families were packed into each one, having been brought up from the lower town at the point of a crossbow. From picking up gossip, Sable knew that Lord Renko had been told about the economic damage detaining merchants would cause, but he had ignored the warnings, just as he had done nothing to stop the riots in the city from spreading.

Sable smoothed down the front of her servant's tunic as she approached the checkpoint by the gates of the residence.

'Good morning,' she said to the Banner soldiers on duty.

One nodded to her. 'Pass.'

Sable went into her pocket and withdrew the stamped permission card, then handed it over to the soldiers. They scanned it as they did every morning, then passed it back.

'In you go.'

'Thanks,' she said.

She walked through the gates and entered a large forecourt. In the centre, wagons were being unloaded, and bewildered merchants and their scared-looking families were being herded by soldiers towards the eastern wing. The emptied wagons were moving off to the right, to leave the compound by another gate so they could collect more inhabitants of the merchant's district. Sable turned away, and took a path to the left between plush, green lawns towards the kitchens.

Beds of flowers stretched off to her left, and beyond that was a walled orchard, where orange and lemon trees were in bloom, the blossom blown by the breeze into drifts by the side of the wall. A large fountain was spraying water high into the sky, using enough water, Sable thought, to last several families in the lower city for days. She reached the door to the kitchens, and waited a moment as two delivery men unloaded tubs and large jars from the back of a cart. One smiled and gave her a wink, but she pretended not to have seen.

They rolled the tubs into the kitchen and she followed, taking a right into a chamber where huge kettles were heating water over a long range. A servant was on her knees, packing coal and wood into the furnace through a small iron opening.

'Morning, Isa,' said Sable as she went to a sink and washed her hands.

'Morning, Sable. You couldn't grab me another bucket of coal, could you?'

'I've just washed my hands.'

Isa shrugged. 'Sorry, my dear.'

Sable walked out of a side door and picked up the small shovel. She filled a bucket, and brought it back in for Isa.

'Thanks.' She emptied half of the bucket into the furnace, then closed the iron door with a poker. She straightened and sighed, her hands on her lower back. 'I'm getting too old for this, and what with my dear husband keeping me up all night with his snoring.'

Sable raised an eyebrow. 'Would you like me to do the rounds of the officers for you this morning, Isa?'

The older woman grinned. 'Oh, would you? That would be lovely. You're a great help, Sable.'

'It's fine,' said Sable, pleased that for once she hadn't needed to engineer the situation. 'Give me a hand setting up the trays, and I'll get started.'

They laid out half a dozen polished metal trays, then began filling them with cups as the water in the kettle warmed up. Sable prepared a coffee pot, and Isa filled it, the aroma filling the small chamber, then Sable carried the first tray out from the kitchens. Her route took her by the rooms of the junior officers of the Banner, and she knocked on the door of Eagle Company, the closest to the kitchen.

Lieutenant Baku glanced up at her as she entered.

I am a harmless, loyal servant; you can continue talking.

The lieutenant turned back to a sergeant who was standing by the table. 'I need you to take some supplies down to Captain Logos in the lower city,' he said; 'he's requested a few items.'

Sable listened as she set down the tray. She had a good memory, and had learned by heart how all of the officers liked their morning coffee. Captain Logos had taken his with two sugars, she remembered. She suppressed the thought of him, and the guilt she felt at what the gods had done to him because of her. She had sent him off to Lady Felice's mansion after convincing him that it was a good idea, and he had been tortured as a result. She shouldn't care; after all, he was a soldier from Implacatus, but she knew from reading his mind that he wasn't an evil man; his only fault was that he had been too clever, and had got a little too close to the truth.

'And,' Baku went on, 'please pass on my regards to the captain while you're there.'

'Yes, sir,' said the sergeant.

The lieutenant bit his lip for a moment. 'How is he?'

'Recovering, sir. He'll be back on his feet in a few days; they didn't leave any permanent damage.'

The sergeant and the lieutenant shared a glance, and Sable didn't need to read their minds to recognise the anger they felt at the assault upon their captain. They were professional mercenaries, not conscripted peasants, and their loyalty was conditional on good pay and fair treatment. Sable had read many complaints from the heads of the soldiers of the Banner since the humiliation of Captain Logos, and she wondered how she could make it work to her advantage.

She picked up the empty tray and walked to the door.

'Servant, wait,' called Lieutenant Baku.

She turned and bowed. 'Sir?'

He held the cup up. 'Excellent coffee.'

'Thank you, sir.'

She gave him a smile, then set off back to the kitchens for the next tray.

It took Sable little over an hour to deliver coffee to the entire group of junior officers, then she went back to the kitchens to help with the preparations for lunch. She hadn't learned much from doing the rounds. The orders were the same as the previous day – bring every merchant up to Old Alea, and detain them so they could be questioned by the gods. The cells under the residence were filling quickly, and more staff were being drafted in to feed them. Sable was avoiding such duties; she didn't want to be down in the dungeons, she wanted to be up in the tower where Lord Renko had his offices, so she could try to locate one of the Quadrants she knew must be hidden away. None of the junior officers had access to that type of information, and only trusted and long-serving staff were allowed near the commander's quarters.

'See those onions?' one of the kitchen hands said to her. 'Start chopping.'

Sable inclined her head and picked up the large knife. She kept her head down as she began working her way through the sack of onions on the worktop, listening to the gossip and chatter of the staff. She picked out a few tidbits of information about the family lives of some of the servants, filing them away in case she needed to call upon them later, and tried to listen closely to the inflections of their accents. As she did so, an old question resurfaced, one that had been bothering her ever since she had arrived in Lostwell – why did the local inhabitants speak Holdings? It was ludicrous to imagine that it could possibly be a coincidence, yet the fact that those living in Khatanax used the same language as Sable's own people perplexed her. She had discovered that the citizens of Kinell used a different dialect, one that was still closely related to Holdings, but anyone in Alea Tanton would be intelligible to someone from her own world. It had something to do with the Creator, the being she had worshipped for most of her life. She should stop calling him that; his name was Nathaniel, and he wasn't a god; not a true god at any rate.

'Have you seen the size of Lord Maisk's harem?' one of the servants was saying. 'Thirty girls, that's three times what old Governor Latude had. He must be insatiable.'

'Nah,' said another, 'he's like a peacock, strutting about, showing off his plumage. The bigger the harem, the smaller the...'

'That's enough,' said one of the overseers. 'I don't want to be listening to that kind of talk. I might get called into the gods' presence if there's a complaint about the food, and what'll happen if they read my head, eh? If they find the "peacock" comment, they'll make my brains explode like they did with poor old Kemal.'

Some of the servants laughed, while a few scowled.

'I know Lord Kemal wasn't popular with some folk up here,' said one with a frown on her face, 'but he was still the patron of the Bloodflies. Half of my old neighbourhood's been burnt to the ground because of his death.'

'Have you been up to Lord Renko's tower?' another servant asked the overseer.

'Yeah.'

'I heard a rumour.'

'Look, I'm not answering any questions about his damn harem, alright?'

'It wasn't about that; it's just that I heard that his lordship has taken an old withered corpse up there for company, and has it laid out on the table in his study.'

The overseer frowned.

Sable darted into his mind. *You can relax; we're all friends here. There's no harm in a little gossip.*

'I probably shouldn't be telling you this,' he said, 'but yeah; it's true all right. It was hard not to stare at it when I was called up there. Lord Renko was treating it like it was precious to him.'

'Who is it?' said the servant.

The overseer shrugged. 'A god, I think, but I was hardly likely to ask now, was I? "Excuse me, Lord Renko, but I was just wondering who that corpse might be?" Can you imagine? My brains would have been on the wall.'

The kitchen staff laughed.

'Anyway,' said the overseer, clearly enjoying being the centre of attention, 'I was...'

A scream rang out from the other end of the kitchen.

'A rat!'

The staff began to scatter. Sable glanced over, and saw the beast scurrying across the floor. She pulled on a tiny bit of battle-vision, aimed, and flung the knife with a flick of her hand. It cleaved the rat in two, slicing through its neck as the tip of the knife sunk into the floor, the blade wobbling.

The kitchen stilled into silence.

Sable smiled. 'Sorry. Instinct.'

She walked over and pulled the knife from the floor, as the kitchen staff crowded round.

'Did you see that?' cried one.

Sable cleaned the knife in the sink as the overseer picked up the remains of the rat.

He turned to her. 'Instinct? What kind of place were you brought up that would create that kind of instinct?'

'There were rats on my parents' farm,' she said. 'I got plenty of practice.'

Don't be alarmed. A servant with skills like that is always useful. Best not to tell any of the officers or gods, though.

'I've seen you around the last few days,' he said to her. 'A coffee-girl, aren't you? What's your name?'

'Sable. I'm from Kinell.'

'I thought your accent sounded a little funny. Well, Sable, you're now our resident rat-eliminator.' He dropped the sliced carcass into a large bin and grinned. 'Who needs a cat when we've got Sable, eh?'

The staff laughed, and went back to work. Isa ambled over to where Sable was standing, as she resumed the chopping of onions.

She raised an eyebrow. 'Nice shot.'

'Thanks, Isa.'

'You might have fooled that dozy overseer,' she whispered, 'but there was no way you learned how to do that hunting rats on a farm.'

Sable eyed her as she chopped the onions. 'Can you keep a secret?'

The older woman nodded.

'I had quite a rough life as a kid growing up in Kinell. I had to fend for myself on the streets.'

Isa seemed satisfied with that lie, and even glanced at Sable with a little more respect. Sable smiled. She got a thrill when someone believed something she had just made up, especially when she hadn't needed to go into their minds to 'persuade' them. She was good at her job, and being an accomplished liar was part of that.

An hour later, and the kitchen was bustling, as lunch for the officers and their staff was being loaded onto trays and trolleys. Sable made sure she was working close to the doors leading to the rest of the residence, waiting. Right on schedule, one of the head servants entered, her eyes impassive as she looked for the overseer.

Sable caught her glance. *Sleep.*

The head servant tottered, then collapsed to the floor, sending a tray of clean dishes crashing onto the tiles next to her. Sable ran to help.

'Lift her head,' she cried as the servants clustered round the fallen body.

The overseer knelt by the unconscious servant. 'Damn it all, what happened to her?'

'It might be the heat,' said one of the others; 'it's like a furnace in here.'

The overseer glanced around. 'You know what this means.'

Everyone except Sable looked away, avoiding his eyes.

'Come on,' said the overseer; 'one of you is going to have to take a lunch trolley up to Lord Renko's quarters. You'll be fine; the gods haven't killed a single servant yet.'

'Nah,' said one, 'Lord Maisk just hustles them off to his harem.'

Sable went into the overseer's head. *Pick me. You know I can do it.*

'What about you, coffee-girl?' he said.

Sable tried to look aghast. 'Me?'

'I'll do it,' said Isa. 'Sable's just a young thing; it wouldn't be fair on her.'

'You can't, Isa,' said the overseer. 'I'm under orders; only send pretty servants up to the gods' quarters. Sorry, but you're too old. No offence.'

'It's fine,' said Sable. 'I'll do it. How bad can it be?'

Several of the other staff pulled faces, but no one spoke.

'It's settled,' said the overseer. 'Load the trolley. Sable – get a fresh apron.'

The servants rushed about as Isa pulled a clean apron over Sable's shoulders and tied it at her back.

'Remember,' Isa whispered, 'keep your eyes lowered at all times, and don't speak unless you're directly addressed. Lord Maisk has wandering hands; make sure you don't throw a knife at him if he pinches your bum.'

'I'll try. Wait, will Lord Maisk be there?'

'And Lady Joaz; they always meet for lunch.'

The overseer pushed the trolley towards her. 'You all set?'

Sable nodded. 'I think so.'

'Alright, coffee-girl,' he said, holding out a signed permission card for her; 'give this pass to the soldiers at the top of the tower. Oh, and good luck.'

Sable slipped the pass into a pocket, gripped the handle of the trolley and pushed it through the swing doors of the kitchen, as the other servants watched, a few with expressions of pity on their faces. She turned for the western tower, and hurried along the narrow service passageway. At the far end was a lift operated by pulleys, where two burly servants were waiting. They nodded to her as she stepped inside onto a wooden platform, then they turned to a large wheel and began moving it round, lifting Sable, the platform, and the trolley up into the narrow shaft.

Sable relaxed as the platform entered the darkness of the lift shaft. She focussed her thoughts, trying to suppress her natural excitement. If she had one fault, she thought to herself, it was that she enjoyed her job a little too much at times, and it tended to make her reckless. Killing the rat had probably been over the top, but she hadn't been able to resist the temptation, partly just to see the looks on everyone's faces.

A light appeared above her head, and the platform emerged onto a wide landing, where two soldiers were posted by a large door. She pushed the trolley out of the shaft, handed over the pass, then waited as the soldiers checked over the trolley's contents and gave her a brief search.

One of the soldiers passed the permission card back to Sable. 'Where's Polly?'

'She fainted in the kitchen,' she said. 'I think it was the heat.'

'Alright.' He nodded to the door, and the other soldier knocked and opened it.

Sable pushed the trolley through the entrance and into a high-ceilinged dining room. A long table stretched down the middle of the chamber, large enough to fit two dozen diners, while a series of stained glass windows were letting in coloured light, splashing the walls in reds, greens and blues. At the head of the table sat a stern-looking man with a grey streak across his hair. That would be for show, she thought to herself, a deliberate choice to show his vast age. To his right sat an enormous man with a thick neck and huge shoulders, and across from him was a beautiful woman in a silver-grey gown, her long blonde hair braided down her back.

The enormous man stared at her as she pushed the trolley towards the table, and she darted into his mind.

Maisk. She recoiled a little at the contents of his thoughts as he leered at her, and she wondered how it was possible that someone who had been alive for so long could be so dull-witted. She was just beginning to ransack his memories for any sign of a Quadrant, when she felt a pressure behind her temples coming from the direction of Lord Renko. She smiled to herself. He was trying to read her mind, presumably to ensure that the new servant wasn't a spy. She could have easily blocked him, but instead allowed him in, to a place in her head she had prepared; a place where he would see nothing except what she wanted him to see – a nervous, frightened servant, in awe of the great and mighty gods. Satisfied, he withdrew from her mind, and she entered his, lurking in a quiet corner unnoticed as he watched her placing the bowls and plates of food onto the table.

She attempted to peer into his memories, but there were so many that she almost reeled. Millennia upon millennia of experiences, a vast library of recollection, and she pulled back, concentrating on his more recent memories as she set out the polished silver cutlery in front of the gods.

'Hurry up,' muttered Joaz, 'or I'll flay the skin off your back.'

Sable bowed her head, while trying to balance her physical actions with her race through Renko's head. They had brought two Quadrants with them, she saw. Maisk and Joaz had used them, but Renko was keeping them safe. There was another one too, that had belonged to Governor Latude. Renko's mind was dwelling on the former ruler of Lostwell. He had a desire to question him again, his curiosity piqued by something; a glimmer of a possibility, a faint hope.

A Sextant.

Conscious that the gods were waiting for her to finish, Sable hurried through the rest of her tasks, then left, unable to snatch more from their heads without arousing suspicion. She bowed low, then turned, feeling Maisk's gaze on her as she pushed the empty trolley from the room.

One of the soldiers chuckled as she approached the lift shaft. 'They let you leave alive then, eh?'

'This time,' she smiled.

'I need to log your name in the book,' he said. 'All servants permitted to access the gods have to be registered.'

She nodded. 'It's Sable.'

'Sable what?'

'Sable Holdfast.'

He leaned over a ledger on a small table and wrote her name down. 'From?'

'Kinell.'

'Right.'

'Tell me, why didn't you ask me before I went in?'

'Because they might have killed you, and it would have been a waste of ink.'

She gave him a look and stepped into the lift shaft. The soldier pulled a cord, and the platform began to lower. She sighed in exhilaration as she descended into the darkness. She had been in the midst of three gods from Implacatus, and not one had suspected a thing. Her nerves cooled as she realised that she hadn't actually discovered the location of a Quadrant, but she was registered; she had access to the gods, and would have another chance. In the meantime, she would need to give some consideration to the object of Renko's thoughts. The Sextant. From its name it had to be related to a Quadrant; perhaps a similar device of some kind. There had been no time to read what Renko knew about it, only that Governor Latude might have the answers. She smiled. Access to the former governor of Lostwell was fairly easy to come by, and the makings of a plan began to form in her mind.

The former governor of Lostwell was drunk when Sable arrived at his quarters later that afternoon, carrying his daily supply of alcohol and narcotics. He had been placed within a large, comfortable cell halfway up the eastern tower of the residence, and had a long chain shackled to his left ankle. The kitchen overseer had been willing to let Sable take the rest of the day off, after she had survived her first trip to the gods of Implacatus, but she had instead persuaded him to let her minister to Latude.

A soldier unlocked the gate and she strode into his cell. The gate was closed and barred behind her, but she was in no danger, the god's shackles preventing him from being able to reach the far wall of the cell.

'Good afternoon, Governor,' she said, setting the tray down onto a table.

'You got my booze, whore?' he slurred, his eyes bloodshot.

'You won't be getting any if you speak to me like that.'

'I'm a god, and I'll speak to you any damn way I please.' He struggled to his feet and staggered towards her.

'You stink,' she said.

He lashed out with his fists, but she stayed out of his range, shaking her head at him.

'I'll report you for this,' he cried. 'Damn bitch.'

She unpacked the jars and bottles onto the table, along with a bundle of weedsticks. She slipped a couple out from the rest and dropped them into her pocket.

'I saw that!' he yelled.

'I'm going to ask you some questions,' she said.

He lunged at the table, but the chain pulled him up short.

'Pathetic,' she muttered, then entered his mind.

You fear me. I terrify you more than Renko does. You will do exactly as I say. You will answer my questions, and you will tell the truth, otherwise I will destroy your mind.

Latude shrieked and fell to his knees, his eyes wide.

That's right; feel the fear flowing through you.

She smiled. 'Shall we begin?'

He whimpered.

'I'll take that as a yes. Right, the first thing I want to know is this – what is a Sextant?'

'A myth,' he said, starting to sob; 'just a myth.'

'So why does Renko want it?'

'That fool thinks it really exists. There was a story, a rumour that it could be found in the tomb of Nathaniel, the Fourth Ascendant, but it wasn't there. Kemal searched the tomb, and the caverns where the rebels had been hiding. There is no Sextant.'

'And what is it supposed to do?'

He sniffled.

'Come on,' she said. 'If you're a good boy, then you can have your booze and drugs.'

He lifted his tearful eyes to her. 'It can create new worlds. According to legend, it's what Nathaniel used to build new worlds; the last such device in existence. But it was destroyed along with the rest of Dun Khatar centuries ago. Renko's hopes are in vain.'

'Renko wants to build new worlds?'

'He says he wants to find it for a different reason, but that's what I suspect. He is proud, and imagines himself the next Nathaniel.'

'And what reason has he given?'

'He thinks it might lead him to the source of the salve. If Nathaniel created a world with salve on it, then the location of that world would be held within the Sextant. It stores the locations of all the worlds it has been used to create, but it's nonsense; as I said, it doesn't exist. Renko is a fool.'

Sable said nothing for a moment, then glanced at him. *Sleep.*

She picked up the contents of the table as Latude toppled to the floor, and placed them within his reach for when he would awaken. Then she crouched by the body and pinched open an eye.

Forget I was here. Forget what we discussed. Forget about the missing weedsticks.

She stood, turned, and knocked on the cell door.

The sun was setting as Sable neared the old abandoned turret where she had been staying with Millen. As usual, he was watching out for her return, and she could see the relief on his face as she stepped through the thick brambles and entered their little hideout.

'How was your day?' he said as she dropped the bag of food and wine onto the bare ground.

'Fine.'

'Any closer to finding whatever it is you're looking for?'

She sat next to him, her back against the stone wall. 'Maybe.'

'Is that all I'm getting?'

She slipped one of the weedsticks from a pocket and lit it.

'All I do,' he went on, 'is sit here every day while you're gone, worrying about you, and when you get back you tell me nothing.'

'Give me a break, Millen. I've brought you food, drink and weed.' And I haven't killed you, she thought to herself.

He rummaged in the bag, and started to unpack its contents onto the ground. Sable grabbed a bottle of wine and climbed up to the sea wall so she could watch the sunset. She sat down on the ancient stones, her legs dangling over the edge, and pulled the cork from the bottle, the weedstick hanging from her lips.

Millen joined her.

'You know the reason I can't tell you anything,' she said, passing him the weedstick. 'It's for your own protection.'

Sable savoured the cool breeze as Millen sat next to her. Below them, the waves were crashing into the base of the cliffs as the vast sky glowed red to the west.

'It's good to see you,' Millen said. 'I missed you.'

Sable took a swig from the bottle, avoiding his eyes. The idiot was in love with her. She should never have slept with him; either that or she should have pushed him off the cliff when they had first arrived at the turret. He was a loose end, a weakness in her armour, but she lacked the heart to kill him.

'Maybe after this is over,' he said, 'we could leave the city and travel...'

'Millen,' she said; 'shut up and enjoy the view.'

CHAPTER 15
AT A CROSSROADS

Torduan Mountains, Western Khatanax – 7th Tradinch 5252

Maddie turned away as Blackrose's jaws tore into the carcass of the mountain deer, a savage gleam in the dragon's eye. For five long days she had raged, her anger devouring her as she had burned, hunted and stalked her way through the high peaks and ridges north of the Falls of Iron. Maddie had kept her head down during that time, saying little, and living off the provisions she had brought from Irno's castle. The dragon's teeth crunched through the bones of the deer, and a spatter of blood landed by Maddie's feet.

To take her mind off the bloody scene in front of her, Maddie's thoughts went back to Karalyn Holdfast, and the way the woman had made her feel. Being under the control of someone else had been one of the worst experiences of her life; she had watched as her own traitorous hands had given Karalyn the Quadrant, while her mind had screamed helplessly in protest. The reasons for Blackrose's rage were obvious, but for Maddie it was more than being denied the chance to travel to Dragon Eyre. For her, having the Quadrant had also meant that, if things got really bad, they could use it to take them back to the City. She had memorised the actions needed to transport them to the roof of

Cuidrach Palace, and it had been a comfort for her, knowing that home was a few moments away.

With that option gone, Maddie felt bereft, and more alone than ever.

The dragon turned her long neck round to face her, blood dripping from her jaws. 'We should go.'

Maddie jumped. 'You're speaking?'

'Clearly.'

'I was wondering if you would ever speak to me again.'

'The rage that gripped my tongue has loosened, though that does not mean my anger is any the less. It has merely become more... coherent. What a fool I was, to have trusted that vile Holdfast witch. To think that I felt pity for her. Damn her; damn them all.'

'The last few days,' Maddie said; 'well, you frightened me. You set fire to half a mountain, and slaughtered Malik knows how many animals. I wasn't sure if you would ever calm down. You were wild.'

'I was betrayed, and then denied revenge upon my betrayer. The roaring ocean waves would not suffice to wash the shame and dishonour from me. I am a queen; a queen! And yet I was held spellbound in that witch's grasp, as powerless as I was in the dungeons of Arrowhead.' She lowered her head, the claws on her forelimbs gouging furrows through the rocky slope. 'And now? I can barely see beyond tomorrow, blinded as I am with anger, and cannot even imagine what the day after will bring.'

'We need a plan.'

'Oh Maddie, my rider, what plan could bring me any hope?'

Maddie thought about suggesting that they try to find some wild dragons, but as it had been Karalyn's idea, she reckoned it would be better not to mention it. She opened her mouth to fill the silence, then closed it again as she felt a low rumble beneath where she was sitting. A moment later, several little cascades of stones trickled down the hillside. Maddie gripped the side of a rock as the rumbling increased. On the mountain across from them a landslide began, slowly at first, then it grew in noise as tons of rocks and boulders slipped down the barren slopes. The rumbling ceased, and a few moments later the rockslides also stopped.

'Another earthquake?' said Maddie.

'Lostwell groans beneath us,' said Blackrose; 'this world is dying; it is a vast grave, welcoming all in its embrace of death.'

Maddie frowned. 'I think I preferred it when you weren't speaking.'

'You mock my pain?'

'Maybe a little. Sorry. It's just that things aren't as bleak as you think they are. We're still alive, and in one piece. We need a new Quadrant, and luckily for us, there are some on this world; we still need to figure out how to get our grubby fingers on one, but we don't have to have all the answers just yet.'

'Were it not for that witch, we would be basking in the sunlight of Dragon Eyre right now.'

'True, but you've been away for twenty years; a lot will have changed.'

'Yes, and all of it for the worse. The subjects of my realm will be enslaved, if they were lucky enough to be spared the greenhides. Those who collaborated with the enemy will be fat and rich, while those with any honour will be dead or in chains.'

'How big was your realm?'

'I once counted over a score of the most noble dragon families as my subjects.'

'That doesn't seem very many.'

'Dragon families can be quite large, and span several generations.'

'And did you have to fight them all to become Queen?'

The dragon narrowed her dark eyes. 'Do you think me a savage beast?'

'No, well, a bit. But I did hear you say that you would have to battle the wild dragons in order to become their big boss.'

'Yes, because they are wild. Even on Dragon Eyre there were a few colonies of wild dragons, outlaws and renegades living on isolated archipelagos. Things were rather more civilised in the rest of the world.'

'So how did you become Queen?'

'My father was King.'

'Ah, so the crown passed from him to you?'

'It did, though there was no physical crown, and it wasn't quite as simple as that.'

'No physical crown? That's a shame, because as you know, I'd like to see you wearing some headgear. Do you dress up baby dragons? If you ever have a baby, can I dress it up?'

'Do you want to hear about how I became Queen or not?'

'Oh, you mean you're actually going to tell me? You never talk about your parents, apart from mentioning how they each gave you a name. I was starting to think that something terrible might have happened to them.'

'Something terrible did happen to them.'

'Sorry.'

'My parents died within a few days of each other. They were hosting a great feast, with dozens of the dragon nobility present. My mother was beautiful and clever, but she wasn't a strong or powerful fighter. A dragon named Oceanwind from a rival house tried to seduce her, and when she rebuffed him, he attempted force. My father discovered what was happening, and intervened, but my mother was mortally wounded in the exchange. In a rage, my father slew Oceanwind. A few days afterwards, while my father was mourning, the kin of Oceanwind ambushed him, and took his life.'

'Malik's ass, that's terrible. Where were you?'

'I had not been invited to the feast, as it was for the heads of the families, and I had travelled to a distant island chain. My uncle, Greysteel, came to me with the news of my mother's death, and together we returned to my realm, and discovered what had happened to my father. Then, we summoned our loyal kin and supporters, and took revenge upon the family of Oceanwind, wiping them out to the last dragon.'

She looked into Maddie's eyes. 'That, rider, is how I became Queen.'

'That was a lot of deaths. Did you really have to wipe out his entire family?'

'Yes. Our kind never forgives hurts to our kin. If we had left any alive, they would have been duty bound to seek vengeance against us. There were those who objected, and some of my friends became enemies because of my actions at the time. I should have killed them too.'

'What did your rider think? I assume you had one back then.'

'It is impolite for a rider to ask about those who came before them, but I will say this – he never once questioned my commands.'

'He? You mean you had a boy-rider?'

'I have had several.'

'How many have you had altogether? Boys and girls, I mean.'

'You, Maddie, are my twelfth.'

She smiled. 'And the best, of course.'

'You certainly talk the most. The riders in my realm were taught from a young age to speak only when spoken to.'

'Do wild dragons have riders?'

'I know of some who did, while others would've rather eaten a human before letting one ride upon their backs. What the wild dragons of Khatanax do, I neither know nor care.'

'Do you want to find out?'

The dragon tilted her head. 'Is that where this conversation was leading? You wish to compound my misery by suggesting we follow the course of action that the Holdfast witch advised?'

'You can take the advice, even if you hate the advice-giver. What harm would it do? Some of them might even be refugees from your world. If you had escaped the fighting pits of that city, Alea-something, then you might have ended up there too.'

'Perhaps, but that knowledge is of no use to us now. The wild dragons will not have a Quadrant in their possession.'

'Alright, so getting a Quadrant is our priority?'

'It has to be, rider.'

'Then we go to this Alea place?'

'Alea Tanton.'

'Right, and we try to find Sable?'

Blackrose glowered at her. 'Not if we can help it. I refuse to place any trust in yet another Holdfast.'

'Ah, but you heard the way the others talked about her? They hate her. Belinda, Vana, Karalyn – none of them had anything good to say about Sable, and Karalyn seemed more than happy to abandon her in Lostwell. Corthie didn't even know she existed; she sounds like an outcast. There's a good chance that she hates the rest of the Holdfasts as much as they seem to hate her.'

'I see your logic.'

Maddie smiled. 'Is that you admitting that I'm right, and that you might be wrong?'

'Don't push your luck.'

The ground rumbled again, setting off a further series of little rock-slides down the mountain slope.

'Let us get into the air,' said Blackrose. 'Like everything else on this accursed world, the ground beneath us cannot be trusted.'

Maddie got to her feet and clambered up the side of the dragon's harness. Blackrose extended her long wings, the deep black glimmering in the sunlight, and they ascended, leaving the barren, grey and brown slopes behind. Nothing seemed to grow on the mountains, their peaks and valleys desolate and lifeless, and to Maddie's eyes it looked as though the scarred and cracked landscape had been tortured. The earthquake rumbled on for a few minutes, sending cliffsides toppling over, and gouging new ravines. In the distance to the north, she could see the land start to level off, but Blackrose flew east, staying close to the centre of the mountain range. They passed a spring, where the river that fed the Falls of Iron began, and the dragon landed to allow Maddie to re-fill her waterskins.

They flew on for another hour, then Blackrose veered to the left as the mountain range curved to the north. To their right, Maddie caught a glimpse of an endless plain stretching out into the horizon to the east.

'The Fordian Wastes,' said Blackrose; 'hundreds of miles of empti-ness and death. As Naxor told us, before the gods' invasion, the land of

Fordia was green and fertile, and now it is a grey, bleak desert, its population gone, its cities in ruins.'

'Did the people there all die?'

'Presumably very many did, but others made their way as refugees to the city of Alea Tanton. They are easily recognisable by the green tinge to their skin.'

'What? They have green... hides? Like greenhides?'

'They are human, or at least very closely related. They are supposedly the original inhabitants of Lostwell, and dwelt here long before the wars among the gods arrived. I knew some of them when I fought in the pits, and they told me stories about their history.'

'You knew some?'

'Yes. The blood sports of Alea Tanton revolve around three teams, one for each of the peoples who live there – the Fordians, the Shinstrans, and the Torduans. I was assigned to the Fordian team, and it was for them that I fought. They loved me for a while, despite my reluctance and shame, but my last memory of them is hearing the boos and jeers when I lay down and refused to fight any longer. They spat upon me as I was dragged from the arena.'

'Assholes,' muttered Maddie. 'And here I was, feeling sorry for them because they had lost their lands in the invasion. Did they ever make you fight other dragons?'

'Only rarely, and never to the death. Each team had but a single dragon, and they kept us alive as we were very difficult to replace. I was forced to kill greenhides, mostly.'

'I remember you telling me that, but if there are greenhides in Khatanax, why haven't they over-run the continent?'

'A huge landmass, far bigger than Khatanax, lies several hundred miles to the west. It is thoroughly infested with the beasts, who have wiped out every other animal that used to live there. Ships leave Alea Tanton, with steel cages on board, and mercenaries trap and capture greenhides for the arenas. In this way, several hundred can be slaughtered each year in the pits for the entertainment of the crowds.'

'They put them on ships? Malik's ass, that sounds risky. I wouldn't want to be stuck on a boat with one of them. Is that how they moved them from island to island on your world?'

'No. There is a far more efficient way to do that – by opening a portal.'

'How does that work?'

'You need two Quadrants, one in either place, and then they are linked together, creating a gateway that allows anyone to walk from the one location to the other. It is how I suspect the greenhides were brought to your world. The gods certainly used that technique to bring their armies to Dragon Eyre.'

They flew on, the miles of barren slopes rolling beneath them. The Fordian Wastes remained on their right hand side, and a road ran along the foot of the mountains, linking the Four Counties to the lands to the north. The slopes began to lower in front of them, and Blackrose swooped up by a high ridge and landed upon a tall rocky outcrop. Maddie gazed down. Where the mountains ended, a high earthen rampart began, heading in a northerly direction. To its right stretched the Fordian Wastes, while on its left were fields, with small farmhouses and structures dotting the landscape.

'That high embankment marks the frontier of Tordue,' said Blackrose. 'It is over twenty miles long, and at the far end the mountains begin again. Apart from this gap, Tordue is surrounded by ocean and mountains.'

'Tordue looks nice,' said Maddie. 'I mean, there are green patches at least, and houses, and trees. I guess it's what Fordia used to look like?'

'Indeed.'

'Is that why we stopped here, so you could show me the rampart?'

'No. This represents a crossroads for us, Maddie. If we fly to the north-east, and reach the mountain range on the far side of the embankment, then we will be approaching the land where the wild dragons dwell. Or, if we turn to the north-west, we shall instead come to Alea Tanton. I do not wish to go in either direction, but this is the choice the Holdfast witch has left us.'

'Are you asking me what I think?'

'I am.'

'Then we should go to the wild dragons.'

'If we do so, there is a good chance you will die, rider. As soon as I am seen, the likelihood is that I will be attacked. I can survive being bathed in flames, but you will not.'

'Oh.'

'The opposite is true in the other direction – you will be able to blend into Alea Tanton, whereas I might stick out a little. Certainly I would be seen, and the gods would become aware that a dragon is near their city.'

'Are you suggesting we split up for a while?'

Blackrose lowered her head. 'Damn that witch. The thought of leaving you alone and unprotected makes me feel sick.'

'And, um... what would I be doing in Alea Tanton, while you were getting cosy with the wild dragons?'

'You know the answer to that, Maddie. Find Sable, and bring me a Quadrant.'

Maddie groaned. 'I don't know if I'm up to it. I'm not a spy or a warrior, and Naxor said that this Alea Tanton place is huge. And dangerous; I definitely remember him saying it was dangerous. How am I supposed to find one person among all those people?'

'Do not lose hope. My heart is already in despair, and I couldn't bear it if you were to follow me down that dark path. Your optimism and cheer is all that has kept me going these last few days. You must be brave. One day, when we are ruling my realm on Dragon Eyre, we will remember this time of testing, and we will recall how we did what needed to be done.'

'Bollocks,' Maddie muttered. 'Fine. How far is it to Alea Tanton? How long will it take me to walk it?'

'The city is still a hundred miles from here,' the dragon said. 'I will fly you most of the way.'

She beat her wings and ascended again, and Maddie clung on as the dragon banked to the left. They passed the line of the rampart, and she could see the tiny figures of soldiers patrolling the road that ran alongside it, then Blackrose levelled out and surged to the north-west, the sun to their left. Beneath them, Tordue stretched out. Enormous fields were arranged in neat grids, with irrigation channels and lines of trees acting as wind-breakers. Huge barns and other buildings lay scattered amid dusty roads, where wagons and carts trundled along.

Maddie saw wheat fields, and corn fields, and long rows of olive trees. Vines sat on terraces facing the afternoon sun, and clusters of citrus orchards lay by the banks of the many waterways that criss-crossed the flat landscape. It seemed like a paradise to Maddie, a beauti-ful, bountiful garden stretching away in every direction; the opposite of the barren wastes of Fordia. Giant lizard creatures were pulling some of the wagons, and she raised an eyebrow.

'Those beasts down there,' she said; 'relatives of yours?'

'Yes, in the same way that you are related to other apes. They are called gaien; the wingless variety. It was into creatures a little like those that the first gods of Dragon Eyre entered, transforming them from dumb beasts of burden into true dragons.'

'So they can't talk, then?'

Blackrose laughed. 'Of course not. Nor can they breath fire.'

Maddie watched the beasts for a moment. 'Good.'

The city of Alea Tanton became visible to Maddie after a further hour and a half of flying. It appeared as a long, hazy smudge on the horizon, and then she realised that the smudge was actually smoke, great palls of it that were hanging in the air above the city.

'We are about ten miles from the edge of Alea Tanton,' said Black-rose, as she banked and started to circle. 'I will set you down close by, as I do not wish to get any nearer.'

Maddie looked down. The view below looked similar to what they had been flying over since entering Tordue, with little rows of buildings next to roads and fields. Outside one of the buildings, a crowd of tiny figures were running.

'It might be too late if you didn't want to get seen,' she said.

The dragon said nothing, then turned for a large stand of trees by a canal. Something whooshed through the air a few yards away, and Maddie jumped.

'What was that?'

A faint noise of pealing bells reached her ears.

'Um, Blackrose? Maybe we should retreat a little; I think you might have set off some alarms.'

The dragon twisted her neck to gaze downwards, then she cried out as her body jolted. Maddie turned, and saw the end of a long steel ballista bolt protruding from the dragon's left flank. Her eyes widened as more bolts came hurtling through the air towards them. One went clean through the edge of the dragon's right wing, piercing it, while another missed her head by a yard. All the while, the bells kept tolling.

Blackrose veered to the east, trying to gain altitude as blood streamed down from her wound. She cried out again, and seemed to hang in the air for a second, then she started to plummet from the sky.

'Mela!' Maddie screamed, clinging on to the saddle harness with all her strength as they dropped. The ground below was racing towards them, but at the last moment the dragon began to pull up, and they tore through the upper branches of the small wood. Blackrose tried to ascend, but her momentum kept them falling, and they crashed into the trees in an explosion of breaking trunks, twisted branches and a cloud of swirling leaves.

Maddie tasted blood in her mouth. She opened her eyes. She was still strapped to the harness on the dragon's back, but was leaning heavily to the right at an angle. Her head was aching from where a branch had struck her, and blood was trickling down from her right temple. She pulled on the buckle, and slid to the hard ground, landing on her side. She gripped onto the branch of a tree, its trunk snapped as if it had been a twig, and staggered forwards. The dragon's descent had gouged a path through the middle of the small wood, laying waste to the trees that had been in her way.

Maddie reached the dragon's head. Her dark eyes were open, and she was gazing at the two bolts embedded into her flank.

'You are alive,' said Blackrose.

'I'm fine,' said Maddie, ignoring the aches and blood. 'What about you? You need to get out of here. Those bells... they're coming; someone will be coming.'

'I think I might have underestimated the anti-dragon defences of Alea Tanton.'

'No kidding? Damn it, what do I do? Should I try to pull the bolts out?'

Blackrose eased her body over a yard or two, grimacing in pain. Her left forelimb reached up to where the two bolts were sticking out of her flesh. She clasped the first, and ripped it out of herself, the long steel barrel dripping with her blood.

'The salve, Maddie,' she grunted. 'There should be a jug filled with the salve that Naxor refined. Find it.'

'Right,' she cried. She scurried back to the harness as Blackrose yanked the other bolt out. She tried to remember when the jug of salve had been stowed. Before leaving the Falls of Iron, they had split the three jugs between them. Naxor had taken one, while Aila and Corthie had been given another. That had left the third, and final, jug with Blackrose.

Maddie searched through the packs and luggage strapped to the dragon's harness, growing more anxious with every moment. They had landed a few miles from where the ballista bolts had been loosed, but she knew that soldiers would already be on their way. They must have thought Blackrose was a wild dragon, come to terrorise the city, and it would have been impossible for them to have ignored her presence.

She found a large pack that was half-wedged under Blackrose's flank, and pulled it open. She groaned. Inside were the smashed remains of the old brandy jug. The salve it had contained was smeared into the ground by the dragon's side. She picked up the largest fragment of the jug, and scooped up as much of the disappearing salve as possible.

'Bad news,' she said to the dragon as she ran back round to where blood was streaming from her wounds.

Blackrose gazed at the broken shard of pottery. 'It will have to suffice.' She leaned forwards and opened her jaws, and Maddie tipped the meagre contents onto the dragon's tongue. Within a few moments, the blood flow from the two puncture wounds had slowed, but they hadn't healed over.

'It has eased the pain at least,' Blackrose said, trying to push herself up.

'Can you fly?'

The dragon collapsed back down onto her haunches, her face contorting.

'You were lying about the pain, weren't you?'

'I do not lie,' said Blackrose. 'It *has* eased. A little.'

Maddie heard a rustling in the undergrowth a few yards away and turned. Two men, dressed in peasant clothes and armed with farming implements, were staring at the dragon, their mouths hanging open.

Blackrose opened her jaws, and sparks ignited.

'Begone!' she roared at the peasants, who dropped the tools and fled. She turned back to Maddie. 'You should go, rider. Soldiers will be coming, with nets and ballistae, but they will not take me alive, I swear it to you.'

'No. There will be something we can do. We can get out of this.'

Blackrose gazed into her eyes. 'I love you for your eternal optimism, Maddie, but the Holdfast witch has destroyed me. If you survive this, promise me you will take vengeance upon her kin for what she has done to us.'

Maddie said nothing. Instead, she rooted around in the luggage until she found a crossbow and a bundle of bolts tied together with string.

'What are you doing?' said Blackrose.

Maddie glanced at her. 'Getting ready to fight.'

CHAPTER 16

A LITTLE TRUTH

A lea Tanton, Tordue, Western Khatanax – 7th Tradinch 5252

The silver swirls rose and bubbled within the small glass vial. When cold, the fluid remained still, but a combination of Van's hand and the sunlight had warmed it a little.

He longed for it, and he hated it. Part of him wanted to open the stopper and consume it until he knew nothing but the euphoric heights it pushed him to, while another part hoped that the darkest fears of the gods would come true, and the source of the salve would dry up forever. For days he had suffered the sickness and pains inflicted upon him in the Governor's residence, when a single dose would have healed him in seconds. During that time, not one of his junior officers or sergeants had asked him why he hadn't taken any; they all knew the reason. Each one had served with Van in the past, and each had seen his addiction in full bloom; the cravings, the obsession. He had lied to them all at one point or another, yet none had judged him for it; half were already on the same path to dependency that he had once taken, it was the nature of the Banner. They were salve-soldiers; it was in their blood.

For over a decade he had been a slave to salve, administering it daily, breaking the rules that the Banner half-heartedly tried to enforce. It was meant for two reasons alone – to treat wounds, and to prepare soldiers for the heat of battle, and, at first, that was why Van had taken it. He could still remember the first time he had been given a sip – a spoon's worth mixed into a glass of chilled vodka just before battle. In the four-hour frenzy that had followed, Van had killed for the first time, thereby indelibly mixing the two experiences together in his mind – salve and death.

Everyone in the Banner knew of the dangers but, like most of the young soldiers, Van had disregarded the warnings. Why should he worry about future heart problems when he was fighting a war? During the years spent on duty on Dragon Eyre, he had been nearly killed a dozen times or more, and it had seemed as if salve was the least of his problems. It wasn't long after that when the first chest pains had arrived. His senior officers had noticed his addiction, and his over-indulgence, but it had taken a near brush with death to finally make him quit. His heart had stopped one night while out drinking and abusing salve, and he had spent the next three weeks in bed believing he was about to die.

He felt a presence on the tower battlements behind him and he slipped the vial into a pocket.

'Sir?'

He turned, and noticed the lieutenant's eyes flicker up from the pocket. 'Yes, Sohul?'

'I have a message from the militia commanders, sir.'

Van sighed. 'Really? Is it not enough that we're down here practically doing their job for them? Can it not wait? I was enjoying the view.'

Sohul raised an eyebrow as he glanced out over the endless miles of slum housing.

'If they want us to go out into those rat-infested streets,' Van said, 'then the answer is no. We're here to facilitate the transport of the merchants up to Old Alea and for no other reason. The Banner soldiers are not theirs to play with.'

'Yes, sir, but...'

'How many have been taken up so far?'

'Merchants, sir?'

'Who else? Yes, Sohul, merchants.'

'Ummm, just over a thousand, sir, if my memory serves me well. I can get the exact numbers for you as of this afternoon's transports.'

Van took out his silver case as he gazed over the city. 'A thousand?' he said, lighting a cigarette. 'Still three-quarters to go, then. They're going to run out of space up there. Any panic in the merchant's district yet?'

'No, sir. There have been no protests since the strict curfew was implemented. Banner soldiers are patrolling the district night and day.' He glanced at Van, a crinkle of worry in his eyes. 'Might I say, sir, that it's good to see you up again.'

'Thank you. I appreciate you taking care of things while I was... recuperating in bed.'

'Yes, sir, although four days doesn't seem long enough for you to have fully recovered from your injuries.'

Van drew on the cigarette. 'I've had a lot worse. Now, be honest with me; do the rest of the Banner soldiers down here know why I was incapacitated?'

Sohul glanced away. 'Yes, sir.'

Van said nothing for a moment. He had suspected that the others knew, but wished it had remained quiet. The last thing he wanted was for the soldiers under his command to feel sorry for him.

'It was impossible to keep quiet, sir,' Sohul went on. 'Too many saw you brought out from Lord Maisk's quarters.' He lowered his voice and leaned in a little. 'The sergeants in particular are a little upset about it.'

'Upset?'

'Yes, sir. There have been murmurings of discontent. And anger, sir.'

'Bloody sergeants,' Van said, 'fussing over me like I was a child. I trust their misplaced sympathy hasn't interfered with their duties?'

'No, sir.'

Van turned, and glanced up at the sculpted cliff face. Wagons were crawling up the long ramp to the gates of Old Alea, passing the gigantic stone features of the gods that had been carved from the rock. Kemal's face was still there, he noticed, despite having been dead for several days. He frowned, and turned back to look at the slums.

'Where's all the smoke?'

'The riots stopped while you were recovering, sir.'

'Why?'

A wry smile crossed the lieutenant's lips. 'Orders were given out from Lord Renko, sir. He took your advice, and appointed a new patron of the Shinstran team, and did everything else that you suggested.'

'Good.'

'He, uh, also made out that it was his idea.'

Van shrugged. 'That's fine. I don't care who gets the credit.'

'The entire Banner knows it was really your idea, sir.'

'If Lord Renko says it was his idea, then it was his idea. Look, Lieutenant, we all signed the same contract, and if that means we get routinely humiliated by our divine superiors, then so be it. When we're back in Implacatus counting our gold, we can have a drink together and grumble about it all, but not before. Understood?'

'Yes, sir.'

'Good. Now, what do the militia want?'

'They want our assistance in a dragon hunt, sir.'

Van narrowed his eyes. 'Explain.'

'An artillery battery shot down a wild dragon that was seen approaching the city. They have the beast surrounded, but the local militia are all busy keeping the peace in the streets, sir.'

'And how far away is this dragon?'

'About twelve miles from the city limits, sir. Almost directly southeast of here. The militia have requested we lend them at least half of Eagle Company. They know that many of us have dragon experience.'

'And they don't?'

'No, sir. Apparently, it's been many years since a wild dragon has flown this close to the city.'

'They want us to kill it for them?'

'No, sir. They want it captured, for the arena games. Apparently, the teams of Alea Tanton would pay a high price for a captured dragon.'

Van said nothing.

'If you want, sir, I can lead a few squads. You are still in recovery, after all, and I don't mind...'

'Forget it. If Eagle Company is going up against a dragon, then I'll lead. Thank you for the offer.'

'Are you sure, sir?'

'Don't look at me like that. I'm fine. A little jaunt into the countryside would be good for me; anything to get away from the stench of the ocean for a while.'

Sohul frowned. 'Yes, sir.'

Van crushed the cigarette butt beneath the heel of his boot. 'Rustle up four squads and have them ready to go in twenty minutes.'

His lieutenant saluted, then disappeared down the stairs leading from the battlements. Van smiled. A dragon. It had been a while.

'What do you mean you have no nets?' said Van as the two officers rode side by side along the country lane. 'How in the First Ascendant's name do you expect to snare a dragon without nets?'

The militia colonel glared at him. 'I would like to remind you, Captain, that I am in charge of this operation. You mercenaries are here as reinforcements only, and Lord Maisk has put you and your forces directly under my command.'

Van glanced around at the mixture of Banner soldiers and local militia trooping down the dusty road. 'You say "mercenary" as if you think it's an insult. It's not, Colonel. It merely means that we are professionals, and if you want my professional advice, you should send someone back to the city for nets. I'm sure the fighting pits have plenty to spare.'

'We have brought shackles and chains,' said the colonel, 'and we have in excess of one hundred in arms, not including the local artillery teams currently surrounding the lizard.'

'And they're sure they hit the beast?'

'Positive. Two strikes to the left flank.'

'It might be dead, then?'

'Witnesses said they saw it alive.'

'I'd like to speak to those witnesses. If that's alright with you, Colonel, of course.'

The militia officer gave a curt nod, then glanced away, ending the conversation. Van shifted in the saddle of the horse he had been loaned, feeling the aches ripple through him with every step. He had smoked a little keenweed to get him through the pain and to keep him alert, and had a flask of vodka tucked into a pocket of his uniform jacket. He glanced around at the countryside. Slaves were labouring in the fields to either side of the road, while large wingless gaien were pulling ploughs through the dry, red soil. The sun was behind them, halfway down the western sky, and he could feel the skin on the back of his neck start to burn. The great majority of the soldiers were marching, dressed for battle, while a convoy of four wagons were at the rear, stacked with chains and a couple of portable ballistae.

Van shook his head in dismay at the rank amateurism on display. Rather than sneak across the fields, the colonel had insisted they go by road, and the cloud of dust they were generating would give the dragon advance warning of their approach. They passed a series of large barns and then slowed as they went through a crowd of peasants and curious onlookers. A line of militia was blocking the road, and Van joined the colonel as he rode to greet them. The crowds parted to let them pass, and the colonel nodded to the militia.

'What's the situation here?'

'The beast fell into those trees, sir,' one of the militia said, gesturing towards a copse a hundred yards to the left of the road. 'We have surrounded the position, but have kept our distance as ordered.'

Van peered at the trees. Even from that distance, it was clear that something had struck them. Trunks were twisted and snapped, and branches were hanging like tattered rags.

'Has there been any movement?' said the colonel.

'None for the last couple of hours, sir, and no sound neither. We thought the beast might be dead, but two farmers have confirmed that it survived the fall.'

'Are they here?' said Van. 'The farmers?'

'This is Captain Logos of the Banner of the Golden Fist,' said the colonel as the militia soldiers frowned up at Van. 'I have been led to believe that he is something of an expert on dragons.'

'Experienced, yes,' said Van. 'Expert?' He shrugged. 'I'd like to speak to those farmers, please.'

'Yes, sir,' said the soldier. 'If you would come this way?'

Van dismounted, and handed the reins of his horse to a nearby Banner soldier. He gestured to one of his sergeants to accompany him, and they followed the militia soldier off the road. They walked back to the crowd of onlookers, and the militia soldier pointed out two men.

'Are you the ones who saw the dragon?' Van asked as they strode forwards.

'That were us,' said the elder.

'Describe the scene to me.'

'Well, sir,' the man went on, 'we saw the creature plummet down through the sky as we was walking back from delivering old Ronald's leather bridles. We thought it was dead, otherwise we'd never have taken a look. We peered through the brambles, and saw it, sir – a great scaly beast, just like I saw in the fighting pits when I visited the arena, except this one was grievously wounded. There was blood on the ground, there was, and a damn lot of it. And there was a girl there too, who was unpacking these great big bags strapped to the side of the beast. We must have made a noise, because the beast saw us, and...'

'Hold on,' said Van. 'There was a girl there?'

'That there was, sir.'

'And the dragon had bags strapped to its flanks?'

'Indeed, sir, just as I was saying.'

Van felt a strange twisting sensation in his stomach. 'Was the girl the dragon's prisoner? A hostage?'

'No. The way the two of them were talking, they seemed to be on good terms, sir.'

Van and the Banner sergeant shared a glance.

'Are you thinking what I'm thinking, Sergeant?' said Van.

'Maybe, Captain. I've never heard of a wild dragon with a rider.'

Van turned to the militia soldier who had led them to the farmers. 'Did you see the dragon before it crashed into the trees?'

'Yes, sir. I was the signaller for the ballistae.'

'And did you see if anyone was on its back?'

The soldier frowned. 'Maybe, sir. Is that important?'

'I'm not sure,' said Van. 'It might be.'

The two farmers were sent back into the crowd, and Van returned to the colonel, who was ordering the soldiers into their flanking positions.

'Colonel,' said Van, 'perhaps we need to rethink our approach.'

'What? Don't be ridiculous. The rules for engaging wild dragons are clear.'

'I don't think we're dealing with a wild dragon, sir. I think we might be going up against a beast from Dragon Eyre.'

The colonel raised an eyebrow. 'Sounds unlikely to say the least, Captain. The mountains due east of here are rife with wild dragons, and you're suggesting that one has appeared without warning from another world altogether? Ultimately, however, it makes no difference. Wild or not, the dragon must be captured. According to the witnesses, the beast is dying, and we need to ensure it is in chains before it succumbs to its wounds.'

'Colonel, if I may? I've dealt with wild dragons and high dragons before. The wild varieties are savage and fierce, but they lack subtlety. If this is really a high dragon from Dragon Eyre, then it will have been trained in war, and will present a far more difficult proposition.'

The colonel laughed. 'A "high" dragon, you say? One might as well refer to a "high" cow, or a "high" cat. It is a beast – a dumb brute, fit only for the fighting pits.'

'Perhaps, sir, but...'

'Enough. You know the plan. I want your mercenaries on the left flank, and we shall take the right. We shall close in on both sides and drive it out from the woods with the ballistae. When you get into your positions, await my signal before advancing.'

Van frowned. 'Yes, sir.'

The colonel turned away, and began striding off to where the ranks of militia were waiting. Van glanced at his sergeant.

'Permission to speak my mind, sir?' he said to Van.

'Granted.'

'These militia are fools, sir. They ask us along because we've plenty of experience in dealing with dragons, and then they ignore our advice.'

Van shrugged. 'Come on, let's get the squads organised.'

He ordered his Banner squads to form four columns, and sent them separately across the fields to the left of the woods, where lines of low hedges and deep waterways offered cover. On the other side, the militia marched in a long arc, forming an unbroken semi-circle over the freshly-ploughed fields, the colonel visible up on his horse. Van crept along a line of hedges at the head of his first squad, then crouched, watching the trees.

Van felt the pain in his chest increase as they waited, his nerves adding to the ache. His mood had changed, and he wished he had allowed Sohul to take his place. He had assumed that they would be facing a wild beast from Khatanax, but the thought that it might be from Dragon Eyre had turned his insides. It wasn't just the fear, it was the memories. Images of battles with the lords and queens of the dragon world filled his head – flames, screams, death. He had sickened of it all, and his final months there had been one long torturous cry of terror, salve and agony. He felt his breath race.

'Are you alright, sir?'

He glanced at the sergeant. 'You know how it is. Memories.'

'Yes, sir. I know how it is. Should I order the squads to take their salve?'

'Not yet. The dragon might be dead for all we know.' He paused. 'If we're lucky.'

'What's it doing here, sir? I mean, if it's really from Dragon Eyre?'

'If it's a rebel, then I guess it might have stolen a Quadrant. But if so, why would it come to Lostwell?' He shook his head. 'They'll never capture it alive. It'll die before it's taken, and it'll kill anything in its way before it goes down. Catching its rider might be the only way to force it to surrender.'

'My thoughts exactly, sir.'

Van unstrapped his sword and passed it to the sergeant. 'Wait here.'

'Sir,' the sergeant said, his eyes wide, 'I must protest. You can't go in there. If the dragon's alive, it will burn you to ashes in a second.'

'And if I don't, it'll burn us all to ashes.'

'But...'

'If it all goes wrong, sergeant, there's only one thing you need to concentrate on – making sure none of the Banner die for this foolish cause. Keep the squads back; if the militia want to get killed fighting a high dragon, let them.'

He hurried off before the sergeant could say anything else. A small part of his mind was screaming in anger at his stupidity, but his legs kept moving, and he reached the edge of the trees. He dived into a thick tangle of undergrowth, and wriggled along the ground, the tall trunks of the trees surrounding him. He squinted ahead, then pulled himself up behind a tree.

'Dragon!' he called. 'I want to talk to you.'

Van listened, but there was no noise except for the rustling of the wind through the trees.

'Dragon, can you hear me?'

He heard a click to his left and turned. A young woman was standing in front of him, pointing a crossbow at his chest.

'I'm unarmed,' he said, keeping his hands by his side. 'I'm here to talk. Are you the rider?'

The woman frowned at him. She had a fierce look in her eyes, but she was holding the crossbow as if she was unsure how to use it.

'How many soldiers are out there?' she said.

'Over a hundred. About seventy or so are city militia, but forty are proper professionals, who have all dealt with dragons before. You haven't got a chance.'

'What are you doing here?'

'I should ask you the same thing,' he said. 'Why have you come to Lostwell?'

She raised an eyebrow. 'What? How do you know we're not from Lostwell? Who are you? Were you sent as a distraction, so that we...'

He whipped his arms out and pulled the crossbow from her grasp, twisting sideways in case she loosed. She yelled in surprise, but no bolt left the bow. She swung her fist and punched him on the chin, but he shoved her to the ground and pointed the bow at her.

'Right,' he said. 'I think you should come with me.'

She edged backwards through the dirt until she backed into a tree. Van stole a glance at the bow in his hands, noticing that it hadn't been loaded properly. He started to frown, then there was a flash of movement to his right, and a huge forelimb slammed into him, sending him flying through the air. He collided with a tree and slipped to the ground, the crossbow landing five yards from him.

'Don't even think about moving, soldier,' came a dark voice from the shadows of the thick branches to his left.

Van hugged his aching chest. He was winded, but nothing seemed broken. Despite his daze, he knew that could only mean one thing – the dragon wanted him alive. The beast's head appeared through the undergrowth, its red eyes glimmering as they stared at him.

'We haven't much time,' the dragon said. 'Rider, load the bow and point it at his head.'

'I came here to talk,' Van gasped.

The dragon tilted its head; her head, Van realised. 'And we are talking, are we not?' She regarded him for a moment. 'You do not seem particularly scared, soldier-man.'

'You might not be the first dragon I've seen close up.'

'No? You might find me rather different from the usual dragons you see on Lostwell.'

'He knows we're not from Lostwell,' said the young woman, who was back on her feet, and gripping the crossbow awkwardly.

'The wild dragons here don't have riders,' said Van. 'As far as I know, only one place does.'

The dragon stared at him. 'And what would you know of that? You are a mercenary, yes? You serve the gods of Implacatus?'

'My Banner works for them sometimes.'

'Be very careful with your next response, soldier-man; have you served on my world?'

Van looked the dragon in the eye, knowing the risk he was about to take. 'For three years.'

The dragon opened her jaws, baring the rows of razor-sharp teeth, around which lightning sparks were coiling.

'Don't kill him yet,' said the woman; 'remember the plan. Revenge can wait.'

Van reached into his pocket and withdrew a cigarette from his silver case as the dragon glared at him. He lit it off a match and took a drag, then felt a pressure behind his eyes.

'I know what you're doing,' he said. 'I've played the truth game with dragons before.'

'Good,' said the dragon. 'Let's see if what you have to say can save you. I doubt it, personally. In fact, I hope it doesn't. For many years, I have longed to slay one of the oppressors of my people.'

'Get on with it, lizard. Ask me your questions.'

'As an officer,' the dragon said, 'do you know the layout of the soldiers surrounding us?'

Van felt the compunction to reveal the truth within his mind, but to him it seemed almost liberating. More than half of everything he usually said was a lie of one sort or another.

'I do.'

'And is there a way past the circle of soldiers – one that a single human could take?'

'Yes. Directly east of here, there is a gap in the lines where your rider could escape. If she follows the hedges and watercourses for a mile, staying low, she should be able to evade detection.'

The dragon nodded.

'What?' said the woman. 'Hang on; I'm not leaving you, not while you're injured and a hundred soldiers are about to start attacking.'

'Fear not, rider. Listen, and you will understand.' The dragon turned back to Van. 'Are you a salve-soldier?'

'I am.'

'Where is the vial that you carry?'

'In my right-hand jacket pocket.'

'Rider,' she said, 'take the salve from him and give it to me. Soldier – if you harm a single hair on her head I will pull your arms off, slowly.'

Van sat motionless as the young woman leaned over him and started rifling through his pockets.

He gave her a wry smile. 'That's the left-hand pocket.'

'Don't get smart with me,' she said.

'That's not a Dragon Eyre accent.'

She took the vial of salve from his pocket and gazed at it for a moment. 'No, it's not.'

'Pull the stopper out,' said the dragon, 'and pour the contents into my mouth.'

The young woman nodded, then moved away from Van. She yanked out the small cork, and began emptying the salve onto the dragon's tongue. As the last drops were dripping out, a sharp whistle blast pierced the air.

'That's the signal for the attack,' said Van.

He watched as the dragon's face contorted for a moment.

'Well?' said the woman. 'Is it working?'

The dragon shuddered, then nodded. 'I am healed, and ready to kill. Soldier – are there ballistae?'

'Two,' said Van, 'and both are directly behind you, where the city militia will be advancing. They have underestimated you, and think you are close to death. They haven't even brought any nets.'

The dragon frowned. 'That was more than I asked. Why are you helping me?'

'Guilt.'

'You feel guilty? Why?'

'I have done terrible things on your world. I have killed many of your kind, and have led soldiers into committing the worst atrocities against your people. I hate myself for it, but it was... it is my job. I am ashamed.'

The woman and dragon stared at him.

'Once,' Van went on, 'I led a company in the destruction of a dozen dragon eggs that a group of rebels had hidden in caves by the sea. We smashed them with hammers and then burned them on a pyre, while the rebels had to watch in chains. The screams of the grieving mothers will live with me forever.'

'Enough!' cried the dragon. 'Your shame and guilt will not save you now. Your crimes against my people demand a blood price.' She turned to her rider. 'Maddie, go. I do not wish you to see what I am about to do to this vile creature.'

The woman hesitated.

'Go!' cried the dragon. 'Travel east for a mile, just as he said, and then you can circle back. We must follow the plan.'

The woman grabbed a bag that was lying by a tree, took one last look at Van and the dragon, then ran.

The dragon waited until she had gone, then turned back to Van. She lifted a forelimb, and slowly extended the claws.

'I know you want to kill me,' said Van; 'but you won't.'

The dragon laughed, a cold, harsh sound that hurt Van's ears. 'Really?'

'Yes, really. I am a broken man. A salve addict, hated by my superiors, while the soldiers under my command pity me. Each day I am consumed by what I did on Dragon Eyre; it would be crueller to let me live.'

'Perhaps.'

'And more than that, you have honour; I see it in you, lizard. Because of me, you and your rider will escape the trap that has been set for you today. It would shame your heart to kill the one who helped you.'

'Do you long for death?'

'Sometimes. On other days, I hope I live long enough to see the gods fall.'

The dragon lowered her forelimb, pushing it down onto Van's chest. He groaned in agony, feeling his ribs bend under the pressure. He gasped for breath, but none came. His eyes started to close, then he felt nothing more.

A bitter liquid splashed onto Van's tongue, and he convulsed as the salve ripped through his body. He lashed out with his fists, then felt hands hold him down.

'Captain! Stay still.'

His heart raced as a mixture of desperate euphoria and dire panic consumed him. His heart felt like it was about to explode, then he started coughing as pain and pleasure tore across his chest.

He opened his eyes. A yard away, a Banner sergeant was holding a half-empty vial of salve, a look of pity and guilt on his face.

'I know you told us never to do that,' the sergeant said, 'but you might have died, sir.'

The Banner soldiers who had been gripping his arms and legs moved back, and Van pulled himself to his feet. All traces of tiredness had vanished, along with any residual effects from the suffering he had endured at the hands of the gods. He felt great; healthy and whole, in the way that only salve could make him feel.

He sniffed the air. 'Where is the smoke coming from?'

'The dragon slaughtered the militia, sir,' said the sergeant. 'At least forty of them are smouldering piles of ash, and another dozen are badly burned. The colonel didn't make it.'

'What about the Banner squads?'

'No casualties, sir. I took your advice, and we stayed back. When the dragon rose into the sky, I ordered everyone into the deep irrigation channels, and the flames passed over us.'

Van nodded, already starting to feel the first pinch of craving for more salve. He lit a cigarette.

'What happened, sir?'

Van said nothing for a moment. The dragon's truth-bewitchment had passed, and he was able to lie again.

'The dragon tricked us all,' he said. 'Her injuries were minimal, and she was waiting for us. In which direction did she fly?'

'South-east, sir.'

'Good. I don't think she'll be back. However, she didn't take her rider along. I want the entire Eagle Company out searching for her. She stole off to the east, but I think she's planning on doubling back in order to reach the city. Her name is Maddie, and she's about twenty, I'd say; long brown hair, armed with a crossbow, and she has a strange accent.'

'But sir, we're expected back at the garrison fortress, and there are numerous wounded from the militia that need to be transported to the city.'

Van walked to the edge of the woods and gazed out. Plumes of smoke were rising from the fields to the south, and he could see dozens of corpses strewn across the ploughed earth, along with the burning remains of two ballistae in the distance.

'I don't care,' he said. 'I want the rider found.'

CHAPTER 17

THE QUEEN OF KHATANAX

Falls of Iron, Western Khatanax – 8th Tradinch 5252

'Morning, Aila,' said Corthie.

She stretched out on the bed, the white sheets tangling round her legs. She opened her eyes, and watched as Corthie placed a tray down onto their little table, then opened the shutters. He was fully-dressed, and was whistling a tune.

She frowned. 'What are you doing?'

'Just bringing you breakfast.'

'No, I meant, why are you up before me? You never get up before me.'

'I've been awake for hours. I got a bit bored waiting for you to wake up, so I went along to the kitchens. I got you toast, cheese, jam, dates, eggs and a few apples.' He sat on the bed, leaned over and kissed her. 'I thought you'd be pleased.'

'I am,' she said; 'suspicious, but pleased. You not sleeping well?'

He shrugged. 'Not really, but don't worry about it.'

'Is it because you haven't had a drink for four days? It is messing with your sleep?'

His smile wavered for a moment. 'Let's not talk about that.'

'But it's a big deal, Corthie,' she said, sitting up. 'We should talk about it.'

'No, we shouldn't. Just let me get on with it, but without trying to analyse everything as we go along.'

She nodded, but bit her lip at the same time. She knew he was doing it for her, and was glad to see him sober, but at the same time she worried that he would resent her for it.

'I've been thinking a lot,' he said, 'about what we should do next. I've already spoken to Belinda and Vana this morning, and we've agreed...'

'Wait,' she said. 'This is all a bit early for me; I've just woken up.' She rubbed her face. 'Why are you so... talkative, if you've not had much sleep?'

He shrugged. 'Coffee.'

'How many cups have you had so far today?'

'Just three.'

'Three? Malik's ass, no wonder you're bouncing around like a puppy.'

He got up and brought the tray over to the bed. She glanced at the full plates and bowls, her stomach rumbling at the sight.

'You've brought enough to feed a small village,' she said, picking up a slice of buttered toast.

'I wasn't sure what you'd want, so I brought everything.'

She resisted the temptation to point out the reason that he didn't know what she ate for breakfast was that he was usually too hungover to ever be around at breakfast-time. She swallowed her bite of toast and picked up a glass of orange juice.

'What were Belinda and Vana saying, then?'

He glanced at her. 'They agreed we should have a meeting, today. We've been sitting around on our arses for days, moping about after Karalyn disappeared.'

'That was because we half-expected her to come back.'

'Aye, but I don't think she is. Four days, and nothing. Right now, she'll be with her twins, and the last thing she'll be thinking about is coming back here.'

'I'm sorry. I know you miss her.'

'She was wrong about us. Her mind was all messed up by what happened to her. I mean, Lennox must have died over four years ago, but to her it was only a few months. She's still grieving for him. That's why she said those things, I think. Our relationship's not doomed; it's the best thing that's ever happened to me.'

'We'll get back to your world one day. That's the plan, right? We'll see your family, once...'

'Once we've made sure that your world is safe first.'

Aila chewed her lip.

'We can't leave here and go back to my home,' he went on, 'not while the gods are hunting for your home. It wouldn't be right; we wouldn't be able to relax, or live in peace knowing that the gods could be ransacking the City for salve. We can't let Emily and Yendra down like that.'

'But you still want to go home?'

He glanced at her. 'Aye. I want to see my mother, and even Keir and Kelsey, I suppose. And Jemma and Thorn, and little Cole. I want to see the house on the Holdfast estate, and ride the horses across the endless grasslands where I grew up. It's beautiful; you'll love it there.'

'And there are no gods?'

'None.'

'Then I'll be the only immortal.'

'Aye, but folk don't have to know that. The Holdfasts are good at keeping secrets; you'll blend right in.'

Aila frowned. 'Karalyn will have told your mother about me. She'll have used me as the reason you didn't go back with her. Your family will hate me.'

His eyes narrowed. 'Why do you have to be so negative? Why is everything a problem? Can we not live our lives without worrying about things that might never happen?' He looked away. 'Sorry. I don't want to fight.'

'I guess having lived through nearly eight centuries gives me a different perspective,' she said. 'I've seen so many generations of mortals come and go. Servants at Cuidrach Palace that looked after me when I was little, and then, before I knew it, their grandchildren were looking after me, and then *their* grandchildren. Sometimes I'd get confused and call someone by their father's name, forgetting that their father had retired or worse, had died. I could count my long-lasting friendships with mortals on one hand; people that I knew from youth to old age.'

'How many times have you been in love?'

'Not often. Naxor and I used to complain about how all of the gods and demigods of the City were related, dooming us to never meeting anyone we could spend centuries with. I guess he thinks he's solved that problem for himself, finding Belinda.'

'Maybe you'll find yourself a god, long after I'm gone.'

She took his hand. 'Don't say that. For you, I wish I was mortal. I wish we could grow old together. You're strong, Corthie, but one day age will catch up with you, and you'll look at me and hate me. Immortality is a curse as well as a blessing. Eternal youth seems wonderful, but it hardens your heart, and makes you cynical, and bitter. I know I seem negative to you; Malik's ass, I am negative, but it's only because I already know what loss feels like – I've felt it over and over, and I've tried to shield myself from it.'

A tear slipped down her cheek, and she glanced away, angry with herself.

Corthie lifted his hand and wiped the tear with a gentle touch of his finger. 'My mother will like you, of that I'm sure. You're strong-willed, a quality she respects. More than that, if we get married, then you'll be a Holdfast, and that's what really matters to her.'

Aila tried to smile. 'Is she like an all-powerful matriarch, ruling over the infamous Holdfasts?'

'Aye. The Empress was always getting angry with her for putting her family first.'

'The Empress?' She shook her head. 'When I first met you, I admit that I assumed you were a low-born warrior, but you're actually like a prince on your world.'

He laughed. 'Far from a prince, but my family is powerful and, aye, rich too. Karalyn will one day be Holder Fast, the chief of the Hold Fasts, the greatest family of the Holdings. As the youngest of four children, it'll never fall to me, but I'm grateful for that. I'd never want the responsibility.'

'I was the ninth child of eleven,' she said, 'so I know how that feels.' She stretched again, feeling the warmth of the new day come in through the windows. 'I should take a shower.'

Corthie glanced at the plates of uneaten food. 'Are you not hungry?'

She caught his eye. 'Not for breakfast.'

He pushed the tray to the side, and took her in his arms.

The meeting was scheduled to take place in Lord Irno's private drawing room, deep within the keep, where thick stone walls kept the temperature cool and pleasant, while outside, the blazing noon sun beat down without mercy upon the land. Both of Aila's siblings were already present when she and Corthie knocked and entered. Wide slats high up on the walls provided some illumination, but Irno had also lit several lamps, and he was sitting in his comfortable chair, reading a book. Vana was busy re-arranging the furniture, pushing chairs around so that they were laid out in a circle.

'Welcome,' said Irno, putting the book down onto a little table next to him, where a glass of raki also sat.

'Sit, sit,' said Vana.

Aila raised an eyebrow at her as she selected a chair. Corthie sat next to her, and she noticed his gaze flicker over to the raki.

'Naxor and Belinda should be here in a moment,' said Vana. 'Now, what would you like to drink? Wine, raki, ale?'

'Eh, just water for me, thanks,' said Aila.

'Aye, me too,' said Corthie.

Vana looked a little put out for a moment. 'We have some wonderful white wine, just in from the port this morning. It has a natural fizz to it; quite lovely.'

'Thanks,' said Aila, 'but water is fine.'

Irno laughed as Vana narrowed her eyes. 'Let them be, sister. If they want water, then get them some water.'

'Actually,' said Corthie, 'I'd love a coffee.'

Vana's features brightened. 'Certainly, champion. Milk and three sugars, was it?'

'Aye, that's right.'

'The door opened as Vana went off to a long side table, and Naxor walked in, his arm entwined with Belinda's.

'Greetings, all,' he said as they strode across the floor. 'I'd offer to help with the drinks, but dear Vana seems to have it all under control. I'll have a glass of that white I overheard you mention.'

Vana rolled her eyes. 'Certainly, cousin. Belinda?'

The god's gaze was on the row of packed bookshelves that lined an entire wall of the drawing room.

'Belinda?' repeated Vana.

She turned. 'What?'

'Would you like a drink?'

'No.'

Naxor emitted a low cough.

Belinda frowned. 'No, thank you.'

Irno laughed again. 'Belinda, feel free to borrow any of my books. Some are in a variety of local dialects, but most are in the Divine Language. I have history, politics, geography, and whole shelves of poetry.'

Belinda nodded as she glanced back at the hundreds of volumes. 'I never saw the point of poetry, but I might read some history. Do you have any fiction?'

'Yes. Much it has been copied from the old glory days of Khatanax. There hasn't been much literature to speak of on Lostwell for some time.'

A smile appeared on Belinda's lips. 'The glory days? You mean when I was queen?'

Irno's expression darkened a little. 'Indeed. Or so I believe.'

Vana came back over to the circle of chairs with a tray, and handed out the water, coffee and wine to the guests. Belinda pulled her attention from the books and sat to Corthie's right, between him and Naxor.

'Thank you all for coming,' said Irno, 'although I think I'm correct in saying that it was Corthie's idea that we all meet. With the departure of Blackrose, Maddie and Karalyn, we should perhaps spend a little time considering what, if anything, we wish to do now.'

Vana was the last to sit. She lit a cigarette and sipped from her white wine. 'I think you all know my feelings on this. I've made no secret of the fact that I am pleased that the dragon and the Holdfast woman have gone. The Falls of Iron is a refuge; a safe place in Khatanax, which is a rare thing indeed. Now, I mean no offence to the champion, but his sister's presence here was rather unsettling, to say the least. What I want is for things to return to normal, which means peace and quiet.'

'But our world's in danger,' said Aila; 'the City is in danger.'

Vana groaned. 'Not this again. I've told you countless times – Sable's word cannot be trusted. Belinda, you would agree, yes?'

'I would, but her story was confirmed by Karalyn. The gods of Implacatus have sent a small army to Alea Tanton, and their mission is to find the source of the salve. Reason dictates that they will make their way to the Four Counties sooner or later.'

Irno settled in his chair. 'I have long feared that this day would come. Salve has made its mark on the gods, and it was inevitable that they would eventually stir. I have to agree with Aila and Belinda's assessment. The Falls of Iron could be in danger. Naxor, it is time you were clear with us regarding the mechanism by which you distributed and sold the salve in Alea Tanton.'

Naxor smirked. 'No chance. It has remained a secret precisely because I have told no one, and I'm not about to start now.'

'Alright,' said Corthie, 'without giving anything away, tell us this – if the gods successfully read the mind of every merchant in Alea Tanton, will that lead them here?'

Naxor raised a finger. 'Vana? Could I try one of those cigarettes?'

'What?' said Belinda. 'Have you started smoking?'

'No. Well, not yet. I was thinking of seeing what it was like.'

Vana lit a cigarette and passed it to him, as Belinda sat back and folded her arms.

'Naxor?' said Corthie. 'Answer my question.'

The demigod glanced at the lit cigarette in his hands. 'Yes.'

Irno frowned. 'Yes? Does that mean they would be led here?'

'Yes.'

Corthie's knuckles whitened as they gripped the sides of his chair. 'Then they're coming?'

'I don't know,' said Naxor. 'Only a tiny handful of merchants in Alea Tanton know anything about the salve trade, and none know the whole picture, but, in theory, if every single one of them was rounded up and thoroughly read, and the gods were clever and good at putting the pieces together, then the name of Gadena would eventually come up, and if he were also interrogated, then it would point to us, here.' He glanced at the others, going from face to face. 'Look, no system is fool-proof. Try to devise the perfect way of keeping the trade a secret, and I'll bet a fortune that none of you could match what I came up with. I am easily the cleverest person in this room, well, the most cunning at any rate.'

'No one is blaming you, cousin,' said Irno; 'but we need to know what we're up against. Should we warn Gadena? He's a decent enough fellow; perhaps we should give him time to prepare, or to flee.'

'We need more information,' said Corthie. 'My aunt is in Alea Tanton. If we could get in contact with her, we could learn what the gods are planning. Naxor, can you reach the city with your powers?'

'Unfortunately not,' he said. 'The mountains in the way are too massive, and my range doesn't reach.'

'Sable reached here fine,' said Aila.

'Yes, well, she's a Holdfast, isn't she?' said Naxor. 'The normal rules don't seem to apply to them.'

'I might be able to reach,' said Belinda, 'once my inner-vision has been restored.'

Naxor glanced at her. 'I do perhaps think you're holding onto a vain hope. Karalyn may well have been lying to you. After all, you've told me that she lied to you in the past. Maybe this was her way of betraying you one last time.'

'No,' she said. 'You're wrong about her. If Karalyn said she'd restored my powers, then she has; it's just a matter of time.'

'Should we send someone to Sable in person?' said Corthie. 'If we can't use powers to contact her, then that would be the next best thing. How long does it take to travel there?'

'Four days by ship, or twelve by land,' said Irno; 'but who would go?'

Naxor smiled. 'Obviously, it would have to be me.'

Belinda glared at him.

'Why?' said Aila.

'Only I know the city of Alea Tanton,' he said. He placed the cigarette onto his lips and inhaled. Immediately, he started coughing, his face going red.

'Serves you right,' said Belinda. 'You going to Alea Tanton is bad enough, but with Sable there? She'd twist your mind just to get to me. You'd be like wet clay in her hands.'

'Then maybe we should go in numbers,' said Corthie; 'the four of us that came from the City. Go to Alea Tanton, and kick the gods' arses for them. Kill every one that travelled from Implacatus, and steal their Quadrants. Why should we sit here waiting? Let's link up with Sable and take the fight to them; destroy them before they have a chance to gather their strength and strike. Naxor has the local knowledge, Aila can infiltrate them with her powers, and Belinda and I can do the killing.'

The room sat in silence for a moment as the god and demigods digested the words of the only mortal in the room.

'I understand your impatience,' said Aila, 'but we could be walking into a trap.'

'I agree,' said Belinda. 'What's our objective? We want to keep the world of Pella a secret from the gods of Implacatus. If we go marching into Alea Tanton, then what's to prevent the gods from sending massive reinforcements? What about this Gadena person? If he's the link between the merchants of Alea Tanton and the Falls of Iron, then we should kill him.'

Corthie glared at her. 'No. Gadena's a good man.'

'Really? Even though he trains soldiers for the gods? And let's not forget that he turned you into a killing machine, Corthie.'

'It wasn't like that. Gadena was kind to me. He was just doing his job. Irno suggested that we should warn him. Naxor – does your range reach his training camp?'

The demigod nodded. 'Yes.'

'So, we warn him, aye? Can we at least agree to that?'

'I don't think that would be wise,' Naxor said. 'I've known him for hundreds of years, and, if it came to it, he would sell us out to save himself. If we inform him that the gods are coming, he might well decide to go to Alea Tanton and tell them everything.'

'Even more reason to kill him, then,' said Belinda.

'No,' said Corthie, his eyes tightening.

Vana shook her head. 'We don't seem to be getting anywhere, do we?'

'So what do you suggest?' said Aila.

'You need to get another Quadrant,' she said; 'then you, Corthie, Naxor and Belinda can follow Karalyn back to her world.'

'And leave you in peace, you mean?'

Vana smiled. 'Precisely.'

'That's not an option any more,' said Irno; 'not if the danger from the gods is real.'

'If there are too many objections to killing Gadena,' said Belinda, 'then we have no choice but to fortify the Falls of Iron and wait for our enemies to come to us.'

Vana looked aghast, but Irno nodded. 'So be it,' he said.

There was a gentle tap on the door to the drawing room, and a servant entered.

'My lord,' he said, bowing.

'Yes?' said Irno. 'I asked for no interruptions.'

'Apologies, my lord, but we have a visitor.'

Irno narrowed his eyes. 'Who?'

'A Lady Silva, my lord. A demigod. She claims to have travelled here from the ruins of Dun Khatar, in order to see Lady Belinda.'

Belinda frowned. 'To see me?'

'Yes, my lady. She arrived by ship from the Southern Cape this morning.'

'And where is she now?' said Irno.

'I placed her in the guest suite on the ground floor, my lord. Shall I send her up?'

'No. We shall go to her.'

The servant bowed. 'As you wish, my lord.'

Irno waited until the servant had closed the door behind him, then got to his feet. He turned to Belinda. 'How did she know you were here?'

'I don't know,' said Belinda. 'I've never heard of anyone called Silva.'

'Then,' said Naxor, 'either she's from your forgotten past, or she's pretending to be. Vana, use your powers to locate her self-healing, and see what else she's hiding.'

Vana nodded, and put down her glass. 'This will just take a moment.'

Aila glanced at Corthie as Vana's eyes hazed over.

'This was a waste of time,' he muttered. 'If we left tomorrow, we could be in Alea Tanton within a few days, and we could put an end to the threat against the City.'

Aila nodded but said nothing, wondering how much of Corthie's desire to take action was due to his boredom, and his need to fight someone, anyone.

Vana blinked. 'She has traces of vision powers,' she said; 'not altogether unlike my own. She can sense when the powers of others are used. I may be wrong, but I think she could have used such a skill to track Belinda here to the Falls of Iron.'

'And that's it?' said Irno. 'No death powers or battle-vision; nothing she could use to surprise us?'

'No,' said Vana.

'Then let's go downstairs and greet our visitor.'

'All of us?' said Belinda, standing.

'Yes. If she can sense powers, then she will already know that we are all here, and besides, I'm curious to learn if this Silva really is a relic from your past.'

They left the comfortable drawing room and descended the stairs to the ground floor of the castle's keep. The servant was waiting for them, and showed them to the guest quarters. Irno knocked on the door, and entered. Aila waited until the others had gone in, then followed. Inside, a woman was sitting on a wooden chair, her clothes soiled from travelling. She looked tired and, for a demigod, Aila thought she appeared quite old, perhaps resembling a mortal in her forties.

The woman gazed up at them, then her eyes widened at the sight of Belinda. She threw herself to her knees before the god, her hands clasping the hem of Belinda's tunic.

'You're alive, your Majesty!' she wept. 'Oh, my lady, my dear lady; you have returned. Praise the Ascendants, my wait is ended.'

Belinda frowned down at the woman, looking a little embarrassed. 'I have no idea who you are. Stop touching me.'

The woman cried out, sobbing. 'How can this be?'

'My memories are gone,' Belinda said, pushing the woman's hands from her clothes. 'Who are you?'

'I am your own Lady Silva, your most loyal and faithful Silva. I served you for centuries, during the golden times, and then throughout our long hiding in the mountains after the gods destroyed Dun Khatar.'

Belinda's eyes hardened. 'Prove it.'

'But, how? You truly have no memory of me?'

'None.'

Silva turned to the others, and her gaze landed on Naxor. 'I recognise you. Before the fall of Dun Khatar, you came to the city several times, bearing salve. You traded with Lady Agatha, and then, after the city's destruction, you never came back.'

Naxor raised an eyebrow.

'Do you recognise her?' said Belinda.

'Maybe?' He shrugged. 'I met a lot of gods and demigods back then. But I never met you, though, Belinda, my darling.'

'Her Majesty never left the side of King Nathaniel while he lay in his long sleep,' said Silva. 'She gave up all of her public duties, and Agatha ruled in her stead.' She reached out with her hands again and touched the god's arm. 'It was I who gave you the salve that returned you to your youth, your Majesty. It was I who ministered to your every need. And when King Nathaniel died, it was I who mourned by your side. I did everything you asked of me, but I'm sorry, I couldn't stop the gods from taking our stronghold when you left with Agatha and the others. They desecrated King Nathaniel's tomb, my lady.'

'Slow down,' said Irno. 'When was this?'

'Seven years ago, my lord. The Queen, Lady Agatha and five others departed Lostwell, to go to the world that King Nathaniel had created for them. I was ordered to stay behind, but the gods of Alea Tanton put us under siege, and... they took the King's body. They were searching for the Sextant, but when they couldn't find it, they took his Majesty's body instead, as a trophy.'

Irno folded his arms across his broad chest. 'I recall some of this. I knew that the gods of Alea Tanton had sent an expedition into the mountains south of the ruins of Dun Khatar, to search for rebels or so I believe, but this is the first I've heard of them finding Nathaniel's tomb.'

'Never mind that,' said Naxor. 'What's a Sextant?'

Silva glanced from Naxor to Belinda, her cheeks glistening with tears.

'Tell him,' said Belinda.

'As you wish, your Majesty,' she said. 'The Sextant is the device that King Nathaniel used to create his new worlds. He made the world that Lord Malik and Lady Amalia travelled to when they fled Lostwell, and then he made the world that caused him to fall into his long sleep.'

'And how long was this sleep?' said Irno.

'Five hundred years,' she said, 'and then, one morning, he died. Such was your grief and anger, my Queen, that you decided to leave Lostwell altogether, and went with Agatha to the King's new world, the last he ever created.'

'And the Sextant?' said Naxor. 'Where is it?'

'I don't know, my lord.'

'How can you not know?' said Naxor.

'Because, my lord,' she said, 'the Queen hid it before she left.'

Corthie laughed.

'I fail to see what's so funny,' Naxor said. 'This device sounds like something we should try to acquire. The gods of Implacatus will certainly want to get their hands on it, should they learn of its existence.' He shook his head and whistled. 'It can create new worlds? And the only person who knew where it was hidden has no memories.'

'Lady Agatha also knows where it is,' said Silva. 'Did she return with you, your Majesty?'

Belinda said nothing.

'Agatha's dead,' said Corthie. 'They all are, except for Belinda. You should know that I killed one of them myself – a god named Gregor.'

Silva wept aloud, and tugged at her hair with her fingers as her lamentations filled the room.

Aila frowned at Corthie, who shrugged.

Irno put his hand on Silva's shoulder. 'Come, sit. Are you hungry?'

She pushed his hand away, and crawled across the floor to a large trunk, which was lying open. She reached in through the piles of clothes, and took out a sword, held in a jewel-encrusted black leather scabbard. She crawled back to Belinda, and prostrated herself before her, holding the weapon aloft.

'For you, my Queen,' she sobbed. 'I kept it safe – your sword. The Weathervane. I kept it for you.'

Naxor smirked. 'The "Weathervane"?'

'Shush,' said Belinda. 'This woman is in pain.' She took the weapon, and placed her right hand onto the engraved hilt. She drew the sword from its scabbard and glanced at the sleek, long blade. The metal was dark, almost black, and its edge glistened in the sunlight filtering through the shutters.

'You fought the Wars of the Gods with that sword, your Majesty,' said Silva, her head lowered. 'You defended Lostwell to the end, my Queen.'

Belinda glanced down at her. 'I'm not a queen any more.'

'You're wrong, your Majesty.' Silva raised her eyes. 'You are the Blessed Third Ascendant; you are the rightful Queen of Khatanax and all Lostwell, and, whether you remember it or not, you always will be.'

CHAPTER 18

THE CREATOR

Alea Tanton, Tordue, Western Khatanax – 9th Tradinch 5252

Sable's eyes opened as soon as the first rays of the sun appeared in the east. She shivered in the chill air of the abandoned turret and pulled the blanket around her more tightly. Within a couple of hours it would be roasting, but the cold bit into her each morning. She could feel Millen's presence lying next to her, and was tempted to cuddle into his body for warmth, but didn't want to encourage him, or give him any false hopes.

She rolled onto her back and glanced up at the cracked and worn stonework above their heads. It took her over an hour to get ready each day for work, and she didn't want to get sacked for being late, but lethargy kept her wrapped up in the blanket. She considered not going into the residence that day. Domestic labour didn't suit her, and she was fed up chopping onions and fetching pails of coal for the kitchen fires.

Seven days, and still no sign of any Quadrant. Renko was good – he kept his mind guarded and his thoughts hidden, and she had only enjoyed a few moments inside his head. The locations of the three Quadrants in his possession were buried somewhere in his voluminous memories, and it was like trying to find a single word on a page within a vast library of books. She had also trawled through the heads of the other gods

– Maisk, Joaz, Latude, but none of them knew where Renko had placed the Quadrants. The Ancient didn't trust them; he didn't trust anyone. Sable had learned much, but none of it was useful to her. Hundreds of merchants had been interrogated in the search for the source of the salve, and dozens more were arriving up the ramp from the lower city every hour, crammed into wagons amid crying children, and then shoved into cramped cells throughout the large basement of the residence.

Millen turned, and his arm brushed her side. His eyes were closed, but Sable was sure he was awake. He had stopped trying to sleep with her, his confidence dented by her constant refusals, and she had begun to regret the one time they had been intimate in the merchant's district. It had seemed like fun at the time, but she wouldn't have bothered if she had known how clingy Millen would be. She frowned. That was her problem. She was supposed to be a ruthless assassin, a cold-blooded killer, but she had a need to be liked, and Millen's obvious feelings for her had made her feel good about herself. It had been the same when she had held Karalyn's sister Kelsey hostage for months. The girl had detested her, and Sable had responded by trying to make friends with her. It hadn't worked, and Sable had no doubt that Kelsey still loathed her, wherever she was.

She had never had a genuine friend, she realised. Her job involved deceiving people into thinking they were friends, but that was all it was – a deception. She glanced at Millen. She could do a lot worse. He was handsome, and had a good heart. He waited for her to get back to the turret every day, and made her meals, and washed her work uniforms. And he loved her. Well, he thought he did. Or, at least, he was in love with the version of her that she had presented to him; but she didn't love him in return. It had been too easy. How could she respect someone who fell for her instant charms, someone who had no conception of the countless times she had been cruel, the countless times she had killed without hesitation or regret? He didn't know her; no one did. Except Karalyn, perhaps.

'You should leave while you still have the chance,' she said.

His eyes opened. 'What?'

'You heard me. I can help you sneak out of Old Alea. There's a way out close to where the aqueduct crosses the walls that's not even guarded. I don't think the Banner soldiers are aware of it. From there, you'll be able to make your way back to the lower city.'

He sat up, and pushed his fingers through his shoulder-length brown hair. 'You want rid of me?'

She glanced up at him from where she lay. 'I don't want your death on my conscience.'

He lowered his head. 'I'm such an idiot. I really thought you liked me. When you asked me to run away with you that day at the arena, I thought, wow, this woman actually wants me. And then, when we were... together in that big house in the merchant's district... but that's where it all went wrong. Did I do something stupid? I mean, you were with Gantu for ages, and all it took was one night with me, and...'

Sable narrowed her eyes. 'Don't be silly.'

He glared at her. 'What else am I supposed to think? One minute you're urging me on, the next you're ignoring me.'

'Let me tell you a secret,' she said; 'I never actually slept with Gantu; not once.'

'But I heard him boast about it, several times.'

Sable sat up. She had no desire to tell Millen the truth about her powers, and how she had used them to send Gantu to sleep, but it rankled that the oaf had been boasting about her.

'He was lying,' she said. 'He was making it up.'

He frowned at her. 'Are you telling me the truth?'

'I swear to you that I didn't sleep with him. That satisfy you? You should get up – your insecurities won't make any breakfast.'

He pulled the blanket off and stood. 'You can be a bitch at times; you know that?'

She nodded. 'It's because I prefer you angry to whiny. Angry I can deal with; whiny just makes me want to slap you.'

He stormed off into the small side room where they kept their supplies, and Sable lit a cigarette, trying to suppress a smile from creeping across her lips.

'Now, my cousin,' Isa said as they washed up the coffee pots in an enormous sink, 'she has a son your age – a lovely boy. I think you'd like him. He's obsessed with the arena games, but so is every man in the city, eh? A real Bloodflies fan, he is, but he has a heart of gold. I could easily have a word with his mother, and...'

'Thanks, Isa,' Sable said, her arms in the hot water up to the elbows, 'but I'm not looking for a boyfriend.'

The older woman eyed her. 'You're twenty-eight and unmarried, Sable. I worry about you. I was hitched at twenty-one, and had given birth to three little ones before I was your age.'

'I don't need a man, and I don't want any children.'

'You say that now, Sable, but you don't want to be a lonely old woman.'

Sable glanced at her.

Change the subject. Never talk about marriage or babies or anything like that with me again. Talk about the weather instead.

Isa blinked, then turned to the little window. 'It's going to be another roasting hot day today. Not a cloud in the sky.'

'Does it ever rain?'

'Up high in the mountains it does, but not so much down here in the lowlands. The old rulers of Khatanax built these great big reservoirs in the hills, and covered Tordue in aqueducts and canals, otherwise it'd be like the Fordian Wastes here, all dried up and lifeless. If anything were to happen to those reservoirs, Alea Tanton would be finished.'

Sable shrugged. 'What could happen that couldn't be fixed?'

'A lot,' Isa said. 'Earthquakes, for one. And it's not safe to go up those mountains any more, not with all the colonies of wild dragons living there. It chills my blood that one of them got so close to the city. Praise the Ascendants that the Banner managed to drive it off.'

Sable nodded. The story of the wild dragon that had been stopped ten miles from the edge of the city had been the number one topic for discussion among the kitchen staff over the previous couple of days.

'I wish I'd seen it,' Sable said.

Isa frowned. 'Why?'

'The only dragon I've ever seen was chained up in the pits. I'd like to have a look at one in flight.'

'You've seen one chained up in the pits? And which pits were these, might I ask?'

'The Central Pits.'

Isa stared at her. 'Please don't tell me that you're a Blue Thumb, I don't think my old heart could take it.'

'I'm not a Blue Thumb. Frankly, I couldn't care less about the stupid teams.'

'Then what were you doing in that arena?'

Sable shrugged. 'I might have been dating a Blue Thumb supporter for a while.'

Isa pulled a face. 'Eurgh. Nasty. That'll be why you've gone off men. I could set you up with a nice Shinstran boy...' She blinked, as if remembering she wasn't supposed to talk about that. 'Anyway, tell me about the dragon you saw. I have a terrible suspicion that I know which one it was.'

'Its name was Sanguino.'

Isa sighed. 'I thought it would be. Those damn Torduans. Sanguino's the Bloodflies' dragon – I assume you know that?'

'Yeah, the arena announcer said that. He also said that they were going to kill it, in just over a month from now, before a big game.'

'He's a "he", not an "it", I'll have you know.' She shook her head. 'The poor beast's been fighting for the Bloodflies for near on thirty years. If they kill him, the city will burn for days. The Shinstrans rioted when Kemal was killed, and they didn't even like him all that much. They love Sanguino.'

With the last of the coffee pots washed and sitting on the drying rack, Sable pulled the plug from the sink to let the water drain away.

'I felt sorry for it, I mean him,' she said. 'They were poking him with spears while he was all wrapped up in chains.'

'It doesn't surprise me, dear. The Torduans are assholes.'

'You mean the Shinstrans wouldn't do the same if they captured the Blue Thumbs' dragon?'

'Certainly not. The Shinstrans have honour, and, much as it pains me to say it, the Deadskins are the same. Both teams have captured dragons over the years, and neither have killed them. Humiliated them, yes, and paraded them about in chains – but they were always handed back afterwards. This is a new low.'

The overseer appeared at the door. 'Hey, coffee-girl-rat-killer, get yourself cleaned up. You're wanted upstairs.'

'But it's not lunchtime yet.'

'Lord Renko's called a meeting of the gods, and I need every servant with permission to serve them up there. It'll be in the Most Noble Ancient's study, not the dining room, so whatever you do, do *not* stare at the body of the old god if you see it. Are we clear?'

'Don't stare at the withered corpse; got it.'

Sable reached for a towel and dried her arms.

'Be careful up there,' said Isa.

'This will be my fifth trip up to the quarters of the gods.'

'I know, and I worry about you every time. I wish you weren't quite so pretty.'

'Umm, alright.'

'You know what I mean, girl.'

Sable pulled on a fresh, clean apron, and Isa tied it behind her back.

'See you later,' she said to the older woman, then went through to the main kitchens. A group of young servants had been lined up, and they set off when Sable joined them. The lead pair of servants were pushing trolleys, and the rest followed them along the service corridors to the lift shaft by the western tower of the residence. The head servant walked up and down, glancing at them as they waited to ascend.

'The first six shall be on food, the last six on drinks,' she said to them. 'Every god in Old Alea except Lord Latude will be present, so best behaviour. Not many of you will have been inside Lord Renko's personal rooms, so I must warn you. Lord Renko keeps a body on his desk...'

'The overseer has already told us, ma'am,' said one of the younger servants.

The head servant glared at her. 'I will dismiss you from your post if you interrupt me again. As I was saying, this... body is precious to Lord Renko. Under no circumstances are you to stare, comment, or otherwise draw attention to it.'

One of the servants raised her hand.

'Yes?'

'Who is it, ma'am?'

The head servant bit her lip for a moment. 'The Fourth Ascendant, King Nathaniel.'

Sable's eyes widened. Nathaniel? The Creator himself? How had she not known? She had heard the corpse being mentioned a few times, but had never once stirred herself into finding out its identity.

'Off we go, then,' said the head servant, gesturing.

The lead servants pushed the two trolleys into the lift shaft, while the rest of them started to climb the stairs. Sable tried to calm her breathing as they ascended the old, worn steps. It occurred to her that appearing nervous would help her fit in, but the reason for her nerves swirled around her brain. The Creator. Was she actually about to see his real body?

They reached the upper floor of the tower, passing the entrance to the dining room. Soldiers from the Banner were waiting for them outside another door, and each servant's name and pass were checked against the logbook. The trolleys were pushed from the lift platform, and Sable was handed a full bottle of raki and a long napkin, which she hung from her left arm. The head servant gave them all a final glance, then nodded at the soldiers, who opened the door.

The servants filed into a large chamber. It was filled with stuffed bookshelves, and large maps and tapestries were hanging from the walls. At the far end of the room were high windows, and the upper portion of each held stained glass images of the gods, while several real gods were sitting on long couches in front of an enormous desk. Despite all of the warnings, Sable's eyes were drawn to the corpse that was lying on the surface of the desk. It was wrapped in white linen sheets, but the dry and shrunken features of its face were visible.

The servants fanned out into the chamber, offering drinks, and a selection of food from silver trays. Sable stood frozen, staring at the body on the desk. Without meaning to, without any real conscious thought, she walked towards it, ignoring Lord Maisk's request for raki.

The Creator. She gazed down at the body. This... being, this man; she had worshipped him for years. Her entire life had revolved around her service to the god who had created her world. A true god, or so she had thought. So many years of loyal faith; he had been the pillar of her life, her one hope for redemption; and it had all been lies.

She burst into tears and dropped the bottle of raki onto the floor.

Behind her, there was silence for a moment, then she heard the sound of someone rushing towards her.

'I'm so sorry!' cried the head servant. 'I'll remove this stupid girl from your presence immediately.'

Sable felt a hand grip her elbow, but she didn't care.

'Wait,' said a voice.

Lord Renko appeared by Sable's side. He glanced at her, then gently pushed the head servant back.

'This servant,' he said, 'should not be punished for weeping at the sight of the Fourth Ascendant. The sight makes me weep too.' He wiped the tears from Sable's face. 'Clean up the mess, mortal girl, and get back to work.' He turned to the other gods in the room. 'It seems we have found a mortal who feels the loss of Nathaniel as keenly as we do. Now, let us continue. Lady Joaz, you said you had an update concerning the interrogation of the merchants?'

Sable and the head servant crouched down by the dropped bottle. The head servant shook her head as Sable picked it up. It had fallen onto the carpet, and was still in one piece, but much of the raki had poured out.

'Yes, my lord,' said Joaz as the two servants put napkins down onto the spill. 'So far, over eight hundred merchants have been examined but, until this morning, there have been no clues or leads regarding the source of the salve trade.'

Sable got back to her feet, and poured some raki into a glass that Maisk was holding out. He was staring at her, a touch of amusement on his lips.

'Until this morning?' said Renko.

'Yes, my lord,' said Joaz. 'A few days ago, I read the thoughts of a dealer in ceramics, and discovered something – a fragment of a conversation that had taken place with a banker friend of his. Today, I located the friend, and it seems that he was one small piece in the jigsaw puzzle.'

'And has this "friend" handled any salve?'

'No, my lord, but he has handled the gold resulting from the sale of salve.' Lady Joaz produced a large notebook from under her long robes. 'He marked the flow of gold in here.'

Renko took the notebook as Sable got into position behind the chairs, waiting for anyone to ask for raki. She kept her gaze away from the body on the desk, not trusting herself to keep her composure if she saw it again.

'Are we sure these payments were for salve?' said Renko as he thumbed through the leaves of the notebook.

'Yes, my lord. It's not written anywhere within the book, but I read it from his mind.'

'There are several large payments made out to someone called Gadena,' said Renko. 'Do we know who this might be?'

Lord Baldwin coughed. 'If I may, my lord?'

Renko glanced at him. 'Proceed.'

'Gadena is a demigod who lives on the edge of the Shinstran Desert. He has a large mercenary camp there, where he trains soldiers. We've hired him a couple of times, to deal with unrest in Kinell.'

'He has also sent mercenaries to other worlds,' said Lady Felice. 'I remember hearing he sent several detachments to Dragon Eyre.'

Renko nodded. 'So someone is selling salve in order to raise troops?

Good work, Lady Joaz, thank you. Lord Maisk, I want you to travel to the camp where this Gadena lives. Take Lord Baldwin with you to show you the way. And Lady Felice, you shall go too. Use your vision powers to stay in communication with me here. I want reports daily.'

The selected gods nodded.

'Am I in command of the expedition, my lord?' said Maisk.

'Yes. Find out what this Gadena knows, and then report to me before acting. Understood?'

'Yes, my lord.'

'I have a further question, my lord,' said Joaz.

Renko nodded to her.

'The cells under the residence were not built to fit more than a few hundred prisoners, and already we have over a thousand crammed in. Should we start releasing those who have been questioned?'

'No,' said Renko. 'None shall leave until our investigations are complete. If you need to make room, start executing some of them. There are bound to be many who have broken the law in one way or another. Mark down the worst offenders, and hang them.'

Joaz bowed. 'Yes, my lord.'

'And are you also searching for information about the other matter we discussed?'

Sable glanced up, and shot her vision into Joaz's mind.

'Yes, my lord,' the god said.

The Sextant, Sable saw in her mind. Renko is hunting for the Sextant.

'And?' he said.

'Nothing so far, my lord.'

'Very well, keep looking.'

Maisk raised his glass again, and Sable went round to stand next to him. His hand touched her thigh as she poured the raki, but she didn't react, suppressing her feelings of revulsion as he leered at her. She pulled back once his glass full, and went to stand by the wall.

'Have you any idea how lucky you are?' the head servant shouted at her as they descended the steps an hour later.

Sable raised an eyebrow. 'For getting felt up by Maisk? I don't feel very lucky.'

'Don't get smart with me, girl; you know what I'm talking about. If I had guessed for a second that you were going to act like that, I would never have let you up there. What possessed you to start weeping in front of that withered old corpse?'

'It may sound stupid to you, but Nathaniel used to mean a lot to me.'

The head servant screwed up her face at her. 'What? You're mad, girl.'

The overseer was waiting for them at the bottom of the stairs.

'Did you hear what happened?' said the head servant. 'Did you hear what this idiot did?'

'Yeah, I heard,' he said. 'That's why I'm here.'

The head servant put a hand to her mouth. 'Oh no. By the Ascendants, what do they want? Is she to be executed?'

'No,' said the overseer, 'though coffee-girl-rat-killer might soon wish she had been. The Most Noble and Ancient Lord Renko wants her for his harem.'

Sable's eyes widened. 'Me?'

'Yes, you. You obviously made an impression on him. Now I have the job of escorting you all the way back upstairs, to show you to where you'll be living.'

'Can I not go home first?' she said. 'I have people there who might wonder where I am.'

'You married?'

'No.'

'Kids?'

She shook her head.

'Then my answer is no. You can send a letter once you're settled in. It'll be censored, so watch what you write.'

'And I'm losing a coffee girl?' said the head servant.

'You can hire another one,' said the overseer, 'we have the budget for it.'

The head servant glanced at Sable. 'Oh dear. Well, you brought it on yourself. Good luck.'

Sable and the overseer watched as the head servant led the other servants back towards the kitchens. A few of them gave sympathetic smiles to Sable, and then they were gone.

The overseer glanced at her. 'You don't seem particularly upset. Most girls get a little hysterical when the news is broken to them.'

Sable shrugged. 'Should I be worried?'

The overseer laughed as they started climbing the stairs back up the tower.

'How many are in Lord Renko's harem?' she said.

'You'll be the fifth to have been selected. The other four are all local girls from Alea Tanton. You're from Kinell, yeah?'

'That's right.'

'You got a criminal past?'

'What?'

'Just checking if you have any secrets. If you do, then prepare to have them sucked out of your head. Lord Renko always checks the minds of the girls in his harem.'

Sable smiled. 'I have nothing to hide.'

'Good.'

'What's he like? Are the girls well treated?'

'How should I know? All I do is send them up there; what goes on behind the doors of the harem is none of my business.'

They reached the door to Renko's private study, then the overseer led her along a passageway to the right. He nodded to a pair of soldiers standing guard by another door.

'Got a fresh one here,' he said to them.

The soldiers nodded, and one opened the door.

'This is where I leave you,' said the overseer. 'All the best. Oh, before I forget, you'll have to let me know where to send your pay. Write me a note, yeah?'

Sable glanced at him, then walked through the door. She came into a dimly-lit chamber, where sunlight was coming through closed shutters in narrow strips.

'Hello?' she said, as her eyes adjusted to the gloom. She sniffed the air. 'Is that dreamweed I can smell?'

She made out a series of long, low couches, where four women were reclining in the shadows. One got to her feet. She had long, blonde hair, and was wearing a dressing gown tied at the waist.

'Oh look,' she said to the others. 'We have a new arrival. What's your name?'

'Sable.'

'Where you from, Sable?'

'Kinell.'

'Well, welcome to Renko's harem.' She passed her a lit weedstick.

'Thanks,' said Sable, taking it and inhaling. She glanced around the untidy room. 'Is this what you do all day; sit about and smoke?'

'Oh no,' she said. 'We drink a lot too.'

Sable relaxed, and focussed her thoughts. The sun had set, and there had been no sign of Renko within the confines of the harem since she had arrived. She gazed out of the window of her tiny bedroom, and let her vision soar through the air, heading south. Her sight flew over the vast fields of Tordue, then climbed the high mountain range. The barren peaks and valleys flitted by beneath her, until she reached the cliffs and saw the Falls of Iron, nestling against the side of the mountains, its lamps lit for evening. She pushed her vision into the castle, and went to the room where she had been on her last trip.

The demigod was sitting alone, reading a book on Lostwell history. Sable smiled, and entered her head.

Good evening, Aila.

The woman jumped, her eyes wide. 'Sable?' she spluttered.

Hold on a moment.

Sable went to the part of Aila's mind that controlled what she saw, and produced an image of herself, to make it appear that she was sitting on the bed next to the demigod.

'How's that?' she said, her image smiling.

'Better,' said Aila, 'but still a bit strange. How are you? I wasn't sure if you'd ever reach out to me again.'

'I'm fine, thank you. I thought I'd drop by to check if my beloved niece has arrived yet.'

'Karalyn? Oh. Well, she came back, and then she left again.'

'She left?'

'Yes, Sable. She took the Quadrant and went back to her world.'

Sable almost broke the connection to the Falls of Iron. Karalyn had left? She started to cry, and as she was mirroring her own position, the image of her that Aila saw started to cry as well.

'I'm sorry,' said the demigod.

'She left?' Sable repeated, the tears streaming down her face. 'She abandoned me? Bitch. I knew she hated me, but I never really believed she would leave me here without a word. What have I been doing these last months? I've been searching for a Quadrant, for her, and she leaves me? And why are you still here? I thought she would have taken you back with her?'

'She left us all here, Sable. She refused to take me, so Corthie said he wasn't going. So she left, on her own.'

A cold fury started to replace the shock of having been abandoned. 'She left Corthie as well? That demented, lying cow.' She wiped away her tears, her eyes narrowing with anger. 'Fine. I half expected her to betray me. Fine.'

'What have you been doing?'

'Working. I got a job as a servant in the residence in Old Alea where the gods live, and today I got selected to join Lord Renko's harem. He's the leader of the gods that have come from Implacatus.'

Aila pulled a face. 'That doesn't sound good.'

'It'll be fine. It means that I'll have access to his personal rooms, where I know he's hiding three Quadrants.'

'But... his harem? Will you have to...?'

'Don't worry about me. Three Quadrants, Aila. As soon as I get my hands on one, then I'll be out of here.'

'Get more than one if you can.'

'Why?'

'Because Karalyn stole the Quadrant from a dragon – a friend of ours. She's trying to go back to her home in Dragon Eyre, but Karalyn took the Quadrant from her. In fact, watch out for a dragon, she might try to contact you.'

'Contact me? How?'

'I don't know, but she knew that you were looking for a Quadrant in Alea Tanton, and she might decide to head that way.'

Sable frowned. 'A dragon was shot and injured a couple of days ago. It flew too close to the city defences.'

Aila's mouth opened. 'Malik's ass. That might be her. What happened?'

'She escaped. The city authorities are saying that they bravely managed to drive her off, but if they shot her down, then they should have been able to kill her.'

'Could you please try to find out? She had a rider – a young woman called Maddie. I'd really appreciate it if you could find out if she's alright.'

Sable paused for a moment. She had little interest in helping a dragon's rider, and almost told Aila as much, but something was stopping her. Aila seemed to like her, even though she hadn't tried to use any manipulation on her. Aila did like her; she could see it in the demigod's mind. Aila needed a friend, and Sable could sense the many times that the demigod had defended her in front of the others who loathed her.

'Alright,' she said. 'I'll do some rooting around and see what I can find.'

Aila smiled. 'Thanks, Sable. Do you know anything about the gods' investigations into the salve trade?'

'Yeah, but nothing has been mentioned about the Falls of Iron. They're after some mercenary training guy.'

'What? Gadena?'

'Um, yeah. You know him?'

'If they find him, then he'll lead them to us.'

'Oh. Well, the gods are going to his camp to question him.'

Aila stood. 'I'd better tell the others. Sable, thank you. I can't tell you how much you contacting me means. If you find Maddie, please let me know.'

Sable nodded. 'Sure. Bye.'

She cut the connection, and her vision returned to her body in an instant. She lit a cigarette, and the smoke drifted up and out through the open window.

Karalyn had gone, and Sable was free from her control, so why did her heart feel like it was breaking? Had her niece despised her so much that she could leave without saying a single word? And Karalyn hadn't just left; she had abandoned Sable on a strange, foreign world, where she was alone.

She thought of Aila, Corthie and the others in the Falls of Iron. Maybe not completely alone. She steeled herself. She would find out if the dragon that had approached the city was the same one that Karalyn had stolen from; and she would find the girl called Maddie.

CHAPTER 19

WILLPOWER

Tordue, Western Khatanax – 9th Tradinch 5252

Maddie kept her head down as she wandered along the dusty path. The setting sun was in her eyes, and she was dazzled every time she lifted her head to glance towards the approaching city. Two days had passed since Blackrose had escaped from the soldiers that had encircled them, and Maddie was hungry and tired. She had ditched her crossbow the night before, worrying that it was more likely to get her shot than be of any use, and had slept hidden in some deep, thick undergrowth, where she had shivered from the cold.

She ducked to the side of the path as she saw another roadblock ahead. She cursed as frustration gripped her. She had been walking for miles, and every way that led to the city was blocked by soldiers. It didn't make sense. Were they hunting her? But how could they know about her? She eased herself into the dried-up ditch by the side of the path, and stared at the soldiers ahead of her. There were only three of them, but they looked well-armed, and were wearing helmets and armour.

Could she bluff her way past? She would have tried if she had been on her own world. There, she knew everything about the City, and would have been able to lie with ease; but on Lostwell she was, well, lost. She knew nothing about the peoples inhabiting the land, or their culture or history, and from the accents she had heard, she knew she would stand out as soon as she opened her mouth.

She felt a sense of panic flicker through her stomach. Even if she made it past the soldiers, what would she do next? Blackrose's plan had involved Maddie finding Corthie's aunt somewhere in a city of millions; it was impossible. The dragon had placed too much faith in her. Maybe her old riders had been expert warriors, or spies who could infiltrate the enemy's defences, but what skills did Maddie have? She swung her bag round and placed it on her lap. Inside, she still had some food; not much, but enough to get her through another day out in the open. She lifted out her water bottle, removed the stopper and took a drink. The water was warm after a hot day in the sun, but she didn't mind.

The sound of birds singing and chirping floated across the vast fields to either side of the road. There were stands of trees, and rows of thick hedges criss-crossing the landscape, but the only other people in sight were the soldiers. She sighed. If she were Corthie or Belinda, she would be able to fight them; if Aila, she would be able to put on a disguise to slip past; if Naxor... well, she didn't know what he would do, but it would probably be something sly and cunning.

She heard a cough from the path.

Her eyes darted up, and she saw the end of a crossbow pointing down at her, held by one of the soldiers she had seen blocking the road.

'You look a little lost, ma'am,' he said, a wry smile on his lips. 'You looking for a dragon?'

Maddie scowled up at him. 'Bugger off.'

He chuckled. 'Name?'

'None of your damn business,' she said from the ditch. 'Leave me alone.'

'That is one strange accent, ma'am.' He glanced down the road. 'It's her. We've got her.' He turned back to Maddie. 'You armed? If you are, tell me now, or things might have to get ugly.'

'As ugly as you? Can a girl not sit in a ditch minding her own business without getting harassed?'

'I'm going to take that as a "no",' the soldier said, swinging the crossbow over his shoulder. 'If I'm wrong, and you do have a weapon, then...'

She threw her water bottle at him. He ducked, and it flew over his head. He raised an eyebrow, then reached down into the ditch and hauled Maddie up to the road, his strong arms pulling her to her feet. The other two soldiers had walked forward, and one grabbed Maddie's wrists, and pulled them behind her back as the other tied a cord to secure her hands.

'About time,' muttered one of them. 'I thought we were going to have to spend another night out here.'

'So sorry for inconveniencing you,' said Maddie. 'Are you arresting me? I haven't done anything wrong. Is it a crime in these parts to sit in a ditch?'

The first soldier nodded along the road. 'This way.'

The other two soldiers took an arm each, and led Maddie along the road. The first soldier picked up the flung water bottle and put it into Maddie's bag, which he slung over his shoulder.

'Has she given her name?' said the soldier on Maddie's left. 'Are we sure it's definitely her?'

'I'm right here,' said Maddie. 'I hate it when people refer to you when you're with them. 'Did she do this?"; "Did she do that?" Why don't you just ask me?'

The soldier narrowed his eyes. 'Alright; what's your name?'

Maddie thought for a moment. Was there any point in denying it? Her accent was what had caused her to be caught. The soldiers didn't look particularly cruel or brutal, but they were alone on a deserted road, and, for once, she decided it was perhaps not in her best interests to antagonise them.

She lifted her chin. 'I'm Maddie Jackdaw, a sergeant in the Auxiliary Work Company, and, before that, a corporal in the Fourteenth Support Battalion, Auxiliary Detachment Number Three.'

One of the soldiers frowned at her. 'Yeah? A sergeant, eh? You in a Banner?'

'A what? A Banner? What's that then? Apart from being, you know, a flag. I know what banner means.'

'Clearly not,' muttered the soldier on her right.

'Are you guys in a... Banner?'

'The Banner of the Golden Fist, ma'am.'

Maddie shrugged. 'Never heard of them. Why are you after me?'

'Orders. Find the foreign girl called Maddie. Something to do with the dragon that was driven off the day before yesterday.'

'First, I'm not a girl, I'm a woman. Second, foreign is kind of relative. I mean, you guys are foreign to me, so why is it that I'm called the foreign one, eh? You thought about that? You're picking on me just because I have a funny accent, well, your accents sound stupid to me. In fact, this Lostwell seems like a stupid place altogether.'

One of the soldiers sighed and shook his head, while another laughed. 'She's right, you know. Lostwell is a dumbass place. We're not from here either, ma'am.'

'Ah,' she said, 'so you're "foreign" too?'

'Let's have some quiet,' said the first soldier; 'we've still got a mile to walk before we come to the command post.'

'But I'm enjoying this little chat,' said Maddie. 'I've not spoken to anyone in ages, as I was using my sergeant skills to evade capture. I mean, I'm pretty proud that I managed to last two whole days on the run. That reminds me, apologies if I'm a bit stinky; I could really do with a bath. Can I have a bath whenever we get to wherever you're taking me?'

The first soldier shook his head. 'You're our prisoner, not a damned guest. I imagine there's a dark little cell waiting for you.'

'Oh. That's a shame. I was kind of hoping...'

'Shut up,' he said, 'before I put a boot up your ass.'

Maddie frowned. 'What would your mother think if she heard you speak like that?'

The soldier stopped on the road. The others halted as he pursed his lips. 'Gag her. I can't take another mile of this.'

The next fifteen minutes passed in silence. The gag covering Maddie's mouth was loose enough to let her breathe, but so tight that any sound she made came out muffled. The soldiers trailed along a series of dusty paths, until they approached a large barn, where wagons and other soldiers were gathered. They were all in the same uniforms, Maddie noticed, and looked professional, reminding her of the infantry companies of the Blades on her own world.

The cluster of soldiers watched as Maddie was escorted into their midst.

'We got her,' said one of her escorts. 'Sergeant Maddie Jackdaw.'

An officer stared at her for a moment. 'Excellent work. Remove the gag.'

The soldier frowned, but did as he was told.

'At last,' said Maddie, flexing her mouth. 'That stung a little.' She glanced around at the crowd of soldiers. 'Were you lot all looking for little old me?'

'Please confirm your name,' said the officer.

'Maddie Jackdaw, just like the man said.'

The officer nodded. 'Right, everyone,' he shouted to the crowd. 'Time to go. Send scouts to all of the roadblocks and recall the squads. I want Eagle Company back in the city before nightfall.'

The soldiers began to scatter.

The officer turned to the three who had brought Maddie in. 'Get her into a wagon.'

'Yes, sir.'

Maddie was led off towards a row of covered wagons, and helped up into the back of one, her wrists still bound behind her back. The three soldiers got in with her, and one attached a shackle to her right ankle, securing her to the chassis. A pair of huge, lumbering lizards were brought to the front of the wagon, and Maddie gazed at them. They looked so similar to dragons, but their eyes were dull and lifeless in comparison. They were just about to move off, when another officer appeared at the rear of the wagon.

'You?' said Maddie.

The officer smiled. 'Yes. Me.' He glanced at the three soldiers. 'Out. I want to speak to our captive alone while we travel back to the city.

'Yes, sir,' they said, then they clambered down to the ground.

The officer climbed up, and took a seat on the low bench opposite Maddie. He reached into a pocket as the wagon began to move, pulled out a knife, and cut the cords binding her wrists. He put the knife away and took out a silver case.

'Cigarette?' he said.

'Em, yeah, alright,' said Maddie, taking one. 'What do I do with it?'

He lit one for himself, then held out a burning match. 'You smoke it.'

She shook her head. 'Nah. I'll watch you do it first, I think.'

The officer shrugged. 'My name is Captain Van Logos.'

'That's a funny name. Why are you still alive? I saw Blackrose fly off, so I assumed she had ripped your head off.'

Van nodded. 'Blackrose?' He frowned for a moment. 'Wait a minute; that name's familiar to me. Blackrose?' He sat back on the bench, his eyes tight, as if he was trying to remember something.

Maddie watched him for a moment. 'Why didn't she kill you?'

He glanced back at her. 'I talked her out of it. Told her it would be crueller to let me live, and I appealed to her sense of honour. That usually does the trick with dragons. Well, high dragons at least.'

Maddie laughed. 'High dragons?'

'Yes, as opposed to wild ones. Tell me, what were you planning to do? Why are you on Lostwell?'

'Are you going to torture me if I don't tell you?'

He raised an eyebrow. 'Let's say yes.'

'Hmm. I'm not sure I believe you.'

'Do you want to take the risk?'

'You don't seem the torturing type, despite the horrible stories you told us about what you did on Dragon Eyre. Do you really feel guilty for what you did? Hang on, why am I asking that? Blackrose was making you tell the truth, so it can't have been a lie.'

'Why are you on Lostwell?'

'Why do you care?'

'Several reasons. For one, I don't want your dragon interfering in our operation here in Khatanax. Secondly, I'm curious. Let me tell you a little secret. I've not told high command that I had Eagle Company searching for you. They think I was merely securing the area in case the dragon returned. None of the gods know that the dragon we were hunting had a rider; they all just assume it must have been a wild dragon.'

'And why would you keep it a secret?'

'Because I haven't decided what to do with you yet. If I have to kill you, then I'll need to be able to dispose of your body without any awkward questions.'

'That's not very nice.'

'I'm not a very nice man. Why are you on Lostwell?'

'Maybe we fancied a holiday.'

'How did you get here from Dragon Eyre?'

'Who says we came from Dragon Eyre?'

Van frowned at her, and Maddie wondered if she had made a mistake.

'The name Blackrose is familiar to me,' he said after a while, 'but I don't recall her fate. I remember hearing her name when I was deployed to Dragon Eyre, and I have a feeling she was meant to be dead. Are you telling me that she was hiding on another world? Is she trying to get back to her home?'

Maddie glanced out of the rear of the wagon at the lines of soldiers marching along the track behind them.

'Look,' said Van; 'forget about the torture. It would be unnecessary. If you don't tell me the truth, then I can take you up to Old Alea, and have one of the gods read every thought in your mind. But then you would belong to them, not to me. And believe me; you don't want to belong to them.'

She turned back to face him. 'Where do you live?'

'Me?' said Van. 'Alright, I'll tell you. I'm from a place called Serene, on Implacatus. The vast majority of the soldiers in the Banner are also from there.'

'Implacatus?'

'It's the home of the Ascendants.'

'Who?'

Van narrowed his eyes as if he was working out if she was ignorant or lying. 'You've never heard of the Ascendants?'

'Nope.'

'They're the twelve oldest gods in existence. So old, they come from a time before there were any gods. Only six of them still live on Implacatus. The Second Ascendant rules, while the Banner were sent here by the Seventh.'

'What happened to the First?'

'She died millennia ago. The Ascendants are assisted in their rule by the Ancients – gods who have lived for over ten thousand years. That's how it works. Any god that reaches ten millennia becomes an Ancient.'

A memory flashed through her mind; something Blackrose had said to her about Belinda, and the Ascendants. She wished she had paid more attention. A trickle of fear ran down her spine, not from Van and the soldiers, but from the thought of having her mind read by a god.

'How would you react,' she said, 'if you discovered that Blackrose wants to go back to Dragon Eyre?'

He lit another cigarette. 'Well, hypothetically, if I were to find that out, then I don't think I would necessarily do anything. I'm never going back to Dragon Eyre, and you have to remember that I don't give a monkey's ass about the politics of it all. The Banner are mercenaries – professional soldiers. We're paid to fight, not to care about the causes we're fighting for.' He blew out a cloud of grey smoke. 'Well, is it true?'

'It might be.'

'Why did she send you to Alea Tanton?'

'Guess.'

He laughed. 'Will you tell me if I guess correctly?'

She shrugged.

'Alright, let me see. Revenge? No. If she wanted to kill an old enemy who had harmed her, then, no offence, but she wouldn't send someone who doesn't know how to hold a crossbow properly.'

'Cheeky sod.'

'You also seem to be fairly useless as a spy, or a thief, so that rules out stealing something such as, let's say, a Quadrant.'

'I could be a good thief if I wanted to be.'

'I doubt that. What else? You're meeting someone?'

Maddie said nothing.

'Who?'

'Why are you on Lostwell?' she said.

'I think you're forgetting who is doing the interrogation here.'

'Answer me, and I might answer you.'

His gaze pierced her. 'Salve.'

Her eyes narrowed for a fraction of a second, and he nodded. 'Interesting response,' he said. 'Perhaps I should hand you over to the gods. If you know anything about salve, then I'll probably get a medal or something.'

'Is that what you want, Van; a medal?'

'What I want is none of your business. Who are you meeting?'

Maddie bit her tongue. The trickle of fear was turning into a torrent. If the gods were looking for salve, and they read her mind, then her entire world was in danger. She imagined hordes of gods and mercenaries arriving in the City; they would tear it to shreds, and it would be her fault.

'Light my cigarette,' she said.

'Sure, Maddie,' he said, striking a match and holding it out in front of her.

She lit the end of the cigarette, and inhaled. Her face went red, and she started coughing. It settled, and she took another draw.

'My head feels a bit woo,' she said.

He smiled. 'Who are you meeting?'

'Me and the dragon have fallen out,' she said, 'and we decided to go our separate ways. I'm heading to the city to look for a job, so I don't starve to death.'

'You're a terrible liar.'

'No, I'm not. I'm an excellent liar. However, I'm telling the truth. See, I'm perfectly innocent, and this has all been a huge misunderstanding. Will you let me go now?'

The wagon came to a halt before the officer could respond. He turned to the rear, where another soldier had appeared.

'Lieutenant,' said Van; 'what's the hold up?'

'Captain,' the officer said, saluting; 'we have new orders, sir. We're to accompany Lord Maisk south, into the Shinstran Desert. We're due to leave at dawn.'

Van sighed. 'The Shinstran Desert?'

'Apparently we have a lead, sir. A mercenary training facility is down there, and the owner might have some useful information.' He glanced at Maddie.

'Hi,' she said.

'Ignore her, Sohul,' said Van. 'I'll need to speak to Major Ahito about this. Stick the girl in the fortress dungeons, but keep her name out of the records. No one is to speak to her until I return; understood?'

Van clambered down from the wagon. He glanced back at Maddie, then threw her the silver case and a box of matches.

'I'll be back for the case,' he said. 'Don't lose it.'

She put it into a pocket along with the matches as Van disappeared round the side of the wagon.

Lieutenant Sohul frowned at her. 'I suppose I'd better get you to the dungeons, then.'

***

Maddie had been hooded, and her wrists had been bound again, before the wagon set off through the streets of the city. She had heard the noises of people bustling on the road on either side of the wagon, but no one had said a word to her for the rest of the journey. She had then been led into a vast building, and escorted down several flights of stairs to the cells. Her hood and wrist cords had been removed, and she had been shoved into a dark, cramped chamber that stank of stale urine. The door had been locked behind her, plunging the cell into darkness.

Hours passed, though she had no way of telling how long she had sat on the damp stone floor of the cell. To alleviate the boredom, and her jangling nerves, she had smoked her way through the contents of the silver case, but that had only made her feel sick. When the cigarettes were finished, she struck the rest of the matches, her eyes taking in the dark stone walls surrounding her with each brief illumination.

She needed to pee, but crossed her legs and held it in. She had tried shouting for attention, but no one had come. To take her mind off it, she thought back to the many times she had been locked up in the cells in Stormshield fortress by the Great Walls of the City, for getting in fights, or for talking back to her superior officers.

Just as she was starting to believe that she had been forgotten, a key turned in the lock, and the door swung open. Her eyes were dazzled for a moment in the bright light of an oil lamp as a man walked in and closed the door behind him.

'Van?' she said, backing up against the cell wall.

'Yes.'

He rested the lamp on the floor and gazed down at her. His eyes seemed strange, as if they had a hazy quality.

'Are you alright?' she said.

Van said nothing. Instead, he sat on the floor opposite her. Maddie frowned, then felt a pressure behind her eyes.

Don't scream or shout.

'Uh, what?'

I'm in you head.

'Why have you got a woman's voice?'

Because I am a woman – it's Sable Holdfast. Aila asked me to look out for you. Right now, I've taken control of Captain Van Logos. I've been in his head a few times, and noticed him come up to Old Alea this evening. And through him, I found you. Now, let's get you out of here.

'Wait a minute. I need a moment to digest this. I don't deal well with people in my head.'

A woman appeared in the cell before her, smiling, with her hands on her hips. 'That better?'

Maddie reached out with a finger, but it passed through the vision of the woman.

'I'm not really here,' Sable laughed.

Maddie frowned. 'You've taken control of Van? You mean, you can make people do things against their will; like Karalyn?'

'Not quite. I'm powerful, but my niece's abilities far outweigh my own. I can only make people do things that deep down they want to do, or at least that they're not completely opposed to doing. I could never have persuaded you or the dragon to hand over the Quadrant, for example.'

'You know about that?'

'Yes. As I said, I've been in contact with Aila. She was worried about you, and asked me to help.'

'Aila's worried about me? I thought she didn't like me.'

Sable shrugged. 'Looks like you might have been wrong about that. I know you're hurting about my niece's betrayal, but she abandoned me here too. I say we work together, to get what we need. I can help you get a Quadrant – I'm so close; but first, you need to get out of this cell before the gods find out who you are.'

'Did Van tell them?'

'No. His mind is conflicted on what to do about you, but Lady Joaz read his thoughts when he was in Old Alea, so they might put the pieces together.' She glanced at the still form of Van, who was sitting with his vacant eyes open. 'He's not evil, and I feel a little bad for all the crap I've put him through. In his heart, he knows he's fighting on the wrong side, which is why I'm able to get him to help us.'

'And where are you?'

'I'm in Old Alea, but I intend to come down to the lower city soon – with at least one Quadrant. I reckon I'll need another day to get my hands on one, and then I can meet you. Do you reckon you can last a day in the city on your own?'

'And you'll steal a Quadrant for me and Blackrose? Why?'

'Do you want my help or not?'

'Yes.'

'Then stop arguing with me. When you get out of the fortress, make your way to the Southern Pits, there are hostels close by. Find one called *The Rosy-Cheeked Pig*, and wait for me there. I'll find you.'

'When?'

'Tomorrow night, most likely; maybe dawn on the following day. Keep your head down in the meantime; got it?'

Maddie nodded.

'I'm going to vanish now, and let Van do his thing. Do exactly what he says, and remember, I'll be controlling him.'

The vision disappeared and Van turned his head to gaze at Maddie.

'Get up,' he said, standing.

Maddie got to her feet as Van swung a bag from his shoulder. He pulled out a long, black hooded cloak and held it out.

'Put this on.'

She took it, and slid her arms into its sleeves, then pulled the hood up to cover her hair.

'Follow me.'

He led her from the cell, and they stole down a silent and deserted passageway. They climbed a set of stairs, and walked out into the warm night air. In the centre of a courtyard, soldiers were loading a long line of wagons, but Van stuck to the shadows by the wall, and they crept by unnoticed. They reached a stout wooden door, and Van pulled a set of keys from a pocket. He unlocked the door, then turned to Maddie.

He pointed. 'Go.'

She frowned at him for a moment, a stab of pity filling her. She shuddered at the power of the Holdfasts, then stepped through the door, which closed behind her with a dull thump. She glanced around. She was on a wide road, filled with traffic despite the late hour. Behind her stretched the walls of the fortress, while before her were packed streets, with tall, ramshackle tenement blocks, and shops selling hot food and cold ale. Carts filled with produce were being pushed along the worn flagstones, and everywhere was noise, and a thousand different smells, all of them better than the dank urine of her dungeon cell.

She smiled, and approached an old woman who was leading a donkey.

'Hello,' she said. 'Can you tell me the way to the Southern Pits, please?'

CHAPTER 20

MIND GAMES

A lea Tanton, Tordue, Western Khatanax – 10th Tradinch 5252

Van woke with a pounding headache, and for a moment he assumed he was hungover, until he remembered that he hadn't been drinking. He retched, then realised that he couldn't recall anything he had done the previous night. He reached for his jacket, in order to get a cigarette, but his silver case was missing. He frowned, and glanced around his quarters. Everything seemed fine, and his clothes were neatly folded on a chair by the bed.

That was odd, he thought, he was never usually that tidy.

He scratched his head, trying to recall what had happened. He remembered returning from the countryside, after securing the area in case the wild dragon had tried to return, and then he remembered going up to Old Alea to speak to Major Ahito about their new orders. That's right, he thought, he was meant to be leaving for the Shinstran Desert at dawn.

He got off the bed and rummaged through his trunk until he found a spare pack of cigarettes, then lit one as he opened his shutters. The sky to the east was starting to lighten and he sat in a daze for a moment, the headache battering away behind his temples.

What had he done after speaking to the major? He must have

returned to the fortress, for that was where his quarters were located, but he had no memory of doing so. He must have had a drink, it was the only explanation, but then who had folded his clothes? He had suffered from a few memory lapses over the years, always related to over-indulging in alcohol, dullweed or salve, and always when he had been off duty. Never while on operation; never.

A fear gripped him. Had he succumbed to the temptation of salve? No, the pain in his head was testament to that. Salve might have induced memory loss, but he would be feeling great if he had taken some of that.

There was a knock on his door. 'Captain?'

'Yeah?'

The door opened and Sohul appeared.

'Is it time to leave?' said Van.

'Yes, sir. Lord Maisk has requested that we make our way up to Old Alea immediately – and we're to bring our two best squads with us.'

'Old Alea?'

'Yes, sir.' Sohul frowned. 'Are you alright? You don't look very well.'

'To be honest, I feel like crap. Do you remember me coming back down to the fortress last night?'

'No, sir. I didn't see you after you left to speak to Major Ahito. I put that prisoner into the dungeons just as you asked.'

'Eh? What prisoner?'

Sohul smiled. 'Sorry, sir. I forgot it was a secret.'

Van stared at him. 'Damn. I'm finally losing my mind. Come in and close the door.'

Sohul did as Van asked. 'Sir?'

'Tell me about the prisoner.'

'Can you really not remember her, sir?'

He shook his head.

'Alright,' Sohul said. 'She was linked in some way to the appearance of the dragon, but you never mentioned how or in what capacity. Her name was Maddie, and you told me to place her into a cell, but not to let anyone speak to her.'

'Is she still there?'

'I would assume so, sir.'

Van scratched his head.

'If I may, sir?'

Van narrowed his eyes. 'What?'

'I heard that the sergeant of the third squad gave you a high dose of salve, sir, after the dragon injured you.'

'So?'

'Could your memory loss be attributed to that? Maybe you're suffering from some sort of withdrawal symptoms.'

'Is that possible?'

'I don't know, sir, but I have heard of salve addiction causing all kinds of problems.'

'I've also lost my silver cigarette case.'

'I can help you there, sir. I saw you give it to the prisoner before you left.'

Van stood and reached for his clothes. 'Alright; let's go pay the mystery girl a visit.'

———

They gazed into the dark, empty cell.

'Are you sure it was this one?' said Van, crinkling his nose from the smell.

'Positive, sir.'

Van glanced down at the logbook in his hands. 'There's no record of her arriving or leaving.'

'That's right, sir. You asked me to keep it quiet.'

'Did you let her out?'

'Of course not, sir. You told me to do nothing with her until you returned from Old Alea.'

Van pursed his lips. 'Not a word of this to anyone. I don't know what in the name of the Ascendants is going on, but if I'm going mad, then the fewer who know, the better.'

Sohul said nothing.

'Swear it,' said Van.

'I swear it, sir. I'll not tell anyone. But...'

'But what?'

'Well, as a friend, I'm a little concerned, to be honest. Perhaps you should go back to bed and get some rest. I can tell Lord Maisk that you're unwell.'

'No chance. I'm not giving that asshole an excuse to have me removed from my position. Look, my headache's lifting, and I feel fine. I can't explain the gap in my memories, but apart from that, I'm ready for anything.'

They closed the cell door and went up the stairs to the fortress's inner courtyard. Two lines of packed wagons were sitting in the centre of the yard, along with the soldiers of Eagle and Bear Companies. Two squads were standing off to one side, and Van and Sohul walked over to them.

The captain from Bear Company nodded as they approached.

'Captain Logos,' he said, 'I understand that you are on your way to Old Alea?'

Van nodded. 'I'm leaving Lieutenant Baku in charge of Eagle Company while I take Sohul and two squads up there. I guess we'll catch up with you at some point.'

'We've been ordered to remain here for now. I suspect you might arrive at our destination before the rest of us.'

'You might be right. Good luck.'

Van gestured to Sohul, and they began to head off to the far end of the fortress, the two squads following.

Van glanced at his lieutenant. 'See? I'm fine.'

They boarded a series of carriages at the rear gates of the fortress, and began to climb the long slope up the side of the cliff towards the gates of Old Alea. Van gazed out of the open window as they went, feeling the cool dawn breeze on his face. He pondered Sohul's words about salve withdrawal for a moment before dismissing it as a possibility. He had come off salve many times in the past, and had never experienced any memory loss. No, something else was happening to him. Perhaps there was a spy in the fortress – someone who had drugged him, and then set the prisoner free, but that wouldn't explain why he had no memory of her. A face flashed through his mind as he thought about the prisoner, a fleeting image of a young woman with brown hair. Was his memory returning?

He glanced at Sohul. As the only two officers, they were sharing a private carriage, and there was no one else within earshot.

'The prisoner,' he said, keeping his voice low; 'did she have long brown hair?'

'She did, yes.'

'And was she quite young?'

Sohul nodded. 'About twenty, perhaps? Is your memory coming back?'

'I hope so.'

He turned to look back out of the window as another possibility entered his thoughts. Were there gods who had vision powers capable of altering his memory? He had never heard of such a power, but there were numerous things that the gods kept secret from mortals. He was fairly sure that Lady Joaz had been inside his mind the previous evening. He hadn't felt her presence, but she had caught him with a lingering glance while he had been speaking to Major Ahito. Had she done something to him? He leaned out of the window and glanced at the convoy following them up the slope. The soldiers of the two squads were sitting on benches on the open backs of the carriages, and he looked for their sergeants.

Sohul raised an eyebrow at him as he sat back down.

'I was checking which sergeants were coming along,' Van said, 'to see if either of them were with us yesterday.'

'I believe it was the third squad who found the girl, sir. We have squads one and two with us today.'

'Damn it. I should have spoken to the third squad before we left.'

'You'll get to the bottom of it, I'm sure, sir. If you're starting to remember the prisoner's face, then give it a day or two, and the rest might come back.'

He glanced at the lieutenant. 'I'm not going mad. Something, or someone, has messed with my head.'

Sohul looked unconvinced. 'And do you have any suspicions about who would, or could, be able to do such a thing?'

'It has to be one of the gods. Imagine for a moment that one of them has a sneaky power that they can use to alter someone's memories. I mean, they can read them, so why not alter them too?'

'I've never heard of a god with such powers, sir.'

'You think I'm paranoid, don't you? Edmond's ass, I *am* paranoid. Bollocks.'

Sohul looked embarrassed for a moment.

'Come on,' said Van, 'spit it out.'

'I, um, would really rather you didn't take the Most High Second Ascendant's name in vain, sir.'

Van laughed. 'He can't hear us. Old Edmond might think he's omniscient, but believe me, he's not. He's just a stuck-up asshole like the rest of them.'

Sohul's eyes darkened, and the lieutenant looked enraged, his fists clenching.

Van raised his palms. 'Sorry. No, I'm sorry, really. I don't know what's wrong with me today. I've lost my memory, I'm paranoid, and I'm babbling a load of crap. I respect your beliefs, honestly, I do.'

Sohul sighed.

'Am I forgiven?'

'Yes, sir.'

'Don't desert me, Sohul; you're all I've got.'

'It's fine. I'll put it down to your... volatile state of mind. You know, as a friend, I blame it on that dose of salve you got a couple of days ago. You've not been yourself since. It worries me that you'll fall back into addiction, and you'll get dismissed from the Banner.'

'You might be right – on all counts. The major's made it pretty clear to me that if I get back onto the salve, then my butt will be kicked straight out of the Golden Fist. Don't blame the sergeant of the third squad, though; he was only trying to save my life.'

They quietened as the carriage came up to the gates of Old Alea. Banner soldiers glanced at the carriages, and waved them through, the corporal on duty saluting Van and Sohul as they passed. They trundled through the gatehouse forecourt, then entered the streets of the high promontory. To their right, the high towers of the Governor's residence were visible over the rooftops of the mansions and servants' accommodation, and they passed down long, tree-lined boulevards until they reached the backyard of the enormous building.

The officers stepped down from their carriage, and waited for the two squads to join them. A demigod courtier from Renko's household was standing by the entrance to the residence.

'Captain Logos?' she said. 'You are wanted upstairs.'

Van glanced at Sohul. 'Wait here with the squads until I find out what's going on.'

'Yes, sir.'

Van walked to the large entrance doors and followed the demigod into the residence. They turned right along a wide, marble-walled corridor, where portraits of the gods hung side by side, and reached the ornate stairwell leading to the upper floors. The demigod said nothing, so Van took her lead and remained silent as they climbed the steps to the gods' quarters. Van knew that Renko lived at the very top of the tower, while the other gods occupied apartments on the floors below their leader. Van was shown to a dining-room, where Renko, Maisk, Baldwin and Felice were seated. Around them, a flurry of pretty serving girls were filling plates and glasses, while trying to avoid Maisk's wandering hands.

'I have brought Captain Logos as requested, my lords and lady,' the demigod said, bowing.

'Thank you,' said Renko, raising a hand to dismiss her. 'Captain Logos, Major Ahito has recommended that you be chosen to lead the advance expedition.'

Van stood to attention. 'I would be honoured, my lord.'

'I'm sure you would,' said Renko, 'however, I feel you have not exactly covered yourself in glory throughout this operation. You gratuitously insulted Lord Baldwin and Lady Felice after all, did you not?'

'I did, my lord; and I was punished for my folly.'

'You were,' said Renko, as Maisk smirked. 'I admit, you wouldn't have been my first choice for this expedition, but Major Ahito continues to display great faith in your abilities. For his sake, as well as yours, I trust you will do your best not to let us down again?'

'You can depend on me, my lord.'

'Hmm. We shall see. Do you know anything about a training camp run by a demigod by the name of Gadena?'

'I do, my lord. I've never been to the facility, but I served alongside some of his battalions while assigned to Kinell.'

Renko nodded. 'We have reason to believe that he may have information vital to the success of our mission here on Lostwell. It appears that he was in receipt of several large payments from the trade in salve, and used those payments to train warriors for whoever was bringing the salve to Khatanax. If word reaches him that the Banner are on the way to question him, then he may panic, and flee. To prevent this, Lord Maisk, Lady Felice and Lord Baldwin will be using a Quadrant to travel directly to the training camp, and they will take you and your two squads along. It is imperative that we discover what Gadena knows about the salve trade, everything else is secondary; understood?'

Van bowed. 'Yes, my lord.'

'Good. Leave us, and wait in the rear yard. Lord Maisk and the others will be down after breakfast.'

Van bowed again, then left the dining-room. He turned to walk towards the stairs, when he saw Lady Joaz approach. He bowed.

'Captain,' she said. 'I hear you are going on a little trip?'

'Yes, my lady.'

'It's a pity we fell out,' she said, eyeing him. 'I used to enjoy your little visits to my rooms.'

He smiled. 'Perhaps we can resume them upon my return, my lady.'

'Oh, I doubt that,' she laughed. 'Not because I wouldn't like to, but because I don't imagine for a moment that Maisk, Baldwin and Felice will allow you to return. Not alive, at any rate. Farewell.'

She walked off towards the dining-room. Van watched her go, then began the long descent back down to the ground floor.

'Form a perimeter,' Van cried, 'protect the gods.'

The soldiers of the two squads moved into a tight circle around Maisk, Baldwin and Felice, their shields facing outwards. Van nodded to Maisk, and the god withdrew a Quadrant from behind his polished steel breastplate. He glided the fingers of his left hand over it, and the area surrounding them went hazy. The rear yard of the Governor's residence vanished, and was replaced by dry, packed sand. A blisteringly hot wind scoured over them, sweeping loose sand up into their faces. Van scanned around them, but saw nothing but featureless desert and barren ridges and slopes.

'Baldwin!' cried Maisk. 'Where are we?'

'I supplied the correct coordinates,' Baldwin said, a hand up to protect his eyes.

'Then where is the training facility?'

Baldwin glanced around, a look of worry on his face. 'Uh, I'm not entirely sure, my lord.'

Maisk scowled at him, then turned to Van. 'Captain, take a squad to the nearest high point and scout around.'

Van bowed, then gestured to Sohul and one of his two sergeants. 'Lieutenant, remain here and guard the gods,' he shouted over the howling wind. 'Sergeant, bring your squad with me.'

The soldiers moved off, with Van leading the way. They hurried over the sands, heading for the closest rock formation. The heat was intense, and Van could feel his bare skin starting to burn. The land around them was shimmering, and the air was filled with hot sand. They reached the shelter of a cliffside, and started to climb. The brown and grey rocks had been eroded into sinuous shapes that seemed to flow, and there were plenty of holes that they could grip onto while they ascended the slope. Van reached a wide ledge, and turned to gaze out over the landscape. To his left stretched a long range of barren mountains, while on the right, the Shinstran Desert led off into the horizon. The rest of the squad joined him on the ledge, and they peered around.

One of the soldiers pointed. Van squinted into the distance.

'I think that might be smoke, sir,' the soldier cried.

Van frowned, then he caught it – a grey tinge to the air, about a hundred yards ahead of them. The wind was gusting the smoke around, dissipating it amid the sand.

Van nodded. 'Let's check it out.'

They edged along the narrow ledge, keeping their backs to the rocks of the cliffside, which began to climb up behind them. The ridge curved in a long, slow loop, and as they got closer to the smoke, Van realised that it was coming out of a tall stone stack, set amid other high clumps and towers of rock. He jumped down from the ledge to the sand and approached the stack. There was a narrow hole near the top, from where the smoke was coming. It was thick and grey close to the vent, but the wind was whipping it away.

The sergeant glanced at him.

'A damn chimney,' Van said. 'The camp is underground.'

They called the other squad over, and the soldiers undertook a search of the area while the gods huddled by the cliffside to shelter from the wind. The temperature seemed to rise with every minute, and the morning sun glared at them from the eastern sky. At last, after a long hour of hunting through the sands, one of the younger soldiers called out to Van. He had tripped over what he had assumed to be dry bones, but which turned out to be a thick iron chain. The soldiers gathered round it and dug it out, revealing a long stretch of chain leading to a massive, iron-framed hatch set at an angle in the side of the rocky slope. The wind had piled sand up next to it, and they used their hands to scoop it away. The gods walked over once the entire hatch had been excavated, and Maisk told the soldiers to stand aside.

The huge god braced his muscles and powered his battle-vision, and with a grunt, he lifted the end of the hatch, wrenching it upwards. Beyond was a dark tunnel, wide and high enough for several soldiers to stand side by side. Van signalled to the squads, and they filed inside. Next came Baldwin and Felice, and finally Maisk himself, who stooped and entered, letting the hatch fall back down with a low clang.

One of the soldiers lit an oil lamp, and they glanced around in the chill gloom. Van shook his armour and clothes, sending streams of sand escaping down to the ground, then he splashed some water on his face.

Maisk gripped the large battle-hammer that he had brought with him, and gestured to Baldwin. 'You shall walk by my side. Kill anything that resists us.'

'Yes, my lord,' the god said.

Maisk turned to Van. 'Have the soldiers stay close to Lady Felice, and follow on behind us.'

Van bowed.

The two gods set off down the tunnel, the hulking form of Maisk towering over the more slender Baldwin. Next came the soldier with the lamp, who pointed the open shutter down the dark passageway, and then Felice and the rest of the two squads. Van stayed close to the lamp-bearer, his hand resting on the hilt of his sword.

'How many mercenaries are down here?' whispered Sohul as they made their way along the tunnel.

'I don't know,' said Van. 'Could be dozens; could be hundreds.'

The tunnel went on in a straight line, heading downwards on a slight gradient, ever deeper into the hillside. They passed a few stout doors to their left and right. All were locked, and some looked as though they hadn't been opened in a long while. After a few minutes, the tunnel opened out into a cavernous chamber. It was lit with a few lanterns, and was lined with stacks of barrels, and crates piled high against the rough walls. An old man was there, moving supplies into a wheelbarrow. He glanced up as the party entered the cavern.

'Halt, mortal,' cried Maisk. 'If you move, you die.'

The old man stared at them, his eyes wide.

'You will take us to Gadena,' said Maisk. 'No tricks.'

'Who... who are you?'

'We have come from Alea Tanton, bearing the full authority of the gods of Implacatus.'

The old man trembled, bowed, then bolted down a nearby tunnel. Baldwin raised his hand to unleash his death powers, but was too slow, and the old man disappeared into the darkness. Maisk glared at Baldwin, then they hurried to follow the old man. They went down the tunnel, then stopped at a junction, where three other tunnels branched away. The soldier with the lamp shone it down all three passageways, but each was deserted.

'Should we split up?' said Felice.

'No,' said Maisk. 'We must stay together. Isolated, we could be picked off one by one. However, we must be prepared for an ambush.' He turned to Van. 'Captain, you shall lead from now on; after all, you are somewhat expendable.'

'Yes, my lord.'

Van glanced at a sergeant. 'I'll take two soldiers and go on a little ahead.'

Maisk pointed at the middle of the three branches, and Van set off, a soldier by each side. They lit no other lamps, instead using the dull glow that shone behind them to guide their steps. Van's eyes squinted in the darkness of the tunnel, but the floor was smooth and level, and the going was easy despite the nerves twisting in his guts. They walked on for another minute or two, then Van heard sounds coming from ahead of them. He glanced back, and saw the rest of the party twenty yards behind them, then pressed on. They turned a corner, and emerged into a well-lit cavern, four times the size of the previous one. Dozens of armed warriors were forming into groups on the floor of the cavern, and one pointed at Van and the two soldiers. Shouts and cries rang through the cold air, and within seconds, the warriors in the cavern had formed a thick line. They were dressed in a wide variety of clothes and armour, and most were armed with swords, as if they had been practising before the party's arrival.

Van raised his empty hands into the air. 'We're here to speak to Lord Gadena,' he cried. 'No one needs to die.'

'It'll be you dying,' shouted one of the warriors.

'You're right,' said Van, raising his voice so that it filled the cavern; 'you can kill me and the two soldiers by my side, but behind me is Lord Baldwin, a god with death powers. If you attack, he will slaughter every one of you.'

The lines of warriors stared at him, but no one moved.

'Lord Maisk is also here,' Van went on. 'He has come from Implacatus. You know what that means. If you resist, then all of you will die. Tell Lord Gadena that we are here.'

A middle-aged man stepped forward from the crowd of warriors. He was protected by a thick steel breastplate, under which a long mail shirt could be seen. In his right hand he held a sword, which he raised and pointed at Van.

'There's no need to tell him; I'm right here. What do you want? This is my private domain, and you have no right to intrude.'

Maisk pushed his way past Van and strode out into the cavern.

'I have every right,' he said. 'I have been sent by the most holy and noble Seventh Ascendant, her Highness Arete. Get on your knees before me, Gadena, and I shall spare your pathetic band of mortal mercenaries.'

Gadena stood frozen for a moment, saying nothing, then he slowly lowered his sword. He glanced at the lines of warriors at his back, then dropped to his knees, placing the sword onto the stone floor before him.

'Forgive me, my lord,' he said; 'I am at your service.'

Van sat with his feet up on a table, smoking a cigarette, his eyes scanning the shelves of fierce-looking weapons that lined the walls of the cavern-office.

'Captain,' said Sohul, entering; 'all trainees and warriors have been disarmed and confined to their barracks.'

Van nodded. 'Good job, Sohul.'

'This place is enormous,' the lieutenant said. 'It could easily fit an army of five thousand. We were lucky, I guess; right now I'd say that there are only about four hundred warriors under training here.'

'Four hundred or five thousand, it doesn't matter,' said Van, 'Baldwin could have killed them all. We weak mortals would have been among the many casualties, but Maisk, Felice and Baldwin would have walked out of here unscathed.'

Sohul shrugged. 'It's our job, I guess, sir.'

'What, to die for these idiots?'

The lieutenant said nothing for a moment, then frowned. 'There was another reason I needed to speak with you, sir.'

'Yes?'

'Lord Maisk wants you.'

Van sighed and stubbed the cigarette out. He got to his feet and strode from the office, Sohul keeping pace next to him. They passed a few Banner soldiers on guard, and went down a long passageway to a row of holding cells. In the first one, Gadena was sitting, strapped to a chair while Maisk, Baldwin and Felice stood round him. The demigod's face was etched in sweat and pain, and his skin had a deathly, greenish tinge to it. Blood was running down his nose and chin, and staining the front of his tunic, the breastplate and chainmail having been removed.

Van entered the cell and bowed. 'Can I help you, my lord?'

Maisk wiped the blood from his hands and glanced at him. 'Time to take advantage of your local knowledge again, Captain. Despite having lived on Lostwell for centuries, it appears that Baldwin and Felice are somewhat lacking in curiosity about their domains.' He turned to Felice. 'Read the captain's mind. Find out everything he knows about the Four Counties and the Falls of Iron, and then contact Lord Renko in Alea Tanton. Tell the Most Noble Ancient that we have discovered the centre of the salve trade.'

Felice bowed low. 'Yes, my lord.'

CHAPTER 21

TRUNKFUL OF TROUBLE

Falls of Iron, Western Khatanax – 10th Tradinch 5252

'I don't understand,' said Aila.

'You're not the only one,' said Corthie. 'You're going to have to try to explain it better, Silva.'

The demigod nodded, but her eyes remained on Belinda, who was standing by the open window, her gaze on the landscape below. Strapped to her waist was the black leather scabbard that held her old sword.

Aila frowned. 'Belinda?'

The god turned. 'Yes?'

'I think Silva is waiting for you to give your permission before she speaks.'

Belinda frowned. 'Answer their questions, Silva.'

'Yes, your Majesty,' said the demigod. She glanced at Aila and Corthie. 'Where would you like me to start?'

'How about when Nathaniel went into his long sleep?' said Corthie.

'Very well. It was during a time of great peace and prosperity on Khatanax. The old wars were long over and, though the other continents of Lostwell had been devastated millennia before, Khatanax remained green, fertile, and rich. King Nathaniel and Queen Belinda ruled wisely from their palace in Dun Khatar, and the peoples of Khatanax were happy. But King Nathaniel remained worried. He feared that the gods of Implacatus would one day resume the old wars and invade, so he decided to begin the creation of a new world, after his failures with the world that Amalia and Malik had fled to.'

'Failures?' said Aila. 'What do you mean?'

Belinda raised an eyebrow. 'Surely, Aila,' she said, 'you must have noticed that the world of Pella doesn't rotate properly? The sun barely rises in the sky each day, and half the world is scorched desert, the other half dark ice.'

'I always thought that was normal,' said Aila.

'It's far from normal,' said Belinda. She glanced at Silva. 'Apologies for interrupting. Go on.'

'No need to apologise to me, your divine Majesty,' the demigod said. 'As I was saying, King Nathaniel decided to try again, and create another world. For this one, he planned to imbue the mortals of the world with god-like powers, despite Agatha and many others advising against it. He said that he wanted to be able to create armies of mortals to fight for our side, in case the gods of Implacatus moved against us. The Sextant was prepared, and his Majesty got to work. Each day, he would go into his new world, and then he would tell us what he had done, until... one fateful day, when he didn't return from his vision trance. This was a little over five hundred years ago.'

'He made a mistake,' said Belinda, 'or so I was told by Daphne Holdfast. She spoke to Nathaniel – once when he was in spirit form, and again when he had taken on a physical body. It was the powers he had given the mortals – something went wrong, and he became trapped in his new world.'

'Two centuries passed,' Silva said, 'and nothing changed. The King remained in his sleep, while Queen Belinda cared for him, passing the authority to rule Khatanax to Agatha. The Sextant was kept ready, in case the King were to suddenly return, but he didn't. Then, unexpectedly, Lord Naxor arrived with salve, and everything began to change. The gods of Dun Khatar were rejuvenated, but so, unfortunately, were the gods of Implacatus. It took them a little over fifty years, from their first taste of it, until they invaded Lostwell in force.'

'When was that?' said Corthie.

'In the year five thousand and seven; nearly two hundred and fifty years ago. Their invasion overwhelmed us, and we had to flee Dun Khatar. Shinstra and Fordia were reduced to wastelands, and our beloved city was destroyed. But we were able to hide. We moved the King's body, and the Sextant, into a hideout in the mountains to the south-east of Dun Khatar, where we were able to evade the new rulers of Khatanax. Agatha had a Quadrant, and wanted to leave Lostwell, but Queen Belinda refused, as she had never given up hope that King Nathaniel would return to us. So she sat by his bedside day after day, waiting, and the years rolled past.'

Aila glanced at Belinda, but the god's face was expressionless as she listened.

'The end of the King finally came,' said Silva. 'One day, he simply died, his life force gone forever.'

'My Auntie Keira hacked his head off,' said Corthie, 'before he could destroy us all.'

Silva frowned.

'It's true,' said Belinda. 'According to the Holdfasts, five centuries of imprisonment within his new world had driven Nathaniel mad. To him, it would have seemed like thousands of years. He believed that the only way to free himself was to destroy his new world.'

Silva glowered a little. 'As you say, your Majesty. However here, in Lostwell, you mourned bitterly. Agatha urged you to action, but you refused to do anything other than lie by the dead King's tomb, weeping. Finally, seven years ago, the gods of Alea Tanton learned the location of our mountain refuge, and gathered in force. It was only then that Queen Belinda was stirred to action. She and Agatha arranged for the Sextant to be hidden, and they prepared to leave.'

'Why didn't they take the Sextant with them?' said Aila.

'I'm not entirely sure,' said Silva. 'Perhaps it was because none of the seven gods who remained knew how to work it; perhaps because of its size.'

'How big is it?' said Corthie.

'About as large as a loaded wagon,' Silva said, 'and very heavy. Perhaps Agatha or the Queen meant to return for it one day, but they never did. The world that King Nathaniel had created, the world that was supposed to provide our side with vast armies, ended up being nothing more than a refuge. Queen Belinda swore to take revenge on those who had murdered the King, but Agatha was only interested in hiding from the onslaught of our enemies. As those enemies closed in on our mountain stronghold, Agatha took the Quadrant, and with Belinda and the other five gods by her side, they departed.'

Belinda turned to her. 'Why did we not take you with us?'

'Agatha forbade it. She said that my powers were useless to her – she only wanted those able to fight. I appealed to you, my Queen, but you were still grieving, and you refused to listen to my pleas. Once you had gone, Lord Kemal and the others assaulted the hideout and broke through our defences. I barely made it out alive. When I returned later, I saw what they had done. I saw the empty tomb, and knew they had taken King Nathaniel's body. Shame filled me, and I made my way over the mountains to the ruins of Dun Khatar, where I used to leave flowers by the colossal statue of my beloved Queen, praying for her return.' She glanced at Belinda. 'It was on my last trip that I sensed the impossible – that you had indeed returned. I recognised the traces left by your powers the moment I approached the statue, and wept for joy.'

Silva dabbed her eyes with a handkerchief, and fell into silence.

'The Sextant might well be lost forever,' said Aila.

Corthie shrugged. 'It's no great loss. Unlike a Quadrant, you can hardly carry it about in your pocket.' He smiled at her. 'Unless, of course, you have plans to make new worlds.'

'I was thinking more of preventing the gods of Implacatus from getting their hands on it. What else can you tell us about it, Silva?'

'It is made of metal,' the demigod said, 'with cogs and wheels and moving parts, but I have no understanding of how to operate it. King

Nathaniel used to say that it was the last one in existence, and that he was the only god with the knowledge to be able to use it.'

Corthie's stomach rumbled and he glanced up. 'Time for lunch?'

'You two go,' said Belinda. 'I want to ask Silva some more questions.'

Aila and Corthie got to their feet, and left the quarters that Belinda shared with Naxor.

'That was a lot to take in,' Aila said as they walked down the steps towards the castle kitchens.

'Aye, but much of it made sense to me,' he said. 'I grew up hearing stories about the Creator, and how he had nearly destroyed my world, and about how he was finally stopped and killed. Karalyn played a big part in it, even though she was barely old enough to walk. What I didn't know, though, was how it was all part of a bigger story.'

Aila. It's Sable. We need to talk, urgently.

Aila paused on the steps. 'You go on to the kitchens,' she said to Corthie. 'I'll just be a moment.'

Corthie nodded. 'Sure. I'll see you down there.'

Aila waited until he had disappeared round the curve of the spiral staircase, then hurried back up to her rooms. She pushed open the door and barred it behind her.

'Alright, I'm ready.'

A vision of Sable appeared in the room before her, her features showing faint signs of worry.

'I made a mistake,' she said.

Aila frowned. 'What?'

'The gods anticipated that Gadena might be sent a warning, and an advance force used a Quadrant to go straight to his training camp. They will be there right now; they left at dawn this morning.'

Aila sat on the bed. 'Oh.'

'I'm sorry.'

'It's not your fault, Sable. Without you, we'd have no idea they were coming at all. Damn it. I guess we'll have to assume that Gadena will tell them everything he knows.'

Sable nodded. 'I do have some slightly better news.'

'Yeah?'

'I met Maddie, and helped her escape from the cells in the fortress down in the lower city where she was being held.'

'Maddie was arrested?'

'Yeah. The dragon got away fine, but Maddie was picked up by soldiers from the Banner of the Golden Fist. But, don't worry, I got her out. Right now, she's waiting for me near the Southern Pits.'

'She's waiting for you? I thought you said you met her?'

Sable smiled. 'Not in person; like this. Listen, I'm going to make my move today. The advance force took a Quadrant to Gadena's camp, which leaves two here in Old Alea, and I intend to steal both of them, then go down and meet Maddie. If all goes to plan, she and I will have left Alea Tanton by this time tomorrow.'

Aila puffed out her cheeks. 'Wow. Be careful.'

'I'm always careful.'

'Before you go,' Aila said; 'have you ever heard of a device called a Sextant?'

'Eh, I have, yes. Why?'

'Apparently, there might be one in Khatanax. A demigod who saw it seven years ago has arrived at the Falls of Iron – an old servant of Queen Belinda.'

Sable pulled a face. 'Queen Belinda? You've got to be kidding me.'

'No. She used to be Queen of Khatanax. I saw her statue in Dun Khatar.'

'Why am I not surprised?' Sable shook her head. 'Back to the Sextant, though, are you saying that someone actually saw this... thing seven years ago? It's not just a legend?'

'No, it's real.'

'Oh crap.'

'Why?'

'Because Lord Renko is looking for it. As well as questioning the merchants about salve, he's been having their minds read to see if he can find it.'

'Does he want to create new worlds?'

'Maybe, but that's not the important bit. I learned that each Sextant stores the locations of every world it has made, which means that if Renko gets his hands on it, then he could use it to find your world, and mine.'

Aila's face fell.

'Does this servant know where it is?' said Sable.

'No. Belinda hid it before she travelled to your world, and, well, as you know, she can't remember anything about her old life.'

'But it does exist?'

'According to Silva – that's the servant's name.' Aila thought about another question she wanted to ask Sable, but bit her tongue.

Sable raised an eyebrow. 'I can read your thoughts, remember?'

Aila flushed. 'Of course, yeah.'

'The answer is yes,' Sable said. 'I used some of my powers on your mind when we first talked. I, uh... this is going to sound stupid, but I wanted you to like me. I'm sorry. I didn't use any powers the second time, or this time, I swear it.'

Aila nodded.

'And now I can feel your anger and disappointment,' Sable said. 'I know everyone hates me, that's the problem with being able to read people's minds. I've messed up every friendship I've ever had, and my own family loathe me. Witness my niece's actions; she was only too happy to vanish without even saying goodbye. And now, I've wrecked our friendship before it even had a chance to start. Sorry. Bye.'

'No, wait!' Aila cried, but it was too late; Sable had gone.

'I don't understand the need for panic,' said Vana. 'We all know Sable is a liar.'

Aila's temper bubbled to the surface. 'Will you forget your hatred of her for one damn minute,' she cried, quietening the room. 'Why would she lie to us? What possible benefit would she get by risking her life to tell us what's going on? She's in Alea Tanton, trying her best to get a

Quadrant, while you're sitting here on your lazy ass doing nothing to help.'

Vana glared at her sister, while the others in Irno's study sat in silence.

'There's an easy way to get to the truth,' said Naxor. 'If the gods have sent forces to Gadena's camp, then I should be able to see them. I can send my vision out now, if we're all agreed?'

'Wait,' said Aila; 'there's more. Sable also told me something about the Sextant.'

Naxor's eyes lit up. 'Does she know where it is?'

'No,' Aila said, frowning at her cousin, 'but she told me that if the gods discover it before we do, then they will be able to find every world the Sextant made. That means the world of the City, and Corthie's world.'

'What?' said Corthie. 'Is that true?'

They turned to Silva, who had been sitting quietly by Belinda's side.

'Yes,' she said.

'Why didn't you tell us that before?' said Corthie.

Silva shrugged. 'I didn't think it was important.'

'Well, it is,' said Aila, 'especially if the gods are searching for it. If they find it, they'll have everything they need to destroy us.'

'Let's deal with one thing at a time,' said Irno from his comfortable armchair. 'Naxor, I would be obliged if you could check on Gadena for us. It shouldn't take too long, and then we'll be able to make a better evaluation of what to do.'

'If it's true,' muttered Vana.

'I also mistrust Sable Holdfast,' he said, 'but I have to agree with Aila on this. Why would Sable go to such lengths to feed us misinformation? And if she saved Maddie from prison, then perhaps she isn't as bad as we once thought.'

'She's an evil witch,' Vana said.

Aila narrowed her eyes. 'Shut up.'

Naxor stood and walked to the side table, where he poured himself a generous measure of raki. He sipped from the glass, then lit a cigarette.

'Vana and Aila shouting at each other,' he said, a wry smile on his lips; 'reminds me of the old days.'

Irno chuckled.

'Gadena's camp,' Naxor went on, 'is at the limits of my range, so it will require a significant effort on my part. Rather annoyingly, it is also underground, and can occasionally be a little tricky to find, especially if the wind has been covering the entrances with sand.'

Corthie rolled his eyes. 'We would be very grateful, o mighty one.'

'Thank you,' he said. 'It's nice to be appreciated.' He took another draw of the cigarette and stubbed it out. 'Right, I am ready to proceed.'

His eyes glazed over.

Aila glanced at Belinda. The god had said nothing during the entire meeting; in fact, Aila realised, she had barely said anything since Silva's arrival. The god caught her glancing at her, and stared back.

'How are you?' Aila said.

'Fine, apart from being annoyed at Naxor smoking.'

'Any sign of your powers returning?' said Corthie.

'No.'

Silva let out a low sob, and Aila turned to her.

'It upsets me greatly,' Silva said, 'to know that her Majesty's powers have been stolen from her. It's so unfair. To think that the Blessed Third Ascendant should be abused in such a manner fills my heart with grief and rage. Someone should pay for it.'

'Well, I'm sitting right here,' said Corthie. 'Any time you want to have a go at a Holdfast, be my guest.'

Silva gave him a look of withering contempt, but said nothing.

'My powers will return,' said Belinda. 'I have faith in the word of Karalyn.'

Silva looked like she wanted to say something, but bit her lip.

There was a groan from the side table, and Naxor's eyes cleared. He spluttered, then took a long drink of raki. He grimaced, as if in great pain.

Belinda walked to his side and put a hand on his arm. 'Are you alright?'

'I will be; just give me a moment.'

The others waited as Naxor stumbled over into a seat.

'Well?' said Irno.

Belinda glared at him. 'He said to give him a moment.'

Irno and Vana exchanged a glance.

'Right,' said Naxor, rubbing his forehead; 'I'm afraid to say that Sable Holdfast was indeed telling the truth. I spotted three gods in Gadena's camp, and as for the dear chap himself, he's currently tied to a chair, having been half-tortured to death.'

'They tortured him?' said Corthie, his eyes narrow.

'Yes. One of the gods has death powers, and it looks as though Gadena was taken to the brink.'

'Then we have to assume,' said Irno, 'that he told them everything.'

'They could have read it out of his mind,' said Corthie; 'they didn't need to torture him.'

'Oh, but Corthie,' smiled Naxor, 'torture can be so much quicker in these circumstances. Don't look at me like that; I'm only stating the truth. Gadena could have buried the information they were after deep within his memory, and what might have taken days to find, torture probably accomplished in ten minutes. Suffice to say, I now believe the Falls of Iron to be in imminent danger of attack.'

The others stared at him.

Irno stood. 'Then we must prepare to defend ourselves. We must assume that the mercenary units currently in Alea Tanton will be sent here, and with multiple Quadrants at their disposal, advance forces could be on the move very quickly indeed. I need to leave, in order to speak with the town garrison. I will order the gates of the Falls of Iron to be closed, and all supplies to be brought within the walls by sunset. Vana – you are my eyes; tell me immediately if you sense any god powers anywhere near the Falls of Iron. Naxor, likewise, if you see anything with your vision. Corthie, Belinda, we may have need of your fighting abilities, so please be prepared.' A grim smile touched his lips. 'Now, if you'll please excuse me.'

He strode from the room, leaving the others wide-eyed.

Corthie glanced at Aila. 'I like your brother. He's calm and in control.'

'He wouldn't have to be if you weren't here,' said Vana. 'Curse the lot of you. We were at peace until you all arrived.'

'The gods of Implacatus would have been searching for the salve with or without us being here,' said Aila.

Vana ignored her, and followed her brother out of the room.

Corthie cracked his knuckles. 'We'd best get ready.'

'My Queen,' said Silva; 'you should not be part of this. If the gods wish to punish mortals for their wickedness, then so be it. It is of no concern to us.'

Belinda glanced at her, but said nothing.

Aila stood, and she and Corthie walked from Irno's study, Corthie casting a wistful eye at the half-full bottle of raki on the side table. They left the room and began heading towards their quarters.

'I don't trust that Silva woman,' Corthie muttered as they climbed the stairs. 'And it's not just because she clearly hates me; she's trying to separate Belinda from the rest of us.'

'Hopefully, Belinda will tire of her soon. She doesn't like Silva fawning over her, and she's not stupid; she'll know what Silva is trying to do. But if we interfere, we might drive her into Silva's arms. Also, it would help it you cut out the little digs at her. Telling her that your aunt cut off Nathaniel's head, and then practically challenging her to a fight, well, it might not be for the best.'

Corthie glowered, but said nothing.

'It's the drink, isn't it?' Aila went on, though a small voice in her head was telling her that she should probably remain quiet. 'It's because you haven't had a drink in seven days. It's making you irritable.'

'No, it's not.'

She raised an eyebrow. 'Right.'

'I'm just worried about the imminent arrival of gods who want to kill us.'

'No, you're not. You're looking forward to it; you'll get to fight again, at last.'

'Sounds to me like you're the irritable one.'

Aila narrowed her eyes and looked away.

They were approaching the passageway leading to their rooms when a crashing noise sounded from above them, as if heavy furniture had fallen over.

Aila glanced up. 'That came from Karalyn's old quarters.'

They ran along the corridor, and climbed the stairs to where Karalyn had stayed before her departure. The door leading to her room was closed, and Corthie pounded on it with a fist.

'Karalyn? Are you in there?'

There was no response, so Corthie gripped the handle and threw the door open. Inside, sitting on the bed was a young woman. She had the same dark skin as Karalyn and Sable, and something in her eyes reminded Aila of both women.

'Hello,' she said.

Corthie's eyes widened, and his mouth fell open.

The woman nodded to him. 'Little brother; except you're not so little any more. Pyre's tits, lad, you're as muscle-bound as Karalyn said you were.' She stood, and walked round the side of the bed. She squinted at Corthie. 'You're just as dopey, though, that hasn't changed.' She stuck her hand out. 'I'm guessing you're Aila, aye? In lieu of my idiot brother having lost the ability to converse like a normal person, let me introduce myself. I'm Kelsey.'

Aila stared at the young woman's hand.

Kelsey frowned. 'Don't tell me you're as slow-witted as Corthie? At least you'd suit each other, I suppose.'

Aila narrowed her eyes. 'Am I not allowed to be a little bit shocked? I mean, what in Malik's name are you doing here?'

Kelsey ignored her, and turned back to Corthie. 'Aren't you going to say anything?'

'Kelsey? I... I can't believe it.' He put his arms out to embrace her and she raised an eyebrow.

'Let's not,' she said. 'I mean, it's nice to see you, but let's not get all touchy.' She glanced at the door. 'It's just the two of you, aye? Good. Shut the door and sit down.'

'We should tell Belinda,' said Aila, as Corthie pushed the door closed behind them.

'Nah,' said Kelsey. 'She can wait. Sit down.'

Corthie and Aila sat on the bed as Kelsey went to a large trunk in the centre of the room.

'Did you bring that?' said Aila.

'Aye,' said Kelsey as she opened it. 'I thought that if I was coming here, I should at least bring some stuff to make it more pleasant. I have whisky, and weed, and books, and um... a few clothes.'

'How did you get here?' said Corthie. 'Do you have a Quadrant?'

'Funny you should ask,' she said as she took a bottle out of the trunk and set it onto a small table. 'Yes and no.'

'What?'

'Yes, I have a Quadrant, but no, that's not what brought me here. Karalyn did it using her weird mind powers. She said she'd done the same to send Belinda somewhere, so that's all it took. Well, she sucked half the life out of Keir to help her, which was pretty hilarious to watch.'

'Why didn't you use the Quadrant?' said Aila.

'Because,' she said, whipping a copper-coloured device from the trunk, 'this one's broken. It used to belong to Agatha, until Karalyn stole it, but then dear old mama in her senility bashed it with a sword, and it hasn't worked since. The Empress gave it to me, to see if anyone here can fix it. Bridget says hello, by the way. I spoke to her before I left.'

She handed it to Corthie, who took it. He held it up, and Aila could see the gouge that marked the upper two inches of the curved edge. While they were gazing at it, Kelsey sat on a stool and lit a weedstick, then opened the bottle.

'Now,' she said, exhaling a large cloud of acrid smoke, 'back to Aila's question. What am I doing here? The short answer is that mother wants her son to come home, and she sent me to make it happen.'

Corthie and Aila's attention went back to Kelsey.

'I assume,' Corthie said, 'that Karalyn told you everything that went on here?'

'Karalyn's an idiot,' Kelsey said. 'For all her weird and wonderful powers, she's clueless at times. Alright, I know about the four-year gap, and the fact that she missed her twins growing up, and everything, but refusing to take Aila? Try to imagine the scene, brother. Keir and I were visiting mother at the Holdfast estate. Thorn, Jemma, and Celine, and all the kids were there too, and into the room walks Karalyn after being gone for four years. Except, she looks exactly the same as the day she left. I'm only a few thirds younger than her now.'

'Thirds?' said Aila.

'They call them months here,' said Corthie.

Kelsey shrugged. 'Whatever. Anyway, in she walks, and there's utter pandemonium. Mother's screeching like a wounded gaien, and then Thorn starts crying, as soon as she realises what Karalyn's return means.' Kelsey shook her head. 'Poor Thorn. She's looked after the twins for so long that I think she started to believe they were really hers. And of course, the first thing Karalyn did was walk up and take them from her.' She snapped her fingers. 'Just like that. It was awful. The twins were crying for Thorn, and called her mum, and Karalyn was freaking out. I thought mother was going to have a heart attack. Keir, of course, just sat there with a confused look on his face. It took a few moments before anyone asked where you were. Then it hit us. Karalyn had abandoned you here. I've never seen mother so upset. She was crying for Karalyn, she was crying for you.'

Corthie groaned and put his head in his hands.

'It took a while to get the full story out of Karalyn, but the end result is that I volunteered to come to Lostwell. Frankly, I would have done anything to escape the madness going on back home.' She gave a crooked smile. 'Mother took a little persuading, but Karalyn whisked most of us off to Plateau City, so we could speak to the Empress, and Bridget thought it was a good idea as well.'

'Why did you need to speak to the Empress?' said Aila.

'Because I work for her. Have done, pretty much ever since Karalyn disappeared in the first place. A lot's happened in four years, but the Empress is pretty much the same. Mother and her went off into a room to talk alone for a while, and when they came out they both agreed that I should go to Lostwell. That's right, Aila, you're looking at the most expendable Holdfast, the only one that mother would agree to let go.'

Aila frowned. 'I'm sure that's not true.'

'Fine; I'm exaggerating, but not by much. Do you know who I empathise with most out of my family? Sable. Bloody Sable. Even though she held me captive for thirds. And it annoyed me, I admit, when I heard that Karalyn had just left her here, without even asking if she wanted to go back.'

'I spoke to Sable today,' said Aila.

Kelsey smiled. 'Aye? Is she alright?'

'Yeah, but she's put herself in terrible danger in order to find a Quadrant.'

'That sounds like Sable. A little reckless; no, very reckless. Sometimes, I think she wants to get caught. Anyway, it's not part of the official plan, but I'm not leaving until I've seen her, and asked her what she wants to do.'

'And Belinda?'

Kelsey shrugged. 'She can do what she likes. I'll ask her, of course, I'm not a complete cow. Tomorrow, we'll work out how to get another Quadrant, or we'll see if we can get Agatha's one fixed, but for now?' She picked up the bottle. 'Whisky?'

Corthie glanced at Aila.

'Have a drink,' she said. 'I think I'll be needing some too.'

'Excellent,' said Kelsey. 'Let's get hammered and swap all our news.'

CHAPTER 22

UNDERESTIMATING

Alea Tanton, Tordue, Western Khatanax – 10th Tradinch 5252

Sable lounged on the long, comfortable couch, her eyes gazing through the open shutters towards the sunset. The other young women of the harem were also stretched on couches, and there was a fug of dreamweed smoke hanging in the air.

Sable turned from the window and glanced at the main entrance to the harem, but the door hadn't opened all day, or during the previous night. The other occupants of the harem had told Sable that this was normal. Lord Renko rarely visited, and sometimes they would be left alone for several days at a time without him making an appearance. She hoped their luck would continue for one more night; that was all she needed – a single night, and then she could be on her way to meet Maddie in *The Rosy-Cheeked Pig*. She yawned, wondering whether it was the smoke or the boredom that was making her light-headed and sleepy.

Someone nudged her elbow, and passed over a weedstick.

'Thanks,' she said. Sable had been making it appear as though she was smoking with the others, but had been careful not to inhale too much. 'Are there any books to read?'

'No,' said the young woman to her left, who had passed her the weedstick. 'We're not allowed any.'

Sable nodded. The young women of Renko's harem, including Sable, were wearing expensive dresses of brightly-coloured silk. They had spent a few hours that morning doing each other's hair and make-up, and then they had waited, and waited. Within the confines of the harem, each woman had a tiny bed chamber, and there was a large, communal bathroom, but no kitchen, and they had their meals delivered three times a day, along with plentiful amounts of raki and dreamweed.

The other occupants had been friendly and talkative towards Sable that morning, but they had grown quieter as the day had gone on; and Sable guessed that their silence was due to a combination of the dreamweed, and their nerves at the approaching dusk. Sable glanced at the other women. At twenty-eight, she was easily the oldest of the five, and she felt a twinge of sympathy for their plight. Not enough to make her want to rescue them; she had a job to do, and couldn't let her feelings get in the way.

'Do you think Lord Renko will visit this evening?' she said.

The other women glanced at her. One shrugged.

'Maybe,' said the one who had passed her the weedstick. 'It's been a couple of days.'

'Does he, uh, pick one of us at a time, or...?'

The woman nodded. 'Yeah. He comes round, chooses a girl, they go away together, and she's back here again the next morning.'

Sable passed the weedstick to the woman on her right. 'And does he pick the girls in a certain order?'

'No,' said the first woman; 'I've been picked twice, while she,' she said, pointing across the room, 'hasn't been picked once yet. You trying to work out if you'll get selected?'

'I guess so,' said Sable.

'You might. You're new, and he must have brought you up here for a reason.'

'Don't worry too much,' said the woman to Sable's right. 'It's not as bad as being in Lord Maisk's harem. There are thirty girls in there, and the stories I've heard...'

'Lord Maisk's away though, isn't he?' said the first woman. 'At least his girls will get some peace tonight.'

'So Renko's not too bad, then?' said Sable.

One of the other women groaned. 'Can we not talk about it? Look, new girl, if he picks you, then you'll soon learn what he's like. I hope he picks you, but he probably won't; you're too old.'

'Ignore her,' said the first woman; 'she's just jealous of your looks and your exotic accent.'

'Lord Renko's from Implacatus, you silly bitch,' said the second; 'we all sound exotic to him.'

Sable closed her eyes as the young women bickered. Part of her was tempted to go into their minds and send them all to sleep, but she found it hard to hate them. They had been whisked off the streets and shoved into a tower, to service the carnal desires of a god who had lived for over ten thousand years. She wondered how many people he had slept with in that time, and whether he remembered even a small fraction of them.

Focus, she told herself, as she felt tiredness seep through her body. She had been up half the night helping Maddie escape, and had nearly exhausted herself by taking control of Captain Logos for so long, not to mention the considerable effort that had been required to wipe his memories afterwards. She knew she had done it partly to please Aila, and the demigod had seemed grateful, but then Sable had blown it by admitting that she had messed with her feelings. Why hadn't she just lied, and denied it? Aila would never have known, and now the demigod hated her like everyone else.

She felt a nudge.

'Don't fall asleep,' said the woman to her left. 'If Lord Renko's going to visit, it'll be soon. If he doesn't pick you, then you can get a good night's rest.'

Sable smiled. 'And if he does?'

'Then you can sleep all day tomorrow.'

Sable stood, stretched her arms, then walked to the window. The huge, sprawling Governor's residence was laid out below, and then the vast gardens where the mansions of the gods were located. In between, lay the narrow streets where the workers and servants lived, and in the distance was the tall wall that surrounded the plateau of Old Alea. Sable made out a line of turrets, and wondered how Millen was doing in her absence. Their little turret was on the other side of the tower, out of sight from where Sable was standing, but she could picture him sitting alone, waiting for her to return.

There was a tap at the door, and a soldier wheeled in a trolley laden with dishes and tall jugs.

'Dinnertime, girls,' he said, his eyes roving over the silk-clad bodies of the five women. 'Oh, and Lord Renko says he'll be along in a minute, so eat fast.'

The soldier deposited the trolley in the middle of the room by a low table, then walked back to the door and closed it behind him. As soon as he was gone, the women got up and gathered round the trolley.

'Look at this!' cried one as she grabbed a plate. 'There's barely enough dinner for two people, never mind five.'

Sable stayed back as the other four stripped the trolley clean of food in seconds, each retreating to a couch with their plates.

The first woman glanced at Sable, frowned, then offered her a piece of bread.

'You have it,' Sable said as she walked to the trolley and picked up a ceramic pot. 'Coffee and cigarettes are all I need.'

'Worried about getting fat?' laughed one of the others. 'There's no chance of that in here; you've seen the size of the portions, haven't you?'

'Lord Renko likes to keep us skinny,' said another.

Sable poured herself a coffee. There was no sugar or milk, but she didn't care. She would have a feast as soon as she had escaped. She took her cup over to the window and lit a cigarette, watching as the sun dipped below the horizon. Street lamps were being lit in the town below her, but other than that, the roads seemed deserted.

The door behind her swung open, and Lord Renko walked in, a soldier a pace behind.

The women in the room put down their half-eaten dinners and stood, then they arranged themselves into a line as Renko waited. Sable frowned, and joined them. Once the five young women were standing together in silence, Renko walked forwards, his eyes glancing at each in turn.

He stopped in front of Sable. She concentrated, and allowed his vision powers to enter her head. As before, she guided him to a part of her mind that she had prepared, where he would see nothing but a nervous and slightly bewildered servant.

Renko nodded to himself, and moved on. He stopped at the next woman in the line, the one who had told Sable that she had already been selected twice before. He raised a finger and pointed at her.

'You.'

The young woman bowed low, her face betraying her despondency. Renko turned and walked from the room, and the soldier escorted the chosen woman out behind him.

The door closed, and the other women breathed in relief.

'Her again?' said one. 'That's three times he's picked her.'

'Who cares?' said another as they returned to where they had been sitting. 'As long as it's not us.'

'Why hasn't he picked me yet?' said a third.

'You sound like you want to be picked. Believe me, you don't.'

'But is there something wrong with me?'

'Just count yourself lucky, shut up, and get drunk.'

Five hours later, Sable sat alone in her tiny bedchamber. The other women of the harem had gone to sleep long before, the toll of dreamweed and alcohol exacting its price. None of them had touched the coffee, and Sable had taken the pot through to her room, where she had drunk cup after cup while smoking her way through her supply of cigarettes.

Sable waited. Her shutters were wide open, but the air had retained the warmth of the day, and it was uncomfortably humid. Below, the streets of Old Alea were quiet, apart from a few patrols of Banner soldiers. Seeing them reminded her of Captain Logos, and she hoped he hadn't been punished for what she had done to his mind. She shouldn't feel sorry for him, she thought; he was an enemy.

A bell in the Governor's residence rang to signal midnight, and Sable took a long breath, then let her vision powers rise from her body. She sent them out of the window, then turned and pushed her sight through the slats of a set of shutters on the floor below. Her vision entered a well-lit room, where Lady Joaz was sitting, a handful of her demigod aides surrounding her. Sable selected one of the aides, and went into the man's mind, so that she could hear the conversation that was taking place.

'But, my lady,' one of the other aides was saying, 'if the source of the salve trade has been discovered by Lord Maisk, why must we continue to read the minds of the merchants? What else is there to learn?'

'Lord Renko has ordered it,' Joaz said. 'The interrogations must continue. Have you compiled a list of those to be executed? We'll need more space in the cells for the merchants that are still to be brought up here from the lower city.'

'I have, my lady,' an aide said, handing Joaz a sheet of thin paper.

Joaz scanned the list. 'Petty bribery, small-scale theft, and some minor forgery of permits? Is that all you could find?'

'Yes, my lady. We have already executed those with worse crimes to their names.'

Joaz shook her head. 'We'd be as well selecting them at random.'

'My lady,' said another, her eyes anxious; 'can I ask what it is that we're still looking for?'

Joaz sipped from a glass of wine, then nodded. 'This goes no further. Lord Renko wishes to keep this confidential, and you know how he feels about those who disregard his commands. He is looking for a device called a Sextant. It was long believed to be no more than a myth, but Lord Renko has assured me that he has evidence that such a device was in Khatanax only a few short years ago. It was in the possession of a group of rebels who had been hiding in the mountains south of Dun Khatar, and it is believed that they hid it before they fled Lostwell. It is an extremely large, heavy object, and could not have been moved around the continent without someone noticing. Lord Renko suspects that it was put onto a ship at the Southern Cape about seven years ago, and then transported to a safe location. If that is the case, then I want you to focus your interrogations on any merchant with ties to shipping; find out if anyone noticed such an object being taken on as cargo, and more importantly, find out where it went. There will be a significant reward for anyone who succeeds in locating this device.'

'What is the purpose of the Sextant, my lady?' asked an aide.

'That is irrelevant. Now, let's go over the names of those to be questioned tomorrow.'

Sable withdrew from the aide's mind, and pushed her vision through a keyhole and into the adjoining rooms. She departed Joaz's quarters and scanned the upper levels of the tower. Maisk's quarters were quiet, excepting the crowded chambers where his large harem was situated, and she sent her vision back up the stairs to the area where Lord Renko lived.

She paused her vision outside the guarded entrance to the Ancient's quarters. She had no desire to see what Renko might be doing with the woman from the harem, but knew she would have to go inside all the same. She had searched every inch of the other gods' rooms in her hunt for a Quadrant, and they had to be somewhere within Renko's chambers. She squeezed her vision through a keyhole and entered.

The small hall at the start of his rooms was empty, with several doors leading off. A light was coming from the room where she had seen Nathaniel's corpse, and she pushed her sight in. Renko was sitting with his back to her in a chair, working his way through a tall stack of papers that were piled on the floor next to him. His desk was still being used to bear the body of the Fourth Ascendant, and Sable kept her eyes averted from it.

Renko glanced up, and for a horrible moment Sable thought he could sense the presence of her powers, but instead he turned to a door.

'Wine,' he said.

The door opened, and the woman from the harem came through, carrying a tray. She was barefoot, and wearing a dressing gown.

'My lord,' she said, offering the tray out to him.

He took a full glass from the tray, then glanced at her as she turned to walk back to the bedroom.

'Wait,' he said. 'Tell me; what do you think of the new girl?'

'Sable, my lord?'

'Yes, I believe that is her name.'

'Well, my lord, she doesn't really fit in with the rest of us. She's older, and she's not from Alea Tanton.'

'Has she mentioned her past to you?'

'No, my lord. She's been quiet.'

Renko sipped his wine, then nodded. 'You may return to the bedroom.'

She bowed and walked away, and Sable followed her, pushing her sight through into a large chamber. The young woman set the tray down onto a side table, where a variety of drinks were laid out, then climbed onto the double bed, puffing out her cheeks. Sable turned her attention from the young woman, and began to search the room. After a few minutes, she saw a small wooden case lying under the bed. It was closed, with no visible keyhole for her to enter. She darted to the door, and checked that Renko was still engrossed in his work, then glanced back at the woman.

You're bored. You're curious. Just what does Lord Renko keep hidden in his room? Aren't you dying to find out? You're not afraid of being caught; this is your third time in his rooms, and you know that he spends most of the night working. Maybe you should have a little look around – to see what you can find? There's an interesting case under the bed. Look for it.

The young woman blinked, then frowned. She glanced at the door, then slipped off the bed and crouched down to peer under it.

Very good. There it is. Now pull it out, slowly and quietly.

The woman reached under the bed and eased the case out.

See if it will open.

She hesitated.

Go, it'll be fun; exciting.

The woman ran her fingers over the case. They found a catch and, with a click, the lid sprang open. The woman glanced at the door to the study, but it remained closed, and no sounds were coming from Renko. She turned back to the case.

Sable looked through the young woman's eyes. Inside the case was a pouch made of soft, brown leather. The woman opened it, and a glint of a copper-coloured metal shone within. Sable smiled.

Gotcha.

That was fun, see? Right, now close the case and carry it to the window. Let's play a funny trick on Lord Renko and hide it for a minute. That'll teach him for taking girls off the street and sticking them in his harem. That'll pay him back a little for what he's done.

The young woman frowned, and Sable could sense the conflict in her mind; the fear battling the unheard voice in her head.

Don't be afraid. It's just a trick; nothing too serious. You'll be fine.

The woman took the wooden case into her hands and carried it over to the nearest window.

Open the shutters, then place the case onto the window ledge.

Sable withdrew from her mind and watched as she swung the shutters wide open and put the case down flat onto the wide ledge that ran under the window.

Excellent. Now, close the shutters and go back to bed.

She shut and latched the shutters, then went and lay down on the bed.

Sleep, and forget everything that happened in the last ten minutes. You have no memory of the case, or having moved it. None. Forget.

Sable released her hold on her vision powers and coughed as she came back to her own body, a headache forming behind her temples. She lit a cigarette, feeling exhausted.

How did Karalyn make it look so easy? She gave a wry smile. She wasn't as powerful as her niece, but she was still pretty damn good. Now all she had to do was work out how the get the case off the ledge.

Sable gripped the grooves in the smooth stone blocks, keeping her eyes on the ledge beneath her boots. Below was a drop of over a hundred feet, from the upper floor of the tower, down to the flagstones of the courtyard, where Banner soldiers were standing on guard. The night air was warm, and a soft breeze rippled over her as she clung to the wall, edging her feet step by step towards the window outside Renko's bedroom.

Her battle-vision was thrumming a steady beat, assisting her perception, and lending her a boost of energy that would have to be repaid at some point in the near future. *Hopefully within a cosy room in The Rosy-Cheeked Pig*, she thought to herself. She had passed the window to the Ancient's study a few moments before, and had checked inside for a second or two. The room had been empty, but that didn't mean he was in the bedroom. He could be anywhere. She would check again when she reached the case, until then she needed to concentrate on not falling.

Her right hand reached over to the next block along, and she shuffled her boots onto the ledge outside the bedroom. Very slowly, she crouched down, and lifted the case. She had brought a shoulder bag with her, and she slipped the case inside, then buckled a strap to keep it secure. She listened for a moment at the shutters, but heard nothing, so she eased her vision in through the slats and peered around. The young woman from the harem was lying on her side on the bed, her chest rising and falling as she slept. Of Renko, there was no sign.

She made sure the bag was safely on her back, then began to descend, dropping so she was hanging from the ledge. The tip of her boots found a toehold in the grooves, and she clambered down a few blocks, her fingers aching from grasping the stone.

Sounds rose up from beneath her, and she risked a glance down as she climbed. Out in the courtyard, more soldiers were gathering, some with lanterns. Officers were herding them into small groups, and sending them off into the grounds of the residence, as if they were searching for someone.

It couldn't be her, she thought. How could they know?

She reached the next row of windows, on the floor where Joaz and Maisk had their quarters, then heard another sound, this time from above her head. She glanced up, and saw the shutters of Renko's bedroom open.

Sable moved quickly. She slid down onto the nearest window ledge and, powering her battle-vision, ripped open a shutter. The room inside was in darkness, and she clambered through, pulling the shutter closed behind her. She was somewhere in Maisk's quarters, but there was still a long way to go before she could get out of the residence. The service lift, she thought, and her feet began to move. Her battle-vision helped her see in the dark, and she raced through the room, and into a hallway. She sent her vision ahead. Outside one of the doors was the main stairwell, where two guards were posted. Sable passed a side entrance to her right, where lamplight was filtering from under the door. Maisk's harem, she thought, hearing the voices from inside.

She crept to the main door of the quarters, put her fingers onto the handle, and readied herself. She took a breath, then flung the door open and rushed out into the hallway.

Sleep.

The two soldiers toppled to the floor, their crossbows clattering off the flagstones as Sable jumped over them. She raced to the service shaft, as sounds grew from the floor above her. The thump of boots approached, coming down the steps, and she turned a corner and reached the lift shaft. She peered into the darkness. The platform was situated a couple of floors below her, so she reached out, and grabbed hold of the thick ropes that connected it to the pulleys. She clambered down the rope as quickly as she could, and her head was just below the level of the floor when the first soldiers appeared on the landing.

'Over here!' one cried. 'Two men down!'

'Take the stairs,' shouted someone; 'get after her!'

'I want her alive,' came Renko's cold voice, 'but more importantly, I want what she is carrying. The contents of that case are extremely valuable, and they must be returned to me whole and undamaged.'

Sable kept still against the side of the lift shaft, listening to the sound of boots tramp down the stairs. She glanced at the rope, then began to lower herself. Her battle-vision was starting to strain. She hadn't eaten much, and she was still tired from the intense use of her powers the previous evening. She could do it though, she had been through worse. She made it to the next level. The stair landing was deserted, but cries were echoing from above and below. She scampered down across the open gap, and had almost made it when two soldiers bounded round the corner.

While one stood, his mouth opening, the other leapt, jumping into the lift shaft, his hands grabbing onto Sable. Her grasp on the rope loosened, and they fell together down the shaft, the air rushing past them. They crashed onto the platform, which shuddered and swung. The soldier tried to grapple her to the ground, but she powered her battle-vision and punched him in the nose. His face whipped back as blood gushed down his face. Sable rolled, and pulled the soldier's long knife from his belt. She lunged out with her arm, ripping through the soldier's throat.

'She's here!' cried a voice from the landing next to her. She turned, and saw a crossbow pointed in her direction.

On instinct, Sable slashed out again, slicing through the thick ropes attaching the platform to the weights and pulleys, and it hurtled downwards as a bolt flew past her head. She tried to brace herself, but the platform was falling too quickly. Down, down, she plunged, passing the bright openings to each level.

Oh crap, she thought.

The platform crashed into the floor of the lowest level, and Sable was battered against a wall, then thrown onto the ground. She grimaced, her lower left leg screaming in agony. Her vision was blurry, and blood was trickling down her forehead into her eyes. Next to her, the body of the dead soldier was staring its lifeless eyes at her, and she saw that her hands were covered in blood. She stared at them for a moment, in a daze, her ears ringing.

She heard shouts, and tried to get up, but her left leg buckled under her, and she crashed back into the broken shards of the platform.

'Don't move!' someone screamed at her.

Her vision cleared a little and she looked up from the ground. Half a dozen soldiers were standing by the lift shaft, each with a crossbow pointed at her head. Behind them, more were coming, and in their midst strode a tall man.

'Move aside,' Renko said.

He halted in front of Sable and looked down at her. His eyes settled on the bag over her shoulder, and he tore it from her. He opened the black case and withdrew the leather pouch, his eyes frantic. He took out one Quadrant, gazed at it, then removed the other. It was cracked, with a long split running down the middle. His face transformed into a mask of pure rage.

'You,' he spat at Sable. 'Look what you have done. I will kill you for this, but not before I have tortured the information I need out of you.' He placed a boot onto her lower left leg, and applied some pressure to the broken bone.

Sable cried out as pain ripped through her.

Renko turned to the soldiers. 'Shackle and hood her, then bring her up to my rooms.'

Two soldiers approached the lift shaft. They each took an arm, and they dragged Sable from the shattered platform. Her left leg caught for a moment on the edge of the shaft as they hauled her away.

Sable screamed, then fell into oblivion.

CHAPTER 23
BY PROXY

Alea Tanton, Tordue, Western Khatanax – 11th Tradinch 5252

Maddie frowned at the menu as the serving-boy waited by the table.

'Do you sell anything that hasn't got meat in it?' she said.

'You're in *The Rosy-Cheeked Pig*, miss. Everything's got meat in it.'

Maddie glanced up. 'But I don't eat meat.'

The serving-boy sighed. 'Then why don't you go somewhere else? No one's forcing you to have your lunch here.'

'That's not very good service. I'm a customer, and you should be trying to help me. Go and ask the chef or cook if they can rustle up something for me without any bits of carcass in it. It can't be that difficult; just make the same, but with no animal bits.'

'Fine; I'll ask,' said the serving-boy, rolling his eyes.

'Thanks, and, eh, maybe one more mug of wine?'

She turned to the window as the boy strode off. The panes of glass were warped and filthy, and she could barely see anything of the street outside. She drummed her fingers on the tabletop. Lunchtime, and still no sign of Sable Holdfast. The woman had told her that she would be in *The Rosy-Cheeked Pig* by that dawn at the latest, but the sunrise had been and gone, and the afternoon had begun. Maddie had stayed in her rented room above the tavern for the whole of the previous day, sleeping off the long walk from the fortress to the location of the Southern Pits, but hunger had driven her downstairs. She checked her purse. She had sufficient coins to pay for lunch and a few drinks, but nothing else. If she needed to rent her room for a further night, she would have to sell the silver cigarette case that Van had given her. She took it out of a pocket and looked at it.

It was beautiful, she thought; engraved by a proper artist, with stylised leaves and flowers covering one side. She turned it over, and noticed an inscription on the back.

To our son Van on his eighteenth birthday.

She groaned. She couldn't sell it; it might be the only thing he had from his parents. It might not be, of course, but could she take the chance?

'Do you eat eggs?'

She glanced up. 'What?'

'Eggs,' said the serving-boy, placing a mug of wine onto the table; 'do you eat them?'

'I don't know. Do they count as meat?'

He sighed. 'That's what I'm here to ask you.'

'What animal do they come from? They're not dragon eggs, are they?'

He looked at her as if she was mad. 'Eh, no. They're from chickens.'

'And what are they?'

'Birds.'

'Can they speak?'

'No, miss, they can't speak.'

Maddie pondered for a moment. The concept of eating eggs that came out of a bird seemed a little odd to her, but her stomach was growling.

'Alright,' she said. 'I'll try them.'

The boy nodded, and walked off towards the kitchen, squeezing between the empty tables of the tavern. Maddie wondered why it was so quiet; shouldn't the place be busy at lunchtime? She picked up the wine and took a sip. If she wasn't careful, she would be drunk by the time Sable arrived, especially with an empty stomach. She was looking forward to meeting the outcast of the Holdfast tribe, and was curious to find out more about her, and also about what Aila had said. Could it be true that the demigod had been worried about her? Maddie was touched. Grumpy old Aila actually liked her, even after she and Blackrose had tricked her into spilling her secrets.

The bell by the entrance to the tavern tinkled as the door opened. A young man walked in, and looked around the interior. His eyes caught sight of Maddie, and he walked through the empty tavern towards her, then took a seat at her table.

'Eh, excuse me?' she said. 'There are plenty of free tables, go and sit at one of them.'

He glanced around, as if worried he was being watched, then shook his head.

'I'll move then,' she said. 'I'm not having some random weird guy sit next to me.'

He leaned over the table towards her and she backed away, raising an eyebrow.

'Are you Maddie?' he whispered.

She picked up the knife from the cutlery on the table. 'Stay away from me.'

'I'm a friend.'

'No, you're not. I've never seen you before in my life. Now, shoo, before I scream.'

'Sable sent me.'

'Or so you claim. And anyway, who's Sable? I've never heard of anyone called Sable.'

He frowned. 'Have I come to the wrong place? This is *The Rosy-Cheeked Pig*, yes? And you look just like the image that Sable placed into my mind.'

'Alright, tell me something that only she would know. And that I'd know as well, of course.'

'Um... you know a lot about dragons?'

She folded her arms. 'More.'

'Alright; Sable helped you escape from the fortress two nights ago, though I'm not sure how she did it. And then she told you to meet her here.'

'Then where is she?'

'She's been delayed a little, and she told me to come and meet you myself. My name's Millen.'

'Sable never mentioned you to me.'

He nodded. 'That doesn't surprise me. Listen, she woke me up last night with a vision message. Did you know she has vision powers, even though she's only a mortal?'

'Yeah, of course I knew.'

'She told me to get out of Old Alea, and come down here. She said it was important, and that she was supposed to be here at dawn.'

'What's causing the delay?'

'She didn't say, but she told me not to worry. She'll catch up with us soon. She said her plan was going well, but there had been a slight complication.' His eyes tightened. 'But, you know, we've not to worry.'

'So you keep saying.'

'Then you believe me?'

'I think that if you were an evil spy, then you would have come up with a better story, so, yeah, let's say I believe you for a moment. What does Sable want me to do? Am I to wait here until she sorts out this "complication"?'

Millen paused as the serving-boy returned to the table with a large bowl. He placed it down in front of Maddie.

'It's your lucky day,' he said. 'Seeing as it's so quiet, the chef has made you something special. It's got beans, and eggs, and all manner of green things floating in it.'

'Vegetables?'

'Yeah.' He glanced at Millen. 'You eating?'

Millen nodded. 'Yes. Sausages, bacon, whatever you've got. And an ale.'

The serving-boy stared at him, an undisguised hostility on his face, then he turned and walked away without a word.

'What was that about?' said Maddie as she picked up a fork.

'He can tell by my accent that I'm Torduan,' Millen said. 'We're not exactly popular in these parts.'

'Aren't we in Tordue?'

'Yes.'

'Then, isn't everyone a Torduan?' she said between mouthfuls.

He raised an eyebrow. 'Sable was right – you know nothing about this place. Are you from Kinell too?'

'What?'

'Never mind. This part of the city's where all the Shinstrans live.'

'Shinstrans? As in the Shinstran Desert? I've been there. It's a horrible wasteland.'

'Shh, keep your voice down. If the locals hear you insult their beloved homeland, they'll be after you as well as me.'

'We got attacked by these disgusting bloodflies. Awful beasts.'

Millen started to look alarmed. He glanced around, as if expecting to be attacked, but the tavern was empty.

'Don't say that,' he whispered. 'The Bloodflies is the name of the Shinstran team; you'll get us lynched. You're lucky there's no one here.'

'About that; where is everyone?'

'It's a match day. The Bloodflies are away to the Deadskins today, so all of their supporters will have crammed onto wagons this morning and headed north.'

'The Deadskins?'

'That's the team of the Fordians.'

A memory of something Blackrose had told her flashed into her mind. Hadn't she been forced to fight for the Fordian team?

'Right,' she said. 'There are three teams, yeah?'

'Look, we don't have time to go over the intricacies of the teams in Alea Tanton right now. We need to go.'

'What? I'm not leaving until I've finished my lunch, and yours hasn't even arrived yet. And where are we supposed to be going?'

'Sable has asked us to do something for her.'

'Does it involve a Quadrant?'

He frowned. 'I don't know what that means.'

'Ha! At last; something I know that you don't. But now it comes to it, I don't think I should say any more. I mean, if Sable had wanted you to know, then she would have told you about them, yeah? Are you good friends with her?'

The man's cheeks turned as rosy as the pig's in the picture that hung up behind the bar.

'I see,' said Maddie. 'More than friends.'

'I wish,' he muttered.

'Oh, now I'm curious. Let me guess – you fancy her, but she's not interested. Oh dear. You seem like a nice guy, but you're not in Sable's league. Did that sound rude?'

'A tad, but it's probably the truth.' He gazed into the middle distance. 'She could get anyone she wanted.'

Maddie clicked her fingers under his nose. 'Hey, stop dreaming about Sable while you're talking to me. What is it that she wants us to do?'

He paused as the serving-boy walked over. He slammed a plate down onto the table, followed by a large mug of ale, some of which sloshed over the side into Millen's lap.

'Oops,' smirked the serving-boy.

Maddie laughed as the boy walked away. 'By the way, I hope you've got money. I only have enough to cover my own food and drink.'

'Don't worry about that,' Millen said as he glanced at the wet patch on his crotch. 'I have gold. Sable and I worked a good job before we went up to Old Alea.'

'Worked a job? You mean you robbed someone? You're a thief?'

'Not usually.'

'Ah, so the wicked Sable has led you down a path of crime? Does she want us to do something criminal?'

'Yes. Does that bother you?'

'It depends. I'm not going to do any murdering, or robbing from old ladies.'

'No?' he said, picking up a fork and stabbing an enormous slice of bacon. 'How about freeing a dragon?'

***

An hour later, Maddie and Millen were on the back of an open cart, being pulled north along a wide boulevard by a set of ponies. Maddie had taken nothing with her but the silver cigarette case and the clothes she was wearing. Millen had paid her bill at *The Rosy-Cheeked Pig*, so she still had a few coins in her purse.

'I still don't get it,' Maddie said, keeping her voice low so their driver wouldn't hear. 'You're one of these Blue Thumb people, so why would you want to do something that will really annoy your own team?'

'Didn't you hear me? They're going to execute him.'

She narrowed her eyes. 'And why do you care?'

'Sable asked,' he said, 'and, well, I guess it's the right thing to do. Not just for the dragon, but for the city. No other team has ever slaughtered a captive dragon before, especially not in front of the opposing team's supporters, and the riots would last for months if that happened.'

'And once we've freed him, then Sable will meet us?'

'She was a little vague on that aspect, to be honest. I guess she'll talk in my head again when she wants to let us know.'

'She's talked in my head too. It was pretty weird.'

'How does she do it? How can a mortal have god powers?'

Maddie shrugged. 'She's a Holdfast. All her family can do crazy stuff. You should meet her niece. Actually, don't; stay out of her way if you ever come across her. Her nephew's alright, though, but don't get on his wrong side; he'd snap you like a twig.'

'Is Sable... really from Kinell?'

'Is that what she told you?'

'Yes.'

'Then, yeah. Sable's from Kinell.'

He shook his head, his gaze lost for a moment. Maddie glanced to either side of the cart. Traffic was crowding the boulevard, with wagons and carriages heading in both directions, while to either side shop fronts gave way to rows of dilapidated tenements and shanty housing.

'Are we still in Shinstran territory?' she said.

'Yes. It's another couple of miles before we reach the area where the Torduans live. To be honest, I wasn't sure I'd ever return. Part of me doesn't want to, but... well, this is something we have to do.'

'Did Sable say how we were supposed to go about it?'

'No. She left the plan up to me.'

'And me. I mean, I am the one with actual experience of freeing dragons. I assume you've never done it?'

'You've freed a dragon before?'

'Oh yes. Indeed. I'm a regular releaser of dragons. But you'll have to tell me everything you know about this one.'

'Alright, his name's Sanguino. He's been with the Bloodflies since before I was born.'

'Where was he before that?'

'He's a captured wild dragon. Must have strayed too close to the city, just like your dragon did.'

She glared at him. 'Sable told you that?'

He nodded. 'She didn't say much; it was a short message, but she mentioned who you were. She said that's why we were perfect for this job – you know dragons, and I can get us into the place where he's being held.'

'And how are you going to manage that?'

'My cousin has a lot of connections with the Blue Thumbs, and I can use them to our advantage. I have a little plan: you pretend to be my girlfriend, and I'll tell them that I'm trying to impress you by showing you Sanguino. We'll say that you've always wanted to see a real dragon up close.'

'A bit of acting, eh? I'm up for that. No kissing, mind.'

He laughed. 'I'm sure I'll manage to resist.'

'What's that supposed to mean? Oh, I forgot, you're obsessed with Sable Holdfast. Do you smoke?'

'No. Do you?'

'No. Well, not really. I had some when I was locked up, and they were horrible, but even so, for some reason I'd quite like one now.'

He smiled. 'I heard they have a tendency to do that. Anyway, listen; I need to tell you something before we arrive at the Central Pits. My cousin, the one I mentioned who has all the contacts, he, um... well, he's probably hunting for me.'

'Hunting... in a good way?'

'In a he-probably-wants-to-hack-my-head-off kind of way.'

'Alright. Why?'

'Because he thinks I ran off with Sable.'

'You did run off with Sable.'

'Exactly.'

'Why would that concern your cousin?'

'He was going out with her at the time.'

'I see. So, we avoid him, then?'

'Ideally. Can you fight?'

'Can I say yes?'

'Would it be true?'

'No.'

He shrugged. 'I'm not much good, either. Best if we try to stay clear of confrontations. We'll need to be sneaky, rather than deadly. And discreet.'

'What, while we escape with a captive dragon? Eh, I don't think that's something we'll accomplish quietly. We'll need a big distraction; an earthquake would be handy.'

'Sure. Can you generate earthquakes?'

'Now you're just being ridiculous.'

'You started it. We'll work something out. First, we have to get in.'

It was fourteen miles from the Southern Pits to the Central Pits, and Maddie could see them loom over the horizon as they approached. The wide road, which Millen referred to as 'the Artery', ran all the way from the gates of Old Alea to the very northern tip of the city, but it split in two just before the Central Pits, then the two roads ran parallel alongside the vast complex of buildings, before joining together again on the far side. As big as the pits were, Maddie noted that they were a lot smaller than the Great Racecourse in the Circuit back home, and consisted of several buildings, instead of one enormous block. She felt a pang of homesickness as she remembered the City, and wished her sister was with her. Rosie was good at planning things, whereas Millen seemed to be willing to leave the details to chance.

The largest building was just beyond the split in the Artery, and was cylindrical. Windows and arches showed that there were four levels, all piled on top of each other.

'That's the arena,' said Millen, pointing. He leaned over and tapped the driver's shoulder. 'Drop us here.'

The driver pulled the cart over to the right hand side of the road, and Maddie clambered down to the worn flagstones. Millen dipped into his pocket and paid the driver, then jumped down next to her.

Millen gazed around. 'Home.'

'There's isn't a game on here today, then? It seems quiet.'

'The Blue Thumbs supporters generally stay at home when the other two teams are playing each other. We like to pretend that it's not happening. Also, there are always extra militia on patrol, in case things get rowdy. The away supporters have to cross Torduan territory to get home, and there are always a few fights.'

They walked across the flagstones towards the arena, then Millen took a path that went by its right hand side. He pulled a hood over his head, and glanced around. Maddie kept up with him as he hurried past a few groups standing outside the arena. Some were eating food being sold from a handful of open kiosks, while others were talking. All, Maddie noticed, were wearing blue sashes across their chests, and the vast majority were men.

'Why the Blue Thumbs?' she said.

'What?' said Millen, his glance furtive as he kept his pace up.

'Why are they called the Blue Thumbs?'

'Blue is the colour of the old flag of Tordue, so it's the colour of our team, to show that we're the original inhabitants of Alea Tanton, and that the other two peoples are incomers; that they don't really belong here. The thumb part comes from an old religious relic; a legend that an Ascendant's thumb ended up in Tordue. It was encased in gold and jewels, and paraded around in front of the army, before they went into battle, like a sacred icon, or symbol, or something.'

'I'd quite like to see it.'

'It's been lost for centuries. It hasn't been seen since the gods conquered the rebels hundreds of years ago, when they destroyed Fordia and Shinstra, and made Alea Tanton their new capital.'

'One of the gods in Old Alea probably has it sat on his mantelpiece; we should ask Sable if she could steal it for us.'

'For all I know, that's what she's there to do,' he said, glancing at her, 'unless you want to tell me the real reason?'

Maddie looked away.

They turned left at a long, squat building, leaving the milling supporters behind. Ahead was a high-walled compound, and Millen approached a side door, where a blue-sashed man was standing, an iron club slung to his belt.

'Here we go,' said Millen, removing the hood from his head. 'This is the compound where prisoners and new trainees are kept. Sanguino will be here, somewhere deep within.'

'Hi, Rodik,' Millen said as they got closer to the door.

The man frowned, then his eyes widened. 'Millen,' he grunted. 'Haven't seen you in a while.'

'Been busy. Just popping in for a minute. I've got someone who is dying to see what goes on in there.'

Rodik eyed Maddie for a moment, then nodded. 'On you go.'

Millen and Maddie stepped past him and entered the building. Millen strode along confidently, betraying no signs of anxiety. Maybe he was good at something, Maddie thought. Well, if he could do it, then so could she.

Light was coming in through high apertures in the ceiling, and she glanced at the storerooms and training halls they passed. Young men and women were practising with spears and nets in one large room, while blue-sashed guards stood watch by the walls.

Millen led her through a maze of passageways, until he came to a door. He knocked.

'Come in,' called a voice.

Millen pushed the door open and walked in, a big smile on his face. He held out his palms. 'Adlin! Great to see you. How are the kids?'

The old man glanced up from a desk of dark wood, its surface littered with coffee cups and ashtrays. He squinted.

'Millen, my boy. Take a seat. And who is this you've brought with you?'

'This is Maddie,' he said. He winked. 'A... friend.'

Maddie pinched his bum. 'I thought we were more than friends, darling?'

The old man laughed as they sat, then his features grew more serious. 'Does Gantu know you're back?'

'Back?' said Millen. 'I haven't been away. I've been, uh, shacked up with Maddie in a little apartment by Butcher's Corner. Gantu knows the address, I've told him often enough. Mind you, he was drunk when I last saw him; he's probably forgotten.'

Adlin frowned. 'He has been searching for you, ever since the Blue Thumbs were last away to the Bloodflies.'

'You're kidding me? Gantu's been looking for me? Why didn't he just come to the apartment?'

'You should also know,' Adlin went on, 'that he was in a considerable rage with you. He was making all kinds of threats. He thinks you went off with that Sable girl he was with.'

'What? That's crazy. I've been with Maddie the whole time.'

'Sometimes,' Maddie said, squeezing Millen's leg, 'we wouldn't get out of bed for days on end.'

Millen looked concerned. 'I'd best sort this out. By the Ascendants, all this time I've been having a bit of fun, and had no idea this was going on. Wait, does that mean Sable's gone missing?'

'According to Gantu,' Adlin said, 'she went missing at the same time as you, during the game at the Southern Pits.'

Millen slapped his forehead and groaned. 'I missed my carriage back, and didn't get home until a few hours later. That's when I spoke to Gantu, but, as I said, he was drunk, and raging at the result. So I went out for a few drinks, and that's when I met Maddie. Anyway, I was actually here for a small favour. I'll deal with Gantu, but first I was wondering if you could do something for me?'

Adlin rested his elbows on the table. 'Of course.'

'Maddie here has a little obsession, and it's to do with dragons. Basically, she really wants to see one up close, and, you know, with a captive dragon in the dungeons, I was hoping you might give us a little tour, so she can see Sanguino before he gets the chop.'

'Please, Mister Adlin,' said Maddie, 'please make a girl's dreams come true.'

'Very well,' he said, sighing, 'though I'm a little too busy at the moment to conduct a personal tour.' He opened a drawer and took out a set of keys. 'These are the spares. The guards at the dungeons have their own set, but use these, and make sure you hand them back before I leave the office this evening. And be careful. Sanguino may be muzzled and bound in chains, but he remains dangerous. I would hate for your lady-friend to be scared half to death.'

Millen took the keys. 'Thanks. I appreciate this.'

He stood, and Maddie got to her feet next to him. She smiled at Adlin, then they left the room.

'Step one complete,' said Millen as he closed the door. 'Do you think we might get through step two without you grabbing my ass?'

'Don't blame me,' Maddie said as they began walking down a long passageway, 'the character I was playing was overwhelmed with lust, and was living in the moment. Are you worried that Sable might get jealous?'

He rolled his eyes. 'This way,' he said, pointing at a set of stairs going down.

They walked past a couple of guards at the bottom of the steps, who glanced at them but didn't try to bar their way. Maddie crinkled her nose at the smell. It reminded her of the cell in the fortress, but worse. A long row of barred chambers ran down the side of a dark stone corridor, each filled with captives dressed in rags. One room contained people with a green tinge to their skins, and Maddie remembered being told about the appearance of Fordians. They glared at Maddie and Millen as they walked by, and a couple spat at them.

'Ignore them,' muttered Millen. 'Don't get distracted.'

'What's going to happen to them all?'

'They'll be executed in the arena. Don't look at me like that; they're all criminals, arrested by the local militia. Some of them will have done terrible things.'

They came to a heavy door in the left hand wall, and Millen opened it. Beyond were more stairs, and they went down again. The lamps lighting the way were sparse, and thick shadows lingered in the hallway at the bottom. Maddie heard a growling, shrieking sound, and her blood chilled.

'I recognise that noise,' she said, her body stiffening. She glanced at Millen, her eyes wide. 'Greenhides?'

He nodded. 'Come on.'

They walked along the hallway, then Maddie jumped as a greenhide charged the bars of a giant cage to their left, its arms reaching out. The claws at the end were bound in thick shackles, and other chains were securing the beast's ankles to the back wall of the cage. Even so, Maddie's heart raced with a familiar fear. The face of the greenhide was demented with rage, and its horrible insect-eyes were staring at her.

'I never thought I'd see these... things again,' she whispered.

'The Blue Thumbs have several greenhides,' Millen said. 'The others will be up in the training areas, though they'll be chained and shackled there too. This one must be particularly wild.'

Two guards were standing by a large door at the end of the hallway.

Millen nodded to them as they approached, and pulled the keys from his pocket.

'Hi,' he said. 'I'm just giving the girl here a little tour. Adlin said it was fine.'

'Good to see you back, Millen,' said one. 'I heard you'd gone missing.'

He nodded to Maddie. 'I was, eh, busy. You know how it is, guys.'

They laughed and let them pass. The door was unlocked, and Millen and Maddie entered a cavernous chamber, its walls carved from the bedrock of the city. Most of the chamber was taken up by an enormous steel cage, from which an overpowering animal stench was emanating. Maddie put a hand to her nose, her eyes watering.

Millen closed the door behind them, and turned. 'Here he is.'

Maddie took a step forward. Lying in the cage was a dragon. Its wings were wrapped in thick chains, and each of its four limbs was shackled to an iron hoop half-buried into the stone floor. A metal muzzle enclosed its jaws, ending just under its eyes, which were glowing a lime green in the dim light. Its scales were red, like Buckler's had been, but much darker, like wine, or blood. All over them were angry-looking cuts and sores oozing blood and pus.

'Wow,' she whispered. 'He's amazing, but look at his wounds. This is horrible. Sable's right; we need to get him out of here.'

'We will.'

'When can we do it?'

Millen shrugged. 'It'll have to be tonight. Any later, and Adlin will notice that the keys are missing. A couple of hours before dawn. We'll come back then, when the place is quiet. I have a plan that might work.'

She frowned at him. 'Might?'

'It'll work,' he said. 'I just need to iron out a few details.'

She nodded, then took a few steps forward, getting closer to the bars.

'Come no nearer,' growled the dragon, its voice coming through the thick mesh of the muzzle.

Maddie halted.

'You disgusting creature,' said the dragon in a low hiss; 'coming here to gloat over my pain. I would enjoy ripping you from top to bottom; I would...' He paused, and the light in his eyes changed slightly. He lifted his head a fraction. 'I sense the scent of dragon on you.'

'I am a rider,' said Maddie, 'and we're going to free you.'

CHAPTER 24
NEVER AGAIN

Gadena's Camp, Shinstran Desert – 11th Tradinch 5252

Van knocked at the door leading to Gadena's private quarters, then entered a brightly-lit chamber, thick with wall hangings and deep carpets.

The three gods inside turned to look at him.

'What do you want?' said Maisk.

'My lord,' said Van, bowing, 'I have come to give you this morning's report.'

'And what makes you think,' said Baldwin, 'that we have any interest in what you have to say?'

Van bowed again. 'The Banner are finding it difficult to keep the trainees under control, my lord. We could shortly have an uprising on our hands.'

'Just do your damn job,' said Felice.

'Yes, my lady, but there are four hundred trainees currently locked in their barracks. With only two squads at my disposal, if they attempt to break out, we would be unable to stop them.'

'Then I will kill them all,' said Baldwin, raising his right hand. 'In fact, I'd enjoy it.'

'Yes, my lord. May I ask what the delay is? I was under the impression that we were to be moving on at dawn this morning. If we intend to stay longer, then arrangements will have to be made to organise food supplies, and the trainees will have to be fed.'

'We shall leave when I say we leave,' said Maisk.

'Why are you boring us with this information, Captain?' said Felice. 'There are far more important things going on that you have no knowledge of. Were you aware, for instance, that last night a spy was captured in the act of stealing two Quadrants from Old Alea? And here you are, distracting us with minor logistical matters.'

'There was a spy in Old Alea?'

'Yes,' said Maisk, 'and she damaged one of the Quadrants. That is why we are still here, you fool. Lord Renko has delayed the opening of a portal and told us to await new orders. Actually, now that you're here, there is something you can do. Fetch Gadena from the dungeons. Lord Renko wishes to examine his mind.'

Van bowed low, then left the room. Sohul was waiting outside in the corridor with a sergeant.

'How did it go, Captain?' said the lieutenant. 'Do we have orders?'

Van frowned. 'Someone broke into Old Alea last night and stole two Quadrants from under Lord Renko's nose. They got them back, but one of them's broken. We could be here for a while.'

'And what about the supply situation? We don't have the resources to guard the trainees and gather enough food for them at the same time. Most of the troopers are exhausted, sir. We have to let some of them rest.'

Van began walking. 'They're not interested, Sohul. They called it a "minor logistical matter". Baldwin offered to kill the trainees, but presumably only after the trainees have killed us first.'

'Then what do we do, Captain?'

Van chewed his lip. 'Withdraw the squads from guarding the barracks and pull them back to the central core of the compound, then block all of the exits.'

'But that will seal us inside, Captain. The trainees would occupy the rest of the compound.'

'I know.'

'And there was a spy, sir?' said the sergeant. 'Do we have any details?'

'The gods weren't in a particularly forthcoming mood. Oh, she was a she. I guess that narrows it down to half the population.'

They came to a junction. 'You go and give the orders to the squads,' Van said, 'and I'll take Gadena to have his mind read by Lord Renko.'

Sohul and the sergeant saluted, and Van turned for the dungeons. The passageways were cold and deserted, with only a handful of lamps lit to guide the way. He reached the row of holding cells and glanced into the interior of the first. Gadena was sitting on a low mattress, his gaze downwards. His injuries had healed, but his eyes had a haunted look to them.

'Good morning,' said Van.

Gadena glanced up, and his expression hardened back into defiance. 'You're still here?'

Van nodded.

'I thought you were leaving at dawn.'

'Plans have changed. Lord Renko wants to speak to you.'

'The most noble Ancient?' Gadena spat onto the floor of the cell. 'Tell him to kiss my ass.'

'Why don't you tell him in person?'

'You should be more careful about who you take jobs with, boy, and I say this as one mercenary to another.'

Van raised an eyebrow. 'You've worked for Baldwin before. You sent soldiers to Kinell.'

'Yes, I did. And I regretted it almost immediately. The gods of Implacatus are filled with nothing but greed.'

Van shrugged. 'I think you'll find they have a good measure of spite and cruelty in there as well.' He took a set of keys from his pocket, and began to unlock the door.

'No shackles, boy? You do know I have battle-vision? I could break you in a second.'

'You could,' Van said, swinging the cell door open, 'but then Baldwin would kill you, and every trainee in this compound. Not because he likes me, you understand; he's looking for any excuse to do it. Now, please follow me; we don't want to keep Lord Renko waiting.'

Gadena got to his feet, his eyes never leaving Van.

'Level with me,' he said as he approached the open door, 'soldier to soldier; are they going to execute me?'

'Not as far as I know.'

The demigod nodded, then stepped out of the cell. He and Van set off down the passageway, the only sound coming from the clip of their boots on the smooth stone floor. They reached Gadena's quarters, where Van knocked and opened the door.

'You took your time,' muttered Maisk. 'Bring him in.'

Van led Gadena into the warm chamber.

'I see you've made yourselves comfortable in my rooms,' Gadena said, planting his feet in the centre of the floor and folding his arms across his wide chest.

'Yes,' said Baldwin. 'I recommend you get some better wine in. The stuff you kept is rank.'

Maisk nodded to Felice. 'Contact Lord Renko.'

She inclined her head, then her eyes hazed over. Van watched from the edge of the room. He hadn't been told to leave, and was curious to learn more about the incident with the spy. After a few moments, Felice's features spasmed, then settled into a thin frown.

'Greetings from Alea Tanton,' she said, but her eyes were still glazed over, and her voice seemed lower, the tone different from normal.

'Lord Renko,' said Maisk, bowing. 'We have Gadena here, as you requested.'

Felice turned to look at the mercenary leader. 'So I see.'

Gadena cried out as if in agony, and fell to his knees, his hands clutching his head. Felice stared at him, her eyes swirling with mist. Gadena groaned, and sunk lower, then fell to the floor, unconscious. Felice raised her head.

'I have taken everything I needed from him. I have new orders for you.'

'Of course, my lord,' bowed Maisk.

'Lord Baldwin is to remain here, as is Lady Felice, but I require you, Lord Maisk to return to Old Alea. I intend to replace you with Lady Joaz for the next stage of the operation. Bring all of the Banner soldiers back with you, except for Captain Logos and two other soldiers of his choosing.' Felice glanced at Van. 'Prepare supplies, and pack civilian clothes. Lady Joaz will instruct you upon her arrival.'

Van bowed low.

'May I ask a question, my lord?' said Baldwin.

'Proceed.'

'With no soldiers in the compound, the four hundred mercenary trainees will revolt. Do I have permission to kill them before they can become a threat?'

'Do so,' said Felice, 'though keep Gadena alive; he may be of further use to us. Place him in shackles, as he may try to prevent the elimination of his students.'

Baldwin smiled. 'Yes, my lord.'

'You did well, all of you,' said Felice. 'I look forward to more such success in the near future. Farewell.'

Felice gasped, and her eyes closed, her head falling forwards.

Maisk stood, his fists clenched. 'Replaced? Did you hear that? Haven't I done exactly what he wanted?'

Baldwin coughed, and glanced in Van's direction. 'Perhaps we should discuss this later, my lord.'

Maisk frowned at the captain. 'Get shackles for Gadena, and summon the Banner soldiers. And you, Baldwin, get to work. Clear out the barracks; I want every trainee in this place dead by the time I leave in fifteen minutes. Go.'

Twenty minutes later, the two squads from the Banner were assembled in a hall close to the central point of the compound. Baldwin had not returned from his trip to the barracks, but the sounds of screams were still filtering through, echoing down the long stone passageways. Felice and Maisk were standing in silence, their dislike of each other plain to see, while Van paused to select two soldiers to remain with him.

'Sohul,' he said, 'you're going back with the others. If all goes well, I imagine I'll be seeing you again soon. You're in charge of Eagle Company until then.'

'Yes, sir. Have you chosen who is staying with you?'

'No.' He glanced at a sergeant. 'Pick me two men. Quiet, dependable, calm under pressure.'

The sergeant nodded. 'Yes, sir.'

A long wail of agony reached the chamber and Van frowned. He tried to suppress his emotions, aware that Felice could read his thoughts, but he found it hard to clear his mind of the hatred he felt for the gods at that moment. He glanced at Gadena. The demigod was still unconscious, and had been wrapped in chains. The moment he awoke and discovered what had happened to his trainees was not one that Van was looking forward to. From the looks on the faces of the squads, he knew that many of them were feeling the same. The equivalent of two full companies of mercenaries, slaughtered for being an inconvenience – it could have been them, and the troopers knew it.

He caught Sohul's eye. 'Never again,' he whispered. 'I'm never working for these bastards again.'

The lieutenant nodded. 'Yes, sir, though I do recall you saying something similar to me on Dragon Eyre.'

The sergeant approached with one soldier.

'Where's the other one?' said Van. 'I asked for two.'

'Yes, sir; the other one will be me, sir.'

Van's composure almost cracked.

'I figured,' the sergeant went on, 'that a captain needs a sergeant, to keep him out of trouble, sir.'

'Alright. Come over and stand by me while the others leave.'

Van nodded to Sohul, then led the trooper and the sergeant over to where Lady Felice was standing. She ignored their arrival, her glance on the floor.

'I'm not waiting for Baldwin to get back,' Maisk said, a Quadrant clutched in his massive hand. He strode towards the gathered squads, and without another word, they vanished, leaving the hall nearly empty.

'Now we wait for Lady Joaz,' said Van. 'Trooper, your job is to watch Gadena for now.'

'Yes, sir,' the soldier said, saluting.

Van turned to Felice, but she was avoiding his glance. 'Is there anything I can do for you, my lady?'

'Just stay out of my way,' she muttered.

'Understood.'

A door swung open and Baldwin walked into the chamber, a gleam lighting his eyes. He glanced around, as if puzzled for a moment.

'Lord Maisk wouldn't wait,' said Felice.

Baldwin nodded, and approached the small group. His eyes roved over the body of Gadena, then settled on Van and the two soldiers.

'Are they all...?' said Felice.

'Of course,' said Baldwin, his stare remaining on Van. 'Every last one of them. Mercenary scum. They think they're tough, but dozens of them wept for mercy, pleading on their knees like cowards and crying for their mothers. Pathetic.'

Van returned Baldwin's stare.

'Do you have something to say, mortal?' the god said.

'No, my lord.'

'Are you sure?' Baldwin said, walking up to the captain until he stood a foot away. 'You look like you want to say something. Have the deaths of those mercenaries upset you? If so, then I could fix that. One more dead mercenary would make no difference to me.'

'Lord Renko wants him alive,' said Felice; 'for now at least.'

Baldwin shrugged. 'We could say that he tried to assault us.'

He raised his hand, and Van felt his heart gripped by the god's power. He swayed, as pain rippled across his chest.

'Leave him,' said Felice.

Baldwin laughed. 'I'm only playing. What's the matter? You hate him too.'

Van felt the pressure lift, and he gasped, his breath sore.

'I loathe him,' said Felice, 'but Lord Renko...'

'Fine,' Baldwin spat. He glanced at Gadena. 'Perhaps we should wake him, so I can see his face when he learns what has happened to his students.'

The air in the centre of the chamber shimmered for a moment, and Lady Joaz appeared, holding the same Quadrant that Maisk had used to depart. She glanced around as the others bowed to her.

'I'm in charge now,' she said.

'The barracks have been cleared, my lady, as per Lord Renko's orders,' Baldwin said.

Joaz nodded, her features expressionless. She looked down at Gadena, and the man stirred. His eyes flickered open.

'Get him onto his feet,' Joaz said.

The sergeant went to the trooper's assistance, and they hauled Gadena up.

'What are our orders, my lady?' said Felice.

'The seven of us are leaving,' Joaz said. 'Lord Renko wants us to scout the Falls of Iron for him, in preparation for the opening of a portal. There is a good chance that the occupants of the place will have been warned that we are coming, so we'll need to be quiet, and discreet. No killings, no distractions; nothing that will raise the alarm.'

'What happened to me?' said Gadena, his voice hoarse.

Joaz turned to him. 'Lord Renko read your memories. He did it quickly, which explains the disorientation you are feeling. You will recover soon. You are coming with us to the Falls of Iron.'

'But what about my trainees? Who will look after them?'

Baldwin started to laugh, but quietened at a glare from Joaz. 'You don't need to worry about them any more,' she said.

'Why?' cried Gadena, his eyes wild as he glanced around. 'What have you monsters done?' He stared at Van. 'What did they do to my students?'

Van said nothing.

'They have been eliminated,' said Joaz.

Gadena wailed, his face reddening as tears streamed down his cheeks. He struggled against the chains, jostling the trooper and sergeant as they gripped his arms.

'Behave yourself, demigod,' said Baldwin, raising his right hand.

Gadena spat at him. 'I will kill you for this.'

Baldwin glanced down at his spittle-flecked chestplate. He pointed at Gadena, and the demigod started to choke, his face paling.

'Baldwin, desist at once,' said Joaz.

'But... he *spat* on me. He...'

'Rise above it,' said Joaz. 'We need Gadena alive. If the time comes to execute him, rest assured that you shall be given the job. Captain, do you have the supplies that Lord Renko requested?'

Van gestured to a heap of packs lying by the wall. 'Yes, my lady.'

'Bring them here and gather round.'

Van slung a pack over his shoulder, and picked up the other two. All had been crammed with food, water, and spare clothes taken from the trainees' rooms. He strode back to Joaz as the others moved in to surround her. Her fingers glided over the surface of the Quadrant, and the chamber vanished in a hazy blur, replaced with open countryside.

Van took a long breath of fresh air. Around them were fields of corn and wheat, with olive groves dotted on the gentle slopes. To the north, a tall line of cliffs stretched east to west like a wall, while behind the small group was a blocky farmhouse, its walls white-washed and gleaming in the sunlight.

'Is this the Falls of Iron?' said Baldwin.

'No,' said Joaz. 'The settlement is three miles from here. I chose this location because the farmhouse is empty, and it will make a suitable base for the moment.'

She set off for the front entrance of the building, and the others followed, the two soldiers dragging Gadena along. They went into the farmhouse, and Van set down the packs in the small front room.

Joaz glanced around. 'Captain,' she said, 'make sure Gadena is secured to a chair, then change your clothing.'

'Yes, ma'am.'

'What about us?' said Felice.

'You are staying here while the captain and I scout out the town.'

'What?' cried Baldwin. 'You dragged us out here to sit in a farmhouse?'

'You have skills, Baldwin,' Joaz said, 'but they are not what I currently require. The captain and I will infiltrate the Falls of Iron, in order to discover who is there that knows anything about the salve trade. That is our mission, not to go in and kill everything that moves. If a slaughter is required, I shall send for you.'

Van took a pack and squeezed into a small bedchamber. All around were the possessions of the locals who lived there – clothes, children's wooden toys, and a stack of unwashed dishes. The locals had fled in a hurry, he thought, as he stripped the armour from his body, removing every trace of his Banner uniform. He pulled on a nondescript set of traveller's clothes, and tightened the belt at his waist. He strapped his sword to the belt, and fitted a knife to his left calf, then returned to the main room.

Joaz eyed him up and down, then nodded. In the other corner of the room, the sergeant and the trooper had finished tying Gadena to a chair, and were securing a gag to his mouth.

'Excellent,' said Joaz. She turned to Baldwin and Felice. 'Make yourselves at home. I'm leaving the Quadrant here with you, but do not use it. The captain and I will be walking to the Falls of Iron, and I shall contact you once we are there.'

The soldiers and gods bowed to her, then Joaz turned and walked from the farmhouse. Van nodded to the sergeant, and followed Joaz out into the blazing sunshine.

'I trust you shall behave yourself?' she said as they joined a farm track heading towards the cliffs in the distance.

'As always, ma'am.'

She smiled.

'Can I ask you, ma'am, about the spy? What happened?'

'It was a servant,' she said. 'She got a job in the kitchens, and then joined Lord Renko's harem. You probably saw her; she used to serve coffee to the officers.'

He nodded. 'Is she dead, ma'am?'

'Stop calling me "ma'am". As of now, we are undercover. I am not a god, and you are not a captain in the Banner of the Golden Fist. We are travellers, making our way to Cape Armour, and merely stopping off in the Falls of Iron. In answer to your question, the captured spy is still alive. Lord Renko has yet to question her; he's been busy trying to repair the Quadrant she damaged. Unsuccessfully, I might add. One of the most precious objects in all the worlds, and she broke it. I believe that leaves under a dozen now in existence.' She glanced at Van. 'As you can imagine, Lord Renko is rather upset. We still don't know how she managed to remain undetected. As you know, every servant working in the Governor's residence has had their minds read, but somehow she was able to fool the mighty Lord Renko.'

They reached a wider road and took it. The fields around them were deserted and silent, and there was no traffic moving on the road.

'You were right,' he said, 'they're expecting trouble.'

'Which means they have a god or demigod on their side,' she said; 'someone with vision powers. Our job is to find out who they are and what they know about the salve trade, and then we report back to Lord Renko. He has the entire Banner on standby, ready to cross via a portal. I admit I'm pleasantly surprised that you survived a full day and night in the company of Maisk, Baldwin and Felice. I imagine that it was only their fear of Lord Renko that prevented them from killing you.'

'Really? I thought it was my charm and good looks.'

Joaz laughed.

'Can I ask something else? It's about the powers of the gods.'

She raised an eyebrow. 'Go on.'

'Are there any gods with the power to remove people's memories?'

'Not that I'm aware of. False visions can implant memories, but they can't be removed. Why? Have you lost some?'

'Yes.'

'Then I would suspect something as mundane as alcohol or dull-weed caused it.'

'And what if I hadn't been drinking?'

'Would you like me to check? When did this happen?'

'The night before last.'

Joaz glanced at him, and he felt a faint burning sensation behind his temples.

She frowned. 'That *is* strange. It's almost as if your mind has been persuaded to forget certain events. I could delve deeper, but it might incapacitate you for a while. Maybe later?'

He nodded. 'At least I know I'm not going mad.'

'I know of no god who could have done this to you.' She paused. 'I shall have to report the escaped prisoner to Lord Renko. She had something to do with that dragon you chased off a few days ago, but your mind has almost completely forgotten all traces of her.'

Van squinted into the distance, trying not to think about the words the god had just spoken. Rising up the face of the cliff, he could see dozens of white cubes protruding from the rock, along with one large building with battlements that shone in the sunlight. Next to it, tall waterfalls were spilling torrents of glistening water down the vertical slope, towards a town nestled at the bottom.

'There it is,' said Joaz; 'the Falls of Iron. Our intelligence states that it is ruled by a certain Count Irno, though no one, not even Gadena, seems to know where he comes from. He supplies iron and foodstuffs to the city of Alea Tanton, and pays his taxes on time. According to the records in Old Alea, this Count Irno arrived shortly after salve was first seen in Khatanax. He'll be my first target when we reach the town.'

They quietened as they approached the settlement. Surrounding it on the side away from the cliffs was a long semi-circular wall of bare, rough stone, with towers every twenty yards. A line of traffic appeared on the road, queuing to get into the town. There were wagons piled high with supplies, with families and animals, all waiting to reach the security of the walls.

Van and Joaz walked by the slow-moving queue, and waited in a smaller line, comprised of those on foot. The queue was moving, as the guards by the gates were letting everyone through. Van eyed the soldiers as they got closer to the walls. They were ordinary town militia, wearing mismatching armour and carrying an assortment of weapons. The walls, too, looked weak and hard to defend. The castle halfway up the cliff face, on the other hand, seemed almost impregnable. Steep stairs cut into the rock led directly up to a forecourt, where tall towers and battlements enclosed a high central keep. It was out of range of any projectile weapons that might be brought to bear against it from the ground, and had access to fresh water from the river that tumbled down from the heights.

He lowered his eyes as they passed through the gates and entered the town. Officials were guiding civilian families to addresses where accommodation had been made available for them, and one approached Joaz and Van.

'Are you residents of the Falls of Iron?' he asked.

'No,' said Van; 'just passing through on the way to Cape Armour.'

'And what is your business there?'

'We were planning on trading,' said Joaz, 'but with the rumours of trouble, we've decided to cut our losses and get a boat back to Kinell.'

The official nodded. 'Head up by the fish pools to your right; there are a few hostels with rooms still available, although I warn you, they won't come cheap.'

'Thanks,' said Van, nodding.

He shielded his eyes from the glare of the cube-shaped white buildings, and they passed crowds of people packing the streets. Merchants were out, selling food and supplies to the recent arrivals, while tired-looking families stood around, waiting to be shown to their temporary dwelling places. They turned right, and walked up the gentle slope in the direction of the cliffs, until they reached a long series of large pools, covered by canvas awnings to prevent the water from evaporating in the heat. Just beyond them was a row of hostels, with taverns and places to eat and drink laid out next to them. The roar of a waterfall filled Van's ears.

'This is a beautiful town,' he said.

Joaz raised an eyebrow. 'It's a little out of the way.'

They picked the first hostel, and paid a small fortune for a tiny room, barely big enough to fit a bed and a side table. They bought some food and wine, and squeezed in. Van laid his pack down onto the bed, then turned away as Joaz got changed out her travelling clothes.

'Ready,' she said.

He turned. Joaz was sitting on the bed, wearing very little.

'Pour me a wine,' she said. 'And don't look so surprised. You've seen every inch of me before now, and there's no way I'm sitting in this humid little room over-dressed. I've sweated enough today already.'

He reached over to the table and opened a bottle of wine. He filled a glass, then passed it to Joaz, before pulling his boots off. He laid his sword by the door, ready in case he needed it.

'Right,' Joaz said, after taking a sip; 'time for a little reconnaissance.'

She placed the glass down and her eyes hazed over. Van sat on the bed and looked at her. She was beautiful, but he knew she didn't care about him. He was just a useful mortal who happened to please her; convenient, but expendable. She might not be as bad as some of the other gods, but he remembered her sitting in silence as he had been tortured by Maisk, Felice and Baldwin. He turned from her before the sight of her bare skin inflamed him, and adjusted the shutters. He peered through the slats, and saw that their view was of the back of the neighbouring building. He sighed, feeling the heat from the midday sun outside. He scrambled over the bed until his back was leaning against a wall, and lit a cigarette, holding it up by the crack in the shutters.

His thoughts went back to Gadena's camp, and the slaughter of the trainees. He had been suppressing it in his mind while he had been walking with Joaz, aware that she could read his thoughts any time she chose. Baldwin needed to die, that was clear. And Felice, and Maisk; all of them. It was true what Sohul had said – Van had previously sworn never to work another contract for the gods, especially during the grim days on Dragon Eyre, yet he had always come back for more. Did he mean it this time?

Joaz coughed, and groaned. She picked up her wine and took a longer sip.

'Any luck?' he said.

'Something's wrong,' she said, a twinge of fear in her eyes.

'Wrong?' he said. 'What do you mean?'

'I sent my vision up to the castle, and I got in fine. But then, when I tried to look for Count Irno, and anyone else who might be with him, it was as if my powers were being blocked. As if... something was stopping my powers from seeing who was there. I pulled back, and went into the head of one of the soldiers on the battlements. My powers are working fine, but not within the inner chambers of the castle.' She glanced at him. 'Give me a cigarette.'

He lit one for her and passed it into her hands, which were trembling slightly.

'I don't understand,' she said.

'Did you get anything out of the soldier's head?'

'Yes. He was aware that guests are living in the castle. Two of them are Count Irno's sisters, but he was unsure who the others were. He also knew that a dragon has been here recently, but has since departed.'

'A dragon?'

She nodded. 'Damn it. What am I going to tell Lord Renko? He won't accept this; he'll think I'm not trying hard enough.'

'We could wait for nightfall,' Van said, 'and get closer. Maybe your powers will work better then?'

'You're not listening. I told you, something is blocking me – like a void, where the powers of the gods are negated in some way. I've never felt anything like it.'

Van glanced at her. For the first time since he had known her, she seemed scared.

'Then we bluff our way into the castle,' he said, 'and scout without powers.'

'I have no battle-vision,' she said; 'you know that. Without my powers I'd be helpless. If I was captured...' She shuddered.

'Then I'll go alone. We'll wait until the middle of the night, and I'll set off. I've sneaked into castles before. You'll be safe here.'

Joaz lowered her face. 'I can't believe I'll have to rely on a mortal. You must tell no one of this; understand?'

'Yes.'

'Damn it,' she muttered, 'and I had plans for this evening, plans involving me, you, wine and this bed.'

He nodded, strangely relieved that he would not have to sleep with the beautiful god. He glanced away, in case she read his thoughts. What was wrong with him? Most men he knew would be envious of his situation, but he was tired of being used.

'I haven't slept since Alea Tanton,' he said. 'I should probably get some rest, if I'm going up to the castle tonight.'

'Sorry,' she said, as he lay down; 'I'll make it up to you another time.'

CHAPTER 25

UNREADABLE

Falls of Iron, Western Khatanax – 11th Tradinch 5252

Aila picked at her lunch as she sat outside in the shade. It had been a long, hot morning, and Corthie still hadn't arisen after they had spent the previous night drinking with his sister. Unlike the Holdfasts, Aila had been able to cure her hangover as soon as she had awoken, and felt fine. She had left Corthie sleeping in bed, and had set out to tell Belinda about Kelsey's arrival, but the god had gone out with Silva for a walk.

She glanced down into the settlement. Traffic was still entering through the gates in the town walls, and the Falls of Iron was filling up with the people from the surrounding farms and villages. Aila frowned. If the gods were bringing an army, perhaps they should be evacuating the town, instead of packing it with more mouths to feed, but her brother had been adamant, and the Falls of Iron was his to rule.

She sipped her chilled coffee. She had found that, with plenty of milk and sugar, a cold version of the drink that Corthie and Vana loved so much was a little more palatable, though she didn't need the lift it gave her.

Aila.

She jumped. That was Sable's voice in her head, but it sounded weak, and tired.

Aila, help me.

'What's wrong?' Aila said.

I'm in chains, lying... somewhere, Sable said, her voice slow and forced. *They put a hood on my head; they don't realise I don't need my eyes to use my powers. They beat me.*

Aila put a hand to her mouth. 'They caught you?'

Yes. I have to go; they're coming. I'm sorry about what I did to you. I'm sorry about everything.

Aila jumped to her feet. She listened, but the voice had gone.

'Sable!'

Nothing.

Aila rubbed her face, then took off for the castle keep. She raced into the cool, stone entrance hall, then sped up the stairs towards Irno's study, leaping two steps at a time. She barged into the chamber without knocking, and saw her brother talking with Naxor and Kelsey.

'Ah,' said Naxor, 'I was hoping to speak to you. I...'

'Shut up, Naxor,' Aila cried. 'Sable's in trouble.'

'What kind of trouble?' said Kelsey, a cigarette in her fingers.

'She's been caught. In Alea Tanton. The gods have her. She's chained, and they've beaten her up.'

'Slow down, sister,' said Irno. 'Tell us everything.'

'I already have! That's all she told me, then she had to go because she said that someone was coming for her. We have to do something.'

Irno frowned.

'Aila's right,' said Kelsey. 'We can't leave my aunt alone up there in the city. We have to get her out. What's the quickest way we can get to Alea Tanton?'

'Without a Quadrant or a dragon,' said Irno, 'that would be by ship.'

'But you said that would take four days,' cried Aila.

'That's for the big merchant vessels,' said Irno. 'My personal galley can do the voyage in half that.'

Kelsey stood. 'We should go now.'

'You should stay here,' said Irno. 'Alea Tanton is a city of three million people. Unless you know your way around it, you'll never reach Sable in time.'

'It has to be me,' said Naxor. 'I know Old Alea, and I can guess where Sable is being held.'

'Where?' said Aila.

'There's a prison under the Governor's residence, and that'll be where the gods from Implacatus will be staying.'

'I should come,' said Kelsey.

'Let me handle it,' said Naxor. 'Irno is correct; you don't know anything about the city or the peoples who live there. Without wishing to cause offence, you'd slow me down.'

Kelsey narrowed her eyes.

'I think Naxor might be right,' said Aila. 'He knows the place, and how to get in and out.'

'Aye, but I don't trust him,' said Kelsey. 'You yourself told me last night about all of the tricks and scams he's pulled to get his filthy little mitts on a Quadrant.'

'This is different,' said Aila. 'This is to do with saving someone's life.'

Naxor smiled. 'Thank you for the vote of confidence, cousin.'

Aila eyed him. 'Don't make me regret it.'

'I shan't. Irno, how long does it take to get your ship ready?'

'I keep it prepared, just in case. It should be able to sail within a couple of hours. Take my carriage to the harbour, and take gold, and anything else you need.'

'Very well. Send a message ahead of me; I'll need to speak to Belinda before I go.' He turned to Kelsey. 'As long as Sable can hold out until I arrive, I will do my utmost to assist her. You have my word.'

He bowed his head a little to the Holdfast woman, then left the chamber. Irno went to his desk and began writing a note.

'Thank you, brother,' Aila said.

'I've mentioned before that I've had some misgivings about Sable, but I'm not going to stand by while she rots in the dungeons of the gods.'

Kelsey scowled at both of them. 'If I had a working Quadrant, I'd get her myself.'

Irno rang a small bell that sat on the desk, and a servant entered. Irno handed him the note.

'Take this to the harbour, and give it to the captain of my galley. Make all haste, if you please; it is rather urgent.'

The servant bowed, and hurried from the room.

'Damn it all,' Kelsey muttered as she paced up and down. 'I'm not even in Lostwell for a whole day, and Sable's already in trouble. Why did my stupid sister leave her here? I'll be having some serious words with her when I get back.' She glanced at Irno. 'You looked at my broken Quadrant yet?'

'No, miss. I will, as soon as I have a little time, I assure you. I must warn you, however, I am no expert in Quadrants. Almost certainly, any necessary repairs will be beyond my skills.'

Kelsey groaned and pulled her hair. 'Where is that half-wit brother of mine? And Belinda, does she even know I'm here yet?'

'Perhaps you should sit down,' said Irno.

'Shut up.'

Irno frowned. 'Really, miss, I...'

'No, be quiet; I heard something.'

'What?'

A low rumble reached Aila's ears, and the ground shook beneath their feet. Aila grasped the back of a nearby chair as it subsided.

She glanced at Kelsey. 'It was only an earthquake; a little one.'

'Karalyn told me about them,' she said. 'She thinks Lostwell is sick.'

Vana rushed into the room, her eyes wide. 'Did you feel that?'

'Yes,' said Irno. 'Nothing to worry about.'

'They're getting more frequent, brother.'

'I've lived with them for three hundred years, sister. Come, sit and give me your report. You were going to check for the presence of gods, were you not?'

Vana sat in a chair opposite Irno. 'I did. There's nothing out there. No traces of any god power for dozens of miles around.'

'That's good news,' he said.

Kelsey stuck up her hand. 'Hello?'

Vana turned and did a double-take. 'Who are you?'

'This is Corthie's other sister,' said Irno. 'She arrived yesterday.'

'And when were you going to tell me?'

'I only discovered she was here an hour ago.'

'I have a name,' said Kelsey.

'I'm sure you do,' said Vana.

'I'm Kelsey, and you must be Vana. I can tell because Karalyn told me about this really irritating demigod who lives here and you fit her description. She also told me that you have this rather odd power, and you can tell if other powers are being used. You can sense them, right?'

Vana frowned. 'Yes.'

'I can too.'

'You can?'

'Yes, and what you're saying isn't true. About half an hour ago I sensed vision powers coming from somewhere inside the little town below us.'

'What? Impossible.'

Kelsey smirked. 'It must be nice to feel so certain about things. However, you are wrong. If you don't believe me, try to use your powers now.'

Vana sighed. 'Another Holdfast? What did we do to deserve this?'

Irno furrowed his brow. 'Do as she says. Just in case.'

'I'll humour her, for your sake, brother.' Vana closed her eyes, then opened them again. She gasped.

'See?' said Kelsey. 'Told you.'

'Is she right?' said Aila. 'Are your powers not working?'

'Try yours,' said the young Holdfast woman.

'Alright.'

You see me as Corthie.

The others in the room looked blankly at her.

'Are you doing it?' said Irno.

Aila frowned. 'Who do I look like?'

'Eh, you, dear sister.'

'Let me explain,' said Kelsey, grinning. They all stared at her. 'I have a unique power. Well, I'm exaggerating, but only a little – Karalyn can also do it, but her range is much smaller than mine. But, she can actually control it, whereas for me it's always on. Anyway, I negate the powers of others. Anyone within my vicinity can't use them. Sorry, maybe I should have mentioned it as soon as I arrived, or maybe I should wear a sign round my neck. Vana, if you go up onto the roof of the castle, or out on the forecourt, you'll find that your powers will start working again. Same with you, Aila.'

'But...' said Aila. 'Wait, how could Sable get into my head earlier?'

'That's easy,' Kelsey said; 'she has dream mage powers – the only ones not affected. Well, not the only ones, strictly speaking. Internal powers aren't affected either. Your self-healing powers, the ones that make you immortal, they still work, as does battle-vision. It's only powers that travel through the air that are negated.'

'Damn Holdfasts,' muttered Irno. 'Is there anything else you can do? Wait, before you answer that, let's go back a moment. You said that you sensed someone using vision powers in the town?'

'Aye. Or attempting to use them would be more accurate. They tried to take a peek into the castle, but I guess I blocked them. That's a little benefit of having me around. No one will be able to use their powers against you, not while I'm in the castle.'

Irno stared at her.

'You mean,' said Aila, 'that if gods come, they wouldn't be able to use death powers against us?'

Kelsey gave a curtsey. 'You're welcome.'

'This changes things considerably,' said Irno, standing. 'I'm going to begin moving civilians up into the castle. We can put them in the caves, where they'll be safe. With this knowledge, we could defend the Falls of Iron indefinitely. At a stroke, the greatest danger we faced has been removed, and best of all, the gods don't know about it.'

'Unless,' said Kelsey, 'it was a god down there in the town, and they've reported their failure back to Alea Tanton.'

'Indeed,' said Irno. 'We have no time to lose. Miss Holdfast, could you guide us to where the source of the powers was emanating?'

'Sure. Just wake my brother up first. And get Belinda too; I want to say hello to the dozy cow.'

It was decided that Belinda would lead the trip to the lower town of the Falls of Iron to confront whoever had been trying to use their vision powers. Aila went along in case she was needed, and Kelsey, to ensure that no one would sense them coming. Corthie stuck by his sister, and the four left the castle along with a wagon full of soldiers as the sun was starting its descent down the western sky. After ordering the soldiers to wait by the main road, Belinda led the others down a side street lined with hostels and taverns.

'Did Naxor get away to the harbour?' said Corthie as they walked by a series of fish pools.

Belinda nodded, her lips set firm.

'I'm surprised you let him go.'

'I made my feelings clear to him,' she said, 'but I'm not his mother.'

'I'm glad he's going,' said Kelsey. 'Someone needs to help Sable.'

Belinda didn't respond.

'Miserable as ever, eh, Belinda?' Kelsey said. 'Don't think for a minute that the Empress has forgiven you. After everything she did for you, and you betrayed her.'

'It was four years ago, Kelsey,' said Corthie.

Belinda halted. 'She told you what happened?'

'Aye. I asked. I guessed you'd done something, otherwise why would you owe Karalyn anything?'

Kelsey nodded. 'Lennox would still be alive if it weren't for her. She opened the gates to Agatha.'

'I did,' said Belinda, 'and I've regretted it every day since.'

Aila tapped her foot on the cobbles. 'Can we stay focussed?'

Kelsey gestured to one of the hostels, the outside tables busy with patrons drinking and eating.

'In there,' she said. 'A small room on the second floor, at the back of the building.'

Aila nodded. 'Belinda, could you use your vision to check what they're up to inside?'

The god raised her face and nodded, her eyes heavy and dark. 'I'll have to move outside Kelsey's range,' she said. 'Wait here.'

Aila turned to Kelsey once Belinda had walked away. 'You should give her a break. She's done a lot of good since then. She played a large role in saving the world I come from, and Corthie would be dead if she hadn't helped.'

'Aila's right,' said Corthie.

Kelsey narrowed her eyes at both of them. 'I can see why Karalyn left you here. You missed the last year of the war, Corthie. The gods slaughtered hundreds of thousands of people, all over the Plateau, and countless more died of famine in Rahain. It's taken four years to slowly put the pieces back together. Four years of pain and struggle. But Belinda's betrayal is what eats at the Empress's heart, especially when she's had one too many whiskies. It wasn't just Lennox who was killed when Belinda let Agatha into our last stronghold. The Empress's friend Calder also died. That was a blow, from which I don't think she's ever fully recovered.'

Belinda appeared from out of the shadows, a tear running down her cheek.

'Hey!' Kesley said. 'Were you listening? I thought you were away using your vision powers? Sneaky cow.'

The god said nothing for a moment, then she wiped the tear from her face. 'I found them.'

'Answer my question,' cried Kelsey.

'Later,' said Belinda. 'First, we do this. Come with me.'

She strode off towards the building. The others glanced at each other, then followed, Kelsey with a deep frown on her face. They entered the hostel, and Belinda stopped at the bottom of the stairs.

'Aila,' she said, 'come with me; I'll need you for this to work. Corthie, stay down here with your sister, and keep any of the staff from going upstairs. Stay ready; we'll be back soon.'

She started up the stairs before the Holdfasts could object, and Aila hurried after her.

'There's a man and a woman inside the room,' Belinda said as they climbed the wooden steps. 'The man has a sword, so I suspect he's guarding the woman.'

'Is she a god?'

'I'm not Vana; I can't tell, but I guess she must be.'

They stopped on a wooden landing, and Belinda glanced at the row of doors.

'What are they doing in there?' whispered Aila.

'Sleeping, or trying to.'

'Then what do you need me for?'

Belinda's dark eyes glanced at her. 'I needed someone, and I also wanted to get away from the Holdfasts for a moment.' She pulled a crossbow from over her shoulder and handed it to Aila. 'Cover me.'

She drew her sword, and put her fingers round the handle of a door. The dark metal of the Weathervane gleamed dully in the dim light, its ancient edge sharp and keen. Belinda wrenched open the door, revealing a tiny room beyond, filled with a bed, upon which two figures were lying. The man's eyes shot open, and Belinda darted forward, placing the blade against his throat before his hand could reach for his weapon, while Aila aimed the crossbow at the woman.

'Don't move an inch,' said Belinda, her eyes tight, 'or you lose your head.'

***

'Are they dangerous?' said Irno, as the small party made its way down into the deep cellars of the castle.

'Not while they're locked up,' said Belinda. 'Kelsey's powers will stop the god from using her vision to let anyone know what's happened.'

They paused as a soldier lit more lanterns along the dark passageway.

'And the mortal?' said Irno.

'He's dressed as a civilian,' said Belinda, 'but I suspect he's a soldier.'

Irno took a breath and glanced around. 'Are we ready?'

Aila stepped forward. 'Remember,' she said, 'not a word about anything secret, or the god will let everyone know if she gets a chance. That means no mention of salve, or the worlds that we come from, or Blackrose, or Quadrants, or anything.'

The soldier nodded to Irno, and they moved off down the cold corridor, passing chambers that looked like they hadn't been used in decades. They reached the end of a passageway, and came to a row of old cells, their walls hewn from the solid rock. Their doorways were barred, and only the last two in the line were occupied.

Irno and the others moved up to face the prisoners.

'I am Count Irno,' he said, 'ruler of the Falls of Iron.'

The woman got up from a worn stone bench and stood in front of the bars. 'Count Irno, why have I been incarcerated within this stinking dungeon? What crimes have I committed within your lands?'

Irno regarded her with a wary eye. 'Don't play us for fools. We know you were attempting to spy on us. Tell us why you have come to the Falls of Iron.'

The woman smiled. 'You have no idea who you're dealing with.'

'Then tell us your name.'

'Or what?'

'Or we'll have you executed as spies.'

The woman snorted, her eyes scanning the group standing outside the cells.

'Your powers won't work,' said Kelsey. 'I can sense you trying to use them. Would it help loosen your tongue if you knew that no one from outside of this castle will be able to see that you're here? If any god is watching, it will look like you've vanished.'

'Then, for your own sakes, you should release me immediately. If my superiors think I have been killed, they will be liable to retaliate with overwhelming force.'

'Let them come,' said Corthie.

'They will obliterate you,' said the woman. 'You've seen the Fordian wastes? How about the ruins of Dun Khatar? Do you want the same thing to happen to the Falls of Iron?'

'Then talk,' said Irno. 'What do you want? Is there a middle ground that keeps everyone alive?'

The woman pursed her lips for a moment, as if considering. 'Do I have your word that neither of us will be harmed?'

'I cannot do that,' said Irno; 'not until I know the purpose of your visit.'

Corthie frowned. 'Have you come from Gadena's camp?'

The woman frowned.

'Is he alive?' said Corthie.

'He's alive,' she said. 'If you wish him to remain so, then I advise you not to harm us.'

Irno shook his head. 'I grow impatient. Your names, please.'

'I am Lady Joaz of Implacatus, and my companion is Captain Van Logos of the Banner of the Golden Fist.'

'The who?' said Kelsey.

'Mercenaries,' said Irno; 'I have heard of them. They work for the gods; carry out their dirty work for them.' He glanced at Joaz. 'Thank you. Now, your purpose here?'

Joaz stared back. 'Salve.'

Aila kept her features still, but her heart began to race.

'Explain,' said Irno.

'The trade in salve,' Joaz said, 'is too important to be left to chance any longer. The rulers of Implacatus have decreed that its source and supply must be brought under control. This is how we all survive this. Tell me where the salve comes from, and how it gets here, and not only will you all live, but you will be rewarded.'

'And what makes you think we have anything to do with such matters?'

Joaz smiled. 'It's too late for that; Gadena has already given you up. An army is waiting to move into the Falls of Iron, and if I do not report back to my superior, they will be coming. Let us make a deal, one that we can all walk away from.'

'This is nothing we didn't already know,' said Belinda. 'If what she says is true, then we should execute them both.'

Irno nodded. 'I think you might be right. Come, let us go. I will order soldiers to bring me their heads.'

'Wait,' said Joaz as they turned to leave. 'You cannot kill us.'

'Oh,' said Irno, 'and why not?'

She gestured to the cell to her left. 'The soldier in there; he doesn't even realise it, but he has already helped your cause. Killing him would be a shameful act.'

Aila glanced into the cell where the man was sitting. He hadn't said a word since they had arrived, and had remained motionless. At the words of the god, however, he stirred, and narrowed his eyes.

'Go on,' said Irno.

'A few days ago,' Joaz said, 'he helped some friends of yours.'

'What?' said the soldier, getting to his feet.

'Be quiet for a moment, Captain,' Joaz said; 'let me finish.' She turned back to the small group on the other side of the bars. 'He was tasked with capturing a dragon that had been shot down. He claims he managed to drive it away, but the truth is that he let it go. I believe this dragon was known to you. Furthermore, he released the dragon's rider, one Maddie Jackdaw, helping her escape from captivity.' She turned to the soldier. 'I read this from your mind, Van, while you were sleeping. Your memories have been altered, to make you forget what you did, but I was able to piece it all together.'

The soldier's face paled, and he gripped the bars.

'You see,' Joaz went on, addressing Irno, 'to execute this man would be to kill someone who has helped you. Also, if he were to return to the Banner, then my superior would be able to read what I have read, and he would be killed for what he has done.'

'Why are you telling them this?' Van cried.

'To save your life,' she said. 'I know how much you loathe the gods, Van, and what you think of me, though you bury it deep in your heart.'

'And what about you?' said Irno. 'Why should I spare your life?'

'It seems clear to me,' Joaz said, 'that you have no one here with vision powers, otherwise you would have read everything you needed directly out of my head. My superior is named Lord Renko, an Ancient from Implacatus. He is cold, and ruthless, but he will be open to negotiations. Tell me what you know about the salve, and I will communicate our deal to him.'

'But your powers don't work,' said Kelsey.

Joaz stared at the young Holdfast woman for a moment. 'My powers do work,' she said, 'just not here. Is that your doing, girl? Have you somehow cloaked the castle, shielding it? How is it done?'

'None of your damn business, and don't call me "girl" again. My name is Kelsey Holdfast, and my family kill gods for fun.'

'Then kill me, and watch as the Falls of Iron is turned into a wasteland, its inhabitants slaughtered, its fields and water supply poisoned for a thousand years. You cannot escape the judgment of the Ascendants. I am but one god among many who will keep coming, until the salve is under our control.'

'That is enough for now,' said Irno. He glanced into the two cells. 'You shall remain here, as my guests. You will not be harmed, yet.' He turned to the others. 'Let us go.'

'We cannot believe a word she says,' said Kelsey, as they sat round a table in Irno's study. 'She knows we can't read her mind; she could be making up any old crap.'

'I should have delayed Naxor's departure,' said Irno, a glass of raki in his hand. 'He could have sorted this out.'

'I believe her,' said Aila. 'What she said about Maddie and Blackrose; it ties in with what Sable told me. Kelsey, does Sable have the power to mess with people's memories?'

The Holdfast woman lit a cigarette. 'Aye, though it's not as strong as Karalyn's power to do the same. Sable's efforts usually wear off after a while, whereas if Karalyn does it to you, it's permanent, as in Belinda's case for example.'

'So Sable could have... manipulated that soldier, and then made him forget about it?'

Kelsey nodded.

'Joaz seems to care about the soldier,' said Corthie.

'Nah,' said Kelsey, 'she just wants us to think that. She's a god; she doesn't give a flying rat's arse about mortals. She was going for the sympathy vote.'

'All the same,' said Aila, 'if he helped Maddie and Blackrose, we shouldn't kill him.'

'Here's what we do know,' said Belinda. 'Gadena has been captured, and his knowledge has led the gods here, to the gates of the Falls of Iron. This Joaz will only be the first to arrive, but when the others do, they will come in force. We must decide – do we defend the castle against them, or do we evacuate?'

'Evacuate?' said Irno. 'Out of the question.'

'You heard what she said,' Belinda went on. 'Do you want your lands transformed into a poisonous desert? It's not too late; we could be at the harbour in a few hours, and then we could sail to the Southern Cape. Silva knows the region down there; we can regroup, and plan our next move.'

'No,' said Corthie. 'We make our stand here, and destroy the army of the gods. Otherwise we'll always be on the run. Look at this castle – it's impregnable; we'll never find a better place to fight.'

'That's the spirit,' said Irno. 'I shall order the gates of the town to be closed and barred. We have soldiers, we have supplies, we have mighty warriors, and,' he said, glancing at the young Holdfast woman, 'we have Kelsey.'

CHAPTER 26

THICKER THAN WATER

Alea Tanton, Tordue, Western Khatanax – 11th Tradinch 5252

Sable felt arms grab hold of her shoulders and raise her a little.

'Pull up the hood,' said a voice, 'but only as far as her nose. Her eyes must remain covered.'

'Yes, sir.'

Sable focussed her powers as the hood was lifted above her mouth. Even weak and in agony, she still had a small grip of her dream vision, and she scanned the room. She sensed six soldiers, two of whom were pointing crossbows at her. Two others were at her shoulders, and one was raising a water bottle to her lips. She felt the cool liquid splash against her mouth, and she drank greedily, parched after lying alone for so long.

She knew it was daytime from the heat and humidity in the chamber where she was being held, but she had lost track of the hours since she had been captured; the broken bone in her leg had seen to that. She had never experienced such pain for so long; it screamed at her, filling her mind and consuming all of her thoughts.

She drank until the soldiers moved the water bottle away, and then the hood was pulled back down over her mouth, and hands lowered her to the stone floor. Footsteps walked away, and the soldiers departed, closing and locking the door behind them. Chains were digging into her wrists, and she struggled to adjust how she was lying, conscious that with one wrong movement, her broken leg would paralyse her with pain.

For a night and a day she had alternated between agony and fitful stretches of shallow sleep. She had contacted Millen in one of her more lucid moments, and had even managed to hide the pain in her voice, telling him not to worry. She had also told him to fetch Maddie and save a dragon, so perhaps she hadn't been as lucid as she had believed. Those two, save a dragon? She must have been delirious to have suggested that, but what was done was done. She no longer had the energy to contact him again; her short message to Aila had proved that. She should have been conserving her strength, but hadn't been able to resist reaching out to the demigod to plead for help. None was coming, of course, she knew that.

She closed her eyes, sweating under the thick hood. All of her clothes were damp with sweat, and streaked with dried blood. It was her own fault. She had made a mistake, somehow, though despite the number of times she had gone over the events, she still couldn't work out what she had done wrong.

The door opened again, and she wondered if she had drifted off to sleep. She flickered her dream powers into action, just enough to sense what was going on in the room around her. A chair was set down onto the floor, then soldiers leaned over and picked her up. She was placed into the seat, and the shackles round her right ankle were secured to a chair leg. Her hood was removed, and the soldiers hurried from the chamber as she blinked in the sunlight filtering through the thin slats in the shutters.

Lord Renko walked in, and closed the door.

'I am wearing eye shields,' he said; 'you will be unable to penetrate my mind.'

She squinted at him through the pain.

'You have a choice,' he went on; 'answer my questions, and I will make your remaining hours as pleasant as possible. Refuse me, and soon you shall be begging for death.' He lifted a glass vial. 'Do you know what this is?'

She shook her head.

'It's salve,' he said; 'the most precious substance in all the worlds. I am going to give you a drop, for two reasons. First, to render you fit to speak, and second, to give you a glimpse of a life without pain. If you are cooperative, I will give more. Open your mouth.'

Sable did not respond, her mind trying to sort out what his words meant as the agony in her leg hoarded her attention. Renko stepped forward and gripped her face, prising open her jaws. He tipped the vial over, and a thick, viscous liquid dropped onto her tongue. She choked for a moment, then felt a surge of euphoric energy pulse through her. She shuddered, then gasped, her head falling forwards. The pain in her left leg receded, and she panted in relief.

'That was a tiny dose,' Renko said. 'Not enough to heal your injuries, but enough to provide some small measure of respite; for a while. Remember, cooperate, and I shall give you more.'

She raised her eyes, her glance catching the vial in his hands. Already she desired more. 'What do you want?'

Renko sat down in the other chair the soldiers had brought into the room. 'I have many questions. Let's start at the beginning with your name.'

'Sable Holdfast.'

He frowned. 'Is that your real name? That's the name you gave when you got a job in the kitchens.'

'It's my real name.'

'Very well,' he said, raising an eyebrow. 'Next, where are you from?'

'An estate called Blackhold.'

'Yes, and where is this estate?'

She smiled. 'You wouldn't know it.' She tried to stretch her aching arms, but the shackles were bound tightly. 'Can I have a cigarette?'

'If you are good, perhaps. You intrigue me, Sable Holdfast; you are the first mortal I have met with powers that only the gods possess. You also have an ability that prevents me from reading your thoughts, otherwise we wouldn't be having this conversation. You are a very powerful woman; you managed to manipulate the girl from the harem into helping you steal the Quadrants, and almost made it out alive.'

'How did you catch me?'

'You're not as clever as you think. The first time I read your mind, all I saw was a young, anxious serving-girl, with nothing to hide. It was a good trick, but you made a mistake. You let your guard down when you looked upon the body of the Fourth Ascendant, the former King Nathaniel. I tried to read your mind again while you were weeping, and found that I could not. With your attention elsewhere, the shields around you were impenetrable, which led me to the conclusion that on the previous occasion, you were merely allowing me to read what you wanted me to read. That was when I knew I had to keep a very close eye on you, so I had you brought up to my harem, to see what you would do next. When you made your move, I was ready.'

Sable said nothing, but inwardly she cursed her stupidity. She had underestimated Renko.

'So, I ask you again, Sable Holdfast; where are you from?'

'I think I've said all I'm going to say.'

A flicker of a smile crossed his lips. 'I know secrets that have been hidden for centuries, secrets known only to the Ascendants and a handful of Ancients. Some of these secrets exist only as rumours. Shall I tell you one such rumour?'

She shrugged.

'Nathaniel used to rule this world with another god called Belinda, as I'm sure you already know.'

Sable struggled to keep her face straight at the mention of Belinda's name, but Renko appeared not to notice.

'Nathaniel was a famed world-builder,' the Ancient went on. 'He made Lostwell, did you know that? And then, he and his rebel companions made this world their home. Do you know how he went about creating worlds?'

'With a Sextant?'

'Ahh, yes, so you do know.'

'Only because I read it from your mind a few days ago. I knew you were looking for it.'

'And I will find it. The Sextant used by Nathaniel still exists, some-where in Khatanax. For five millennia, Nathaniel had the Sextant here, and this is where those rumours come in. Over the centuries, our spies would sometimes tell us that the great King was busy, locked away in his chambers, working on something. It is my belief that he was creating new worlds. He was a genius, with a brilliant mind. If anyone could create salve, and mortals with powers, it would have been him.' He smiled. 'What do you think of my theory so far?'

'Seems a little speculative. Where's your evidence?'

'Oh, Sable; you're my evidence. You, a puny, weak mortal woman, except you're not so puny, or weak. You have battle-vision, and the ability to enter the minds of gods, and the power to manipulate thoughts. If I were to take you back to Implacatus, the Ascendants would be dumbfounded. Some might see you as an abomination; a walking blasphemy; an aberration to be eradicated.'

'That's nice.'

'Where is the Sextant, Sable?'

She shrugged.

'Do you come from a world where mortals have powers?'

'Where's my cigarette?'

'What did you intend to do with the Quadrants?'

'I thought they'd make a nice wall decoration for my bathroom.'

He leaned forward and slapped her across the face with the back of his hand, sending her and the chair flying to the ground. He stared at her for a moment as she gasped in pain on the floor, then he righted the chair.

'Interesting,' he said, 'how you have no healing powers.'

She spat out blood onto the floor in front of her.

'I want a list of all your contacts; everyone you know in Khatanax. Time is running out for you, Sable. I have other matters that will soon demand my attention.'

'Good, then maybe you'll give me some peace.'

He laughed. 'Of all the things coming your way, peace will not be one of them. I have tried to be reasonable. I have tried to be conciliatory, but my patience isn't limitless. My anger with you, on the other hand, is considerable. You broke a Quadrant, for which the penalty is death; there is no avoiding that. As a consequence of your actions, my plans have had to be delayed. So, let me ask again; what did you intend to do with the Quadrants you were attempting to steal?'

'Get me a cigarette, and I'll answer.'

Renko frowned, then went to the door of the chamber and leaned outside to speak to the soldiers posted there. He returned a few moments later with a lit cigarette, and held it out for Sable. She inhaled, keeping it balanced on her lips.

Renko sat back down on his chair and watched her. 'I'm waiting.'

'What was the question again?'

'The Quadrants, Sable; what were you going to do with them?'

'I can't remember.'

'Who do you know in Khatanax?'

'No one.'

Renko sighed. 'Very well, you leave me no other choice. I assume you are familiar with Lord Maisk? He has not long returned from a task I had set him, and currently he is sitting in his rooms, stewing in a foul temper. He's a sadist, Sable; he loves hurting people, especially pretty girls like you. I had hoped to keep this civilised, but your attitude is suggesting to me that perhaps it's time to leave you and Lord Maisk alone for a while. Maybe his approach would garner more answers; that is, unless you want to start cooperating?'

Sable kept her face steady, despite the near panic that was starting to ripple through her. Renko had been right; she would rather die than face torture. She would break, everyone did. Shame filled her at the memory of all the times she had been the one doing the threatening and questioning. Had the crimes of her past finally caught up with her?

'Let's try again, shall we?' said Renko. 'Give me some names.'

She thought of Corthie, the nephew she had never met, and Aila.

Would they forgive her? But what if her answers led the gods to her own world; the world where her sister Daphne lived, the world that, despite all of its betrayals, she still loved? She glanced at Renko. If she riled him up enough, then maybe his rage would give her a quick death.

'I will tell you this,' she said; 'if you harm me, the Holdfasts will come for you, and they will kill you all. Did you ever wonder what happened to Agatha and the other rebels?'

Renko stared at her. 'Tell me.'

'I will. They came to my world, and we slaughtered them all. Every one of them, and the same thing will happen to you, and any other god who tries to hurt us. I'm a Holdfast, and I can see that you don't yet understand what that means, but believe me, one day you will, when you are writhing in your own blood. The gods will fall, and we shall not stop until every last one of you is dead.'

The Ancient said nothing for a moment, then he got to his feet and walked from the room. Sable spat the cigarette out, and waited.

An hour passed before the door to the chamber opened again. The pain in Sable's leg had slowly returned over that time, but it was still far less than before. She glanced up from the chair as the door swung open, and saw Lord Maisk enter. He had a smile on his lips as he closed the door behind him and turned to regard her.

'Well, well,' he said; 'you.' He laughed. 'A mere servant, a coffee-girl; you're the one that has Lord Renko in such a rage? I'm going to have fun with you. The most noble Ancient told me I could do whatever I wished; he no longer has any need for answers from you. I can be as quick, or as slow, as I like.'

He took a step forward, his eyes roaming over her. He placed a hand against her cheek, gently at first, then he gripped her hair and forced her head upwards as he leaned over her, leering.

'What shall we do first?' he said.

'How about you jump out of the window?'

He laughed again. 'You have spirit; good. Soon you'll be whimpering and pleading for mercy, but there's no fun if you're like that from that start.' He released her hair and took a knife from a pocket. 'I think the fingers will be first to go. Yes, the fingers, and then the face.'

He pushed the chair over, and it toppled forward. Sable's knees took the brunt of the fall, cracking off the stone floor. He reached round to where her hands were shackled behind her back, and she braced for pain, but instead felt the chains loosen and come free. Her arms swung forward in aching relief, and she hugged herself.

'Look at you,' he said, as he unshackled her right ankle; 'pathetic mortal. I want you struggling, not lying there in a heap.' He kicked the chair away and crouched down next to her, the knife glinting in his hand. He wrenched her left arm free, and placed a boot on her wrist to hold it in position. 'We'll start with the little finger, then work our way up.'

Sable closed her eyes as Maisk brought the knife down, then she screamed as a blinding pain flooded her body. Dizziness and agony engulfed her and she fought off unconsciousness. She had to reach for her battle-vision, to block the pain, to make her fight back.

Maisk held up the severed finger before his face, his eyes delighting in his prize.

Sable's right hand darted out, reaching for the god's eyes, and scratching them with her nails. He cried out and staggered back a step, then stared down at her.

'You think that's going to help you?' he spat, wiping a streak of blood from his cheek.

'No,' she gasped, holding up the thin, clear disc that she had clawed from his right eye, 'but this might.'

Fear; overwhelming fear.

He staggered, his eyes wide as Sable bore into his mind.

Get on your knees.

Maisk fell to the floor, his knees hitting the stone.

Cut your own throat.

Maisk stared at the knife in his hand.

Sable focussed all of her strength, channelling everything she had into her powers.

Do it! she commanded.

Maisk's hand shook, his eyes staring at disbelief at Sable, then, with a single sweeping motion, he slashed the blade across his own neck, spraying blood across the room. He dropped the knife, then collapsed to the floor, convulsing. Sable stumbled over to him, dragging her broken leg across the ground. She picked up the knife, seeing Maisk's flesh already starting to heal. She knelt by him and drove the blade back into his throat, sawing and hacking through the muscles, tendons and, finally, his spinal cord. His head rolled to the side, the eyes lifeless.

Sable gazed down at her bloody work, then fell, the knife clattering off the flagstones.

She awoke shaking, her leg and hand burning in agony. There was almost no light within the stone chamber, but she could sense the giant body of Maisk lying close to her. She panicked for a second, trying to scramble away, before she remembered. She lifted her left hand, and saw the silhouetted outline of her fingers in the gloom. The smallest one was missing. She threw up, but as she hadn't eaten anything, only water and bile came from her mouth. She lay her head down on the blood-slicked flagstones. She had done enough. Her tormentor was dead; what else could anyone expect of her?

She had killed a god, just as Corthie, Karalyn and Daphne had done before her. She wondered if that meant she was now a true Holdfast. She started to cry on the stone floor, pain and revulsion at what had happened overcoming her as her body shook.

'Daphne,' she whispered, though she had no idea why. 'Help me.'

She tried to close her eyes, but the pain wouldn't let her rest; it gripped her, spiralling out from her left leg and her torn hand, twin centres of agony. She lifted her head and started to crawl towards the door. Her right arm pulled her along, and her right leg kicked out, the boot slipping over the pools of blood.

She summoned what remained of her battle-vision, and felt a low thrum. Enough for a few minutes, she guessed, and then oblivion would take her. It wasn't sufficient, she thought; she wouldn't have been able to get out of the residence in that time if she had been fully fit, never mind grievously wounded.

Hide, screamed the animal part of her brain, anywhere; just get out of that room, and leave the stench of fear and death behind. She reached the door, and hauled herself up with her right hand, her left leg hanging uselessly. She tried to sense if there were soldiers outside in the hallway, but a wave of nausea and exhaustion surged over her and she had to stop. She steadied herself on her right foot, and turned the handle. The door creaked open, revealing an empty hallway.

Where were the soldiers? A small part of her had almost hoped they would be there, and then she would have been put out of her misery, or they would have tied her back to the chair, or... anything other than having to continue onwards. She looked down. Her boots were covered in blood, but both her leg and hand had stopped bleeding. She crouched, taking her time to ease herself down, and began to loosen her boots. Getting the right one off was easy, but she could hardly bring herself to look at her lower left leg, never mind attempt to get the boot off. She steeled herself, and gazed at the wound. No bone was visible, but the flesh around the injury was bruised and swollen. She tugged at the laces, picking at them until they were so loose, she could slip the boot off without moving her ankle.

She panted, exhausted after her efforts. What would Daphne tell her to do? Get up and stop being a baby, probably. She narrowed her eyes. Why was she thinking of her sister again? They hated each other, and were half-sisters, she reminded herself. Sable's mother had been a queen, which should have made her a princess. Still, Daphne was all she had, her only real family. She leaned against the doorpost and closed her eyes.

Pain streaking up her leg jolted her, and she started moving without thinking about what she was doing, as if her mind had given up, but her body refused to. She pulled herself up and closed the door, then staggered down the hallway, her left leg trailing as she leaned against the wall. She came to a junction and squinted, her sight blurry. She should recognise where she was, she thought. Where was she? For a moment it wouldn't come to her, then she remembered. The Governor's residence. The top floor of the western tower. Lord Renko's quarters. She gazed around. Ahead of her was the door to the harem, while to the left was a passageway leading to the Ancient's study and bedchamber.

Voices echoed up from the stairs behind her, and she almost froze. Go, she screamed to herself, and started to move again, taking the corridor to the right, into a part of Lord Renko's quarters that she had never been in before. There was an alcove, and she stumbled into it as the voices got closer.

'Why are there no guards outside the prisoner's room?' said Lord Renko, his voice coming from the hallway.

'Lord Maisk told them to leave, my lord.'

'Why?'

'He... uh, said he didn't want anyone listening, my lord.'

'I see.'

There was a silent pause.

'I can't hear anything in there,' said Renko, 'so I must assume he has finished. However, I have no desire to witness his handiwork. Post a guard on the door and send for cleaners in the morning.'

'Yes, my lord.'

'Lord Renko!' cried a different voice from further down the stairs.

'Yes?'

'I bear an urgent message from Lady Felice, my lord,' came the second voice. It belonged to a demigod, Sable remembered as she slumped against the alcove wall.

'Go on.'

'She contacted me five minutes ago, my lord. There's no sign of Lady Joaz within the town of the Falls of Iron. She visioned to the others to tell them that she'd arrived, but when Lady Felice tried to vision back to her this evening, there was no response. Lady Felice has searched every-where, but there's no trace of her.'

Renko groaned. 'So, she's been killed, or she's fled. Please tell me that she doesn't have a Quadrant with her.'

'No, my lord. Lady Joaz handed over the Quadrant to Lady Felice before she left for the town.'

'Praise the Ascendants for one piece of good news today. Wake Major Ahito and inform him that the entire Banner will be sent by portal to the Falls of Iron at dawn. Until then, I have work to do, and I am not to be disturbed; is that understood?'

'Yes, my lord.'

There was the sound of a door slamming, and then footsteps trailed away down the stairs. Sable emerged from the alcove, and looked down the hallway. Empty. She turned back and glanced around. There was only one more door to take, and she made for it, dragging her bare left foot behind her.

She opened the door to the harem and almost fell in. A solitary lamp was burning on the little table in the middle of the square of couches, where four young women were sleeping. Sable eased the door shut, and stole forwards, almost choking on the thick reek of dreamweed smoke. She passed the first couch, clinging on to it as she stumbled along, then grabbed cigarettes, weedsticks and a bottle of raki from the table, stuffing them into the pockets of her bloody tunic. She staggered to the door that led to the bedrooms, and passed through, then crawled the last stretch to her old room. Her clothes were still inside, right where she had left them. She clambered up onto the bed and kicked the door shut, then lit the lamp on her bedside table.

She lit a weedstick, her entire body trembling with nervous exhaus-tion, then ripped a strip from her bed sheet. She wrapped it round the stump on her left hand, then straightened her left leg, just as she had been shown to do in the army, except then it had always been to other people. Pain tore through her, but it had been the pain that had stopped her from giving up; without it, she would have drifted into oblivion on the blood-soaked floor next to Maisk's body.

She had made it, she thought as she stubbed out the weedstick and extinguished the lamp. No doubt, she would be caught in the morning, or earlier, but at least she had made it back to her bed. She pulled the covers over her bloody clothes, and wondered if the Holdfasts would be proud of her.

CHAPTER 27

AS FORETOLD

Alea Tanton, Tordue, Western Khatanax – 12th Tradinch 5252

'There he goes,' said Millen as he and Maddie crouched in the dark shadows by the Central Pits. 'In another minute, the second guard will walk round that corner, and then we'll have five minutes before the other guy comes back.'

Maddie squinted at the high-walled compound in front of them. 'Are you sure?'

'We've been watching them for over an hour, Maddie; yes, I'm sure.'

Maddie yawned. 'We're doomed.'

'What? You having second thoughts?'

'No. I still think we should do it, but our chances are slim to none. I just thought you should know that I'm the unluckiest person around.'

Millen rolled his eyes.

'I'm being serious,' she said. 'Back on my world, I was the sergeant in charge when the greenhides broke through our defences and went on to murder half of the City. Me.'

'Was it your fault?'

'Not exactly, but I was there. Everyone was panicking, and we didn't close the gate in time. But I was in charge; I should have stopped it. I could have stopped it, if only I'd been thinking straight.'

'Sounds like you're blaming yourself for something you had no control over.'

'Exactly. It was bad luck; that's what I'm saying.'

'There's no such thing as luck. Look, there's the second guy. Right, all we have to do is wait for him to pass, and then we run for the side door. Get ready.'

Maddie groaned. 'Maybe we should wait for Sable.'

'No. She told us to get the dragon, and she'd meet us afterwards.'

'But she hasn't been back in contact. Anything could have happened to her.'

'I'm not going to think about that; I'm not going to let her down.'

She frowned at him. 'Please don't tell me you're only doing this to impress her? Malik's sweaty crotch, that's it – we're definitely doomed. We're going to get caught trying to steal a dragon just because you want to get into Sable Holdfast's pants.'

'We're not stealing a dragon, we're rescuing one.'

'I notice you're not denying the pants-thing though. Why do guys never do crazy stuff like that for me?'

'I don't know; maybe being the rider of a fierce dragon is a little intimidating?'

'I never thought of it that way. I could live with being intimidating.'

Millen grabbed a large bag and slung the strap over his shoulder. 'Let's go.'

Maddie glanced up. The second guard had disappeared round the flank of the long building. Millen leaped to his feet and ran off, and she followed, her glance darting from side to side across the empty plaza. Sounds of cheering and partying were coming from the late-night bars and taverns on the other side of the arena, where Blue Thumbs supporters were celebrating the death of the Deadskins' captain during the game with the Bloodflies the previous day. Millen had been pleased when he had heard the news, telling her that the death would keep the locals occupied all night.

They ran to the side of the compound, and Millen reached into a pocket for the set of keys as Maddie huddled against the wall, her heart racing. She watched as Millen tried several keys in the door, none of them working.

'Didn't you check which key it was?'

'I didn't have time,' he said.

'What? We've been hanging around for hours. What do you mean you didn't have the time? You should have...'

'Let me work,' he hissed.

She glared at him as he tried another key. It fitted, and he turned it. The lock clicked, and he pushed open the door. They hurried inside, and Millen closed the door and locked it behind them.

'I hope you remember which key you used,' Maddie said as they stood in the darkness. 'In case we need to leave in a hurry.'

'We won't be leaving by this door,' he whispered; 'the dragon's hardly likely to fit through, is he? And keep your voice down; there might still be people around.'

There was a narrow window slit above the door, and they waited until their eyes had adjusted to the gloom. Maddie saw a short passageway ahead of her, with doors leading off on either side, and a set of stairs going up. Millen set off, the bag over his shoulder clanking as he walked. They went to the first door on the right, and Millen put his ear to it for a moment, then eased it open.

'So far, so good,' he whispered as he peered through; 'the way's clear.'

They went through the door, and entered a room that was in pitch darkness. Millen closed the door, then knelt by the bag and took out a small lantern. He lit the wick, then angled the shutters downwards, providing a low glow of illumination. In front of them, a large training hall was deserted, the weapons and armour all piled up neatly by the walls.

Millen strode into the room and selected a short sword, then attached the scabbard to his belt.

'You should get yourself a weapon,' he said.

'And what would I do with a sword? I'd probably only cut myself, or you.'

'I thought you used to be a soldier? A sergeant, you said.'

'Yeah, I was, but I've never actually, you know, stabbed anything. We were more of a crossbow-sort-of-army.'

He gestured to another wall, where racks of crossbows stood.

'Oh,' she said. 'Um, sure.'

She went over and selected a bow, then pulled the strap over her shoulder.

Millen raised an eyebrow. 'You might need some bolts too?'

'I knew that.'

She picked up some short, wooden bolts tipped with steel, and shoved them into a pocket.

'Just imagine you're back in the army,' said Millen, 'and we're conducting a raid. We're going to be slick, and professional.'

'Right.'

He smiled. 'Come on, Sergeant Jackdaw, we have a dragon to rescue.'

He picked up the lantern and they set off again. They reached a long passageway, and took it until they came to stairs going down.

'Remember,' he said, 'down here is where the criminals are kept. There will be guards, but they should be posted at the other end of the compound.'

'Should be?' she groaned. 'Be honest, are you making this up as you go along?'

'Of course not. Don't worry, my plan is as close to perfect as possible. Trust me.'

They stole down the stairs, the only sound coming from the low clanking from Millen's bag. At the bottom of the steps, Millen shone the lantern down the passageway. In the distance, Maddie could see the row of large cells that they had walked past the previous day. The light from the lantern attracted attention as they neared them, and a few captives came close to the bars to see what was happening.

'Don't look at them,' Millen whispered. 'We don't want them getting excited.'

Maddie glanced at the cells from the corner of her eye as they passed. Inside, most of the captives were sleeping, bunched together in the cramped conditions, but a few were on their feet, staring at Millen and Maddie.

'Hey!' one called out.

Maddie turned.

The man spat at her. 'Torduan scum.'

'Keep walking,' hissed Millen. 'If the guards come, we're screwed.'

They reached the second flight of stairs and descended again. At the bottom, the door leading to the caged greenhide was locked, and Millen began trying different keys.

'We should free those captives,' Maddie muttered from the shadows.

'Why? They're criminals.'

'Yeah, but weren't we looking for a distraction? Imagine, they'll try to run outside, and the guards will have to chase them.'

'And then the guards will catch them, bring them back, and search the place looking for whoever let them go.' He glanced at her. 'I know you feel sorry for them.'

'Of course I do. They're going to be killed in all manner of horrible ways for the enjoyment of a bloodthirsty crowd. This is not a nice city.'

'Did I say it was?'

'Some of them looked quite young.'

Millen shrugged as he selected another key.

'What's the youngest age you can get executed here?'

'Twelve, I think.'

Maddie narrowed her eyes. 'You lot are sick in the head.'

'I told you, half of them are murderers, the rest will be thieves or something. They're bad people.'

'For the sake of argument, you could be twelve and steal some food for your starving family, and then end up getting killed in the arena for it?'

'I guess so. I don't really think about it, to be honest. The law's the law.'

He picked the right key, and the door swung open. As soon as they peered through, a low growling came from the left.

'Quick,' said Millen, 'shut the door before the greenhide wakes everyone.'

Maddie swallowed, the sound from the creature chilling her blood. She closed the door, and edged away. Millen shone the lantern towards the cage, and the beast's eyes shone back.

'See? It's safely locked up.'

The greenhide launched itself at the bars, its jaws trying to rip the steel gate loose. Its limbs darted out, slashing through the air as it shrieked in rage. Maddie stared at it as visions of her previous life on the Great Walls flashed through her mind. An urge to shoot it with her crossbow swept through her, and she almost unslung the weapon from her shoulder.

'Come on,' said Millen, 'don't stand there gawking at it. It'll quieten down once we get to the dragon's chamber.'

Maddie tore her eyes away from the greenhide and followed Millen to the next door along, where they stood for another few minutes as Millen selected the correct key. He opened the door and they entered the room with the enormous cage. Inside, the dragon was lying down, but its right eye was half open, a green gleam coming from it.

Maddie walked up to the cage. 'Hello.'

'You again,' muttered the dragon. 'Go away.'

'I told you; we're here to rescue you.'

'You ridiculous insect. I am the mighty Sanguino; I have no need of rescue, especially not from pathetic beings such as yourselves.'

Maddie put her hands on her hips. 'Don't give me that. They're going to execute you at the next games. Do you want your supporters to watch you be killed in front of them?'

'You lie. No dragon has ever been executed at the games. Several have died honourably in combat, but no captured dragon has ever been put to the sword. In a few days, I shall be released, and allowed to return home.'

'You stupid lizard,' Maddie muttered. '"Home"? The Southern Pits aren't your home, they're your prison. And I'm not lying. Millen, tell him.'

'She's right,' he said. 'The Blue Thumbs are going to execute you in public.'

The dragon raised his head a foot. 'But you are a Blue Thumb, boy. I know why you're here – you're trying to trick me. Perhaps some of you do wish to see me die; if so, then a foolish attempt to escape would be the perfect pretext for it. No, I think I shall remain here.'

Millen and Maddie glanced at each other.

'Don't you remember being free?' said Maddie.

'I am a warrior,' said the dragon; 'a renowned champion of the Bloodflies. My old life is over.'

'But do you remember it?'

'No.'

'Come on. Imagine yourself soaring over the mountains, feeling the wind and the sun on your scales. Freedom, Sanguino. Right now, you're no better than a slave, humiliating yourself in front of a baying crowd.'

The dragon's eyes narrowed and he raised a shackled forelimb. 'I would eviscerate you for your insults, insect, were it not for these chains.'

'Yes, the chains of slavery.' She nodded to Millen. 'Bring the bag over.'

'What?' he said. 'You heard the dragon. He doesn't want to be rescued.'

Maddie glared at him. 'Is something wrong with you? You drag me all the way here, and now you're trying to wriggle out of it?'

'I'm not trying to wriggle out of anything; I'm just considering the difficulty of freeing a dragon who has no desire to be free.'

'I am free!' thundered the dragon. 'You insects are mocking me, and I grow tired of it.'

'The bag, Millen,' said Maddie.

He sighed, and brought it over, setting it down in front of the cage. Maddie crouched by it and loosened the straps. Inside was a collection of tools that Millen had stolen from a blacksmith the previous after-noon, with thick bolt-cutters, saws, pliers, hammers and steel pins.

Maddie picked up the bolt-cutters and approached the padlocked gate of the cage.

'Desist, insect,' cried the dragon. 'If you open the cage, it will be assumed that I acquiesced in this nonsense.'

'Tough,' muttered Maddie as she raised the bolt-cutters. She slid the end over the chain by the padlock and grunted. 'A little help, Millen?'

He shook his head and came over. He grabbed the bolt-cutters with her, and together they squeezed. There was a crack, and the broken chain fell loose. The dragon got to his feet, his eyes wide. He tried to circle round, but the thick shackles on his limbs were hindering him.

'Stop at once,' he growled. 'Stop, now.'

'Shut up, dragon,' said Maddie. 'I'm getting tired of listening to your whining.'

'You are trying to get me killed, insect.'

'No, we're trying to save your life. Listen, do your dragon trick on us, and I'll prove it.'

'Trick? You want me to perform tricks for you? You unbearable human wretch. If you continue with this, then I will tear you limb from limb.'

'The truth trick,' she said. 'You know, when you can make us tell the truth.'

The dragon glared at her.

'Eh, what are you talking about?' said Millen.

'Come on,' said Maddie, 'you must have heard about it? Dragons can make people tell the truth.'

'No they can't.'

'They can,' she cried.

'You are delusional,' said Sanguino. 'Dragons do not have such powers. I wish it were true, but it isn't.'

Maddie paused. Blackrose had never told her that her truth-powers were limited to her alone. Maybe it was only dragons from the ruling families who could do it – 'high' dragons, as Captain Van had called them.

'Alright,' she said, 'but you have to believe me. Do you think I'd be risking my life to rescue you if I was lying to you? They *are* going to kill you. Imagine what it will feel like, to see thousands of Bloodflies supporters watching as the Blue Thumbs murder you in front of them. It's shameful, I agree. It would be a dishonourable death; a sordid end for one so mighty and powerful. Even Millen here, a Blue Thumb, thinks it's going too far. But imagine instead, the looks on the faces of the Torduans when they discover that you have foiled their evil plan. They will be enraged, while you can laugh at them. Wouldn't you enjoy laughing at them?'

The dragon hesitated for a moment. Maddie was starting to sense that Sanguino wanted to leave, but it was fear that was keeping him inside the cage, rather than any notion that he would be released.

'And imagine,' she went on, 'how happy you would make the Shinstrans if you were to escape. All of your loving admirers would cheer and celebrate; it would be your finest victory. Mothers would name their children after you, and songs would be sung about how you taught the wicked Torduans a lesson.'

The dragon stared at her. 'I will kill you if you are lying to me.'

She nodded. 'I know.' She picked up a steel pin and a hammer from the bag, then swung the cage door open a foot. 'I'm coming in. I'm placing myself at your mercy. Would I do that if I was lying to you? You're a glorious creature, and you don't deserve the fate the Torduans have planned for you.'

She placed her crossbow into the bag, then slipped inside the cage, leaving Millen standing wide-eyed, the bolt-cutters in his hands. Maddie slowly moved round the wounded and scarred flank of the dragon.

'I'm going to start at the back,' she said, 'and free your rear limbs. Alright?'

The dragon swung its neck round to watch her, but said nothing.

Maddie knelt down by the chains attached to Sanguino's back legs. She lifted the pin, placed it over the shackle, then drove the hammer down. A dull clang reverberated through the chamber, and Maddie glanced around, her heart thumping in her chest. She brought the hammer down again, and the shackle fell to the floor. Maddie wiped the sweat from her brow. One down, three to go. She made her way round the vast bulk of the blood-red dragon, releasing the shackles until all four of his limbs were free. He stretched his forelimbs out, extending the claws. They had been filed down, Maddie noticed, their ends blunt and ragged.

'Alright,' said Maddie, standing and feeling her tunic stick to her back with sweat. 'Now the wings. Millen, get in here.'

The young man didn't respond, his eyes on the dragon as it flexed its freed limbs.

'Millen!' she hissed. 'I need you and the bolt-cutters. Move your ass.'

He glanced over to her, his face pale, then entered the cage. He edged past a large forelimb and reached Maddie.

'Lift the cutters up,' she said, pointing at a thick cluster of chains securing the dragon's wings. 'We'll go for those first.'

Millen raised the bolt-cutters, and Maddie helped guide them into place. Millen braced his feet and brought the handles together, sweat pouring down his forehead. He strained and grunted, and the chain snapped, and fell loose to the floor.

He stopped, panting,

'That might do it,' she said. 'The other chains look like they'll pull off. Now, if we...' She paused, her ears catching something.

'Someone's coming,' cried Millen.

'Quick, out of the cage,' said Maddie. 'We can hide. Sanguino, lie down and pretend your shackles are still attached. If it's just a guard, we'll wait for them to leave, and then come back, alright?'

The dragon said nothing, his lime green eyes staring at her.

Millen and Maddie jumped down from the cage. Millen grabbed the bag, while Maddie swung the gate closed and draped the chains over the bars so that, at a glance, it looked as though the gate was still locked. The sound of boots grew louder, and they scurried into the shadows by the back of the cage, where Millen extinguished the lantern.

The door opened, and a lamp shone through. Figures were standing behind it, but the light was making it impossible to see how many were there. Maddie squeezed back against the wall, Millen's elbow digging into her waist.

'Light more lamps,' came a voice, and Millen let out a low moan of despair.

Someone began to light a series of wall lamps, and Maddie blinked. At least a dozen blue-sashed guards had entered the chamber. At their head stood a large, well-built man, the veins on his neck bulging. He gazed around the room.

'Over here!' cried a guard, pointing into the corner where Millen and Maddie were huddling.

Millen got to his feet, his hands up. 'Gantu, I can explain.'

The well-built man stared at him, rage seared across his face. 'You little bastard.'

'It was just a prank!' Millen said, his voice high and nervy. 'I only wanted to show my girlfriend the dragon again.'

Adlin entered the room, and stood by Gantu's side with his hand extended.

'The keys, please, Millen.'

'Of course,' Millen said. He rushed forward and dropped the set of keys into Adlin's palm. As soon as Adlin had them, Gantu swung his fist, catching Millen on the side of the head, and driving him to the floor.

'You're going to pay, boy,' he screamed down at Millen, his finger pointing.

At the other end of the chamber, a guard pointed his crossbow at Maddie, and she got to her feet, sliding her bag into the shadows behind her with a boot. She glanced at the prone body of Millen. Blood was coming from his mouth, and he was groaning on the floor.

'This is the girl,' said Adlin as Maddie approached.

Gantu stared at her. 'This isn't Sable! Where's Sable?' He turned back to Millen. 'Where is that bitch?'

'I have no idea, Gantu; honestly. I haven't seen her for days. I've been with Maddie.'

'Who?'

Adlin pointed at her. 'I believe he means this girl. She was with him when they came for the keys yesterday.'

Gantu turned back to her. 'What were you doing down here, girl?'

'What Millen told you is true,' she said; 'I wanted to see the dragon again. It's my fault, sir; please don't hurt him. I begged him to do this; he didn't want to.'

'Excuse me,' said Sanguino, his rich voice echoing through the chamber. 'I am trying to sleep.'

They all turned. The dragon was lying down with his eyes closed, his limbs hidden beneath him.

'Be quiet, reptile,' sneered Gantu. 'Save your breath for the arena.'

Sanguino half-opened an eye. 'Am I to fight again?'

Gantu laughed. 'I'm going to enjoy watching you die, but more than that, I'm going to enjoy watching the faces of the Shinstran scum when they see you butchered on the sands.'

'If I were free, I would kill you for that.'

'Yes, but you're not free, are you, beast?' Gantu said. 'You're chained, shackled and muzzled. Now, go back to sleep.'

Millen tried to stand.

'What do you think you're doing?' said Gantu. 'You think you can run off with my woman and not suffer for it?'

Adlin pursed his lips. 'Perhaps he's telling the truth, Gantu.'

'I know what I saw!' Gantu cried. 'One minute he and Sable were sitting next to me in the Shinstran Pits, the next they were both gone. You want me to believe it was a coincidence? Are you calling me stupid?'

Adlin took a step back and lowered his eyes. 'No, Gantu, of course not.'

Gantu stared down at Millen. 'Either you tell me where Sable is, or I'm putting you and the girl into the cells upstairs with the criminals, and tomorrow I'll cheer as you're torn to shreds in the arena.'

A loud roar shook the chamber. For a second, Maddie thought it had come from the dragon, but then a huge chunk of stonework fell from the ceiling. It struck one of the guards, then the floor rumbled and shook, throwing everyone off their feet. Maddie cowered on the ground, her hands over her head as the building swayed and groaned. A split opened up in one of the walls, and the air filled with dust and the sound of grinding stone.

The ground settled, leaving a cloud of thick dust hanging in the flickering light of the lamps. Another sound rose, of a clattering over flagstones, and Maddie raised her head.

'No,' she mumbled, then pulled herself to her feet. Around her, the guards were also starting to rise, and one was helping Gantu get up as the clattering sound grew nearer. Maddie ran to Millen, and grabbed his arm.

'Into the cage!' she yelled in his ear.

He gazed around, his hair and clothes coated in dust. 'What?'

Maddie hauled on his arm, half-dragging him along the floor.

'Get back here,' growled Gantu as he stood.

Maddie swung the barred gate and bundled Millen into the cage, and then the door to the chamber burst open, and a deafening shriek arose.

'Greenhide!' cried a guard, as Maddie kicked the cage door closed. She backed away, still dragging Millen, and collided with the dragon, whose eyes were staring out into the chamber.

The greenhide stood in the doorway for a second, its jaws open, then sprang. Even with its claws bound, its teeth were still lethal, and it jumped at the first guard and bit his head off with a lunge of its jaws. The other guards screamed and tried to run, but the greenhide was too fast. It tore through them in seconds, hurling bodies to the side and lashing out with its fearsome jaws. Gantu stared at it in disbelief then, with a snap, his head was sheared off. Adlin was next. The old man tried to run, but was gathered into the beast's limbs and crushed. Blood sprayed across the floor and walls as the greenhide hunted the remainder of the guards. It ripped the arms from the last man, then paused, its eyes scanning the chamber. It caught sight of Maddie and Millen and bounded forward.

Sanguino pushed the two humans behind him with a giant forelimb and raised the other towards the greenhide, baring his claws. The greenhide's eyes widened, and it skidded to a halt, its feet slipping on the blood. The dragon moved its claws closer, and the greenhide turned, and raced from the chamber, its limbs skittering off the flagstones until it disappeared into the distance.

Maddie hugged the dragon's limb. 'Thank you.'

Sanguino arced his long neck towards her. 'I believe you now. Shall we leave this place?'

Maddie rushed forwards and swung the gate open to its fullest extent, as Millen walked over to gaze at the headless body of his cousin lying amid the scattered body parts.

'Millen,' she called; 'get the tools. We still need to get Sanguino's muzzle off.'

He stared at the body a moment longer, then turned and retrieved the bag from the corner. He passed it through the bars to Maddie, his hands trembling.

'An earthquake,' he said. 'How did you know?'

Maddie frowned as she started to remove the muzzle from the dragon's jaws. 'What?'

'How did you know there would be an earthquake? Are you a witch?'

She laughed before she could stop herself. 'Maybe my luck has changed.'

The muzzle fell free, and the dragon strode through the gate, stretching out his blood-red wings and limbs. His eyes scanned the multitude of wounds and sores running down his flanks, then he sniffed at the corpse of Gantu.

'Where now?' cried Maddie.

The dragon glanced upward at the huge gaps in the ceiling. 'Through there.'

Maddie and Millen stood back as the dragon reached up, his great claws enlarging the holes, and sending chunks of masonry and rubble to the ground. When the hole was big enough, he glanced down at them.

'Follow me.'

Maddie and Millen ran after the dragon as he hauled his vast bulk up through the broken ceiling. They clambered up the pile of rubble, leaving the bloodstained bodies behind them as they reached the next level. The dragon set off down a wide passageway, and the two humans raced to keep up. At the end was a ramp leading up to the ground floor, barred with a huge, solid door of wood that had remained undamaged in the earthquake.

'Stand back,' said Sanguino, then opened his jaws.

A streak of lightning crossed his teeth, and then an explosion of flames leapt from his mouth, enveloping the wide door in fire. It splintered under the blistering heat, then sagged and burst into fragments, revealing the night sky beyond.

The dragon turned its neck to face Maddie and Millen. 'I assume you are also running away?'

Maddie nodded.

'Then you'd best climb up onto my shoulders.'

'Can you fly?' said Maddie. 'I mean, after being chained up, are your wings alright?'

'Why do you continue to insult me, insect?' he said, though there was a softer gleam in his eyes. 'A mere month and a half in chains is not enough to hinder me. I am mighty and strong, and I can fly better than any eagle.'

Shouts and cries rang out behind them, but Maddie didn't turn to see if it was coming from guards chasing them, or guards being chased by the rogue greenhide. She clambered up the dragon's right forelimb, then helped Millen up onto his shoulders, where they sat and held on.

Sanguino strode up the ramp and emerged onto the wide, open plaza, where people out on the street screamed, and fled at the sight of him. He extended his long wings, and they rose into the dark, night air.

'By the Ascendants,' gasped Millen, his knuckles white from clinging onto the folds on Sanguino's shoulders.

Maddie smiled at him. 'You get used to it.'

'What about Sable?' cried Millen.

'We've done as she asked,' said Maddie. 'She'll find us.' She glanced forward. 'Take us out to the ocean, Sanguino.'

'The ocean?' the dragon said.

'Yes. If we go inland, we'll have to cross the anti-dragon defences and, believe me, we don't want to do that.'

'So be it,' said the dragon, 'and then, once we are clear of the city, I will soar over the mountains, free, just as you foretold.'

The blood-red dragon circled higher above the tightly-packed streets and slums of Alea Tanton, the lights of the city glittering for miles. He turned to the west, and put on a surge of speed. They crossed over another mile of buildings, and then shot out over the sea, where the only light came from the moon and the stars, and the bright foam of waves crashing against the shore.

CHAPTER 28

SAVAGE

Falls of Iron, Western Khatanax – 12th Tradinch 5252

Van re-positioned himself, his side and arm sore from lying by the cell door for so long. He twisted the nail in the lock, moving his hand as he tried to reach the inner mechanism.

'Will you stop that?' said Joaz from the neighbouring cell, her voice echoing through the empty stone corridor. 'You're been trying for hours and I'm getting sick of the noise.'

'We don't know how long we'll be left alone for,' he said from the ground; 'they could post guards here at any time.'

His fingers slipped and he dropped the nail. He sighed, then reached out for it. It had taken him three hours to prise the damn thing out of the side of the box mattress, and he wasn't about to lose the only chance they had of getting out of their cells. His fingers scrabbled over the worn flagstones until he grasped hold of it. He glanced at it for a moment, then reached up and poked the end back into the lock.

'There you go again,' muttered Joaz. 'If, by some miracle, you do manage to pick the lock, what are you going to do then?'

'What do you mean? I'll be freeing you and then we'll run for it.'

'What, and take us back to the Banner; to Renko?'

'Yes.'

'Hmm.'

He paused in his efforts. 'What's that supposed to mean?'

'It occurs to me that there's a flaw in your plan. If you rescue me, and we escape to Lord Renko, then I will be obliged to tell the Ancient everything I know, otherwise he would read it out of my mind anyway. Therefore, I'll have to tell him about you letting that dragon go, when it could easily have been killed by the militia. And then, you released the dragon rider too. Now, don't think for a moment that I haven't been pondering the meaning of there being a dragon with a rider in Khatanax – I too have served on Dragon Eyre. So why did you let it go? I admit that I wasn't able to piece all of that together; your memories are too fragmented. On the other hand, I'm not sure Renko will care about your motivation. He'll kill you, you know that?' She snapped her fingers. 'You know what he's like when he's angry; your brains would be sprayed across the nearest wall. If you want to live, then you either need to abandon me or, if you were ruthless enough, kill me, to make sure I cannot tell Lord Renko what I know.'

'Then,' Van said, 'I guess we're lucky I'm struggling to pick this damn lock.'

Joaz laughed, but it was devoid of any joy.

Van lowered his arm to rest it for a moment, and thought about the god's words. She was right, as she usually was. But what was the alternative? He had signed the contract, just as every other member of the Banner had, and had sworn to do his duty while that contract remained valid. His first priority was to protect the lives of the divine members of the expedition, even at the cost of his own, and many Banner soldiers had died over the years to defend the gods.

'That's better,' said Joaz. 'I could hardly think straight with all that horrible scraping going on. Tell me, what did you make of that young woman who was among those who visited us?'

'Which one?'

'The mortal one.'

'Which one was that?'

'Really? It seemed obvious to me. Out of the five who were here, three were gods or demigods, and two were mortals.'

'I didn't know you had the power to tell them apart.'

'I don't. Call it long experience perhaps, but I can easily tell the difference. It's something about their bearing, the way they carry themselves. The mortals were the tall, muscular man, and the short, dark-skinned woman. It was she who seemed to be claiming the ability to negate powers. Normally, I would greet such a claim with the derision it deserved but, well, my powers are in fact negated here, so something is causing it. Kelsey Holdfast, she said her name was; does that mean anything to you?'

'No.'

'It troubles me. A mortal with the ability to block the powers of the gods cannot be other than a threat to our rule. This information must get to Lord Renko.'

'I thought you wanted me to stop trying to pick the lock?'

'He'll be wondering where I am by now, and why I haven't reported for so long. Lady Felice will have informed him the moment she lost contact with me. He probably imagines me to be dead.'

'And what will he do in that case?'

'I'm not sure, but if I had to guess, then I would say he will launch an immediate invasion of the town, using all the force at his disposal. Presumably, Lord Maisk will lead, with Lord Baldwin and the Banner soldiers under his command. I...' She paused, as the sound of footsteps echoed along the passageway towards them.

Van moved back from the gate, sliding the nail into his boot as he did so. A figure appeared, and Van recognised her as the one who had held the sword to his throat when they had been captured.

She halted in front of the two cells.

'Good morning,' she said.

Neither of the prisoners responded.

'I want some information,' she went on, 'but first, I want to tell you who I am.'

'Really?' said Joaz. 'I hardly think I'm likely to care.'

'My name is Belinda, and I'm the Third Ascendant.'

Van blinked. From the cell next to him was nothing but silence.

'I imagine you think me a liar,' the woman continued, 'or maybe mad. However, it's the truth. I am the Queen of Khatanax. Can I ask, what do people on Implacatus think happened to me? Am I rumoured to be dead?'

'Well...' began Joaz, her voice hesitant; 'I, uh...'

'It's not a difficult question. Am I supposed to be dead or not?'

'No one is completely certain of the fate of the Third Ascendant,' Joaz said, her voice a little more confident. 'It is known that she was with King Nathaniel, of course, but there has been no sign of her for a very long time. The rumours concerning her fate are split. Some say she disappeared with Lady Agatha when the last rebels were driven from Khatanax, while others say she must have died before that.'

'Why must she have died? Why do they think that?'

'Because, they say, she was so powerful that she would never have allowed the rebels to have been defeated. Only the Second Ascendant is, or was, more powerful than her, and he hasn't left Implacatus in millennia.'

The woman nodded as Van watched her intently. It was rubbish, of course, he knew that. The very idea that the person he was staring at was the second most powerful being in existence was ludicrous; but something about her expression made him believe that she, at least, thought it was true.

'I did go with Agatha,' she said after a while.

'Where?' said Joaz.

'None of your business.'

'May I ask if she still lives?'

'She's dead, along with Gregor, Racine, Asher, Gorman and Witten. Every one of them was killed except for me.'

'Why are you telling us this?'

'Because you're the first god from Implacatus that I've met, and I was curious.'

Joaz laughed. 'If you are who you say you are, then you'd know that the Third Ascendant is from Implacatus, so therefore, I'm certainly not the first you have met.'

'You're right. You're the first I remember meeting.'

'This could be easily proved one way or another,' Joaz went on. 'If I could be taken to somewhere out of the range of Kelsey Holdfast, then I could communicate with Lord Renko. He is an Ancient, and has sometimes talked about the olden days he spent in the company of King Nathaniel. They were friends for a while, so he most certainly would have met Queen Belinda. This would have been before the creation of Lostwell, indeed before the civil wars of the gods had begun. If I could speak to Lord Renko, he would be able to confirm if you are who you claim to be.'

The woman smiled and shook her head. 'I don't need confirmation; I know who I am.'

More footsteps were heard hurrying along the passageway.

'Belinda!' cried a man's voice. 'Come quickly; the Falls of Iron is under attack.'

The woman glanced at Van and Joaz, then turned and walked away, her footsteps fading into the distance.

'Under attack?' said Van. 'The Banner? It must be.'

'Never mind that,' said Joaz. 'Start picking the lock again; I need to get out of here, so I can tell Lord Renko what just happened.'

'Why? Do you believe her story?'

'It sounds crazy, but yes, I do. I've seen portraits of all of the Ascendants, and she looks just like the image of her in her younger years. We all think of the Third Ascendant as an old woman, but if she was here when salve first arrived... Damn these bars. I must let Lord Renko know about this. Van, get me out of here.'

He slid the nail from his boot, and got back to work.

Two hours later, Van was no closer to picking the lock. In the cell next to his, he could hear Joaz pacing up and down, and muttering to herself.

Despite what Joaz had said, he still harboured doubts about the woman's claims to have been the Third Ascendant. It was true that he pictured the god as a wise, old woman, just as the many statues on Implacatus portrayed her, and he knew what the effects of salve would have been, but he had trouble believing it. How could she have forgotten her past?

To take his mind off it, he went through the standard Banner plans for occupying towns such as the Falls of Iron. With two Quadrants at their disposal, the gods could set up a portal, and funnel the soldiers through in one surge, so it would all depend on whether Felice or Baldwin had managed to get inside the town. If they had, then the battle for the lower levels of the Falls of Iron was probably already over, and the castle where he and Joaz were being held would be under siege.

He lowered his aching arm from the outside of the lock on the cell door, and rummaged in a pocket for his cigarettes. He sat up and lit one, flexing the fingers on his right hand.

'Don't stop,' said Joaz.

'My arm needs a rest.'

'You don't understand,' she said; 'I must get out of here.'

'I know, but it's not working. I wish I knew what was going on down in the town.'

'I'm losing my patience, mortal. Get back to work, now.'

Van frowned. For a few, brief, scattered moments during their captivity he had almost imagined that he and Joaz were friends, but from her tone he realised that would never be true. She might be fond of him, but she would never see him as her equal. He tried to sort through his feelings towards the gods. Some of them were rotten to the core, grown arrogant and cruel on limitless power, while others inspired nothing but fear. Joaz had been right earlier; if Renko discovered he had let the dragon and her rider go, then the Ancient would kill him without a second thought. He glanced at the bare stone walls of the cell. Perhaps he was better off where he was.

A crashing sound came from the end of the dark passageway, followed by shouts.

Van stood, and leaned against the bars. Soldiers were running down the long hallway, their armour and uniforms immediately recognisable.

'Praise the Ascendants,' cried Joaz, her voice lifting as Banner soldiers piled into the end of the passageway.

Van stared in disbelief as Lord Baldwin strode towards the cells. At least twenty soldiers were around him – two full squads of the Banner's finest.

'Get these doors open,' Baldwin shouted.

Soldiers moved forward with long steel bars, and began to lever them under the barred gates to both cells.

'Lord Baldwin,' said Joaz. 'This is a pleasant surprise.'

He performed a little bow, a smile on his lips.

'What's going on down in the town?' she asked.

'The entire settlement is under our control, my lady,' Baldwin said, 'and the castle is under siege.'

'Stand back, Captain,' said a sergeant close to the bars, 'the gate's going to fall inwards.'

Van retreated to the rear of the cell as the soldiers continued to work.

'How did you know we were up here?' said Joaz.

'Lord Renko took a chance, ma'am. Something is blocking the use of vision powers here, and he suspected that you may have been captured rather than killed.'

Van's cell door toppled towards him as half a dozen soldiers levered it off its hinges. It fell with a clang and a cloud of dust, and Van stepped out into the passageway, his back slapped by the soldiers surrounding him. Others were working on the door to Joaz's cell as she waited by the rear wall.

'Did you come here by Quadrant?' she said.

'Yes, ma'am,' said Baldwin.

She smiled, and Van could see the relief shining on her face. The captain turned to the closest sergeant.

'Did you encounter resistance on the way in?'

'Minimal, sir,' the sergeant said. 'There were a couple of militia guards close to where Lord Baldwin's Quadrant brought us, but the way to the dungeons was clear. Everyone's up on the battlements.'

Van nodded. 'Good work, Sergeant.'

'Thank you, sir, and might I say how good it is to see you again? You had some of the lads quite worried.'

'Stand back!' cried another soldier, and Joaz's cell door collapsed inwards, crashing to the flagstones. She waited for the dust to clear, then strode from the cell.

'This way!' Baldwin shouted. 'Follow me.'

The god raced back down the passageway, and the two squads of Banner soldiers formed up and began to move after him, flanking Van and Joaz.

'Wait,' said Joaz; 'what are you doing? We need to get out of here.'

Whether Baldwin hadn't heard her, or whether he had chosen to ignore her, wasn't clear to Van as they followed the soldiers down the hallway.

'Lord Baldwin!' Joaz cried.

Van glanced at the sergeant as they ran. 'What's he up to?'

'He told Lord Renko that he could bring the castle to its knees on his own, sir.'

Joaz turned. 'Lord Renko's here? In person?'

'Yes, ma'am. He's set up his command post in the lower town.'

They burst through a door and out into the open air. Van glanced at the sun's position in the eastern sky. Mid-morning. Around them was a small forecourt, the whitewashed stone walls of the keep and the battlements towering above them on either side. A solitary militia soldier of the Falls of Iron was crossing the courtyard, and he stopped to stare as the Banner soldiers approached. Two raised their crossbows and loosed, and the man fell, his blood spilling over the cobbles.

'To the battlements!' cried Baldwin, raising his arm. 'Kill them all!'

'Wait!' shouted Joaz. 'That's a direct order, Lord Baldwin. Stay where you are.'

The god frowned and turned to her. 'We have a chance to destroy this nest of traitors, my lady.'

'No. We must return to Lord Renko immediately.'

'Lord Renko told me to seize any opportunity to eliminate the enemy forces, ma'am, and his orders outweigh yours.'

'You don't understand,' Joaz said, her eyes tight. 'It isn't only vision powers that are being blocked; your death powers won't work either.'

Baldwin gave her a glance tinged with scorn. 'I'm sorry, my lady, but how could you possibly know that? You have no death powers.'

Joaz's eyes reddened with rage. 'Then try them.'

At that moment, two warriors emerged from the keep to their left, and Baldwin turned to face them. Van recognised them both. One was the woman who had claimed to be the Third Ascendant, and the other was the tall mortal who had also been outside the cells when they had been questioned. The mortal man was coated in steel armour, and was carrying a great war hammer, at the end of which were three large greenhide talons.

Baldwin smiled and raised his hand, but nothing happened.

The two warriors charged into the midst of the Banner squads, the woman slashing out with a long sword, and the man swinging his clawed hammer. Van stared, his mouth falling open. Both of them were moving too quickly for the soldiers to be able to respond, and within seconds several were lying dead, their limbs and torsos sliced or hacked to pieces by powerful blows.

'They have battle-vision!' a soldier cried, moments before his head went spinning through the air in a spray of blood.

The warrior-woman took a crossbow bolt to her guts, but didn't flinch, her sword carving its way through the soldiers in a blur of dark steel.

'Get us out of here,' cried Joaz, but it was too late. The two warriors had driven a wedge into the squads, separating them into two halves. Van and Joaz were on one side of the carnage, while Baldwin stood on the other, his feet backing away, his eyes wide with terror.

The giant mortal leaped into the soldiers surrounding Joaz. Van was shoved to the side and flung to the cobbles. He glanced up to see the warrior swing his blood-soaked hammer, the blow cleaving Joaz where she stood, the long greenhide talons cutting her to pieces. Baldwin cried out, then there was a shimmer in the air and he vanished.

Van pulled himself up. All around him, his soldiers were falling in a torrent of blood.

'Lay down your weapons!' he cried, raising his empty hands. 'We surrender!'

The warrior woman pulled back a step as the soldiers threw down their swords and crossbows, but the man pressed on as if he hadn't heard. Van gazed into the warrior's eyes, and recognised the lust for death that lay there. The tall warrior lashed out with the clawed hammer, and another two soldiers fell, ripped to shreds. Van backed away to the edge of the keep wall, his palms still raised, as the warrior kept hacking and swinging.

A young woman, tiny in comparison to the warrior, ran out from the keep. She jumped into the fray, heedless of the risk, and stood between the warrior and the last few survivors from the two squads.

'Corthie! Stop!' she screamed, her arms out as if to shield those still living.

The warrior brought his hammer down, then pulled back at the last second as he saw the young woman. The clawed weapon swerved down to the side, gouging out chunks of bloody cobbles from the ground.

The small forecourt fell into silence as the warrior faced the young woman.

'They had surrendered, Corthie,' she yelled, her voice strong, but her eyes revealing the terror she felt within.

The warrior glanced around at the carnage. Aside from Joaz, the bodies of twenty Banner soldiers lay scattered over the cobbles, their blood pooling.

'Did they?' the warrior said. 'I didn't even notice.'

'Pyre's tits, that was insane,' said the young woman. 'Brother, what has happened to you?'

'I was killing the enemy, Kelsey,' he said. 'Isn't that what I'm supposed to do?'

'I've seen him like that before,' said the woman who claimed to be

Queen Belinda, 'except then, it was against greenhides.' She glanced down at the dismembered body of Joaz as she sheathed her sword. 'You killed another god.'

Corthie turned, and nodded, his eyes dark.

Another woman appeared out of the door to the keep. She put a hand over her mouth as she stared at the scene of carnage.

'Aila,' said Kelsey, 'take your boyfriend back inside. Belinda and I will deal with this.'

Corthie glowered at the young woman for a moment, then strode away, Aila going back into the keep with him.

Kelsey turned to look at the survivors. 'Three?' she said. 'He left three alive.' She shook her head. 'My brother's a maniac.'

'Thank you for saving us,' said Van.

Kelsey looked up at him. 'You again?

Van nodded. He walked over to the body of Joaz, and knelt by the remains. He lifted a hand, and closed the god's lifeless eyes. By his shoulders, he felt the presence of the other two survivors. One was shaking, his face pale and drawn, while the other was staring at his slaughtered comrades scattered over the cobbles of the courtyard. It reminded Van of the inside of a butcher's shop, with limbs and shorn body parts lying out as if on display. His heart sickened, not only for what had happened, but with the knowledge that, over his many years of service, the Banner had also slaughtered unarmed soldiers and civilians who had surrendered.

'What happened here, Belinda?' said a man's voice.

'One of the gods jumped in using a Quadrant,' she said. 'They released the two prisoners, then Corthie and I caught up with them here.'

There was a pause. 'You and Corthie did this, alone?'

'I got a few, but it was mostly Corthie and his Clawhammer.'

Van glanced over at the woman everyone was calling Belinda. She was standing talking to Count Irno, while Kelsey waited a few paces away as militia soldiers began clearing the corpses from the courtyard.

'Are you really the Third Ascendant?' he said.

Belinda and the others glanced at him.

'I am,' she said.

'Get these Banner soldiers into the dungeons,' Count Irno said, gesturing to the militia near by. 'Actually, leave the officer here. He may be useful.' He turned to Belinda. 'A herald has arrived to speak to us.'

Van stood as militia soldiers approached. They took hold of the two surviving Banner troopers and escorted them away in the direction of the cells. Other militia approached Van, their crossbows levelled at his waist.

'Should we shackle him, sir?' said one.

Irno glanced over, and stared at Van. 'Bind his hands behind his back, but no chains.'

'Yes, sir.'

Van's arms were hauled back, and his wrists were bound with tight cords.

'Escort him to the battlements with us,' said Irno, then he and Belinda set off, heading for a set of steps rising up the side of the high curtain wall. Kelsey tagged along as Van was led off behind them by two soldiers.

'That god,' she said as they walked; 'were you in love with her?'

Van eyed the young woman. 'No.'

'Were you friends?'

Van shrugged as they started to climb the steps. 'She was a god.'

'So?'

'Gods don't have mortal friends.'

'She tried to save your life when you were locked in the cells,' Kelsey said. 'She told us what you did with the dragon. She must have been fond of you at least.'

'Maybe. Look, if you're trying to apologise for what your brother did to my men, then forget it; I don't want to hear it.'

Kesley raised an eyebrow. 'I wasn't going to apologise. I'm not responsible for what my brother does.'

'Then why did you intervene? He could have taken your head off.'

She glanced at him. 'Impulse. It was pretty stupid.'

'It was, but I'm grateful nevertheless.'

They reached the top of the battlements, which were crowded with local militia. Irno was there, standing next to Belinda and a few militia officers. The guards pushed Van along until he was positioned close by, and he looked out over the town. Below them, the streets were filled with soldiers, but other than that, the place looked peaceful.

Irno glanced at Van. 'Will the Banner kill my people?'

'They'll do whatever Lord Renko orders them to do.'

'Lord Renko?' said Belinda. 'Is the Ancient down there?'

'So I believe,' said Van.

'The god who appeared in the castle with the Quadrant,' said Belinda; 'what is his name?'

'Lord Baldwin.'

Belinda nodded, then glanced at Irno. 'Where's the herald?'

'He's coming,' said Irno. 'I have instructed the militia to let him pass through the castle, but stay close to me, in case it's a trick and he tries to attack.'

Soldiers along the battlements parted, and a herald in the uniform of the Banner of the Golden Fist approached. His eyes glided over Van for a moment, then settled on Count Irno.

'I have been sent here by the most Noble and Sacred Ancient, Lord Renko,' he said, inclining his head slightly. 'Am I addressing Lord Irno, Count of the Falls of Iron?'

Irno kept his face impassive. 'You are.'

'Lord Renko sends his greetings,' the herald said, bowing again, 'and wishes me to present you with the following ultimatum. You have until dawn tomorrow to surrender the castle of the Falls of Iron to him, along with all of the occupants currently residing within its walls.'

Irno narrowed his eyes. 'Or what? Renko must know by now that his god powers won't work against us, and he saw what happened to the squads he sent into the castle. Lord Baldwin, I assume, has informed him of the fate of Lady Joaz?'

'Indeed, my lord, he has. The most Noble Ancient Lord Renko has the following to say on the matter – that if the castle is not surrendered in its entirety, then the civilian population of the town of the Falls of Iron will be put to the sword, starting at dawn's first light tomorrow.'

Irno said nothing, though the lines around his dark eyes tightened.

'Do you have a message, my lord,' the herald went on, 'that I can take back to the most Noble Ancient?'

'Yes,' said Irno. 'Tell him that the Falls of Iron will be his grave, and the grave of all those who harm my people.'

The herald bowed. 'Thank you, my lord. I shall now take my leave.'

'Give him clear passage out of the castle,' Irno called out as the herald departed, making his way down the stairs as the militia soldiers watched from the battlements.

Irno turned to Van. 'Will they do it? Will the soldiers of the Banner follow such savage orders?'

Van nodded. 'The soldiers of the Banner always obey orders.'

'You didn't,' said Kelsey. 'You let the dragon go.'

'And look where it got me.'

Irno frowned. 'If Renko starts killing my people at dawn,' he said, 'then your life will be forfeit in return; I will hang your corpse from the walls, so that your men can witness what becomes of those who commit acts of barbarism. Do you understand, Captain Van Logos?'

'I do.'

'So far,' said Kelsey, 'only one person in this conflict has committed an act of barbarism that I'm aware of – my brother.'

'Do not interfere, Miss Holdfast,' Irno said. He gestured to the guards holding Van's arms. 'Get him out of my sight.'

CHAPTER 29

UNLEASHED

Falls of Iron, Western Khatanax – 13th Tradinch 5252

Aila gazed at the shadows flickering on her bedroom ceiling. It was a sticky, humid night, and she had opened the shutters to let in the air, but they had also allowed the light from the fires burning in the town to seep through. Bonfires had been built under the tall walls of the castle, so that the soldiers of the Banner could keep watch on the battlements throughout the night. Next to Aila, Corthie was lying on his back, sleeping. He had ignored her advice and got drunk the previous evening, once the terms of the ultimatum had been made known. Kelsey, though, had refused his offer to have a few drinks with him, and had made her feelings at his behaviour plain.

Aila sat up and glanced down at him. He seemed so peaceful, so unlike the huge steel-clad warrior who had butchered the unarmed soldiers in the courtyard the day before. He had sworn to Aila that he hadn't noticed the Banner squads lay down their weapons, and she believed him, but what did that say about the frenzy that had overtaken his senses? She remembered watching him fight greenhides from the battlements of the Middle Walls back in the City, and how had been so lost in combat that he hadn't heard the shouts recalling him. But back then, it had been beasts he had been destroying, not men who had surrendered.

And he had slain another god, a being undone in a few seconds of violence after living for thousands of years.

Should she be worried? After all, these things happened in war, and Corthie wasn't the first who had committed such acts, nor would he be the last. She knew he wasn't an evil man, but if he couldn't control himself, then what else might he be capable of?

She slid out of bed and walked to the table by the window. There was a jug of water sitting there, with a cloth on top to keep the dust out, and she poured herself a mugful. The light from the bonfires had created a dull, red, flickering glow over the town that seemed to herald its end. She glanced to the east, but there was no sign yet of the sun. Good, she thought. She was dreading dawn, and what it would mean for the hundreds of civilians trapped in the settlement below.

The water in the mug was lukewarm, and she grimaced at the taste. She glanced back at the bed, but knew she wasn't going to be getting any more sleep that night; her mind was buzzing, and filled with the images of carnage.

A walk, she thought; she would go for a walk around the castle to clear her head. She placed the mug back onto the table and pulled on some clothes, selecting a light, cotton dress due to the intense humidity. She strapped on a pair of sandals, and crept past Corthie's slumbering form to the door. Once out in the corridor, she took a turn to the right, then went down a quiet and deserted set of stairs to the ground level of the keep. She went out into a courtyard – the one where she usually ate breakfast, not the one where Corthie had slaughtered the soldiers – and walked to the low wall at its edge. The great line of battlements stretched out before her, just a few feet lower than where she stood. The walkway at the top of the wide walls was filled with the town's militia, standing at their posts in case the Banner attempted a night attack.

'Having trouble sleeping?'

She turned her head. 'Hi, Irno. Yes, as a matter of fact. It's so hot here, but I guess that's not the only reason.'

He nodded, his gaze out on the town beyond the line of the battlements in front of them.

'What about you?' she said.

'I haven't been to bed,' he said. 'I saw little point in trying to sleep, when I knew I would fail. I've been working instead; checking on the stores of water and crossbow bolts, and talking to my officers. And looking through lists of names.'

'Names?'

'Yes, the names of all of the civilians who didn't make it up to the caves in time, and who remain in the town. There are over six hundred of them; families, old folk, children. The great wealth that I used to make this place prosperous; a place where no one starves to death, has become the cause of its destruction.'

'Money from the salve trade, you mean?'

'Precisely. For three hundred years it has made me rich, but all that is now at an end. No matter what happens next, there will be no more salve trade, at least not as we know it.' He frowned. 'I thought the loss of my wealth would mean more to me, but now that it comes to it, I would give all of my gold to save the lives of the people trapped below us. I have doomed them.'

'The greed of the gods has doomed the town, not you.'

'I always feared this day would come; the day the wolves of Implacatus came seeking the source of the substance they worship; the blessed salve. How I hate it now; how I wish salve never existed.'

Aila said nothing for a while as they stood side by side next to the low wall. She thought back to her youth in Pella, when she had trailed Irno around the palace, following him because she considered him the best big brother in the whole City. Unlike several of her other siblings, Irno had always made time for her, and had always seemed to be without a care in the world.

'You remind me of father,' she said.

He glanced at her. 'In a good way or a bad way?'

'A good way. Father was a strong leader, who loved his people and fought for them when he had to. The Reapers trusted him because they knew he was there for them; they knew he was on their side. And, what "bad way" are you talking about? I can't remember father having any bad ways about him.'

'No?' said Irno. 'I guess, as the youngest daughter, you were a little spoiled by father; you didn't see his temper much, but he had a rage about him; a fiery red-hot rage. As the eldest, I probably saw it more than the others. You know, in battle, he fought in the same manner as Corthie Holdfast.'

'Did he?'

'Yes. I once saw him carve up more than two hundred members of the Taran militia that Prince Michael had sent into Pella. He went into a battle frenzy, like a trance, and cut down anyone in his path, even those who had discarded their weapons and were trying to flee. The entire harbour front was covered in bodies.'

'Where was I at the time?'

'With Princess Yendra in the Circuit, I think. When the last Taran had fallen, father sent all of their heads by wagon to Prince Michael in Maeladh Palace. Then he went and got drunk.'

'Malik's ass,' she said; 'I've fallen for someone who's like my father.'

Irno smiled. 'Not if you didn't know father was like that. There are probably a few things about him that you might not realise; for example, he had a harem containing dozens of young Pellan women.'

'I know; I was born and raised there.'

'Of course. I forgot.'

'It's alright; there were so many siblings I'm surprised we could remember each other's names, let along where we were all brought up.'

'Only four of us now remain, and three of them are within these walls.'

'How is dear Vana?'

'Terrified. If she had a Quadrant, I think she'd return to the City.'

'Maybe Naxor will bring one back with him.'

'At this point, I'd rather he brought Blackrose.'

'What will happen at dawn, do you think?'

'I believe the word of the herald they sent. At dawn, they will start to kill the civilians in the town, while we watch helplessly from the battlements. If Lady Joaz had survived, then we might be able to bargain for their lives, but I doubt they'll stop because we have three Banner soldiers locked up, even if one of them is an officer.'

'And what happens next?'

'Next?' Irno shook his head, a despairing laugh leaving his lips. 'I can't even think about that yet. My mind is filled with what will occur at dawn.'

'But there will be an "after",' said Aila. 'We will still be under siege, and Lord Renko will still be sitting in the town below us.'

Irno caught her eye. 'Then we'd best hope Naxor has that Quadrant with him when he returns.'

'My lord!' came a cry from the lane that ran in front of the keep.

They turned, and saw a militia soldier hurrying towards them.

'There's been a disturbance, my lord,' the soldier said as he arrived before Irno and Aila. 'Someone was in the dungeons, trying to free the three mercenary prisoners.'

'What?' cried Irno. 'Have more Banner soldiers appeared within the walls?'

'No, my lord.'

'Then who was it?'

The soldier lowered his eyes. 'Kelsey Holdfast, my lord.'

———

'Just what were you playing at, young lady?' cried Irno as Kelsey stood before him, two militia soldiers at her back.

She raised an eyebrow. 'It's been a while since anyone called me a lady.'

Irno's face reddened further, his eyes bulging. 'You went against my orders.'

'Aye, but your orders were stupid.' She nodded in the direction of the three occupied cells behind her. 'These soldiers are going to be executed, despite having surrendered, in retaliation for what the gods might do at dawn. Don't get me wrong, if the gods carry out their threat, then that makes them worthy of a gruesome death, but these three haven't done anything except follow orders. If you kill them, you'll be no better than the gods you hate.'

'If you're trying to make amends for the behaviour of your brother, then...'

'Of course I'm not,' she spat. 'I'm trying to stop you from making a mistake.' She tilted her head. 'I didn't get very far. It turns out I'm not very good at trying to break into locked cells.'

'You naive child,' Irno said, his tone a little more gentle. 'These men you tried to save, do you really think them innocent?'

Kelsey shrugged.

'Let me tell you a little about the Banner of the Golden Fist,' Irno went on. 'There are many Banners, and what I'm about to say applies to them all. For hundreds of years, they have worked for the gods of Implacatus, carrying out their dirty work for them; suppressing populations, and invading and occupying worlds that have tried to resist the rule of the gods. They have carried out atrocities that would consume your heart if you were to hear of them in any detail; massacres of children, whole towns and villages wiped from the face of their worlds, entire tribes annihilated. If Blackrose were here, she would be able to relate some of the terrible deeds they performed on Dragon Eyre.' He pointed at the three cells. 'These men are not innocent, Kelsey; they are the willing accomplices of the tyrants that rule Implacatus. You say they were only following orders, but tomorrow at dawn their comrades will massacre hundreds of civilians. Will they be merely following orders too?'

Kelsey bit her lip. 'It's still wrong. Are we supposed to be as bad as them, or are we supposed to be better? What are we trying to aspire to?'

'Noble words,' said Irno, 'but they come at a cost. Sometimes, the only way to fight evil is with evil.'

'No. I'm not accepting that.'

Irno turned to the three barred chambers where the soldiers were being held. Each man was hidden in the shadows at the back of his cell, and none had spoken since Aila and Irno had arrived.

'Captain Logos,' Irno said. 'Please step forward.'

A figure emerged from the gloom of the central cell. Van Logos approached the bars, a lit cigarette in his left hand.

'Count Irno,' he said.

Irno nodded to him. 'Captain, I would be much obliged if you would please relate the most recent atrocity carried out on one of your operations. I think a certain Kelsey Holdfast needs to hear it.'

Van took a long draw on his cigarette. 'Two days ago...'

'Two days,' cried Irno. 'Did you hear that? He only has to go back two days.'

Van waited.

'Please, continue,' said Irno.

'Two days ago, Lord Baldwin killed four hundred mercenary trainees who were living in Gadena's camp in the Shinstran Desert.'

Irno's smirk fell away, and his face paled as he stared at Van.

'He used his death powers,' Van went on, 'because, basically, the trainees were an inconvenience. We didn't have the manpower to both guard and feed them at the same time.'

A look of hatred and disgust swept over Irno's face. He turned back to Kelsey. 'Do you now see what we're fighting against?'

'If they're so evil,' said Kelsey, 'then why are you trying to emulate them? And think for a moment; what good will their deaths do? Imagine the scene – the soldiers in the town start carving up the townsfolk until they're wading in blood, and you hang three bodies from the battlements? Do you think anyone will even notice? And those who do, will they think anything other than how weak and pathetic it makes you look?'

Irno took a step back as Kelsey pointed her finger in his face.

'If the gods and soldiers carry out their carnage tomorrow,' she went on, her finger getting ever closer to Irno's chin, 'then our response should be nothing but cold silence and contempt. Don't sully our hands in the blood of those not responsible. For Pyre's sake, Irno, be a leader.'

'Listen to her,' said Aila; 'she's right. We can't act the same way as the gods and still claim to be any better than them.'

Irno lowered his eyes, his face ashen. 'Very well; you win. The three soldiers shall not be harmed. We will stand on the battlements and watch as our people are slaughtered, and do nothing, for there is nothing we can do.'

'That's not true,' said a voice from the shadows of the corridor.

Aila turned. 'Corthie? I thought you were sleeping.'

'I woke up and noticed you were gone.' He walked forward, wearing his full armour, the Clawhammer slung over his back. 'I've been thinking. I didn't mean to kill those men; I honestly didn't see them throw down their weapons. My battle-vision... it devours me at times.' He glanced at Aila, Irno and Kelsey, then turned to the prisoners. 'That's why I'm down here; to apologise. I'm sorry.'

Van remained by the bars of his cell, but said nothing.

Aila walked over to Corthie. She wanted to embrace him, but every inch of his body was covered in steel or thick mail.

'What did you mean before?' said Irno. 'Is there something we can do?'

'Aye,' said Corthie. 'I'm going down to the town; I'm going to fight the Banner.'

'What?' said Aila. 'You can't.'

'I must,' he said. 'If this is who I am, then I have to. It's the only way.'

'But they'll kill you.'

He smiled. 'No, they won't. Maybe if I was meeting them on an open field of battle, where their numbers would weigh against me, but in the narrow streets of the town? They'll never get close enough to me. I can burn battle-vision for hours, just as I did countless times in front of the Great Walls, and I'm immune to the gods' death powers. Unleash me, and I'll kill them all.'

'You're not a wild animal, Corthie,' said Aila.

'No, but I am a killer. I was born to fight.'

A tear slid down Aila's cheek.

'My heart is against this,' said Irno, 'but I will not try to stop you, Corthie.'

'This is insane,' said Kelsey. 'You're not a god, brother, you're just a man; a mortal.'

'You're right,' he said. 'I am just a mortal, but there has never been another mortal like me, and there never will be. This is my purpose, and my life, and I am the one who has to live it. If I can save the civilians down there, then I have no choice but to go.'

'No,' said Aila, the tears falling down her face.

He touched her cheek with a gauntlet-covered hand. 'I'll need you when I get back. If I know you're here, it will make it bearable.'

'You're breaking my heart, Corthie; don't go.'

He smiled, then turned and strode down the passageway, the sight of him lost in the shadows. Irno glanced at Aila, then hurried after him.

'Amalia's breath,' Aila sobbed, 'this can't be happening.'

Kelsey put her arm round her shoulder. 'We should go with him to the gates, to see him off.'

'I can't bear it.'

Kelsey began steering her down the passageway.

'Wait,' said Van. 'Tell Corthie to head straight for the gods. If he kills them, then the soldiers of the Banner will surrender or pull out. Without orders or commanders, they won't continue to fight.'

Kelsey frowned at the soldier, then led Aila from the passageway. They emerged into the darkness of the night, but a glow was forming on the eastern horizon, heralding the new day to come. The castle lay still and quiet around them, the shadows deep by the high walls.

'We need to pass on the soldier's message,' said Kelsey. 'We should go to the gates.'

'No,' said Aila; 'I can't. I'm not ready to say goodbye.'

'Then I'll go. Stay here.'

Kelsey withdrew her arm from Aila's shoulder and ran off. Aila remained where she was. She wiped her face, her tears dried up. Her heart felt empty and hollow, her mind flooded with images of the only time she had ever seen Corthie fighting, when he had destroyed greenhide after greenhide in front of the Middle Walls. She had sworn that she would never watch him again; it had been too much to take.

She heard footsteps behind her.

'What's going on?' said Belinda. 'Why is Corthie heading towards the gates?'

Aila paused, feeling for a moment as if she had lost the ability to speak. Belinda narrowed her eyes as she glanced at Aila's tear-streaked face.

'He's going to fight, isn't he?' she said.

Aila nodded.

'I'd better go.'

'Are you going to stop him?'

'No, Aila,' she said, 'I'm going to help him.'

Aila stared at her.

'I can assist him, just as I did when we fought beyond the walls on your world.' She gazed into Aila's eyes. 'I'll make sure he comes back.'

Belinda hurried off before Aila could say anything, leaving the demigod alone in the shadows. She glanced around, feeling helpless. What could she do? She couldn't watch from the walls, and there was no way she could go back to bed and sleep. The thought of food made her feel sick, and there was no one to talk to who would understand how she was feeling. She wandered for a minute, her feet following the twisting paths and lanes that wound round the castle keep. Militia soldiers were scurrying about, most of them heading for the battlements as the light in the eastern sky grew. A sense of excitement was palpable on some of the soldiers' faces, as rumours spread and grew about the mighty steel-clad warrior who was going to fight on their behalf.

Aila entered the keep and found herself outside the ale room. The place was in darkness, but she tried the handle, and the door opened. She walked inside and lit a lamp, the place reminding her of Corthie. She took down a jug of raki from a shelf and walked over to the table where Corthie had sat for night after night when they had first arrived in the Falls of Iron. She sat, and wept, then filled a mug with raki.

Aila's eyes flickered open. A pale gloom hung in the ale room as the sunlight beat against the closed shutters. She lifted her head from the table, and wiped the drool from her face. Her head was pounding, and she focussed her self-healing powers, dispelling the pain in a surge of healing.

She glanced at the empty jug of raki. How long had she been unconscious?

Outside, a low sound was building; a rumble, and she thought for a moment that it was another earthquake.

She frowned. No, not an earthquake.

The rumble grew louder, and she got to her feet and walked to the door. She opened it, and a roar of cheers rang through her ears. Drums were being beaten, and voices were crying out all over the castle. Aila emerged blinking into the strong light. The courtyard was filled with people, and the battlements to her left were packed with militia soldiers raising their swords and crossbows into the air.

Aila gazed at the crowds. Every face was pointing in the same direction – towards the cobbled path that led up from the gates of the castle. She pushed her way through the tight press, trying to get a better view. A flash of steel armour glinted ahead of her, but there were too many bodies in the way for her to see who was wearing it.

A path was cleared on the stairs leading up to the battlements, and Irno sprang up a few steps then turned to face the crowds, his hand raised.

'This morning,' he cried, 'we, the people of the Falls of Iron, have witnessed a miracle!'

The crowds roared, and the drumbeat picked up, the vibrations rumbling through the crowded courtyard.

'A few hours ago,' Irno went on, 'there was nothing but fear and despair in our hearts, and a bleak night seemed to herald nothing but the grimmest of days. Instead, our people have been delivered from their woes by the two mightiest warriors ever seen on the soil of Khatanax – one a god, the other god-like.'

He gestured downwards as the crowd cheered their joy into the skies. Two figures began to climb the steps, and the noise increased. Corthie lifted the Clawhammer above his head, and Aila pushed through the crowds, trying to get closer to him. His steel armour was covered in dents, scores and blood, and he was clutching onto his helmet, which had been almost sheared in two. Next to him stood Belinda, the dark blade of the Weathervane held in her right hand. Neither were smiling, and they both looked drained, their eyes dark.

The crowd surged forward at the sight of them, flooding the courtyard, as the soldiers on the battlements hammered their swords against their shields.

'Behold our saviours!' cried Irno, his eyes wild. 'Corthie Holdfast and Belinda, the Third Ascendant.'

Aila put her hands to her ears as the noise grew to a fierce intensity. She glanced up, and saw Corthie's eyes gazing at her. He bounded down the steps, and the crowd wrapped itself around him as dozens, hundreds of them tried to get close enough to touch the warrior who had saved them. He pushed them aside, and made straight for Aila. Taking her by the hand, he barged his way towards the keep, ignoring the cheers, the pleas and the weeping. They made it to the entrance, and Corthie closed the large iron-framed door behind them, dulling the sounds of the frenzied crowds outside.

Keeping hold of Aila's hand, Corthie strode for their quarters without a word, and when they reached their rooms, he shut and locked the door, then sat, his head in his hands.

Aila touched his face, and felt the tears on his cheeks.

'I did it,' he said, his voice barely rising above a whisper.

'You did.'

'I feel sick. I killed... hundreds. And Baldwin, I killed him too. If the survivors hadn't used a Quadrant to escape, I'd still be down there, killing.'

'You saved the civilians.'

'Aye.'

'Then you did a good thing.'

He glanced up at her. 'Am I a monster?'

'You're Corthie Holdfast,' she said, kissing him, 'and that's all I need to know.'

CHAPTER 30

DESIRABLE

Alea Tanton, Tordue, Western Khatanax – 13th Tradinch 5252

Sable awoke. For one terrible moment she thought she was inside a coffin, and wild imaginings arose of her having been buried by mistake, lowered into a grave while still alive. Around her were wooden walls, trapping her body on every side as she lay. She tried to move her arms, but there was no room, and they remained down by her sides. She struggled as panic clouded her mind, then rapped the fingers of her left hand against the wood. The wound there screamed into life, and she almost broke down as she remembered what had happened to her finger. Then she remembered her broken leg, and as soon as the memory crystallised, she felt the agony from it wash over her. Her breathing became more frantic, and she was about to cry out when a light appeared to her left.

'Shush, Sable,' came a woman's voice; 'keep quiet.'

Sable turned her head. The side slat of the box where she lay had opened, and a young woman was peering in at her.

'Where am I?'

'You're still in the harem,' the woman said, 'we've been hiding you from the soldiers.'

Sable squinted into the brightness beyond the young woman, and saw the large bathroom that they shared.

'We took all of the towels out of this cupboard, and carried you here,' the woman said. 'The soldiers searched the place, but with no gods around, no one could read our minds, and they didn't find you.'

'No gods?'

'No,' the woman smiled. 'Latude's still in prison, and Renko is away fighting somewhere, so we've been left alone for more than a day.'

'More than a day?'

'Yes, Sable. We found you in your bed yesterday morning, but before that, we'd heard what you'd done.' She raised a cup of water. 'Here, take a sip.'

Sable let the woman hold the cup to her lips, and she drank greedily, the water soothing her parched mouth.

'We were awoken by screams,' the woman said. 'They were coming from a cleaner who had been sent into the room where you had been taken. We thought that asshole Maisk had killed you, but then we realised from the cries that it was Maisk's body that had been found. You killed him.'

Sable nodded. 'Yes.'

The woman smiled. 'Then we noticed the bloodstains trailing along our floor, and discovered you unconscious in bed. You had lost a lot of blood, but we set your leg and patched you up as best we could. And we cleaned up the blood.'

'You did all that for me?'

'Of course, Sable. You're one of us, and... you killed Maisk. You actually killed a god, and not just any god, but a sadistic asshole god who treated us girls as if we were dirt. We would have done whatever it took to protect you.'

Sable looked at the young woman. Had she and the others really risked their lives for her?

'Can you help me get out?'

'Yes,' the woman said, 'but only for a little while.' She turned her head towards the bathroom door. 'Someone give me a hand.'

The other three women of the harem came through the door.

'She's awake,' said one.

'How's her leg looking?' said another.

'Shut up and help me,' said the woman crouching by the cupboard. 'Let's get her out.'

'Is it safe? The soldiers could be back.'

'They won't; they've already searched the harem, and there are two of them standing outside our front door. We'll be safe in here.'

They reached down, and Sable was pulled from the cramped cupboard, and helped to sit on the edge of the bath. She gazed at the bandage on her left hand.

'He cut my finger off.'

'We know; we saw it,' said the first woman. She glanced at the others. 'One of you should be by the front door, listening for anyone coming.'

'You just told us it was safe.'

The door to the bathroom opened and a man walked in.

He smiled. 'Hello, girls.'

The women from the harem shrieked, and one of them pulled a dinner knife from the folds of her dress.

'Woah,' the man said, raising his hands. 'I'm a friend.' He glanced towards the bath. 'Sable Holdfast?'

'Yes?' she said.

'My name's Naxor. Aila and the others sent me to help you.' He turned to the woman holding the knife. 'Would you please put that down? You're making me nervous.'

Sable darted into the man's head. 'He's telling the truth.'

The woman with the knife scowled. 'How did you get in?'

'I sent the two guards outside your quarters to sleep. In fact, we should probably move them in case anyone else comes along.' He tapped the side of his head. 'I'm a demigod, and I have vision powers.'

Sable turned to the four women. 'Please leave me with Naxor for a moment.'

'Good idea,' he said, 'and perhaps you could find somewhere to hide the two guards while you're gone?'

The women edged past the man at the door, keeping their eyes on him. When the last had left the bathroom, Naxor eased the door closed.

'How did you find me?' said Sable.

'I guessed you'd be somewhere in the Governor's residence. I just stepped off a boat this morning; it's waiting for us at the harbour. All we have to do is get down there, and we can be on our way to the Falls of Iron.'

'That might be tricky,' she said. 'I broke my leg.'

Naxor smiled again. 'Then it's a good thing I brought some salve along, isn't it?'

He was wearing a small pack over his shoulder, and he dropped it to the bathroom floor then crouched down next to where Sable was sitting. As he was opening the bag, his eyes caught sight of the bandage on her left hand.

'Been through the wars, have you?'

'Why don't you read it out of my head?'

He raised an eyebrow as he took a jar from the bag. 'I think you already know the answer to that. Tell me, can every Holdfast block powers?'

'No. I couldn't; not until Karalyn did something to my head. But, whatever she did, it only worked because I'm a Holdfast.'

He opened the jar. 'But Belinda can also block powers.'

'That's because Karalyn had to rebuild her mind from scratch after she vaporised everything.' She gave him a suspicious look. 'You and Belinda, eh?'

He halted what he was doing. 'Please don't read my mind. It's very rude, you know.' He handed her the jar. 'Take a mouthful of this; no more, mind, just a mouthful.'

She raised the jar to her lips with her right hand and drank. The effect was almost immediate and Naxor took the jar from her before she could drop it. A surge of well-being and healing rippled through her, tingling every nerve in her body. She felt her left leg glow with warmth as the bone knit itself back together. The bruises faded, and she gasped, her eyes closing. She opened them again, and saw Naxor staring at her.

'That was amazing,' she said. She looked at her hand. 'There's no pain, but I guess my finger isn't going to grow back, no matter how much salve I take?'

'I'm afraid not. It would if you were a god but, well, you are quite clearly a mortal.'

She smiled and got to her feet. She put a little weight onto her left leg and it felt steady; better than steady, it felt strong. She glanced down at Naxor as he resealed the jar and placed it back into the bag.

'I don't suppose you have a sword hidden away in there that I could borrow?'

'No,' he said, 'but the two sleeping guards do, and if your fellow harem girls have brought their bodies in, then you can take your pick.'

Sable stretched her arms and legs. 'I could dance,' she said; 'I feel great.'

Naxor looked away, his cheeks reddening a little, and she smiled. They came out of the bathroom, and found the other women of the harem in the main sitting room of their quarters. The sleeping soldiers had been dragged onto the carpet, and the women were still moving them when they noticed Sable.

'You're walking!' said one.

Sable sat on a couch and laced up a pair of sandals. 'Naxor had some salve.'

'Can we have some?' said another.

'No,' said Naxor; 'it's to be used for healing broken limbs, not for recreational purposes. I didn't bring it all the way here so that you girls could use it to get a rush.'

Sable stood and faced the four women. 'Thank you,' she said. 'You saved my life, when you could have let the soldiers find me. I'll never be able to repay you, but you should take your chance and get out of here. Go back to your homes and your families.' She paused. 'I'll never forget what you did for me.'

'What are you going to do now?'

'Naxor and I are leaving; we still have a lot of work to do.' She leaned over and unbuckled a sword from one of the soldier's belts. 'Take care.'

Sable and Naxor turned, and they walked from the room.

'That was very heartfelt,' he muttered.

'You should know,' Sable said, 'that after having read your mind, I'm not sure that I should completely trust you.'

He smiled. 'And we've only just met. It's curious, but I've been told by many people not to trust you, so I guess we're in similar positions.'

She turned along the passageway.

'The stairs are the other way,' he said.

'We're not going to the stairs,' she said; 'we're going to search Lord Renko's quarters. Were you seen entering the building?'

'No. The place is almost deserted.'

'That's because Lord Renko has taken the entire Banner to the Falls of Iron.'

'What?'

Sable reached the door to Renko's rooms. 'They left yesterday.' She turned the handle, and it opened.

'I know what you're thinking,' she said as they walked into Renko's study. 'The answer's yes, we're looking for a Quadrant.' She closed the door behind them and gazed around. 'There's a good possibility that Renko has both with him in the Falls of Iron, but maybe not.'

'"Both"? I thought there were three in Alea Tanton.'

She glanced at him. 'I might have accidentally broken one.'

Naxor frowned, then noticed the corpse lying wrapped on the large desk.

'It's Nathaniel,' said Sable, keeping her eyes away from the body.

'What? But...'

'Later. For now, just shut up and search.'

They started looking through the suite of rooms. Sable tried under the bed, but the box had gone. As she was rummaging in a tall wardrobe, the sound of voices floated up from outside. She hurried to the window, and glanced down through a gap in the shutters. Below her in the mansion's large backyard, soldiers were gathered in small groups.

Some were wounded, while others were shouting, their voices tinged with fear and alarm.

'Naxor,' she hissed.

He walked through from the study.

'The Banner are back,' she said; 'well, some of them.'

He joined her by the window. 'I'd say maybe three hundred? The rest must still be at the Falls of Iron.'

The front door of Renko's quarters opened, and an angry voice echoed through.

'I don't care about your feelings, Felice,' Renko shouted. 'Pull yourself together.'

Naxor raised a hand, ready.

'No,' whispered Sable. 'He has eye shields.'

They glanced at each other, then dived under the double bed just as Renko's boots came into view.

'This might be the worst day I've experienced in a thousand years,' the Ancient said, 'and you're weeping like a fool.'

'I'm sorry, my lord,' said Felice, her shoes visible by the doorway.

A large case was thrown onto the bed, and Renko began packing. 'I have to return to Implacatus immediately,' he said, 'and somehow try to explain that not only have I failed to find the source of salve, but that I managed to lose both Lady Joaz and Lord Maisk.'

A vase smashed off a wall. 'Damn the Holdfasts!' Renko cried. 'First some wild beast named Corthie destroys almost an entire regiment of soldiers, and then I return to discover that Sable has escaped.'

'That beast killed Lord Baldwin too,' said Felice, sobbing.

'Yes, him as well.' He sat on the bed, his legs inches from Sable's arm. 'But his death pales into insignificance next to the news that Queen Belinda has returned, and that she's allied herself to a family of god-killing mortals who can resist our powers.'

'Was it really her, my lord?'

'I know what I saw!' he cried. 'It might be thousands of years since I've seen her looking so young, but it was definitely her.' He stood. 'Here, take this. I shall use the other to transport myself and the body of the Fourth Ascendant back to Implacatus. You are now in charge of Lostwell, Governor Felice. Congratulations.'

He picked up the case from the bed and strode past Felice into the study. He stood by his desk, then there was a faint shimmer and he disappeared. Sable and Naxor raced to be the first out from under the bed.

Naxor rolled, then got to one knee and raised his arm at Felice. 'Sleep.'

Sable went straight for the god, reaching her as she toppled over. She plucked the Quadrant out of her hand, then whipped it away as Naxor stretched to snatch it.

'I'm afraid not, Naxor,' she said. 'I'll be keeping this.'

He glared at her, as if ready to pounce.

'Don't feel bad,' she said; 'I did lose a finger for it.'

Naxor's features softened, and he smiled. 'As you wish. However, I feel the need to point out that, without me, you won't be able to use the Quadrant, and, as we saw, there are now several hundred Banner soldiers around the residence. How exactly are you intending to get out of here?'

'I've already read the knowledge of how the Quadrant works from your mind, Naxor,' she said. 'I'm not an expert, yet, but I'll learn.' She glanced at the copper-coloured device in her hand, her eyes on the engraved lines and markings. 'I already know enough to get to the harbour.'

Naxor laughed. 'Are you going to leave me here?'

'No,' she said. 'I'll transport you to the harbour with me, and then we can take separate boats out of Alea Tanton. You can go back to the Falls of Iron, and I'll... well, I'll go where I please.'

He lit a cigarette.

'Pass me one of those,' she said.

'Sure.' He lit another one, and held it out for her. 'Let me make you an offer.'

She took a draw of the cigarette. 'Alright. I'm listening.'

He sat on the double bed. 'Give me the Quadrant, and you'll live like a princess for the rest of your days.'

'Go on.'

He glanced at her, his eyes betraying his coiled nerves. 'I shall take you back with me to the City.'

'What city?'

'My City,' he said, 'the City of Pella, Tara and the Bulwark. The City where Aila and I come from, and where Corthie used to fight the greenhides. There, you will live in a palace, with gold, and servants, and as much luxury and comfort as you can possibly imagine. You'll be welcomed with open arms; after all, you're related to the great champion, and you have a set of skills that even the mighty gods would envy. I know the King and Queen who rule there; they'd be delighted to have someone of your calibre choose to live next to them.'

'And what would you do?'

'Can you keep a secret?' He laughed. 'What am I saying? Of course you can. Unknown to almost everyone, there is a mine of untapped salve two hundred miles from the City. I have seen it; it contains enough salve to last the gods for millennia to come.'

'I thought the trade in salve had become rather risky?'

'A substance of that value will always find buyers. I'll have to rebuild my network of merchants, but that shouldn't prove too difficult. Great wealth and power await us, Sable, and for you, a lifetime of safety and comfort. For this dream to become a reality, all you need to do is give me the Quadrant, and we could be in the City within seconds.'

Sable nodded. 'What about us? Would there be an "us"?'

Naxor's eyes lit up. 'I would very much like that. You are the most beautiful woman I have ever seen, Sable, and you have more heart than…'

'Than Belinda?'

'I wasn't going to say that, but yes.'

'I thought you loved her?'

'Belinda and I want different things. I was after a bit of fun, whereas she, well, she seems to be taking the whole relationship thing a little more seriously than I'd like. You understand that, yes?'

She thought back to the way she had treated Millen. 'Yes, I do.'

'You and I are very similar,' he said, standing and coming closer to her. 'We want the same things, and are disliked by those jealous of our success. But why should we abide by their rules? We could do great things together, Sable; great things.'

She pondered his words. What he was offering would change her life; it would be a fresh start, in a new place where no one would know her, or judge her for the terrible things she had done. And, it would destroy Belinda, a woman who loathed her. She went into Naxor's mind, and saw nothing there she wasn't expecting. He saw Sable as a means to an end. He desired her, that wasn't a lie, but he would never love her, not in the way she wanted to be loved. He was telling the truth about the City, though, and about her life in a palace, and the wealth and power that would bring her, but did she care about any of that?

'Do you want me?' she said.

'Yes, Sable,' he breathed, getting ever closer; 'I want you.'

'Get on the bed.'

'What, here? But soldiers could arrive any second.'

'I thought you liked a little danger?'

He smiled, his eyes filled with desire for her. He jumped up onto the bed, and started to remove his clothes.

She shook her head. 'Sorry, Naxor; you're not my type.'

Sleep.

His eyes widened in shock for a moment, then he collapsed onto the covers.

You will awake in an hour, and when you do, for an entire day you will forget about the boat waiting for you in the harbour.

She leaned towards the bed and removed Naxor's cigarettes from a pocket, then stepped back over the sleeping body of Lady Felice on the carpet. She gazed at the Quadrant in her hands. She had done it; she had accomplished what she had set out to do, and now, she was free.

The harbour, she thought. Her fingers traced the engraved lines of the copper-coloured surface, and with a shimmer, she was gone.

NOTE OF THE CALENDAR

The Divine Calendar is used on every world ruled by Implacatus (for example, on Lostwell and Dragon Eyre). As all inhabited worlds were created from the same template (and rotate around their sun every 365.25 days), each year is divided into the same seasons and months as that of Implacatus itself.

Each month (or 'inch') is named after one of the Twelve Ascendants (the original Gods of Implacatus). Through long years, the names have drifted some way from their originals, but each month retains its connection to the Ascendant it was named after.

In the Divine Calendar, each year begins on the 1st day of Beldinch.
- Beldinch (January) – after Belinda, the Third Ascendant
- Summinch (February)– after Simon, the Tenth Ascendant
- Arginch (March) – after Arete, the Seventh Ascendant
- Nethinch (April)– after Nathaniel, the Fourth Ascendant
- Duninch (May) – after Edmond, the Second Ascendant
- Tradinch (June)– after Theodora, the First Ascendant
- Abrinch (July) – after Albrada, the Eleventh Ascendant
- Lexinch (August) – after Leksandr, the Sixth Ascendant
- Tuminch (September) – after Tamid, the Eighth Ascendant
- Luddinch (October) – after Lloyd, the Twelfth Ascendant
- Kolinch (November)– after Kolai, the Fifth Ascendant
- Essinch (December) – after Esher, the Ninth Ascendant

AUTHOR'S NOTES

JANUARY 2021

Thank you for reading the Falls of Iron and I hope you enjoyed it. Writing this book marked a new era in my life, as it was my first as a full time author. I began it the morning following my departure from my old day job, and getting to this stage represents the culmination of years of hard work. I owe many people thanks for their support in helping me fulfill what has long been a dream of mine; so, thank you all!

RECEIVE A FREE MAGELANDS ETERNAL SIEGE BOOK

Building a relationship with my readers is very important to me.

Join my newsletter for information on new books and deals and you will also receive a Magelands Eternal Siege prequel novella that is currently EXCLUSIVE to my Reader's Group for FREE.

www.ChristopherMitchellBooks.com/join

ABOUT THE AUTHOR

Christopher Mitchell is the author of the Magelands epic fantasy series.

For more information:
www.christophermitchellbooks.com
info@christophermitchellbooks.com

Printed in Great Britain
by Amazon